# FIVE BROTHERS

PENELOPE DOUGLAS

BERKLEY ROMANCE
New York

BERKLEY ROMANCE
Published by Berkley
An imprint of Penguin Random House LLC
1745 Broadway, New York, NY 10019
penguinrandomhouse.com



Book design by George Towne

Library of Congress Cataloging-in-Publication Data

Names: Douglas, Penelope, 1977- author.
Title: Five brothers / Penelope Douglas.
Other titles: 5 brothers
Description: First edition. | New York : Berkley Romance, 2024.
Identifiers: LCCN 2023052707 (print) | LCCN 2023052708 (ebook) |
ISBN 9780593816578 (trade paperback) | ISBN 9780593816585 (e-book)
Subjects: LCGFT: Romance fiction. | Erotic fiction. | Novels.
Classification: LCC PS3604.O93236 F58 2024 (print) |
LCC PS3604.O93236 (ebook) | DDC 813/.6—dc23/eng/20231120
LC record available at https://lccn.loc.gov/2023052707
LC ebook record available at https://lccn.loc.gov/2023052708

First Edition: July 2024

Printed in the United States of America
5th Printing

The authorized representative in the EU for product safety and compliance is Penguin Random House Ireland, Morrison Chambers, 32 Nassau Street, Dublin D02 YH68, Ireland, https://eu-contact.penguin.ie.

## PRAISE FOR THE NOVELS OF PENELOPE DOUGLAS

"Penelope Douglas showcases [their] knack for creating compelling central characters and thus reversing all our expectations about them. [They] deliver a multilayered love story that strikes every emotional chord along the way—a story that is beautifully complicated, infinitely angsty, and completely impossible to put down."

—Natasha Is a Book Junkie

"Beyond addictive! Visceral and cuttingly edgy, *Punk 57* will own you from the first page to long after you turn over the last. Penelope Douglas slays it!"

—Katy Evans

"Douglas launched this series and held nothing back. They delivered a medley of emotions I never thought I could feel at once. I was afraid, intrigued, anxious, and enamored. A must-read!

—B.B. Reid

"*Credence* consumed me with its sinfully unique taboo story and gorgeous imagery. Truly a one-of-a-kind book that I can't recommend enough."

—Carian Cole

"The seductive tug highlighted by the character-driven storyline held me in its grasp until the very end. Douglas's ability to draw such powerful emotions from the reader is truly fascinating."

—Abbi Glines

"Misha and Ryen's fiery romance will have your heartstrings twisted in knots and have you wanting a pen pal of your own. They're fire and ice, and I couldn't get enough."

—H. D. Carlton

"Penelope Douglas does many things very well. One of the best of those things is their ability to make something taboo seem irresistibly satisfying. With *Birthday Girl*, they twist the older man / younger woman taboo and make it compelling, sensual, and a wonderful treat."

—Eden Butler

## TITLES BY PENELOPE DOUGLAS

### *The Fall Away Series*

BULLY

UNTIL YOU

RIVAL

FALLING AWAY

THE NEXT FLAME
(includes novellas *Aflame* and *Next to Never*)

### *Stand-Alones*

MISCONDUCT

BIRTHDAY GIRL

PUNK 57

CREDENCE

TRYST SIX VENOM

FIVE BROTHERS

### *The Devil's Night Series*

CORRUPT

HIDEAWAY

KILL SWITCH

CONCLAVE
(novella)

NIGHTFALL

FIRE NIGHT
(novella)

*For 1438 Garfield Avenue*

## AUTHOR'S NOTE

*Five Brothers* is a stand-alone romance that takes place in the same world as one of my other books, *Tryst Six Venom*. Reading *Tryst Six Venom* isn't necessary, but it would be helpful. The Jaeger brothers are featured a lot in that book.

## DEAR READER,

This book deals with emotionally difficult topics, including dubious consent, mentions of domestic abuse, sexual assault, and discussions of suicide. Anyone who believes such content may upset them is encouraged to consider their well-being when choosing whether to continue reading.

# PLAYLIST

"Afterlife" by Avenged Sevenfold
"Blood in the Water" by Ayron Jones
"Careless Whisper" by Seether
"Coming Down" by Five Finger Death Punch
"Happy Together" by Filter
"Heron Blue" by Sun Kil Moon
"High Enough" by Damn Yankees
"In the Woods Somewhere" by Hozier
"Raise Hell" by Brandi Carlile
"Shout" by Tears for Fears
"Shout 2000" by Disturbed
"Something in the Way" by MXMS
"Take the World" by She Wants Revenge
"Twist of Fate" by Olivia Newton-John
"Waking Up Beside You" by Stabbing Westward
"Where the River Flows" by Collective Soul
"Whispers in the Hall" by Chromatics
"Your Woman" by GYM

# FIVE BROTHERS

# 1

## Krisjen

*Don't walk alone at night.*

I grip the hem of my plaid skirt and glance behind me. The dark empty road disappears into the black void, like a tunnel under the canopy of trees. The midnight moon reflects only enough light to make the leaves look blue, while the mid-October breeze blows my hair across my cheek.

I face forward, continuing to walk. My heart pumps hard in my chest.

*Don't walk alone at night.*

I don't think my parents ever told me that, but I learned it well enough. The world is full of things that want to hurt us because they can. Because we make it easy.

Women shouldn't have too much muscle on our bodies. We shouldn't be too smart or learn how to manage money. We don't need to know how to navigate a crowd, lead the way through a city or an airport, or choose the car we want to buy. Let the man drive if there's one in the vehicle with you, and the dinner reservation should always be in his name.

Those are things my parents *did* tell me.

Everything in life is about power, and it wasn't that I was taught that I didn't have any. I learned that men would like me better if I didn't show it.

The forest closes in on both sides of the road, and I feel figures that aren't there. Hidden in the trees. Watching me. As if danger can tell when we're unprotected and show up at that exact time and place. Summer camp serial killers always know when a girl has traipsed off away from her group, don't they? No matter where the summer camp is. Even if he's in a different one.

But instead of being afraid, I look up, the semi-clear night offering a spray of stars so bright that I'm glad I'm out alone, after all. Deep on this dark road, away from the lights of town.

I clench my school skirt in my fists as the soft fabric of my shirt sticks to my damp skin. My breasts chafe against the cloth.

Jupiter will be visible in a few months. I forget what's visible this time of year, but it's nice to see anything. Coastal Florida towns in hurricane season aren't a joke. The clouds always roll in.

I don't hear the engine behind me.

"Need a ride?" someone calls out.

I jerk my head, my heart skipping a beat. I look over, meeting green eyes that peer at me from the driver's side of his truck. I move off the road, to the gravel, as his vehicle crawls up next to me.

His arm drapes over the door, and he's not wearing a shirt, every inch of skin that's bared on his chest, neck, and muscles tan.

He works outside. And often shirtless from the looks of it, because there are no lines.

A boy from across the tracks.

His black hair is pushed back under a backward baseball cap, and his eyes gleam in that way that I know by now. Men have been looking at me like that since long before they should have.

I swallow. "No, thank you."

I continue walking, waiting for him to press the gas and keep going, but he doesn't. The muscles in my thighs tense, ready to run. I move farther and farther away, feeling his eyes on my back.

"You know what you need?" he says, and I see his truck come up again out of the corner of my eye. "A girl like you should have a boyfriend."

A lock of my chestnut hair floats on the wind and then falls back against my face. I squeeze my skirt again, the tails of my white shirt hanging almost as low as my hem.

"Someone to take care of you and drive you," he says. "Would you like a man?"

His words climb my skin. I look ahead of me, down the road. More dark. More empty. No one knows I'm out here.

"Come here," he says, almost a whisper.

My mouth goes dry.

He's not asking.

I hear his door creak open, and I stop, slowly turning and watching him jump out of the cab.

*Run.*

Leaving his door open, he drops his chin, slowly approaching me as if I were a dog he needs to leash before I get away.

*Run*, I tell myself.

I take a step back, but he reaches out and catches the lock of hair hanging down my cheek.

He doesn't look at it, though. He looks in my eyes.

He's young. Not much older than me, but definitely taller. Broader.

*Too close.*

I spin around, but before I can take the first step away, he's grabbing me and hauling me back against his chest. I gasp, feeling one of his hands cover my breast and the other one slide down between my legs.

He exhales in my ear, stroking the slit beneath my underwear. "Oh God, you got something good, don't you?"

He moans.

I squirm, whimpering, "No . . ."

He reaches inside my panties, stroking me as he sucks in air between his teeth. "Get in the truck." He spins me around and releases me, but he pushes me toward his car before I can run. "I'm your man now, honey," he growls.

I look side to side as he shoves me, his open door blocking my escape to my left and him blocking me on my right. I scramble into the truck, flipping over and crawling backward as far as possible to the other side until my back hits the door.

I grab the handle behind me, but the locks click just before I yank. I pull up and down, trying to get out, but his eyes are on me as he climbs in and slams the door. I can't move. I clench my thighs.

His gaze travels down my body to my legs and everything he can see with my skirt hiked up. I pull it down.

"Goddamn," he murmurs, his tongue moving inside his mouth.

He kicks the truck into *Drive* and hits the gas.

"Where are you taking me?"

"Somewhere I can pay my new girlfriend a little attention," he replies.

His eyes dance as he watches the road, a trickle of sweat streaming down his chest. I watch it glide over every ripple in his abs.

His dark hair is blacker near his ear where the sweat has matted it, and I watch him bite his bottom lip as he stares ahead. Smooth, young neck. Every muscle flexed as he holds his arm out straight and fists the steering wheel. No tattoos. Just a scar on his eyebrow—a small slit where the hair no longer grows.

I dig my nails into the seat behind me.

I should try harder to get away. Hit him. Kick him.

He pulls off the road, down a gravel path, and then takes a sharp left into a small lot surrounded by woods. It's where people come to play with their ATVs. The woods are filled with trails.

But the lot is abandoned at night.

It's just us.

He parks and shuts off the engine, the cab turning nearly pitch black.

I feel hands grip my ankles, and I'm yanked down the seat as he kneels between my legs and hovers over me.

"I want to go home," I say.

He doesn't reply.

Reaching under my skirt, he peels my panties down my legs and over my shoes, staring at my naked skin. "Oh God, you are a pretty little bitch."

Pushing up my shirt, he comes down, sucking one of my nipples into his mouth as he strokes me between the legs with one of his hands.

"Mmm," he groans.

I grip his wrist under my skirt with both hands, trying to take his hand out from between my legs, but his muscles flex underneath my fingers, holding tight. Flicking my nipple with his tongue, he moves to the other breast, and I shove at his chest, whimpering, but he pays me no mind as he takes his pleasure.

Like he doesn't see me.

Like I'm just here for fun.

He pinches my nipple between his teeth, and a shock shoots through my stomach to down between my thighs. I release him and drag my fingers up my stomach to the waist of my skirt.

"Yeah, your wet little cunt is ready for me, isn't it?" he coos.

*Yeah, baby.*

I clutch the hilt of the knife hidden in my skirt and raise my arm, pressing the blade to his neck.

He stops.

I feel my smile in my fucking throat.

His hot breath hits faster against my skin as he hovers over my breast, and I lift my head, feeling like I'm floating as I get into his face.

"Get off me."

God, how he just stopped. That was awesome.

I could do whatever I wanted to him right now.

Slowly, he sits back in his seat, and I follow, keeping the blade at his neck as I slide my leg over his thighs.

Straddling him, I settle in his lap. "Put your hands on the roof," I order.

He raises his arms, still barely breathing as he places his palms above his head.

The steering wheel presses into my back, and I lean into him, the hard flesh of my nipples pressing through my shirt, against his warm chest.

He holds his breath as I slip my free hand down, digging in his pocket. I pull out a few folded bills and hold them up, smiling a little before dropping them inside my shirt pocket.

I press the blade harder. "Hands behind your head."

He pierces me with his stare but does what he's told.

I could probably escape right now. He might not grab for me. Or try to take away my weapon. A guy like him—good-looking and used to having whoever he wants—probably thinks I'm not worth any more trouble.

I could leave.

But I don't.

I shift, rolling so slowly over the bulge in his jeans and sliding my hand up his chest.

"On second thought," I taunt, rising to my knees so the breast poking through my shirt is level with his mouth. "You are built for fun, aren't you?"

I press myself into his mouth, and he seizes the invitation, nuzzling my collared shirt off my shoulder, baring a breast. He sucks it into his mouth. His hot tongue nibbles and teases so soft, and I grip the back of his neck, holding him to me to make sure he doesn't stop.

I come down, kissing his mouth and whispering against his lips, "Open your jeans and take it out."

I roll my hips into him, panting and groaning as he rips at his belt and unfastens his fly.

He tries to take my hips, but I dig the blade into his neck. "Don't touch me."

He pulls away, and I attack his mouth, feeling the hard, hot flesh of his cock brush against my clit.

I stare down into his eyes. "You still want me?" I whisper.

He nods, his mouth hanging open as he breathes hard. "God, yes."

I linger, rolling my hips and taunting him, but he's ready to go. He dives behind me, reaching for the glove box, and I kiss his neck and trail up his jaw and to his temple.

But then he goes still, and eventually, I stop kissing.

Looking behind me, I see his hand clutching a condom box upside down. As if it's empty.

He throws it down onto the floor and shuffles through the contents of the glove box, looking for a condom that must've spilled out. Papers and napkins and tools I don't recognize slide onto the floor, but when he stops, he's still empty-handed. Nothing.

He has nothing. No protection.

I tense. "There were two left," I tell him.

He glances up at me, a pained look in his eyes. He swipes his hand through the compartment again in vain.

I drop my arms from his body. "Trace . . ."

He shoots up, letting his head fall back and locking his hands on top. "Shit," he murmurs to the roof.

My stomach drops a little. We were together three days ago. He had two condoms left in that box. His brothers don't use this truck.

I try to catch his eyes, but he won't look at me. "Are you serious?"

Without waiting for him to answer, I climb off, plopping back into my seat and setting the knife down.

"Come on," Trace says in a gentle voice. "Please don't be mad, Krisjen."

He reaches for my hand, but I take it away, buttoning my shirt the couple of notches I undid earlier to look like sexy serial killer bait on the dark road in the middle of nowhere.

He hesitates, but the mood is gone. He zips up his fly and fastens his belt, our little role-play switching back to reality. I'm eighteen again, graduated and no longer in Catholic school, and he's twenty, trying not to make an enemy out of one of his sister's best friends, because he knows he'll be running into me a lot in life.

"Please don't make me feel bad," he says softly. "I didn't think you were exclusive to me, either. You're not in love with me, are you? I'm an idiot."

I close my eyes but almost laugh, because he is an idiot.

And I'm not in love with him.

But now I can't lie to myself anymore. I am absolutely not special to him. I'm probably just the only one who texted back tonight.

I did like him, though. He goes along with my role-playing fantasies where I overpower someone trying to overpower me.

I bow my head, rubbing my tired eyes.

"Krisjen, seriously." He takes my hand. "I'm sorry. I didn't think we were like that."

"Don't apologize," I tell him, pulling my hand back. It just makes me feel more pathetic. "You're right. We're not getting married."

I meet his eyes, saying his name in my head. *Trace Jaeger.*

And Milo Price. My ex-boyfriend. The two men I've slept with.

I always thought it would be only one. When I was twelve, I imagined my true-love experience would be passionate kisses on seaside cliffs as my dress blew in the wind. He would be a poet. And secretly a duke. With a castle. Like, I literally thought that's what would happen, because I had lofty ideas and never figured in my desperation for attention.

But that's not what happened. I was a sophomore, invited with some friends to junior prom, which ended at a party where I gave it up to my boyfriend on a stranger's bed, and it was all over in eleven minutes.

I've slept with two men.

And counting.

Trace won't be the last.

"Other guys will do what you do to me," I murmur.

"Exactly like me?"

"Probably harder."

He snorts, sitting back in his seat. "Well, you know you can still come over when you need a break from your future husband five or ten years from now. When you need it good and dirty."

He's trying to make me smile, but I don't. I look out the window instead. *Ten years from now* . . . God, will I still need him in order to feel alive?

An image flashes in my head, but almost immediately I realize it's not my mother. It's me. With her hair. In her clothes. In her life.

He tries to take my hand. "Come here."

I resist.

"Come here," he whispers.

But gently, I pull my hand away before he can take it.

Trace is a people pleaser. He hates anyone being mad at him. Comes from years of dodging four older brothers who are all tornadoes.

Macon, Army, Iron, and Dallas.

His sister, Liv, dates my best friend, Clay, but Liv is pretty calm compared to the rest of the Jaegers. Which I'm sure *also* comes from years of dodging five older brothers who are all tornadoes. She loves them all, though.

Their parents died within two months of each other more than eight years ago. The oldest, Macon, was forced to leave the military to come home and raise his siblings. Trace's older brothers are pretty much his only memories.

"We could go on a date," he says. "You have my money."

"You mean your allowance?" I pluck the folded bills out of my breast pocket—a twenty on the outside and, knowing him, it's probably a one on the inside. I hand it back before pulling my underwear on.

He returns the bills to his pocket. "I'm a man who makes his own living, thank you."

*Mm-hm.* "I'm not letting you take me on a date out of guilt."

"Well, I'm still up for sex, too," he adds, flashing his adorable smile. "I mean, this was all your idea, and you got me pretty worked up." He gestures to the hard-on in his jeans. "The part where you robbed me was pretty hot."

I force a frown, but only because I'm mad that I want to smile. He's trying hard to make me feel better, and for some reason, I feel an urge to let him know his effort is appreciated.

Turns out, I'm a people pleaser, too.

"I was trying to be tough like your sister and Clay," I mumble, teasing.

I thought I was doing well, but now, I don't know.

He touches my face. "I'm glad you're not violent," he says quietly. "I like that you're soft with people. Don't change that."

It's nice of him to say, but being that way doesn't seem to work out for me. Being gentle just makes me an easy target.

"Don't change, okay?"

*Yeah, okay. Whatever.*

"Just take me to your house." I push up my sleeves and fasten my seat belt. "I need to pick up my car."

"Krisjen . . ."

"It's fine, Trace." I don't look at him. "We're not a couple. We never were."

I lied to myself. I did it to myself.

I'm pretty sure I was officially a booty call from the start. One night last spring I followed Clay across the tracks into Sanoa Bay, the original settlement of St. Carmen.

Officially, we're all St. Carmen now, but the Bay—where Trace and his family live—doesn't like to hear that. They're possessive of their land, and they want to rule separately.

They're wild.

We hide everything.

They're poor.

We're not.

They're Swamp.

We're Saints.

Clay fell in love with Liv, the bad girl from the wrong side of town, and I fell into insanity with one of that bad girl's brothers.

But it was never love like it was for Liv and Clay. Trace doesn't think of me after I leave his bed, and if I'm being fair, I don't think much of myself, either.

He turns the key, starting the engine, and in a moment, he's pulling onto the road and heading left, toward the swamps.

We cruise past the gates of my house, and I glance to see the upstairs lights still off before Trace turns right onto the dark lane and then takes a another left, across the bridge and over the wetlands.

I take out my phone and DM my brother.

**Running to the Bay to grab my car. Be back soon.**

Marshall is almost thirteen. He usually has his headphones on so he won't hear Paisleigh if she wakes up.

A text rolls in. **How did you know I had the old iPad?**

I laugh to myself. **Because you're smart, like me.**

I took all of his tech when I put them both to bed two hours ago, but I didn't ask for the one device he thought was still a secret. Maybe I should have. If my parents had been stricter with my bedtimes, maybe I'd be in college right now like all my friends.

But I also know Mars is going to do what he wants to do. I'm strict enough that he knows I care about him getting a good night's sleep, but not so strict that all he learns is how to hide from me. There will be bigger battles than iPads and cell phones.

If he's anything like me.

**Love you. Give Jason a hug for me.**

**Leave my pillow alone**, he fires back.

I laugh out loud, and I see Trace look at me out of the corner of my eye. My brother has a pillow with Jason Momoa's face on it. It's a good-looking pillow.

My phone vibrates with a text. **And nice flowers**, Mars taunts. **Mom dug them out of the trash.**

**And I promptly threw them back in**, I tap out my reply. **Good night. Sleep tight. I love you.**

I tuck my phone back in my pocket, turning the volume up on Trace's radio as he speeds me away from those white roses in the garbage at my house.

I love getting flowers, but not from strange men.

I'm tempted to reach out to my father and grandparents to let them know that my mother is trying to marry me off, but I'm not sure they'd care.

And I'm not asking my father for anything. He doesn't want to support his family, so I don't think he'll care that my mom is trying to find a way to do it instead by making me marry someone rich.

Droplets of rain spatter the windshield, but I crack my window, inhaling the scent of the wind. The gentle lights of St. Carmen and the soft glow of the gas lamps on Main Street disappear in my sideview mirror as Trace exits the overpass. We bounce over the tracks, the road turning pebbly and loud under the tires as he coasts into the wild landscape of the Bay.

Old shacks that have been here for a hundred years serve the area's best gumbo and fresh seafood, and we pass unkept land, the dark porches of hidden houses just peeking through the brush.

I rub my hands together in my lap.

There's a part of me that's asleep until I come here. Maybe it's the heat, which I feel just a little bit more, or maybe it's the land, chaotic and overridden as if the trees are trying to take it back.

Over hundreds of years, Seminoles and Spaniards claimed, fought, lived, warred, and then eventually built together.

And when more Europeans came and wanted the swamp and the beautiful views of the sea, the Bay became one nation unto themselves—one wall against the world.

Communities stop working together over time once they no longer have to, but the Bay is unique. After five hundred years, they're still fighting to survive. That one common goal has kept them together.

St. Carmen has passion, too, but it's not nearly as fun.

Trace speeds down the dirt road, passing a few homes and businesses along the main street, and then swings the car around in a U-turn, pulling up in front of his house. Half a dozen trucks and other vehicles are parked outside, the downstairs lights illuminating the windows.

We hop out, and I look next to the fence, seeing my Rover still parked where I left it.

"Son of a bitch!" someone bellows from inside the house. "I could've been killed!"

I inhale a deep breath. *Iron Jaeger.* One of Trace's older brothers.

I know his voice by process of elimination. He's the only one I rarely hear yell, and I know all the others' voices. If it were Macon, the oldest, I'd probably just turn around and leave.

Guys come barreling out the front door, running down the walk and out into the rainy dirt road. Their girlfriends wait by the cars, laughing and shielding themselves from the weather.

Music inside makes the house vibrate as the Seminole flag blows over the garage door. Ivy and moss climb the exterior of the ancient pink stucco of the dilapidated Spanish mission-style mansion, and I inhale like I always do, because you can eat the air here.

Stepping through the arch of the heavy wooden front door, I hear one of the shutters on the second or third floor flapping against the house. Screams pierce the air, and I wince as more people rush toward me.

I leap, Trace pulling me into his arms and out of the way. The music cuts off as they squeeze past me, out the door.

"What the hell is going on?" I mumble.

But Army Jaeger, the second-oldest, answers instead. "An alligator slithered into the pool."

He pulls on a T-shirt. His black hair is soaked, drops of water sliding over the giant octopus tattoo that spills over his shoulder and onto the left side of his chest. I used to think he rarely wore a shirt because he knew how good he looked without one, but I eventually figured out that he simply liked to save time. When his brothers aren't causing him enough trouble, he's taking care of his infant son. At twenty-eight, he's the only one with a kid.

"Iron fell in when we tried to haul it out," he adds.

Of course he did. One of the Jaegers is always on the verge of getting killed.

"Is everyone okay?" I ask.

But he just waves me off, grabbing a baseball bat from behind the coatrack. His short dark hair gleams with water. "Yeah, just keep your eyes peeled. We lost it, but it could be hanging around. We're going to search for it."

*Awesome.* I look over, seeing Iron throw back his beer, muscles tense and his clothes soaking wet. His black hair is slicked back. He started growing it out this summer, and his tan is still deep everywhere I can see. The vein in the side of his neck bulges underneath a tattoo.

But then another Jaeger steps up. "Great," Dallas says in a snide tone. "Trace calls, you come running."

Dallas's green eyes are always looking at me like he's imagining me on fire.

I turn my attention back to the remnants of the party and the damage in the living room. "We drove, actually."

Trace lets out a chuckle and tosses a flashlight to his brother. "Be careful."

Dallas takes it, pushing his hair back over the top of his head and slipping on a ball cap. He's a year older than Trace. Twenty-one. And he doesn't like me.

He doesn't like me *a lot.*

Army, Iron, Dallas, and Trace. That's four.

Army's infant son, Dex, bawls upstairs.

"Why's that kid still up?" Dallas barks.

"Because y'all are too fucking loud," his father growls, heading out the door.

A girl calls after him. "Army, seriously. Should I wait in Liv's old room or what?"

I look over at the half ponytail on top of her head and the bright red lipstick that matches her tight skirt and shirt. I cross my arms over my chest, covering the paint stain from helping Paisleigh with her art earlier tonight.

But Army just tells her, "Stay out of my sister's room."

He bolts through the door with Dallas as Iron starts to follow, swallowing down the rest of his bottle.

"How are you?" I ask him.

He doesn't look at me, just shakes his head and sighs as he sets the beer down.

My grandfather is the district judge who always seems to have Iron in his courtroom for one arrest or another. Breaking and entering, theft, and, most recently . . . assault. Iron loves to get into fistfights. Something he still hasn't grown out of at twenty-four years old.

Unfortunately, his luck ran out this summer. His last arrest resulted in bail, a court date, and finally a plea bargain. He'll serve time. He has to surrender in a week.

I'm not responsible, but I also feel like I shouldn't be in his house.

"Iron, you coming?" Dallas calls out.

Iron casts me a look, his eyes softening with the hint of a smile. An hourglass with a snake wrapped around it is inked on the side of his neck, and several more tattoos cover his body. I've never looked at length, but I know he has a palm tree with Sanoa Bay's latitude and longitude on his forearm, and a huge alligator on the bottom left of his back.

He shrugs. "Nothing better to do, I guess, right?"

I half smile back, always liking him. Maybe even more than Trace. Iron is completely different around women and children. I once saw him stop and park his motorcycle, take an old lady's groceries, put them in his saddlebags, and drop them at her house so she wouldn't have to carry them. It was kind of funny, because she thought he was stealing them at first and tried to hit him. Now, they're on a first-name basis, and she has him run her husband and his wheelchair to physical therapy for her once in a while. Not on the motorcycle, of course.

Engines start up outside as Iron, Dallas, and Army leave. Trace stays behind, and I have no idea where Macon is, but the garage was closed when I got here. If he's home, that's where he is.

No parents.

Just five brothers.

All in the same house.

I think some of them want to move out, but they wouldn't know what to do without each other on a daily basis.

"Drink?"

I glance at Trace as he twists off the tops of a couple of beers. The same hourglass with a snake wrapped around it rests against his skin, forged in iron, and secured with three thin leather bands around his right wrist. All of his brothers wear the same bracelet. It's the Tryst Six family crest. Tryst after their mother, Trysta, and Six because there are six children. Not sure who came up with the name. I'm pretty sure they didn't give it to themselves.

Trace holds a bottle out to me. I hate beer. I'm sure I told him at some point.

"Where are my keys?" I ask.

"You know where they are."

He holds a bottle in each hand, taking a long swig out of one.

I blink at him. "Would you go get them, please? Like a gentleman?"

We went out on their boat last time I was here, and he drove me home from there. I need my car back now.

But he just teases, "You may have left other things. May as well go look."

I arch a brow, reading into his ploy to get me into his room. I start up the stairs. "Like my vibrator?" I grumble. "I used it here more than at my house."

"So rude."

He starts up the stairs after me, and I keep my laugh to myself. I didn't come a lot with Trace, but to be fair, I didn't expect to.

Nor do I think he was trying that hard.

I'd read somewhere that the majority of women can't orgasm through penetration, so I gathered I was part of that majority.

Sometimes I made him slow down so I could help myself get there. I used my vibrator a lot here, as it turns out.

He's a good kisser, though. Touching him and being close to him felt good, and for a while, feeling him helped me forget about my troubles.

For a while anyway.

At the top of the stairs, I pass his sister's closed door and smile a little, because I know I'll see her in a few weeks when she's home for Thanksgiving. The bathroom and Macon's room are on the right, his door closed as well, and I spot Iron and Dallas's room ahead, to the left of Trace's.

Army's is closed, his son's cries now quiet, and there's a door in the far corner, always shut. I've never seen anyone go in or out of there.

"Why didn't you want to come to the party?" Trace asks, following me into his room as I go to his desk that's simply a dumping ground for discarded junk.

I start moving things, looking for my keys. "You mean the one today as opposed to the one yesterday?"

I meet his green eyes for a quick glance, seeing him smile. I look away, feeling that familiar flutter in my tummy. That easy smile was all it took when this one-night stand started six months ago.

"You're not the only thing I have to do in life, Trace."

Doors slam downstairs, the house growing quieter as engines fade away down the street.

"Oh, come on, Ms. Conroy." He sets one of the beers down, coming up behind me and taking my waist in one hand. "You love coming down here to the servants' quarters to get serviced."

I shake my head, lifting a tackle box and prying up a greasy car part. "You don't need me," I tell him. "There are plenty of girls hanging around your house."

I glance at the mussed bed.

He nuzzles into my ear. "I like to think about seeing you around town for the next fifty years," he tells me, "pretending to be a sweet, southern wife when I know what you look like underneath me. I'll see you. You'll see me. We'll smile as we pass on the sidewalk, remembering. Clock's ticking, Conroy. May as well have some fun while you can."

There's a lightheartedness in his twenty-year-old voice that I love, but it always gives me pause, too. He's never serious, and after six months of playing around together, I'm starting to suspect it's on purpose.

I stop looking for my keys. "You know I don't think of you like that, right? As a servant, I mean?"

His family has more money than mine at this point. My parents are locked in a divorce battle, and my father left us nothing while they duke it out. The Jaegers, on the contrary, probably aren't as poor as they like to seem.

But Trace just teases, "Shh, don't break the fantasy."

I spot my keys on his bedside table and grab them, turning around to face him. "I'm going home."

"Will you come back sometime?"

I'm taken off guard by the question.

*No.*

I won't be back.

There's nothing here that's good for me, and it's time I got my ass in gear. I need plans. Some direction. College, maybe?

But I still have no idea what I want to do with my life.

I never wanted to be a lawyer, a stockbroker, or a CEO.

All I ever wanted was to love waking up. To be counted on to make someone's life better.

And I want a man who breathes me. Who craves me and needs me.

I'm not going to find any of that in Trace's bedroom.

"Maybe I'll see you around town." I smile a little. "Over the next fifty years."

He takes my face in his hand, his nose nearly brushing mine. "You need one more good memory to take with you."

I shift my mouth away, about to push his hand off, but someone knocks on the door.

"Trace?" It's a woman's voice.

The door opens, and I peer around him as he releases me. A brunette peeks her head inside his room, and I think she was downstairs with Army's date. I think her name is Carissa.

She sees me, smiles, and bites her bottom lip. "Need anything?" she asks us.

I stare at her. *Do we* need *anything?*

Why would . . .

I turn to him, but he's just watching me.

He leans down, planting his hands on the desk at my sides and gets in my face. "Tell her I'm yours tonight," he says.

*What?*

It takes about a second and a half for me to realize she's his backup plan. I shove him away and start for the door.

*Jesus.* So either I claim him or she will?

When I whip open the door, the girl slides out of my way. "You can stay," she tells me. "We can both play."

"Krisjen's not brave," Trace says like I'm not here. "Or is she?"

I'm not letting him bait me. "No, I am." I toss him a glance. "Maybe I'll do that someday. I'm just not going to do it with you."

And I walk out, slamming the door behind me.

*Motherfucker.* I'm half-tempted to call his sister and rat him out, but she wouldn't be surprised, and I have some pride left.

Plus, she loves the hell out of him.

Trace has always been deliberately irresponsible, but unlike Milo, he's nice. Not very considerate, but not once did I ever get the impression it was personal. I didn't love him, so I didn't worry about it.

But that was personal. I was well aware he wasn't going to miss me when this was over, but it's not like him to rub things like that in.

Rain hits the windows, and I head down the stairs, barely noticing the house is now quiet and dark. Lightning flashes outside, and I fist the keys, opening the front door. I take a step but stop, remembering the gator.

Looking around, I scan the yard and the dirt road beyond the fence, spotting lights from the fire station next door and the repair shop across the street. Music beats against the walls of the bar far off to my left, but most of the cars have cleared out of the Jaegers' place, and I don't see anyone—or anything—outside.

I would love an escort to my car, but I'm not about to ask Trace for help. I leap out into the yard, pulling the door closed behind me, and run to my car. Drops hit my head as I round the front of the vehicle, but before I can hit the button to unlock it, I know something is off. The car isn't level. I drop my eyes to the front tire on the driver's side, seeing it's flat at the same time I notice a gash in the rubber. Right there. Plain as day.

I drop my head back, growling. "Ugh!"

*Goddammit, Aracely.* Seriously. She's not even interested in Trace. What did I ever do to her?

And I know it's her. She pulled the same shit with my friend Amy this summer, which I sympathized with, because Amy hooked up with Dallas and Iron. Both Aracely's exes.

I can see her being aggravated that a Saint is sleeping over here. Having fun with their men (as she would see it). But Trace was never hers. And I thought she liked me.

I guess she thought she'd put up with me until I left for college, and since I didn't, she's now letting me know that my time is up.

The wind stirs, rain blowing sideways, and I climb into my car and pull out my phone.

I dial Maker Street Tow Service, but the line just rings. I hang up and try again, but it goes to voicemail.

I start to dial Clay but stop. She worked tonight. And she has classes.

I hover my thumb over my phone. Mom, Dad . . .

Milo would come and get me. For sure. They'd all come and get me, but they can all fuck off. Can I drive on a flat tire?

I think that hurts the rims or something, but I push the button, turning over the engine anyway. Shifting into *Drive*, I press the gas and nearly topple over, grabbing the steering wheel in both hands for support. "Damn," I blurt out.

Shutting off the engine, I dash back out into the rain and run around the car, seeing the rear passenger tire is flat, too.

I throw out my hands. "Jesus, Aracely. Do you want me to leave, or are you trying to keep me here?" I call out to the empty street, just picturing her watching all this from the woods.

*Goddamn.*

Locking my car, I run back into the house and up the stairs. Swinging open the door to Liv's room, I spot someone asleep on the bed and stop.

Face down, no shirt . . . I have no idea who it is, but I can't crash here.

"Come on," I gripe under my breath.

Snatching the blanket off the bottom of the bed, I close the door and walk back downstairs. I can hear laughter followed by moaning somewhere behind me, and I kick the couch before I drop my keys to the coffee table, kick off my sneakers, and then plop down on my back, pulling the blanket over me.

I'll look nice and pathetic still here in the morning. I can't even change the tire once the rain stops, because I need two of them now. Hopefully, I can reach a tow service in the morning.

I tap out a text to my brother.

**Car trouble. Stuck in the Bay. Be home in the morning.**

I reach behind me, finding one of the many chargers they keep around the house, and plug it in my phone.

Drops of rain catch the moonlight on the windows, lightning filling the room for a second. Small sounds drift downstairs—a laugh, a thud, a creak—and I can't help but stare at the ceiling, listening. Anyone would think I might be upset that all those sounds are probably Trace, but all I'm wondering is if he was that loud with me so anyone downstairs would've heard.

I remember hearing Liv and Clay once. Last year, during an away game when we were on the lacrosse team. They were enemies—hated each other—but we were all on the same team, sharing a hotel room one night. I was in one bed with Amy, and they were in another bed together. And I woke up and finally knew my suspicions were correct. They didn't hate each other at all. I swear I could hear the sweat under the sheets as they went at it.

When I felt Amy start to stir next to me, I triggered the alarm on my phone and pretended to wake up, because Amy seeing them wouldn't be the way Clay would want everyone to find out she was into girls.

Or maybe just into Liv. Their need for each other is still so strong. I've never felt that with anyone.

I've never felt like someone wanted me more than anything.

*"More?"*

But it's not Trace saying it.

It's someone, though.

One of many silly fantasies.

*I back up as he stalks toward me, a gleam in his eyes.*

*"Just a little bit more," he taunts.*

*I let my eyes fall down his naked chest to where the jeans hang low on his hips, and I can smell the water in his hair from when he jumped in our pool after he tended to the lawn.*

I close my eyes, breathing hard and my stomach already swirling a little.

*He closes the distance between us, and I back up, running into my closed bedroom door. "Don't you have to check in with your boss?" I ask.*

*My nipples strain against my shirt as he takes my chin and runs his thumb down my bottom lip. "I'll tell him I had to stay and negotiate my tip."*

*His tip . . . um, oh, right. I pull some money out of my pocket and hold it out to him, but he just smirks, taking the money and tossing it onto my dresser.*

The pulse between my legs throbs, and I place my hand under the blanket, pressing my hand there.

*He slips his rough fingers underneath the hem of my shirt.*

And my heart races against my chest as I use my hand to do the same.

*I don't breathe as he pushes my shirt up, up, and up, over my breasts, letting it rest there as his gaze heats my skin.*

The cool air in the house hits my nipples, and I feel them rising straight up as I push down the blanket and rub myself harder and harder.

*He grabs the backs of my thighs and lifts me against his body. "Open your legs," he growls softly.*

*I widen them.*

I widen them.

*And circle his waist as he carries me to my desk chair, dipping his tongue out just enough to taste my lips again and again.*

I squeeze one breast, my clit hammering as I roll my hips in and out against my hand and tip my head back.

*I straddle him in the chair, and he grabs my hips, pulling me in against his cock. "Now open your mouth and give me your tongue, girl, and don't tell your mother what we did while she was gone."*

I ride my hand like I ride him, feeling his eyes on my tits and his fist in my hair. I move faster, feeling my breasts sway back and forth, and I bite my bottom lip to keep quiet. But my breathing is getting too fast and shallow.

*Oh God. I . . .*

*I . . .*

I blink my eyes open, seeing a figure looming at the entryway between the stairs and the living room, and heat rushes under my skin.

*Oh shit.* I gasp, pulling my hands off my body, pulling my shirt back down, and opening my eyes wide until he comes in view.

*What the fuck?*

He lifts a beer bottle to his lips and tips it back, taking a drink.

*Trace?*

My heart pounds against my chest. "Oh my God," I murmur.

I can't swallow. My throat is so dry.

I peer through the darkness. It's not Trace. This one's taller, though I can't tell who it is exactly. The rooms are almost pitch black with the cloud cover overtaking the moon outside.

But great. Fucking awesome.

It's got to be one of the Jaegers. Jeans. No shirt. *Just like my dream.*

I pull the blanket up over my bottom half, my skirt still hiked up.

I try to calm my breathing, rubbing my eyes. "Aracely slashed my tires," I say. "I'll be out of here as soon as I can get ahold of a tow truck."

Whoever it is doesn't say anything, and after a moment, I risk another glance. He still stands there.

*Watching me*, I think.

I squint, trying to make him out.

"What?" I blurt out. "Why are you staring at me?"

I sit up, keeping the blanket over me, and swing my legs over the side of the couch. "You can brag about this," I tell him, feeling around in the dark for my shoes. "Someday, when I look, act, and smell like a pristine pair of fifteen-hundred-dollar heels, and I'm married to a lawyer or a banker who tastes like glue and campaigns for family values at church every Sunday, you can say you once watched me fuck myself on your couch, right?"

It's almost too funny, and I would totally understand if he laughed. Should I do it again, so he can video?

I look back up at him, waiting for some kind of response. "Who is that?" I ask.

I can't see his face. How long was he watching?

"Should I leave?" I almost whisper. "Walk home?"

He doesn't say anything. But his head tilts to the side a little.

"Would you like to give me a ride?" I press. "Get me off your couch?"

He stays frozen.

*Jesus. What the hell is his problem?*

As if tonight hasn't been bad enough. I'm stuck in Trace's house, where I'm perfectly welcome as long as I'm going in the morning. The trouble is, I don't feel much more comfortable at home.

"Trace is upstairs screwing someone else," I say in a soft voice, watching the bottle hang at his side. "And it's weird, because I don't care."

I look at him, shaking my head as the tears well in my eyes. I have no idea why I told him that. Maybe it'll make him leave.

"I kept coming here, because I really had nothing else to do." I laugh under my breath, but only for a second.

Needles prick my throat, and I lower my gaze, remembering the laughs Trace and I had. How I actually thought that, even though I didn't love him, he wasn't laughing like that with anyone else, because I certainly wasn't.

"I guess . . ." I fist the blanket. "I guess I didn't want to think it was meaningless, either, though, you know? Because then it would mean I was just as shallow as . . ."

I don't finish the sentence. Mommy issues are boring.

"Why do I do that?" I say more to myself but still feel him there, watching me. "Why do things *have* to mean anything? Why is it either all in or empty? If it's not enough, then it's nothing to me. Why?"

My chin trembles, and I must seem so ridiculous to him. What do I have to cry about? "Empty . . ."

The word comes out as a whisper, and I can't even see him breathe as the bottle hangs from his fingers and rests against his leg. He doesn't leave, though.

I stand up and fold the blanket. "I can't afford to go to college," I drone on, "because my dad took all the money, and even if he hadn't, the kids . . ."

I stop, staring at the floor as the tears spill over.

I choke out the words. "I can't leave them alone with her."

After what she's trying to do to me, there's no way in hell I trust her. Or my father. I hide that he now lives on Barony Lane, just a mile away with his girlfriend, and not in Atlanta like my brother and sister think. How else was I supposed to explain to them why their father suddenly doesn't see them?

"My mother wants me to marry Jerome Watson." It hurts to talk, the tears lodged in my throat. "A thirty-two-year-old corporate tax lawyer, whom I've met once, who's looking for a pretty wife so he'll want to fuck her over and over again, a healthy one who can take care of his house and stay knocked up for years to come, and a young one who's too ignorant and naïve to challenge him."

The tears keep coming, but I don't feel sad. "I'm scared," I breathe out. "I didn't think making life better for the people around me would involve spending my life with someone I don't love."

I blink long and hard.

"But what does it matter, right?" I force a laugh. "Nothing I do will make a difference. May as well help my family and numb myself with pretty shoes and handbags while I'm at it."

As if that will distract me from knowing I was sold, because contrary to what he and my mother discuss about *my* future, I'm neither ignorant nor naïve.

I toss the blanket down, wiping away the tears. *Screw it.* I'll sleep in my car.

But then he's there, his body pressing into my back and his hands squeezing my waist.

I gasp. "No." I try to push his hands away.

*No more. No more.* I drop my head back into him, trying to push against him, but I'm not sure if I'm fighting to get free or fighting because I want to hit someone. Tears stream down my face, and I suck in breath after breath.

But then I feel it.

His shallow breaths against my temple. And his arms slowly slipping around my body, holding me to him.

Slow. Tight. Strong. Warm.

I go still, his heat covering my back as his chest rises and falls against my spine, and I relax just enough to feel him hold me up. One arm wraps around my stomach, the other hand reaches around to cup my cheek as he grazes his mouth over my hair.

"We're not dead yet," he murmurs over my skin at my temple.

And then he turns my head, and before I can see his face, his mouth covers mine, swallowing my whimper. His tongue dives into my mouth, and I can't breathe as he holds me strong and keeps me locked against his body.

Fuck . . .

My lungs scream, and fire covers my skin. I gasp, pulling my mouth away and inhaling air, but it takes only a second before he's fisting my hair and biting my neck.

I cry out, electricity coursing down my thighs and up to the top of my head. I close my eyes, my heart leaping into my throat as he forces my shirt over my head, my arms flying up as he tears the fabric off me.

Pulling his mouth off my skin, he holds my tummy, unzipping my skirt, and I look down, watching his hand in the dark. The same Jaeger bracelet they all wear—three thin straps of brown leather entwined—circles his wrist with the emblem of the snake wrapped around an hourglass in the middle.

My skirt drops, and he takes my hand, guiding it down between my thighs as he gently peels my panties off until the tips of my fingers touch my wet clit.

"Keep going," he whispers, kissing my hair.

A light sweat covers my forehead, and I can't move. I can't even think.

He devours my neck and kneads my breast as heat rushes between my legs and covers my body. I pant, whimpering. "Oh God," I moan. "Stop, stop, please. I can't breathe. I can't breathe."

But he thrusts into me from behind, his jeans creating delicious friction on my ass. Almost touching the sensitive skin deep inside.

I bite my bottom lip so hard, I feel a sharp pain.

And I can't stop. I don't even care. I pull my underwear all the way off before I lean back into him, resting my head against his chest and rubbing myself slowly, riding my hand and knowing that he's watching.

I close my eyes again, loving the feel of his hands on me, and smelling his hot skin, which reminds me of wood and earth and fuel and grease. Loving how the Jaeger boys wear their work on their clothes, and don't get their muscle any other way.

He grows harder, resting his chin on the top of my head as he just holds my right hip in one hand and grips my ass with the other.

I rub the nub, starting to feel the tingle. A little more. I suck in a breath. A little more. I like him watching me. His fingers curl into my skin, digging, pulling, wanting me to fuck myself harder.

"Ah," I groan. "Ah." I roll and bounce harder and faster, and then . . .

He growls, yanks me back into his body, and cuts off my breath again, kissing me.

But before I can come, he leads me down onto the couch, flat on my stomach, and comes down behind me. I immediately lift my knee, opening myself up, and listen to him rip off his belt.

I squeeze the couch in my fist, my stomach pressing into the cool leather.

His hand presses into the sofa, next to my shoulder, and I moan as his fingers glide down my spine.

I feel his breath on my ear. "Krisjen," he whispers, and goose bumps cover my body. "Don't tell Trace about this."

Trace won't care, but I nod anyway.

He works the head of his cock inside me, takes hold of me on both sides where my thighs meet my hips, and thrusts.

I stretch as he bottoms out, and I cry out for a moment before his hand comes over my mouth.

His chest heaves again and again against my back. And then he stops moving—breathing—and I think he's going to say something, but he doesn't. His nose presses into my hair, and he inhales instead.

My pussy contracts around him, and I shift a little to ease the pressure. He's so deep.

And then . . . he rises up, takes hold again, and pumps his hips. Again and again, slow at first, letting me adjust to him, and then he's thrusting so fast and hard all I can do is hang on.

My hair sticks to my back, and I tighten my legs around him, loving the feel of his hands squeezing me. I said I came here because I had nothing else to do, but this is all I want to fucking do.

He grips my hips, sucks my shoulders, bites my back, and it's so hard not to moan too loudly. I don't care who sees. I just don't want him stopping.

I feel my orgasm build again, push myself up on my elbows, and start backing into him. He leans over me as sweat trickles down my back, and I feel his hot breath in my hair.

I feel everything. The thick air on my skin. The clouds over the house. The leather underneath me, now damp with my sweat.

His hands holding me like I'm not dead yet.

Tears burn behind my eyelids, and I smile as he comes down, holding the front of my neck and pulling my head back to meet his. I grasp his hand, feeling the leather bands and warm metal around his wrist.

I arch my back, meeting each thrust as he pumps into me, and then I suck in air again and again until . . . my thighs course with heat, my insides burst open, and the orgasm explodes inside of me. I moan through his hand over my mouth, growing so fucking wet as it spreads through me. His body jerks in short, slow thrusts, and then he lets out a growl in my ear, and I feel him come inside me.

*Oh God.* I breathe hard. *Oh God.*

I inhale in and out, trying to calm down as I collapse onto the couch, exhausted.

But before I can catch my breath, I hear his voice in my ear.

"Someday," he says as he squeezes my throat, "when you look, act, and smell like a pristine pair of fifteen-hundred-dollar heels, and you're married to a lawyer or a banker who tastes like glue and parades you around like his little trophy . . ." He flicks his tongue over my ear, taunting me. "I can wonder if it's my son he's playing Daddy to."

I round my eyes, my pussy clenching around his cock one more time as he pulls out and fastens up his jeans and belt.

I lie there for a second, my body already aching at his absence. But by the time I flip over and look around, he's gone.

"Holy shit." I scan the dark, empty living room. "Who the hell was that?"

# 2

## Krisjen

I startle awake, not moving a muscle as I take in the sunlight coming through the windows. And the heat in the room.

I draw in a deep breath, immediately feeling the ache in my neck as my cheek and stomach press into the leather couch.

Leather couch.

Not my couch. I roll my eyes in every direction, taking in the room. The Jaegers' living room.

And everything comes flooding back. "Oh shit." I flip over, the blanket resting against my bare skin, and feel a crick in my neck from sleeping too hard.

I blink against the light streaming through the curtains. It's morning. I pat the blanket, feeling my body underneath. I'm still naked. Shit, I fell sleep.

"Yeah, I'll think about it," I hear Trace say, and see him walk across the foyer in a towel as he opens the door for Carissa, the girl from last night. "See you."

She walks out, and I hurriedly search, finding my school shirt and pulling it on.

Fuck, where is my skirt? I search the floor.

Oh my God. What did I do?

"Is that Krisjen's car?" he asks. Half of his body hangs out the open door, talking to someone, and I lean over, quickly feeling under the couch for the rest of my clothes.

The smell of bacon and coffee fills the air, making my mouth water, and it hits me that someone is cooking. Someone had to come downstairs and pass me, half-covered, on the couch. I clench my teeth.

Trace comes back inside, closes the door, and I lie back down, the blanket still covering my naked bottom half.

"Oh, hey." He sees me on the couch.

"Hey."

"What are you doing?" he asks.

I can't seem to calm my breathing. "Um . . ." I search for words. "My tires. They're flat. I wanted to wait for the rain to stop to call a tow truck."

He sits down on the edge of the couch. "No, we'll take care of them. I'm good for something, right?"

He looks down with a friendly vulnerability in his eyes that turns everyone to putty in his hands.

I'm a little mad at him, contrary to what I told . . . whichever one of his brothers last night.

*Oh my God, I don't even know who it was . . .*

But I should be angrier at Trace. I'm just not. What happened after I left his room has overshadowed whatever happened before.

I fist the blanket, staring up at him but still feeling the other one inside of me.

He cocks his head. "Are you okay?"

"I'm fine. I meant to be gone already." I start to sit up. "I'll be out of here soon."

"You don't have to rush." He stops me. "Krisjen, don't pay me any mind, okay? I'm a shithead."

"It's fine. I'm fine."

Guilt nips at me, because I'm really glad I left his room last night. What happened afterward was certainly weird. Would I do it again? Yes.

"But you did come with me, right?" he asks, studying me. "Like you didn't fake it all summer, right? You were just teasing me about that?"

I finally let out a chuckle. I don't want to lie, but I don't have the heart to burst his bubble. Honestly, I never really minded. I didn't come with Milo, either. I just liked being touched. Being close to someone.

But last night . . .

On the couch . . .

That was something I didn't know existed.

I have every confidence Trace will get better with time, but I don't think it will ever be like that with us.

He stands up, tsking. "You're so mean to me. I always had an orgasm with you."

I snort, but as soon as he disappears into the kitchen, I scurry to find my skirt. I spot it on the side of the coffee table and grab it. Standing, I pull it on and zip it up.

Dallas rounds the banister just as I finish and slows as soon as he sees me. I go still.

His gaze never leaves mine as he heads past me, and while his eyes are the same color as Trace's, they look completely different on Dallas.

I glance down, seeing the bracelet on his wrist. My stomach sinks. Whoever it was last night would probably still be wearing it this morning.

He enters the kitchen, and I bolt for the bathroom. Down the hall, into the half bath under the stairs. I close and lock the door, pulling up my skirt and sitting on the toilet.

Jesus Christ. How could I not stop him last night? At least to wear a condom? I'm sure I'm not pregnant. I've been on birth control since I was fourteen, but every single Jaeger sleeps around. Except Liv, of course.

I grab toilet paper and wipe, feeling the slickness between my legs as he leaves me. I clean myself up and flush, looking in the mirror.

I'm breathing hard again, but I just stare, letting myself process.

A bracelet. Bare chest against my back. Tall. He smelled amazing and tasted like meat with a hint of bourbon. And the beer he'd just swallowed.

He didn't speak much above a whisper, he had rough hands, and there was so much heat on his tongue. All of the brothers could probably fit most of that description.

Fuck.

I look down at my body, not seeing any visible marks yet, but I feel them. An ache between my legs, some red on my neck from when he squeezed it. My arms are sore and my scalp hurts, but I'm not in pain. In fact, I fight not to smile as I feel all of it. Proof that he had me in his hands.

Could it have been Trace? He would've felt comfortable enough to go after me like that. None of the others have even looked at me twice. I didn't see any tattoos, and Trace doesn't have any yet, but then again, I didn't see much of the man's skin at all. Just the hands, wrists, maybe a forearm. Iron has a tattoo there. Would I have noticed it in the dark?

I grab someone's brush on the edge of the sink and smooth out my hair, then take the tube of toothpaste and put some on my finger, wiping it over my teeth and rinsing.

I have to leave. If it was Dallas, he won't be kind about it this morning. *God, please let it not be Dallas.* He hates Saints. He's never been civil to me, let alone kind. As far as he's concerned, we're good for one thing.

And I really hope I didn't give that one thing to him last night.

I head out of the bathroom, fold the blanket in the living room, and search the coffee table for my keys.

But they're not there.

Spinning around, I scan the floor and then drop down on all fours, looking under the couch. Nothing. Did someone pick them up?

I hear Trace's laugh, followed by Dallas's cursing. There's at least one other person in there, cooking. I groan, smoothing out my clothes and hair as I inch around the corner to look in the kitchen.

Army stands at the stove, flipping bacon with a dish towel hanging out of his back jeans pocket, the sun making his dark brown hair and the skin on his back look golden. The tentacles of the octopus tattoo drape over his shoulder blade.

His one-year-old son, Dex, jumps up and down as he stands on Trace's lap, the half-eaten Cheerios and banana left at his high chair. His new white sneakers with the black Nike symbol are always on his feet because he's just learned to walk, and his uncles couldn't wait for all the new doors that was going to open. Soccer, climbing trees, walking dogs . . . But I think it'll be a few years before he's ready for any of that. Doesn't stop them from buying him shoes, though.

My keys sit on the counter, and I can feel Dallas's eyes on me as he takes a seat at the table. I move toward Army, reaching around him at the stove. "Excuse me."

He glances over his shoulder, seeing me as I snatch my keys back and turn to leave. I don't know how they ended up in here.

But Trace pulls me to the table. "Sit."

I pull away. "Stop."

"I'll fix your tires after breakfast," he says. "Stay and eat."

"I can handle it myself." I head out of the kitchen. "I don't need your help."

"I fixed her tires already."

I look up, seeing Iron head into the kitchen. He meets my eyes, sweat covering his neck and chest, and I don't realize I'm frozen until my lungs ache from no air. He walks around me, to the table, and I stand there for a second.

How did he know I had a problem with my tires? I guess that explains how my keys weren't where I left them.

But before I can say thank you, I hear Dallas.

"You fixed her tires?"

I can hear the disgust in his voice.

"Her grandfather is sending you to prison for forty-two months, Iron. Forty, if you behave yourself, which you won't."

"Maybe fixing his granddaughter's car will win him some points," Trace jokes, and grabs my arm, hauling me over.

I fall onto the seat next to him but immediately pop back up.

I'm not staying.

"This isn't funny!" I hear Dallas yell. He glares at me from the other side of the table. "Get the fuck out of here. Macon says no girls at the table anyway."

"Clay eats at the table," Trace points out.

"Clay's more to Liv than just a piece of ass!" Dallas cocks an eyebrow at me. "Unfortunately."

"Jesus, enough," Army growls at him. "Goddammit. I'm sick of your shit." He dumps the plate of bacon on the table. "I want some peace at this table for once."

Dallas opens his mouth.

"Shut up," Army barks again before Dallas can argue more.

The table falls silent as Army puts his kid back in his high chair and everyone starts loading their plates. It's almost comical how they fight nonstop, and Dallas just insulted me several times in the span of thirty seconds, but I still see them as more of a family than I've ever witnessed before. I've seen them eat more meals together in the six months I've known them than my family has in my entire life.

I look across the table where Iron has taken a seat next to Dallas. I know I told Trace I could take care of the tires, but it wouldn't have been that easy. "You didn't have to do that," I tell Iron. "I appreciate it, though. Thank you."

"We can be gentlemen from time to time," Army adds next to me.

I look up as he holds a loaded plate out for me, his smile unusually soft. "Sit."

A hickey mars the skin under his ear, the red-purple mark fresh. My heart kicks up a beat, and I stare at it, trying to remember if I kissed the man's neck last night. I absently take the plate and sit down in the empty seat at the foot of the table.

"Eat," Iron tells me. "The car has a few issues you need to have a mechanic look at. I'll walk you out when we're done."

I nod, but I can't eat. My stomach is doing somersaults. No one speaks, and I look over, seeing Dex smiling at me. I wink at him, remembering my brother and sister. Pulling out my phone, I tap out a text to Mars, letting him know I'll be home soon.

But when I look up, I see Trace watching me. He looks away when I meet his eyes.

Then I spot Dallas casting a sideways glance, followed by Iron and Army. Their bracelets catch the sunlight coming in from the windows. Leather and iron. With the same symbol that's tattooed on Iron's neck and on the left side of Dallas's chest.

I float my gaze from one wrist to another as if I'll recognize the feel of the skin or the wear on the leather by sight. Which wrist did he wear his on last night?

"Did you find the gator?" Army suddenly asks.

I look up, noticing Macon entering the kitchen. The oldest and the head of the house.

He pulls off his greasy, sweaty T-shirt and tosses it into the laundry room. I watch him fill a glass with water, his broad back tanned and toned, and it does that thing where his muscles bulge on each side of his spine, making it look indented. His jeans hang low as he watches the water fill the glass like none of us are here.

There's a three-inch vertical gash on the right side of his back—an old wound—and another small one on his upper arm. And those are just the ones I can see. Macon doesn't have tattoos. He has scars. Maybe from when he was a Marine. Maybe from here in the Bay. He's thirty-one, and the only one, other than Liv, with brown eyes. They got them from their mother.

I catch Dallas watching me, and he just shakes his head.

Macon sits at the head of the table, Army placing a plate in front of him.

"You should've let me come with you," Army tells him. "You wouldn't have been able to handle it on your own anyway."

Macon says nothing, just starts eating.

Dallas opens his mouth, but Macon cuts him off before he has a chance to speak. "Shut up and eat."

I cast Dallas a look, trying to hide my amusement, because I know he was going to bitch that I was at the table.

But when I look away, I catch sight of Macon's wrist.

And his bracelet.

My smile falls, and I raise my eyes, watching him ignore us as he chews.

It *couldn't* have been him. It wouldn't have been him.

My stomach swims. *It's on his right wrist.* Same as Trace. Same as the guy last night on the couch.

I float my eyes around the table. They all wear theirs on the right wrist.

"I called Collins and Barrow," Iron tells his brother. "Asked if we could wait till midday for the grass to dry a little."

Macon nods, the rain last night throwing off their schedule, but I'm sure they're used to it. Florida has weather. "Swing by Trade Winds a day early, then," he says, "and do the maintenance in the solarium."

Iron shifts in his seat.

"And wear a shirt this time," Macon gripes. "I don't ever want another phone call from those fuckin' people."

I bite back my smile; all the places they're talking about are in St. Carmen. The Jaegers will let us pay them for landscaping, gardening, pool cleaning, and carpentry, but other than that, they don't want to be reminded that we exist.

"Mariette phoned," Army tells him, finally taking his seat. "Her latest hire already quit, and no one wants the day shift."

Macon scoops up more food onto his fork. "Call Aracely."

"No answer."

"Just deal with it," Macon mumbles.

Bags hang under his eyes, and his arm looks like it weighs a hundred pounds when he picks up his coffee cup. He pushes his plate away, barely eaten, and rises, leaving the room. Back into the garage.

*Don't worry, Dallas.* Pretty sure Macon didn't even notice I was at the table this morning anyway.

I stand up, setting my plate down next to Trace, because I know he'll eat it. "I'll wait outside," I tell Iron. "Take your time."

Sanoa Bay never seems to sleep. Kids run around where their older siblings and parents played last night, and I can never tell if people are just getting in or just going out for work. There's always music drifting from someone's garage or someone's house. Always from Mariette's Restaurant, and always from the bar next door to it after 4:00 p.m.

It's a community in the way my neighborhood isn't. The only thing I hate over here are the dirt roads. They're a reminder that the Bay is just the poor part of St. Carmen and not its own town. If it were, it would have autonomy over its own revenue and be able to afford the bare minimum. Like streetlamps and sidewalks.

Iron leans under the hood of my car next to me, and I hear him talk, but I don't know what he's saying.

He's been kind this morning. Really helpful like he never has before.

But my grandfather is sending him to prison for three and a half years, so maybe he thought seducing me last night would be a great way to get back at my family? And now he feels guilty about it? Was it him, then?

Army was attentive at breakfast, too. He's usually rushing around, overwhelmed, because he's running a business *and* trying to shield Macon from whatever will set him off, and I'm eighteen, so what do I matter to a twenty-eight-year-old single father? But he was calm this morning. He smiled at me. Why?

Dallas was as angry as ever. It can't be him.

Trace looked guilty when he saw me on the couch, too.

But he did walk that girl out, so I doubt he came down after me last night and left her in his room. It wasn't him. Definitely not. I know what he feels like, and that wasn't it.

Macon's the only one who acted typical this morning.

And I don't think it's his style to sleep with his little sister's friends, either. He's way older than me.

"Krisjen."

It had to be Army or Iron. Right? I mean . . .

"Krisjen!"

I blink, coming back into focus. Iron still leans under the hood, but he's staring at me. Oh my God. Was I thinking out loud?

But he just smirks in that way that makes the color in his eyes look like a shamrock. "You have no idea what I'm talking about, do you?" he asks.

Talking? What? Oh, the car.

I shrug a little. "Could you write it down? I'll pass it on to a mechanic."

It's not like I'm fixing any of this myself.

He laughs under his breath, standing up and closing the hood. "I'll give you a ride home. Just leave it here for a few days. I'll fix it."

"No, that's okay," I say it as gently as possible. "I won't be back."

He looks at me, and I don't mean that to sound insulting. Last night ended much better than it started, but I need to focus now. If I don't get ahead of my mother, she's going to have my future figured out for me.

But he just slips my keys into his pocket. "I can drop it off when I'm done, then."

"Why do you want to fix it?" I study him, definitely having an idea why but deciding not to press it. If he's not going to talk about last night, then it's either not him or it wasn't a big deal, so I play along. "I'll put in a word with my grandfather, but all you had to do was ask. Not that my input will help you anyway. He barely knows I exist."

"I don't want to hear about your grandfather, and I don't want you to talk to him for me." He takes a T-shirt hanging off the handlebar of his motorcycle and pulls it on. "He warned me the first time I was busted and the second, and I didn't listen. Not sure I still would if I could go back and do anything differently."

He's not lying. My grandfather gave him chances.

But my grandfather also knows, as do I, that if Iron's last name was Ames or Collins or Price, his punishment would be no more than being the butt of a joke within his father's circle as he smokes a cigar on the golf course while they all complain about their kids.

Prison rarely makes a person's life better. It's more likely than not that Iron will be perpetually in and out of jail.

He steps up to me, takes my backpack, and slips it into his saddlebag. "I would like you here after I go away, okay?"

I hesitate.

"You don't have to fuck Trace to be his friend." Iron looks over at me. "He's lonely. Dallas is always in a bad mood, Army is a lot older and has a kid, and Macon doesn't talk to anyone. It would be nice for Trace to know you're around. I know he acts like a tool, but he's twenty."

I always liked Trace. But I don't want to be walked on. He and I started at the wrong place. We can't just be friends now.

"His only memories of our mother were after she'd gotten to her worst," he tells me. "He was never nurtured, not the way the rest of us were or how Liv was, because she was the only girl. Trace missed out on a lot. He needs a woman in the house."

*After she'd gotten to her worst . . .*

Their mother died by suicide more than eight years ago. Two months after their dad died of a heart attack.

She'd been depressed long before that, though. That's about all I know. Trace doesn't talk about it, and I never pressed Liv for details. They were so young, I doubt they really knew the full measure of what had happened with their mom. Macon and Army will remember the most.

I just shake my head. "I can't pay you for the car," I admit. "And I've got my own problems, Iron. Trace will be fine. Everything's going to be okay."

"Nothing has ever been okay," he whispers, looking down for a second. "I'm used to it. Trace is still young."

I watch him, both of us falling silent.

He's worried. He knows he probably wouldn't have avoided this if he could go back and do it over, because Iron lives for people to give him a reason to hit them, but he doesn't feel good about what he's done, either. Did it just finally dawn on him that his family needs him, and in a week, they'll be without him for years?

He clears his throat, digging out a set of keys, and I see they're not mine. "Do you have another car at home?" he asks.

"My dad's old Benz."

"Does it run?"

"Yeah." I nod. "It should."

He sighs, gesturing for me to climb on his bike behind him. "You don't have to pay me," he says. "I need something to do this week."

He starts the bike, and I take the helmet he hands me, pulling it on and fastening it as I sit down behind him. Wrapping my arms around him, I hold tight as he takes off, through the green and shade of the swamp, over the tracks, and onto the two-lane highway as his tires finally touch pavement.

He revs the gas, sending the bike lurching, and I squeeze my arms around his waist, pressing my body close to his.

He's warm. And tight under my hands.

My friend Amy said he was good. She said he and Dallas didn't let her get any sleep.

Thoughts of how he might've been with her versus me—if it was him last night—hit me, and I push them away.

It's not worth dwelling on. I won't be going back over there.

We cruise into the main village of St. Carmen, a street sweeper cleaning the spilled palms and flowers from the storm last night as potted ferns and perennials swing from hangers under streetlights. Shops begin to open, and I unlock my fists, pressing my fingertips flat against his stomach. The wind blows my hair over my back. And while thoughts creep in that I'm practically doing the fucking walk of shame when Clay and the rest of my friends are busy with classes, making something of themselves, I force myself to appreciate this moment. It feels better than school. Better than home.

I wish he'd keep going. Down the coast. To the Keys. Cuba. Anywhere.

I always feel too much guilt. *I should be doing this. I should be doing that. I shouldn't sit down. I shouldn't wake up late. I shouldn't drink or party or skip a workout.* I rest my cheek against his back, close my eyes, and fly through the wind.

Before I know it, he pulls up to my house, and I see the gate is open.

My mother is home. *Great.*

He slowly pulls down my driveway, and I spot my mom's new Maserati parked off to the right. She bought it, because she's still married to my father, and while I'm sick of her, I'm kind of excited to see my father react when the first payment comes due.

Iron stops behind it, out of direct view of the front of the house. It's nice how he's trying to save me from getting yelled at, because he knows no parent wants their daughter getting brought home—in the morning—by a Jaeger.

I sit there, not letting go, though. "Is it weird I'm enjoying this town more with all my friends gone to college now?" I ask him.

I feel him take something out of his pocket.

"I mean, Clay is still in town," I say as I climb off the bike, "but she's busy. I don't have to see too many familiar faces from high school. It'll only be embarrassing when they come home for the holidays and I'm still doing nothing."

He flicks his lighter, mumbling over his cigarette as he lights it. "At least you won't be in jail."

Puffs of smoke rise into the air. I don't remember that smell last night. Iron doesn't smoke a lot, but he smokes every day.

"True," I say.

If I were him, I'd be depressed, knowing where I was going to be in a week. It's almost better to just get arrested and go, without the opportunity to dread it.

"It can always be worse." He peers over his shoulder at me. "And once in a while, it will be. Stay in the moment. This could be it, right?"

*This could be it.* The Tryst Six motto. A reminder that time is the most valuable commodity and no one can buy more of it.

We can try, but the clock ticks and it never stops. It never slows.

"For what it's worth," I tell him, "I'm sorry."

"It's not your fault."

"I know. I just . . ." I'm not sure what I'm trying to say. He did the crime. Multiple times. Blew the chances he was given. He chose this. "I just know you're good. A good person."

Despite his troublemaking.

His eyes soften, and I can see the wheels turning in his head as he looks at me. Finally, he gets off the bike and digs into the saddlebag, the cigarette hanging out of his mouth. "I know how you can pay me back," he tells me. "For fixing your car, I mean. Mariette needs help at the restaurant, and you don't seem to have a job."

He pulls out my backpack.

But I shake my head. "I told you. I'm not going back over there."

"Done looking for love in all the wrong places?"

"Isn't that a song?"

He comes around and holds out the straps of my bag. I slip my arms through, feeling his fingers graze my skin. My skin tightens, tingles spreading.

"I enjoy this town more this time of year, too," he says in a low voice. "The college kids are gone, and the snowbirds haven't arrived yet. For a little while, it's just ours. Nothing else really changes. It's always summer here. But the nights do cool down a little, and the streets are quiet enough that you can hear the wind in the palms. The air smells better. We finally come outside. It's the locals' turn to play."

A taunt laces his tone, and I swear I feel his breath on my neck.

He's right. I never really thought about it like that. Saint or Swamp. We're both still locals.

"I'll kind of miss you, kid," he almost whispers. "I hope you had some fun in Sanoa Bay at least. While you played."

A jolt hits me low in the belly, and I turn around, but he's already climbing back on his bike. I watch him speed off, and for a second, time slows as he leaves, turns, and disappears behind the hedge wall.

A knot twists in my stomach for just a second. I said I was done there, but it suddenly hits me that I don't know when I'll see him again. I almost take a step as if I'll catch up to him, but I shake it off and head inside.

I'll miss him.

I step into the house, hearing the buzzer on the stove going off, and rush into the kitchen. Bateman, Paisleigh's nanny, pulls a sheet of fresh-baked pastries out of the oven, and I exhale. I forgot he was going to be here today.

"Morning," I call out, dumping my backpack on the chair next to my sister as she sits at the island. I lean over her. "What are you working on?"

"Drawing dinosaurs."

Her hair, just a shade lighter than mine, is styled in two reverse French braids that Bateman undoubtedly did when he got her up this morning. I think my mother stopped doing her kids' hair with me.

I peek at the triceratops walking underneath a rainbow. "Nice," I tell her. "You know they weren't purple, though, right?"

"We don't know for sure that they weren't," she replies too assuredly for a five-year-old. "No one is actually sure what they looked like, just made guesses based off nutrients they found in the bones and other things like climate and vegetation at the time."

She goes to a really good school.

I kiss her head. "Touché."

She continues drawing, and I ask Bateman, "Is she upstairs?"

He nods, his eyes flashing toward the ceiling.

I grab my phone and head up the staircase, that job at Mariette's feeling like heaven right now.

I scroll through my notifications as I head up, spotting a few pictures of Liv and Clay at breakfast this morning. I smile. Liv's in town. I didn't expect her back before the holidays. She went up north to Dartmouth for college. Clay loves her to death, but it's really fucking cold up there, so Clay stayed home for school.

But I think the real reason is that she's reconnecting with her parents. Years ago, they lost her younger brother to leukemia. Now they're divorcing, but it's only made all of them closer. She doesn't want to lose that.

And I also see a follow request from Jerome Watson.

I close my eyes, exiting out of social media.

I pass my brother's closed door and stop at the doorway of my mom's bedroom as she comes out of her bathroom, dressed in a pretty white dress with short sleeves, a square neckline, and a tight fit around her body.

It's mine.

She pops her head up, carrying some toiletries to an overnight bag. I guess she plans on being gone tonight, too.

"Oh, you're here," she chirps. "Good. Sit down."

I shuffle to the chair at her vanity, seeing all her jewelry in a pile on top. What is she doing?

"I'm taking your brother to church," she tells me. "You come, too."

She hasn't attended since my father left nearly a year ago. She wanted to avoid the stares and fake sympathy. I know why she's going now.

Jerome Watson will be there.

"Why don't you marry him?" I ask her.

At forty years old, she's only eight years older than him. They're closer in age than he and I are.

"Because I'm not having any more kids," she retorts.

And I'm certainly not having any anytime soon, either. "I'm not going to church. And I'm not accepting his friend request, so you can stop encouraging him."

She zips up the leather satchel, removes her glasses, and walks over, reaching around me to get her perfume. "He will make sure your brother and sister stay with me instead of your father and that paid-for piece of ass," she bites out, not missing a beat. "He will make sure I don't grow old in some assisted-living center surrounded by early bird specials and denture cream. He will secure the lifestyle you've always known. You'll have everything, Krisjen." She peers down at me, spraying a shot of Guerlain, and cocking an eyebrow. "You're coming to church, and he's going to bring you home. You may stop off for lunch, and then later in the week, you'll invite him over for a barbecue, where you'll laugh and play with your brother and sister and show him what a good girl you are before you present him with those caramelized onion, roast beef, and goat cheese focaccias you make so well."

She leans down, planting her hands on my armrests. I turn away as she gets in my face.

"Then you'll move on to a few dinners, where I will let him bring you home later and later and your dresses will get tighter and shorter, and then, finally, I will let you know when it's time to let him seduce you, because he's going to want a test-drive before he commits."

I fold my lips between my teeth to keep my chin from shaking.

"You're going to do what you have to, and you're going to blow his mind, do you understand?"

I swallow hard. I refuse to give her a fight.

"Now, I'm not crazy," she states. "I know I sound horrible, and when I was your age, I probably would've wanted to kill my mother for saying the things I'm saying to you, but that 'follow your heart and persevere' bullshit rarely works for most of us. You have to grow up and fuck people you don't want to fuck, because there is one thing that's worse on this planet, and that's being poor. I guarantee, no matter how much you hate him, you're going to hate Paisleigh growing up in the Vista View Apartments a lot more. We need you, do you understand?"

*Fuck . . .*

"You let Milo fuck you because you wanted a popular boyfriend." She goes back to her bed and slips her feet into her heels. "May as well get some purses and shoes out of the next one."

Every muscle in my body tightens as she disappears into the bathroom again, and I get that fantasy of shoving everything I can into a backpack and hitchhiking out of here flashing through my mind. Anywhere. Seattle. Montana. Alaska.

But I would never leave Paisleigh and Mars.

I don't want my parents to die, but sometimes I have other fantasies that include them mysteriously disappearing. Prayers or running away aren't going to save me, though. I'll just have to figure a way out of this. I'm smart.

I leave her room, grab a quick shower, and change my clothes.

I can't be here today. I need my dad.

If he would just pay her off and show up for his kids . . . He doesn't even have to show up for me. I'm grown.

They need him, though. If he acted fairly, I might have options.

And the irony of that isn't lost on me, either. Begging for one man to save me from another.

No. I'll figure it out. I need to think. And not in church.

I jog downstairs and pick up a banana out of the fruit bowl. I wrap my arms around Paisleigh. "Wanna spend the day with me?"

She nods quickly.

I dig my wallet out of my backpack, grab the keys to my dad's old car, and quickly sweep her into my arms.

"Just get her clothes and lunch ready for school tomorrow and then you can go, okay?" I tell Bateman.

He narrows his eyes. "Are you sure?" But he sounds a little excited by the prospect of an unexpected day off.

"Yes." And I practically run with Paisleigh out the door before my mother comes downstairs.

I put my sister in the back seat of the Benz, strap her into the booster, and then unlock the top, putting it down on such a sunny day.

"Yay!" She giggles. "And turn up the music!"

"You got it, princess." I start the car, my dad's old cassette tape still in the player. Olivia Newton-John blasts over the speakers as we cruise to the only place I feel safe, shouting the lyrics as we cross the tracks.

# 3

## Iron

I enter the house, tossing my keys into the dish next to the door. I grunt at the semi-hard-on still going in my jeans. I fucking swear she was doing that on purpose. Pressing into me, holding on to me so tight, breathing on my neck . . . I almost ran a red light, not paying attention.

Aracely stands in the living room, wiping down one of the end tables. She sees me, tosses down the cloth, and saunters up to me. The flyaways from her messy bun fan across her face, and her winged eyeliner makes her brown eyes look even sexier. She still kind of does it for me. Too bad she's fucking crazy.

"Did you slash her tires?" I ask.

"Well, how else could you be the hero?" she coos. "Did she hold you nice and tight on the back of that bike like I used to do?"

And then she strokes the can of furniture polish in her hand exactly like she used to . . . stroke me.

I chuckle. I broke up with her when we were teenagers so I wouldn't have to deal with her every day, yet here we are. "I used to think your antics were fun," I tell her, "but then I turned eighteen and grew the fuck up."

"And yet you're the one going to prison," she shoots back,

pulling out something from her back pocket. She holds up a pair of white cotton panties. "Found them in the couch."

"They're not mine."

She reaches out, yanking me by the ear.

"Ow!" I pull away. "Celli, dammit . . ."

She gets in my face. "I would've expected something a little fancier for a St. Carmen girl."

She means Krisjen.

She tosses the panties at me, and I catch them, firing back, "A St. Carmen girl knows it's not the wrapper that sells the candy."

She scowls, walking away, and I can't help but smile after her. I'm going to miss her.

We pay her to clean up a couple of times a week, but I think she'd do it for free, honestly. She's determined to be a part of this family.

She's already dated Dallas and me, but I have no doubt someone's going to marry her eventually. Just not me. She's way too possessive. Even six years after we've broken up.

Although, I'm sure it's more because I gave a Saint a ride home. The women in the Bay are territorial. They don't like the rich girls coming over here and stealing their men. Even for a night.

But, I wonder how wealthy Krisjen actually is. I don't expect her to pay me for repairs. We're friends. Kind of. But why wouldn't she have the money? Something's going on.

I head into the kitchen, sticking the underwear in my pocket, and open the fridge, taking a swig out of the orange juice container.

Army zips up Dex's lunch bag and screws on the cap of his water bottle. "Did she question you about the underwear?" he asks me.

I can hear the laughter in his voice.

I smile, nodding and putting the juice away. "I'll make sure Krisjen gets them back."

Or not. From the sound of it, we won't see her again. Or at least I won't before I leave.

Army slams the dishwasher shut, starts it, and pulls on his T-shirt. "All right," he calls out. "I'm dropping the kid off at Jasmine's and heading in with Dallas and Trace. You can ride with me unless you want to get a head start on the pools at the Bay Club and Fox Hill."

"I'm not going in." I pull my phone off the charger, checking for messages. "I'm done," I tell him.

I feel his eyes on me.

I refuse to look at him.

"Iron . . ." he says.

But I ignore him. "Is Macon in the garage?"

"Iron . . ."

I hesitate, then look over my shoulder. "What?"

He stares at me, and I know what he's going to say without him uttering a word. "You know what." He shakes his head. "It's your funeral."

I walk to the door and pull it open, seeing Macon down in the garage working on a green seventies Wagoneer. Its owner is a regular customer. A collector in St. Carmen who trusts only Macon with it.

This is what he does most of the time now. He runs the business side of our landscaping and pool-cleaning services, but he rarely leaves the house to do it. Army is the boss everyone sees. He's a lot easier for people to talk to. Macon hasn't crossed the tracks in months. And before that, very rarely.

I close the door and walk down the three steps, as Dallas passes the open garage with the day's cooler he just filled up with the hose. I hear the tailgate of the truck fall open, and Dex's cry as Army carries him down the street to the babysitter.

Macon's phone rings, and I dart my eyes between him and his

cell that he's pretending isn't there. A half-empty bottle of bourbon sits on top of the toolbox behind him.

I square my shoulders. "The developers are going to come whether you answer that phone or not."

He doesn't look up.

I step closer, wiping the sweat off the back of my neck. "Look, I found some issues with Krisjen's car," I tell him. "I'm going to stick around here today and work on it."

"No, you're not," he says, still twisting the wrench. "We need you on the job."

"They'll be fine without me."

He tightens the bolt, the muscles in his arm flexing enough that I almost take a step back.

"So it's not bad enough you're leaving me shorthanded for three years," he says, "but you can't even pull your weight until you go?"

"I have eight more days of freedom I'd like to enjoy."

He looks up. "Oh, you had your fun," he points out. "Losing your freedom was the price, remember?" He tosses the tool down and turns, digging in a drawer and pulling out some needle-nose pliers. "Tell her to take it to a mechanic in St. Carmen. She's not wasting our time just because you think you're going to get laid." And then he stops again, scowling. "And I'm sick of these girls hanging around. You understand? At least Aracely pulls her fucking weight. Y'all stop bringing them home."

He goes back to work, while I just stand there, watching him, whatever argument was on my lips disappearing altogether. There's no use talking to him. There never was. He got saddled raising us eight years ago, and he's been angry at the world ever since.

I can't say I remember him being any different before then, though. All I wanted when I was sixteen was for him to smile. Or say that I did something well. But he was always a ghost.

I don't even think he cried at our parents' funerals.

"Macon . . ." I murmur.

He removes the engine cover, turning it over and placing it on his workbench.

I speak a little louder. "Will you look at me, please?"

He dumps the bolts inside the cover and turns back to the car as if I've already left the garage. He hates me.

I take a deep breath and tip my chin back up. "Krisjen has no money," I tell him. "She needs me to fix the car."

"I'll fix the fuckin' car," he growls. "Like I don't have enough to do. Just get to work, because soon enough you get to sit on your ass all day, and you're still gonna need money from me."

I swallow the fucking rotten taste in my mouth, because he's not wrong. He's never fucking wrong, and I'm always a piece of shit.

According to every interaction I've had with him the past eight years, I'm all but useless.

I feel stupid enough. If I could go back and change it, I would hope I wouldn't get into that fight. I wouldn't have gotten drunk, let my temper get the better of me, and hurt the wrong person so badly over something I don't even remember that I put him in the hospital.

I knew it was a mistake. I always do, but it's like I can't stop myself.

I'm not worried about going to prison. I'm worried it won't change me.

"I fucked up." My eyes start to burn with tears I fucking hate myself for. "I fuck up."

But he doesn't spare me another glance.

I reach into my pocket, tossing Krisjen's keys on the table. "The alignment, the brakes," I tell him, "the radiator is leaking, and I'm guessing the oil is as thick as mud."

A snarl hits his lips, and I almost smile, but I don't.

When I head out of the garage, Trace is climbing into the bed of the truck and Army's crossing the street, minus Dex.

"Give me the keys." I hold out my hands.

Army smiles, shaking his head, because he knows Macon won. He tosses the keys, and I catch them.

"Don't laugh," I say.

"Hey, nothing to be ashamed of," he teases. "I'm older than you, and he still scares the shit out of me."

"And that's nothing to brag about."

"No, but staying alive is."

Army starts to turn, but I spot Dallas back by the truck, stealing glances at us and trying to get the beer into the cooler before Army sees.

I pull Army's arm, distracting him to give Dallas time. "Hey."

Army stops and turns back, facing me.

"You need to handle Aracely," I tell him.

He looks confused. "She's not my girlfriend."

"She wants to be." I pull off my T-shirt and stick it in my back pocket. "She'll listen to you. Tell her to stop doing dumb shit, please."

He smiles. "Like taking advantage of a St. Carmen princess?" he muses, because he knows she slashed Krisjen's tires. "Like we *all* like to do from time to time? Since when do *you* give anyone a ride home?"

"I'm a gentleman."

He cocks an eyebrow.

"Well, I'm the *most* gentlemanly."

He snorts. "Probably true."

"Well, no one wants me to be a gentleman," Dallas says, coming up to my side. "That's for sure."

He grins at Army, our older brother's eyes shifting between us as Dallas hangs his arm across my shoulder.

"Look." Army sighs. "I know you're the middle children and all, but your rebellious stages are long overdue for a fucking conclusion, so wrap it up, because I'm exhausted." And then he flicks Dallas on the forehead. "And get the goddamn beer out of the cooler. It's eight o'clock in the morning, and I'm not an idiot."

He walks off; Dallas and I head for the truck.

"Can we start drinking now?" I gripe.

"Noon." He gives my shoulders a squeeze. "It'll give you something to look forward to."

He climbs into the back with Trace, and I open the cab, tossing in my shirt. "God, it's so fucking hot still. I think I'll camp out on the beach tonight. I can't deal with his shit for the next eight days."

"Macon's on my case almost as much as yours," Dallas chimes in. "You can stick around and buffer before I have to deal with him by myself for the next three and a half years."

"What the fuck is his problem all the time?" I say under my breath.

"It changed the moment he had to become our father instead of our brother," Dallas says.

But I disagree. He was never a brother like Army is.

"He needs to fucking let it go," I say. "Anger isn't going to keep me from prison."

"He isn't angry."

I turn to Trace, whose voice chimes in. He hangs his elbows over the side of the truck.

"He's worried," he tells me. "What the hell does Macon have when we're gone?"

He looks past me, and I follow his gaze, seeing Macon toss two tires out of the garage. The sun beats down on his back, his head hanging like it weighs a ton.

"He has no woman who loves him," Trace goes on. "No kids of his own running around. He has nothing but us. Liv left. You're going," he says to me, then looks at Dallas. "And how long are you gonna stick around without him here?" He doesn't wait for an answer. "I'll be next, and Army will stay only because he has Dex in tow. What will Macon have to do with his life then?"

I grind my fingers into my palms.

But before I can ponder what he said for too long, I hear his low voice turn to a bite. "Oh, what the hell?"

I look up, seeing what he sees.

Milo Price walks out of the small motel next to the bar down the road.

A burn swirls in my stomach. A feeling I know well and one that I love.

He's dressed only in jeans as he leans against a column and lights a cigarette.

The motel's got six units, which are almost always empty, except for an hour here or there when guys like him pay to slum.

"What the fuck is he doing here?" Army strolls up, tossing his tool belt into the truck.

I take a step but stop, a white nineties Mercedes-Benz convertible cruising past right in front of me. Music blasts, and Krisjen heads straight for Mariette's, sliding perfectly into a spot right up front.

"What is she doing back?" Dallas asks.

I glance at her ex, still standing in front of the motel, and I can tell the moment he sees her. I dart my gaze back to her, but she doesn't see him.

Dallas and Trace climb out of the bed, and I slam the door closed, all of us stepping toward the road. Krisjen climbs out of the car a hundred yards down the street, takes a kid out of the back seat, and holds their hand as she goes into the restaurant. Milo watches her, and I wait till she's gone before I charge over to him. He isn't welcome here, and it has very little to do with her. He's got to be another level of stupid to think he can show his face after what he did.

With my brothers on my heels, I head straight for the son of a bitch.

He sees me coming and straightens up. "Easy, man." A fucking smile dances across his lips. "I'm not looking for trouble."

"Iron . . ." Army tries to calm me.

But I don't listen. "You're not welcome here," I bite out.

Milo sucks on his cigarette, the scar my sister's girlfriend left down the side of his face last spring still red and fresh. I'm surprised he forgot the warning to stay away with it staring him in the mirror every day.

"I paid," he assures us.

Camilla Gonzalez steps out of the room behind him, fixing the cups of her tank top. She stops, seeing us.

"Get inside," I growl.

*Goddamn her.*

She steals back into the room, and I take a step into Milo. "Stay away from our women."

"When you have plenty of fun with ours?" He casts a look toward Mariette's and the Mercedes parked in front of it, indicating Krisjen. He snickers. "You all want them because they're young, tight, and clean between the legs. They giggle and wear pink, but damn, they feel good, don't they? Your sister knew it. She loves Saint pussy, too."

I jolt, a hand gripping my arm from behind to stop me.

"And they get wet around any cock wearing a tool belt." Milo shakes with laughter. "But, Iron, they don't stay. Our women need money to look that good."

"Clay doesn't need money from Liv," I tell him. "And if you were any fucking good in bed, you would realize they'll always cross the tracks for the things you can't give them."

He takes a drag and blows out smoke, his eyes never leaving mine.

"Did you know there's a ring of wife swapping in St. Carmen?" he tells us. "My dad has fucked everyone's wife. I followed my mom to a party one night where she was the belle of the ball."

I frown.

It's becoming easier to understand why he's so fucked up. God, these people are ugly.

"People marry for lots of reasons," he explains, "that aren't about love, and they get unhappy. To keep it together, they share with one another. Within their circle, that is, because there's no danger of falling in love or breaking up families. They're all in business deals together, so everyone has too much to lose and enough motivation to keep it quiet."

Is that true? They fucking pass their wives around?

Milo lowers his voice, taunting us. "I hear Jerome Watson is after Krisjen." He grins, and something starts crawling up my throat, my gut turning to brick. "She will get so much attention as a young St. Carmen wife. Maybe down the road, I'll get my turn with her again."

I bite down on my teeth, and he releases a sigh, a memory playing behind his eyes. "My favorite thing about Krisjen," he whispers, "is that she hits back."

I launch for him, grabbing him by the back of the neck and pushing him to the ground. *Motherfucker.*

Someone grabs me from behind. "No, goddammit!" Army bellows, wrapping his arm around my neck and hauling me back against him.

I growl, fighting to get away, and he throws me off to the side, getting in my face.

"Stop it!" Army yells at me. "He's baiting you!"

He turns, and I glare at Milo, knowing we should've fucking killed him last May.

Army points his finger in Milo's face. "Get the fuck out of here!"

Milo backs off, toward his car, but pauses to spit on our ground. "Enjoy your last week, Iron." He breathes hard. "By the time you get out, nothing will be yours."

And I know exactly what he means.

We watch him drive out of the Bay, and I wipe the sweat off my lip.

Why can't they just leave us alone? They have everything. Our land is a fraction of what it was, and they just keep coming for more.

All of this will be gone by the time I'm out.

I see Krisjen carry drinks to people on the deck, and I head for her.

"Iron," Trace calls out.

I ignore him, watching Krisjen head back inside.

"Krisjen," I call.

She turns her head, sees me, and rolls her eyes. "I know . . ." She enters the restaurant, and I follow. "It took about three seconds after you left for me to realize that I did not want to be subjected to my mother today, so I'm taking you up on your offer. But just for today." She nods, assuring me. "I won't be back. I mean it."

She's being playful, but it's the wrong time. "Just go now."

She turns and looks at me, and I feel my brothers stopping behind me.

"I mean it," I tell her. "Leave."

Someone lets out a hard breath. Probably Trace. He wants to be on my side, but he doesn't know what I'm doing.

Krisjen frowns, straightening as we all confront her. "What's wrong?" she asks us.

"You heard him," Dallas tells her. "Go."

"We're not a fucking tourist attraction," I point out. "Dick for you girls to ride until you've had enough. Slum somewhere else."

"Iron, knock it off," Trace barks. "Krisjen's not like that."

"We're a joke to them," I say over my shoulder. "To all of them. They use us."

"Like you and Dallas, or any of you, were looking for love all the times you went after St. Carmen tail?" She sneers. "Please."

"The difference is . . ." I walk up to her, lowering my voice. "We would marry you."

Her chest caves a little.

"If we loved you," I tell her. "I'd be so fucking proud if you were mine. Any of us would be. Would you show me off to your friends? Jump at the chance to live over here in the gutter with us?"

A lump moves down her throat, but her stern expression doesn't waver. "If I *ever* loved any of you, then maybe."

Dallas snickers behind me, but she doesn't fight me further. Ripping off the apron around her waist, she grabs the little girl, who I can only assume is one of her siblings, and rushes out of the restaurant.

"No! I don't want to go!" the little girl screams. Her sketchbook falls from her hands, her crayons still on the table.

"I'm sorry," Krisjen chokes out. "It's okay."

"What did I do?"

"Nothing, honey. I've got you."

Trace sweeps up the sketchbook, and we all walk after her, down the steps of the restaurant.

"Trace will deliver your Rover when it's done," I tell her.

"I'm taking it now."

"It's not drivable."

She whips around. "Like I give a shit!"

Army quietly laughs, and I follow as she heads to her Rover, which is still parked in front of our house. She leaves her dad's Benz at Mariette's. Is she actually going to take her little sister home in a car that's unsafe?

"You're stubborn," I taunt. "I always liked that. But no one can ever accuse you girls of being smart. That's for sure."

She puts her sister into her back seat, closes the door, and turns to face me. "See this?" She grabs herself between her legs. "I was born with all the tools I need to make as many sons as it takes to see this shithole burned to the ground."

"Ohhhh." Trace laughs.

Army snorts. "Damn."

"Shut up," I growl at them. That isn't funny.

I face Krisjen. "He smacked you around? Milo? He hit you, right? More than once?"

Fire lights up in her eyes. She knows I was at the lighthouse party last spring and saw. We let Milo have it that night, not that it did much good.

I get in her face, backing her into the car. "You know what he tried to do to my sister last spring. And if you would've spoken up before that—about what he was like—maybe he wouldn't have had a chance to try anything."

"Spoken up to who?" she shouts. "The police who are hired by the city council his mother sits on?"

I glare down at her.

"Or my grandfather, who is grooming Milo's cousin to replace him as district judge?" she says next, water pooling in her eyes. "Or maybe the school administration that accepts his family's donations? Or my classmates who never would've taken my side over his? Who?"

A beautiful blush crosses her cheeks, and I can almost feel the heat of her breath as she holds the tears at bay.

"Maybe I'm stupid." Her chin trembles, but she looks determined. "Because maybe he said all the right things one night when I thought he was all I had and I felt sorry for him." She laughs at her own dumb thinking. "Or maybe I wanted to believe he cared about me. Maybe I was naïve and I had lofty ideas about love and thought that his having violence in him didn't make him a bad person and the struggle would make it worth it."

Her words wind through me. *I have violence in me.* I'm not bad, though. I'm nothing like him . . .

"Or maybe I liked it." She smiles bitterly. "Because nothing felt good, so when it felt really fucking awful, the blood made me feel like I was surviving something. And that made me feel powerful."

I feel the crooked bone in the middle finger of my right hand that I once broke in a fight. The left nostril that I can never breathe through because it didn't set right after another altercation. And all the scars from all the times I lived to bleed, because it was the only time I felt strong.

"Or maybe I wanted it," she goes on, "because then I could hit back, and Mrs. George next door to me growing up never did. No financial independence to leave with her three kids. She was so quiet, because her husband had all but killed her, and she'll stay with him forever. And maybe sometimes I hoped Milo would take a swing just so I could swing back at him, and Mr. George, and my father, and everyone who stands on weaker people."

A tear spills down her cheek.

She's killing me.

"I wish you all could have all the money you ever wanted, so you can see that's not the answer," she says. "I liked coming here, because no one covers the bruises. Your women have their own motorcycles, and everyone's either laughing or howling. It's . . . different. I wanted friends, and you guys don't throw people away." Her voice lowers to a whisper, and I can tell she's struggling not to cry. "It's a good place."

She turns, but I grab her. Pulling her into me, I wrap my arms around her and bury my nose in her hair.

She tries to push away. "Stop it."

I don't let her go. "I'm sorry." I squeeze my eyes shut, feeling them watering. "I'm so sorry. I'm a prick. Jesus."

She shakes in my arms, and I pull back, looking down at her.

She shakes her head, refusing to look at me. "You think I have nothing inside of me."

"I don't think that."

She tries to turn, but I won't let her.

"You're not stupid," I tell her. "It's not your fault that you have a heart and tried to give it to him. I don't even know why I went after you this morning. I'm sorry."

I'm pissed at myself and my fucking mistakes, and I resent her family and her circle, but I like Krisjen.

She tears away from me, opening her car door. "Just let me go."

But I press my hand into it, slamming it shut. "You're not going back there today."

She turns, scowling at me.

I look down at her. "I don't want you around those people."

# 4

## Krisjen

What is his problem? As if I didn't feel like a big enough loser waiting only ten whole minutes before I followed Iron back over to the Bay when I said I would never be back again.

Now he's kicking me out.

But then . . .

*Oh wait, no, stay.*

I shake my head, his mouth so close I can feel his breath. At some point I really need to learn that men are just *not* worth the trouble.

"What the hell is going on?" Macon barks, and I see him out of the corner of my eye, walking out of the open garage.

Everyone stands there, but I'm not saying anything. This isn't on me.

Finally, Army pipes up, "Nothing!" And he pushes Trace toward their work truck.

"Then get to work!"

Iron's eyes don't leave mine, and I shouldn't, but I smile just a little, because he has to leave, and now, so can I.

"Iron, let's go!" Army shouts. "We're late." I hear the others climb into the truck. My smirk grows, the challenge hanging between us.

Iron jerks his head, looking at Macon. "Give me your knife."

"Why?"

"Just give it to me, Macon!"

Iron holds out his hand, and Macon hesitates as the truck's engine starts up. He digs in his pocket and pulls out a pocket knife, tossing it to Iron.

Iron swipes it midair and twists around, heading back toward the restaurant down the street.

We all stand and watch as he stalks toward the stairs, but then he stops at my dad's Benz, unsheathes the blade, and it hits me what he's going to do.

"No!" I growl, but I'm too late.

He bends over, stabs the front left tire, dragging the blade through the rubber to widen the gash.

"Ah!" I cry as laughter goes off in the truck behind me.

Iron runs over, tosses the knife back to Macon, and smiles. "Change that one, too?"

"You son of a—" Macon bites out, charging up next to me as we both watch Iron-fucking-Jaeger pull himself up and over the side, hopping into the truck bed.

"What the hell are you doing?" I scream.

He flashes me a white smile.

I ball my fists. "You asshole!"

He lets his head fall back as he laughs. "Go, go, go!" he shouts to Army in the cab.

They all howl as Army speeds off.

"Whoo!" Trace hollers.

"Goddammit!" Macon calls after them.

"I can order an Uber, you know!" I shout.

"We'll be back at five o'clock!" Iron calls out, leaning up on his knees as they drive off. "Tell Mariette we want our usual, and can you make those stuffed mushrooms you brought on the Fourth of July?"

"I'm not making you shit!"

"But I'm going to prison, Krisjen."

He sounds so fucking innocent, like I'm going to feel sorry for him. Trace covers his face with his hands, unable to stop his laughter.

They disappear down the street as Macon and I just stand there. Paisleigh giggles inside my car.

"God—" Macon says through his teeth. "Son of a . . ."

I look up at him, his scowl darkening as he turns from the truck that just sped off down to me.

I shrug. "It's not my fault,"

"Just . . ." he grits out, holding up his hands like he's going to strangle someone before gesturing to Mariette's. "Get over there and work this off. So help me God, I'm going to fucking explode right now."

I don't have a chance to argue further before he walks back into the garage, but I'm not sure I would've anyway. I would just leave. If I had a car.

I kick a rock, looking over at the Mercedes that now sits as lop-sided as my Rover did last night. *Fuuuuuck* these boys.

Dammit!

I grab my sister out of the car and walk back to Mariette's, shouting at Macon as I pass by the garage. "I'm keeping my tips!"

I spy the clock over the menu on the wall and pick up my pace, setting the sandwiches down in front of the two old ladies and collecting their empty dish of appetizers.

I wanted to be gone before five, so Iron can't gloat when he walks in and sees me here.

The day went quickly, though. For my first time working *ever*, it's not that bad. It feels like I'm being helpful, and I like that. Bring 'em drinks. Take their orders. Refill sodas. Clear plates.

It's kind of fun. I like people.

And the best part is I kept busy. The other server left early, so I've been swamped since noon, and although it was stressful to cover that many tables by myself, it was also strangely satisfying to multitask. Refill at table four, clean fork needed at table eight, order's up for table thirteen, hot sauce for table one . . .

I did something today. And did it well. I was never a great student, and an even worse athlete, but I'm good under pressure. Who knew.

"Hey, back again?" I ask, dropping menus in front of two road workers I just saw at lunch.

The one to my right grins, his blond mullet sticking out of his trucker hat, but honestly, he makes it work.

"We like pie," he teases.

The other one laughs, and I set their waters down as I dart my eyes to the wedding ring on his finger.

"Well, be sure to take some home to your wife," I reply.

The other one chuckles, and I don't look back as I walk away.

I wipe down a couple of tables, positioning place settings, when the screen door flaps closed behind me.

"Krisjen! We had so much fun!" my sister boasts. "I love those boats!"

What? I turn and watch her run to me, wrapping her arms around my neck as I scoop her up. Jasmine Cabrera walks in with her five-year-old, and Dex in a stroller. She babysits a few of the neighborhood kids, while her husband is away half the year fighting fires all over the country. I think he's in Arizona now.

I eye Jasmine. "You took her on an airboat?"

"I babysat for free."

I'm about to say something, but then I close my mouth, no matter how inappropriate it is for Paisleigh, Dex, or her—being four months pregnant—to ride on one of those things. My sister looks like she had a blast, and no one died, so okay.

I plant Paisleigh in a chair and pull the plate of macaroni and cheese I ordered in front of her as the rest of them take a seat and start eating. Jasmine holds Army's kid in her lap, feeding him, and I look down at the boy, noticing his eyes are blue, unlike his father's. He must get them from his mother. Wherever she is.

He chews, looking up at me, and I stick out my tongue and cross my eyes. He still just stares.

I check the clock again. It's almost five thirty.

"Eat up, kiddo," I tell Paisleigh.

I shoot my brother a text. **Be home soon.**

Then, I bring up my camera and squat down next to my sister, in selfie mode. She immediately giggles and follows my example, making a funny face for the camera before I snap a shot.

I send it to Mars and my mom. As if she's bothered to check with me at all today to make sure Paisleigh is safe. Tomorrow the kids will be in school, so if I decide to make this a job, it'll be easier. I don't have to worry about Paisleigh being at home and ignored by her.

"Krisjen!" someone shouts behind me.

I jump, recognizing Trace's voice. On a whim, I open TikTok and start filming my facial expressions, because I figure I can make something funny out of this later.

"Krisjen!" Trace bellows again. I roll my eyes, hearing several sets of boots trail behind me. I move the camera up to see him and his brothers.

"Where's dinner?" he asks.

I look over my shoulder. "It's in the kitchen. Get it yourself. I'm not serving you in front of everyone."

"Just in private, then?" He flashes a smile as they all sit, and I catch sight of Iron watching me. "I'm really dirty," Trace shouts. "Want to shower?"

Still holding the phone, I walk over to his table and snatch the tip left in the middle. Trace rises and grabs for me, but I hook my leg behind his, sweeping his leg out from under him, and push him back down in his seat.

His brothers laugh, and I walk away. "If he only wants to hang out with you when it's dark outside, he's a"—and I lower my voice to whisper as I talk into the camera—"fuckboy."

"Ohhhhh," Trace laughs like a good sport.

Army sits down with his son in his arms. Iron—I see through the camera—is staring at my ass.

I think it was him last night. It has to be. Has he ever noticed me before? Picking up signals is one thing I am good at.

But he is going to prison for three years. Pretty sure anyone looks good to him right now.

I stop filming, trim the footage, and add a background tune. I post it and stick my phone in my back pocket, seeing some people come in out of the corner of my eye.

"Hey, what are you doing here?" a familiar voice says.

I whip around and catch Clay and Liv just stepping through the door. I smile big, a flutter hitting my stomach as I wrap my arms around Liv, hugging her. And despite the fact that it's only been eight weeks since she left for school, my eyes burn a little. I don't mind the town being empty of all the people I used to know in school, but I miss *her.*

I clear my throat, stepping back. "Long story," I tell her. "But they needed help, and I was free. Staying long?"

"No . . ." She hooks her thumbs through the belt loops on her jeans. Her nipple pokes through one of Clay's tank tops, which she probably borrowed because she forgot how hot it is here. Dartmouth will be getting snow soon. "I head back tonight," she tells me.

Just flew in for the weekend to see her girlfriend. How sweet. I'm jealous.

"I'm glad you're around, though." She rubs my arm. "Is Trace behaving himself?"

"God, no." I peel off my apron. "But everyone loves him anyway."

"Liv!" Army shouts.

She looks over at her brothers and then whispers to Clay. "Gimme a minute."

She walks over to the table, Clay calling after her: "Grab a pie!"

I wait until Iron rises and wraps his arms around his sister before I grab Clay's hand and pull her to the end of the counter at the back of the restaurant.

I'm glad I still have one friend who stayed home for college.

"I need to tell you something." I sit down, but she remains standing. "I've been dying to talk to someone."

"As long as you're not pregnant . . ." she says.

My face falls, and I just sit there, my mouth hanging open like I can't bear to tell her.

Her blue eyes bug out. "Oh God. No."

I snort. "I'm kidding."

She sighs, relaxing. "Well, what is it, then?"

I glance around, making sure we're not in earshot, and lower my voice, leaning in close. "I had sex with someone last night. Not Trace."

She stares at me like she's waiting for the rest. "Okay . . . Um, were you safe?"

"Well, the thing is—"

"Does Trace know?"

"It's . . . not that kind of relationship."

"Okay, so who was it?"

A lump gets caught in my throat. "Fuck, I have *no* idea."

She gapes at me. "What?"

I can't help but let out a little laugh. "It's hard to explain, but with the darkness in the room and the angles and . . ."

"All right, okay." She holds up her hand, stopping me. "So you just didn't see his face? Like, seriously? Where was this?"

"In the Jaeger house." I hesitate before finishing. "I know it was one of them. On the couch." I watch her eyes go round again. "I was just so lost in what we were doing, I don't know. Clay, it was the best thing I've ever felt. All of it. Every second."

A gleam hits her eyes. "Really?" she teases. "Better than your showerhead?"

Oh God. I drop my face into my hand. I actually told her about that, didn't I? A long time ago. She, Amy, and I were making margaritas. I overshared.

"I don't know," I whine. "Maybe I was just better with him? Or maybe I was on my game and he was on his game and it was just great that one time and would never be like that again; I have no idea, but shit, it was amazing."

And it had almost nothing to do with the part where he was inside me. The hands, the arms, the heat from his mouth on my cheek—my hair—and how when he pressed himself into my back and wrapped himself around me, a part of me wasn't missing anymore. That's what it was supposed to feel like the first time. Every time.

*God.* A light sweat travels down my chest, and . . .

Clay shoves something in my face, and I blink, seeing her snap her fingers to get my attention.

I spaced off.

"And you're sure it was one of the Jaegers?" she presses.

I nod. "He was wearing the bracelet, and I've been with Trace enough to know those weren't his moves."

He's a possibility, but not a likely one.

"What do I do?" I ask her, lowering my voice again. "I mean, I'm not expecting round two, but I want to know who it was."

"Ask them."

"Oh, right. That'll be hilarious. 'Hey, guys. Which one of you left your handprint on my ass last night?'"

Some diners turn in my direction, and I shut up. Shit. I'm

talking loudly again. I look over, spotting Iron and Army glancing in my direction.

Clay shakes with a laugh. “He left a handprint?”

I show her my neck and the reddish-purple busted blood vessels right above my collarbone. “He left marks everywhere,” I say. “Do you want to see the insides of my thighs?”

Liv stops right behind Clay and cocks an eyebrow at me.

I swallow. “You walked into that one out of context. Sorry, babe.”

She knows better anyway.

She steps up to Clay’s side, amusement in her eyes. “What’s going on?”

“Do you really want to know?” Clay folds her smile between her teeth.

Liv heads behind the counter, toward the kitchen. “Probably not,” she mumbles. “I’ll get the pie.”

I smile after her, then look to Clay. “So, what do I do? How do I figure out which one it was?”

“Well, I’m guessing more of him than just his dick touched you last night, right?” she presses. “See which one starts acting familiar with you. Putting his hands on you. Looking at you differently. Being flirty.”

I look over at the guys’ table, Trace fitting together six packets of sugar, ripping them open in unison, and pouring them all in his iced tea at the same time.

“Any of them besides Trace doing that today?” she asks.

Iron chews his ice.

“Maybe,” I murmur. “I mean, we can probably rule out Dallas, right?”

“Did it feel like him?”

I look at Dallas’s back, a bad taste hitting my mouth. “Well, it wasn’t hate-fucking, but . . . it was aggressive, I guess.” I shoot her a look. "God, if it was him, I probably don't want to know. It wouldn't be him, right? He hates Saints."

She kind of flinches, tilting her head side to side, thinking. "I'm not sure how much that's true. I wouldn't rule him out, honestly."

"Oh God."

"Relax." She laughs quietly. "My guess is Iron. But I sure wish I could stick around and watch this one play out."

No, thanks. I'd rather endure this mess only I could get into without my friends spectating.

Liv comes out with a pie box, holding it by the string.

"I've got to go," Clay tells me.

I rise and move with her toward the door. "Lighthouse?"

"Back to my mom's, actually. She's away." She does a little dance. "We're gonna skinny-dip before Liv's flight."

I've seen girls skinny-dip in the Jaeger pool, but obviously Liv's going to want Clay naked in private. Understandable.

"Have fun," I tell her.

She gives me a hug. "Are you going to be okay? We can stay over here if you're uncomfortable . . ."

"Go." I push her toward the door. "I'll be over on my side of town tonight. I'm not staying."

Liv embraces me quickly, and they both leave, climbing into Clay's old Bronco. I'll see Liv at Thanksgiving, but . . . this was the last time she'd see Iron outside of . . .

My throat tightens.

*Three and a half years.*

But instead of sadness and pity, I'm mad at him. Then I lock eyes with him, seeing his narrow on me, because he can tell something is wrong. But I just head over to Paisleigh instead. She's stopped eating and is tearing her napkin into strips, puzzling them back together.

"Ready to go?" I chirp.

"Can we come back tomorrow?"

"You've got school tomorrow."

She drops her head back in dramatic disappointment like kindergarten is living hell. I pick up her sketchbook and markers, stuffing everything into her backpack. I take her hand and start to walk out, but I crash into someone and look up. Two men have entered the restaurant, dressed casually in slacks in a pathetic attempt to blend in, but they're Cucinelli. My father wears them. Tourists don't.

Their short-sleeved button-ups are pressed, and I can smell the leather scent all rich men pick up somewhere in their day. Their briefcases. Shoes. BMW seats.

The dark blond one doesn't look at me, but I know him. I squeeze Paisleigh's hand.

"Ouch," she whines.

They take a seat at a small table next to the windows, and I pull her behind me, over to the Jaegers. "Is one of my cars ready yet?" I ask Army.

"I don't know. I—"

"Probably," Iron interrupts, starting to rise. "Here, I'll walk over with you. Macon needs dinner anyway."

"It's fine. I can do it myself."

I don't want to get into it with him again. He stranded me over here with my little sister today. I mean, I could've gotten a ride somewhere, I'm sure, but he doesn't think, and it's not cute.

He stares at me. "I'll take you."

"You've been enough help," I snap.

Trace scarfs down his food, Dallas standing next to the window, eating a sandwich and never really relaxing. Army is nearly finished. On workdays, they skip lunch, and my stomach growls as I realize I did today, too.

I reach over and grab the food off the counter that I'm taking to go for Mars, Paisleigh, and me, but I stop and lean in a little, speaking low as I look at Army. "The two guys by the window," I tell him. "One is from the health department. The other is Garrett Ames."

His eyes flash to the table mid-chew, the last bite of his burger pinched between his fingers. He swallows. "How do you know the first one is from the health department?"

"He goes to my church."

"You go to church?" Dallas asks.

Trace snorts, and I hold back my eye roll. They literally sent their sister to the same Catholic school.

I lock eyes with Army again. "Garrett Ames doesn't come to places like this, is my point," I whisper. "Just letting you know."

I'm not sure what they can do to find out why he's here, and with a health inspector, but it's not for the food. Whatever magic the Jaegers weave, arms they twist, or people they bribe to hold on to everything they have here, they better get on it.

I see Iron staring at the men, his shoulders squared and his jaw flexed.

"Walk me," I tell him, changing my mind.

He doesn't seem to hear me, and I can only imagine what he's planning.

"Walk me," I growl.

He needs to get out of here before he tacks on another five years to his sentence. Jesus.

Pushing away from the table, he grabs his phone and takes the brown bag stapled shut on top of the counter. We leave, Iron holding open the door for my sister and me.

"You coming back tomorrow?" he asks, his stride slowing to match mine, because mine matches Paisleigh's short one.

"Why?"

I'm not sure if I'm asking why I should take the job, or why he seems to want me to, but he just stares at the ground, and I'm taken aback by the smile that he's almost hiding.

"I shouldn't have said that shit this morning," he tells me, "but you were fun, kid. I'd rather wake up tomorrow and see you around than not."

I was fun? What does he mean?

The Jaegers' garage door is open, light pouring out as Macon leans under the hood of a car, his arm completely buried somewhere in all the parts. Both of my cars sit outside.

"How's it going?" Iron asks him as we head in.

Macon digs in his pocket and tosses me the Mercedes keys. I let go of Paisleigh's hand, catching them. "Thank you."

"A few days on the other one," he says.

Reaching into my pocket, I pull out what I earned today in tips, my temper cooled since I spouted off to him this morning. I set the stack of folded-up bills on the edge of the car he's working on. "This is what I have in tips. I can Venmo the difference this week if you let me know what it's all going to cost."

I'll dig up the cash somewhere.

I take his bag of food from Iron and walk over, setting it on the worktable as he looks at the money. "They make that much?" he asks Iron as if I'm not here.

Iron just smirks. "*Krisjen* makes that much."

I start to turn but notice the nearly empty bottle of Jim Beam next to the food. No glass. Then I look down into the huge gray Rubbermaid trash can, glancing at Macon before I peel away a few paper towels and spot at least two other unopened bags of food from Mariette's.

And the neck of another empty bottle.

"Garrett Ames is at the restaurant," Iron tells him. "Krisjen says the man he's with is from the health department."

Macon continues to dig under the hood. "Don't pretend to worry like you're going to do anything about it. I'll handle it, like I have every single year they try to come for the Bay."

I take my sister's hand again, the keys and bag of food in my other. "Find something they want more," I muse out loud, looking up at all the old license plates bolted to the ceiling. Maine, South Dakota, Arizona . . . Strange that I've been to Fiji and Athens but haven't even seen the Grand Canyon or Mount Rushmore. "Or give them a reason to find it unappealing here, I guess."

I leave with my sister, buckling her into the car and setting the food safely on the passenger seat.

But before I climb in, I look up.

Macon stares at me from under the hood, and I pause, frozen for a moment.

He never looks at me.

I can count on one hand the number of times he's spoken to me.

A flutter hits my stomach, but before I can read the look in his eyes, he turns back to his work and refixes the ever-present lock in his jaw.

I climb into the car, my forehead cooling with a light sweat.

# 5

## Krisjen

I don't realize I'm speeding out of the Bay until I run over a pothole and nearly hit my head on the roof of the car.

I slow down, checking my rearview mirror like I pissed off Macon in some way and he'll send someone after me.

Why was he looking at me? That's not a good sign.

Not that it would be unpleasant to have the attention of someone who looks like him, but I don't think anyone has ever given the impression they *want* to be on Macon's radar. In fact, I'm pretty sure his usual avoidance of making direct eye contact is a mercy on his part, because he *knows* he scares people. If he gives you his attention, you immediately worry you've been caught misbehaving.

Did I say something? I don't even remember.

Just then, my phone rings, and I snap my attention back to the present. Steering the car with one hand, I dig in my purse with the other. I finally find my phone, glancing at Paisleigh in the back seat. Her head sways against the seat, her eyes starting to fall closed.

Marshall's name shines on my screen, and I swipe, answering it.

"Hey," I say. "I'm on my way. I have dinner."

"Can you come and get me?"

The car veers into the wrong lane, and I jerk the wheel, correcting myself.

"What? Where are you?"

I check the clock on my dad's dash, but it still reads 2:04 from when it stopped running years ago.

"Fox Hill," he replies.

I clench the phone. No one's playing golf this late. And the family men are home at dinner.

All that's left are the plotters, pushers, and playboys—and twelve-year-olds who have "victim" written all over them. Dammit. "Be there in ten."

I hang up before I scream at him. "Shit!" I whisper-yell, tossing the phone and kicking the floor. I hit the gas, flying to the country club and slowing down only while on Main Street, because a speeding ticket will just delay me more.

The highway curves to the right, but I keep straight, coasting between the two large stone pillars and down the dark drive. Trees line both sides of the private entrance, immediately secluding visitors in a quiet landscape that makes you feel like you're deep in the country.

Without slowing down, I race past the guardhouse. The security detail checks in members as they arrive, but after six o'clock on a Sunday, it's empty.

Cruising up to the clubhouse, I pull in behind a black Audi that I know belongs to Clay's father because it's new, and apparently a source of friction between him and her mom—his soon-to-be ex-wife. Something about frozen money until they decide how much belongs to who. Why do divorcing couples think that's a good time to go buy a flashy car? I hope she takes it. *Go, Mrs. Collins.*

I crack my window, turn off the engine, and tilt my mirror, seeing Paisleigh's head hanging off her neck like a tetherball. Taking my phone and keys, I climb out and close the door, dialing my brother.

He breathes hard in my ear.

"I'm here," I tell him, checking that my sister is still asleep through the window. "Where are you?"

"Upstairs."

"So come down."

"They won't let me."

I freeze. "Who?"

But he just snickers. "Do you seriously have to ask?"

He hangs up, and I stick my phone in my pocket as the sprinklers kick on out on the course. The doorman peeks around the corner to see if I'm coming or not, but I just stand there.

I know who's up there, and have a vague idea of what he wants. I also know that while he's a little stupid, coercion is his strength.

*Milo.*

I lock the car doors and stalk up to the clubhouse. Rafe rushes to open the door, tucking his other hand behind his back as he smiles at me.

"Keep an eye on my sister, please?" I tell him.

He shoots up straight, glancing at my car. "Huh?"

"She's asleep in the back seat," I call out, running inside and up the stairs. "I'll be quick! I promise!"

"Ms. Conroy!"

But I ignore his protest, swinging around the banister and down the hall to the right.

Mahogany paneling on the walls gleams in the soft light of the sconces, and I brush past the painting of my grandfather holding a cigar and standing next to a silver-haired Great Dane. He doesn't have a Great Dane. Never did. He has four King Charles spaniels. And cigars make him sick.

Deer antlers jut from the wall, and I jump out of the way before I'm stabbed in the eye. I push through the closed door at the end of the hall, letting it fly open as I enter the Wainwright Room, and stare at my brother where he stands next to the two-seater table, waiting for me.

His blue eyes raise just enough but then drop quickly again. He knows he fucked up. I jerk my chin at him. "How did you get here?"

"I picked him up."

Milo sits at the table, doling out a hand of solitaire like he's a king hovering over maps and planning a war.

Or like he has any idea how to play anything other than Go Fish.

My former boyfriend decided not to attend college right away, either. Instead, he's been interning at his older brother's law office, but probably using most of his mental capacity on just learning to tie a tie every morning.

"So this is your life now?" I ask him, glancing at his friends, whom I don't know, who are sitting on the couches near the fireplace. Two guys, one girl. New faces, because nearly all of our high school friends went off to school this fall. "Taking your petty pleasures wherever you can get them?"

Milo smiles, his black hair combed and shiny, not a strand out of place. "I just wanted to lure you back to your side of the tracks tonight. Where you belong."

How did he know I was in Sanoa Bay?

I step closer, glaring down. He still hasn't looked at me.

"You don't give a shit about me," I say in a low voice. "You never did. Your pride is hurt because I like them more than you."

His small grin locks in place as he stares at the cards, and for a moment, everything stops, because I know that look. The look of him angry and on the cusp of violence.

I shouldn't have said that. It'll only bring attention onto Liv's brothers.

"Did you know your sister is in bed with a Jaeger?" He looks up at Mars.

But instead, I order my brother, "Let's go."

"In a year, they'll be gone." Milo continues placing cards. "The government will declare eminent domain and sell the land out from under them because it's more valuable as a resort. Tryst Six will end."

I shoot my brother a glare. "Now."

But when he meets my eyes, I notice his pupils. They're huge. The blue is barely visible.

I lean over the table, swiping my hand over the white residue on the glass.

My heart pounds in my ears.

"You son of a bitch," I whisper.

"He wanted some," Milo explains.

I tremble. Macon would handle this beautifully. Like a fucking Spartan. And all I can do is swear at him? I want a knife. A weapon. Something.

I swing my arm across the table, sending his cards to the floor, and get down in his face.

Slowly, he rises, and I know everyone in the room is watching us. We stand toe to toe, his eyes cast down at me, only slightly taller as he grins.

And then . . .

He swings his hand out, and I twist away, rearing back to shield myself from the blow.

But it doesn't come.

He drops his arm, chuckling as his friends join in and the room fills with laughter.

I drop my hands, steeling my jaw.

"You don't even know, do you?" he taunts me. "You have all the power in the world. Not me."

He grabs me between the legs, and I yell, pushing him, but he pulls me in, holding me tight.

"You could stop all of this," he breathes down on me. "If you learned to use your head, you'd already see that. You have all the power and no clue how to use it."

What the fuck is he talking about?

"But you were never that bright." He kisses me, his wet mouth making me gag.

I twist away, pushing him off, and charge for the door. "Mars!" I yell.

With my brother behind me, we leave, but I refuse to give Milo the satisfaction of seeing me run. I grip my brother's wrist, damn near digging my nails into his skin.

"Krisjen," Mars says, but it sounds less like he's trying to slow me down and more like an apology. I'm not even that mad at him, although he knows Milo and I ended things badly. He doesn't know most of it, but he knows enough, and he never should've taken his call or gotten into his car tonight.

But it's not his fault. It's mine. Iron was right.

I drag my brother down the stairs and across the lobby, but I hear a male voice behind me. "Ms. Conroy."

I stop, remembering Clay's father is here. But when I turn, I see it's not him after all. Jerome Watson walks up to me from the lounge, every seat at the bar behind him nearly full, and every one of them men.

He looks at me with a gleam in his gray eyes, and I keep my hand on my brother's wrist. I wish it were Clay's dad.

He stops, his white shirt wrinkled but still tucked into his black suit pants. His tie and jacket are probably discarded somewhere in the bar. He smiles, only a few dark blond hairs out of place at his temple. Still a full head of hair, though. At least there's that.

"I missed you at church this morning," he says.

He glances at Mars and then reaches into his pocket, pulling a twenty and holding it out to my brother. "Here, why don't you get a snack?"

But I push Mars toward the door, handing him my keys. "Paisleigh's in the car. Wait for me there."

He casts a worried glance between Jerome and me, but he does what he's told. I face the older man again.

His lips curl into a smile. "Your TikTok was cute."

I arch an eyebrow. He has TikTok? *Yay.*

He inches closer, and while I would never back down from Milo, I have no problem backing up from this guy. I retreat a step.

"You don't have to be afraid of me," he tells me. "I hope you're going to be the one who knows me best."

My tongue feels like sandpaper. I don't want to get to know him.

He looks at me, and I feel like I'm naked. I know what he wants. I know what my mother is promising him. I don't have to do anything I don't want to do. That's a fact.

But it's also not a solution.

He lowers his voice. "May I see you sometime?"

I open my mouth to refuse, but then I close it again. What had Milo said? *You have all the power in the world.* I don't know what he meant, but I'm sure he meant something.

Jerome Watson is connected to everyone capable of making and breaking the Bay.

Before I can dwell too long, I hear myself tell him, "Maybe."

Maybe he'll be useful after all.

He smiles as he cups my cheek. But he doesn't kiss me.

He walks back into the bar, and I wipe his touch off my face as I leave the club.

Rafe opens the door for me, and I head out into the middle of the driveway. Mars sits in the passenger seat, playing on his phone, while Paisleigh's dark form is still passed out in the back seat.

I don't go to the car, though. What did Milo mean?

I need to think.

I walk onto the green, between two trees, and stand still as the long shot of the sprinkler passes over my head. Water rains down on me, and I close my eyes and let my head fall back. A couple of nighthawks sing in the woods far ahead of me on the other side of the course, and I stay there as the sprinkler makes another round, and then another.

There's a way out. That's what Milo meant. For me, for the Jaegers, I don't know, but if he were lying, he wouldn't have been vague. He was being vague to taunt me.

The problem is I'm actually not that smart. I could have an aneurysm trying to crack this.

"I hate these people," I say to myself. So many games. I hope Clay keeps Liv far away from it, because I would pity anyone marrying a Saint. Especially a Jaeger.

"Krisjen?" someone calls out.

I pop my eyes open and spin around as Army Jaeger emerges from the shadow between the trees.

I square my shoulders, watching him approach with his hands in his pockets and his eyes always steady. Like he never blinks.

He wears a forest-green T-shirt, the muscles in his chest just visible underneath, and I've always liked how his hair perpetually looks like he's just a week or two overdue for a haircut.

What is he doing here?

I wipe the water and hair away from my eyes, glancing at Rafe still by the door, but I don't see anyone else. I look back to Army. "Are you guys on call or something?" I grumble. "Someone needs an emergency lawn mowed in the middle of the night?"

His eyebrows shoot up. "Ouch."

But I can see the smile behind his feigned offense.

"Sorry," I chuckle.

Iron's got my claws out today. And then Milo. And then Jerome.

He pulls out a wad of cash and hands it to me. "I just wanted to give this back to you."

I take it, puzzled. I recognize the torn five-dollar bill as part of the tip money I gave Macon earlier tonight.

I try to hand it back. "I want to pay for the repairs."

"You did. You worked. That's all we needed."

"And my Rover?"

He's quiet, as if he's waiting for me to answer my own question. My dad's car only had a flat tire, but according to Iron, my Rover has a lot more that needs to be done to it. It's going to cost a lot.

Then it hits me.

"I'm not working at Mariette's full-time," I tell him, slipping the money into my pocket. "I don't belong there."

"Too low-class for you?"

"I didn't say that."

He narrows his eyes, takes a step into my space, and I back up, but he keeps coming. "Let me tell you something, Conroy." He's never called me by my surname before. "Mariette has been working that joint since she was eleven. She's never left the state, much less the country. She had no choices, so you know what she did? She played the hand she was dealt. She's there seven days a week and has created a fucking culture inside those four walls. It's not a restaurant. It's a home. Kids have celebrated birthdays there. Couples have laughed through wedding receptions there, and a shit ton of people have lost their virginity either in the bathroom or in the parking lot, so I'm not going to stand here and listen to a rich girl tell me that where Mariette has spent three-fourths of her life is worthless and that she's too good to be a waitress there."

He raises his eyebrows, challenging me as he looks down like he's waiting for me to get a clue.

I didn't realize my mouth was hanging open until it goes dry, and I have to swallow to generate saliva. He's always so calm. "I meant . . . the Bay." Heat breaks out across my neck. "I don't belong in the Bay, because I'm using you to hide from my responsibilities. And my future. I like it too much there, to be honest. That's what I meant."

He stares down at me.

I would never think I was too good for Mariette's. I'm positive I want to do something else with my life, but it's not like I believe waitressing is beneath me, either. I just need to get serious and find a way to escape my parents without abandoning Mars and Paisleigh.

Army finally lets out a quiet laugh, his expression softening. "And we like you there," he tells me. "You fit in. Most of the guys you served at lunch today are next door at the bar right now, talking about your smile. One called you 'damned cute.' Another said 'pleasant.' I even think the word 'delightful' was used at some point."

I smile, laughing under my breath. It feels good to hear that.

"And a few are talking about your legs," he adds.

His eyes drop to them, and heat rises to my cheeks.

Does he notice my legs?

Out of all the brothers, Army is the one who puzzles me the most. He has no hobbies. No interests that I can tell. No friends of his own that he doesn't share with his brothers. He doesn't hunt. Fish. Read. Brew his own beer or weld weird garden sculptures. He doesn't ride like Iron. Kill time on boats like Trace. Party and party some more like Dallas.

He's at work. Or home. Always ready for when he's needed. Like a firefighter.

Exactly like a firefighter, in fact. He's indispensable.

Macon takes care of the land, the finances, and holds all the power, because he has the will to do what no one else will. Not even Army.

But the younger siblings talk to Army.

He's the one they tell bad news to, and they entrust him to tell Macon, because Army is the only one who can face their older brother. He holds him back. Calms him down. Puts it into the right words so that it deals the smallest blow. He mans the bomb. Army has to stay calm, because the house needs one emotionally stable adult.

Who does he talk to?

I cross my arms over my chest and look away, uncomfortable under his constant gaze.

"It's too late in the semester to start classes," he points out, "so join us until you start college in January."

I chew the corner of my mouth. I'm not sure I'm going to college, but it's a possibility.

"We need you." His voice is firm. "I mean, when you don't know what you want to do for yourself, be useful to someone else. It's better than lazing about, right?"

He sounds like my teachers.

I love it across the tracks, but what I said last night still holds true. There's nothing over there that's good for me right now.

But I do need a job. I don't want to be around my house all the time where Milo, my mother, or Jerome Watson knows where to find me anytime they want.

I don't want to shop or go to the beach or catch up on Netflix. I want to be around people.

It's better than doing nothing for the next three months. Just while the kids are at school. It'll give me time to find out how to stay close to my siblings on my terms. Not my mother's.

"I'll think about it," I say.

A job is a good idea, but I'll get one here in St. Carmen instead.

Army nods slowly, looking like he knows I'm just being nice, but what can he do? They'll find help. I'm not sure why he's trying to convince *me* to come back.

He turns to leave, but I stop him. "How did you know where to find me tonight?"

At first, I thought he was here for something relating to the landscaping and the work their business does, but he said he came to give me back my tips. Wouldn't he have just gone to my house?

He twists back around, looking like he's holding his breath and trying not to grin.

He closes the distance between us, his words a whisper as he leans down to my face. "We have cameras in the clubhouse," he says.

I gape at him. "Are you serious? And you're just telling me that? Like you can trust me?"

Why would he admit that? My family comes here. Or we did. I'm sure my dad can still afford his membership.

But Army just studies me. "Maybe we have dirt on your crowd. On Milo. Garrett Ames."

I take the last step up to him. "And my father?"

He smiles. "Maybe," he taunts. "Who knows?"

Oh my God. They could have stuff I might be able to use.

Or stuff I'd want deleted. Especially if it's about my family. A lot of talking goes on at Fox Hill. They might've picked up a lot of useful info.

My chest rises and falls.

He plucks my phone out of my pocket and taps his number into my contacts.

I gaze up at him and then down to his chest at my eye level. His sternum dips underneath his T-shirt, and I get warm everywhere.

"I'm not sleeping with you," I tell him. "You're too old for me." Just so we're clear.

We both know that any woman around his family, and not related to his family, is on the menu. If I'm coming over there every day, I want it understood that I'm not. Women love a hot, single dad, but it's little weird that his son's mother is never mentioned.

He doesn't say anything or even look at me, just fights a smile tilting up his mouth.

"What?" I ask.

He smiles like he has a secret.

He shakes his head, but he starts smiling more. "Nothing."

He hands me back my phone, and I take it, brushing his fingers as I do.

Time slows as the wheels in my head turn. I don't think it

would've been Army last night. He'd said "I can wonder if it's my son he's playing Daddy to."

Army already has a son, so wouldn't he have said "one of my sons" instead?

He starts to walk away, my gaze lingering on his back.

It's really not a good idea for me to be over there five days a week, eight hours a day.

I hesitate a moment before saying, "I need to help get my brother and sister off to school in the mornings," I inform him. "Tell Mariette I can be there by seven thirty."

What the hell am I doing?

He looks back at me over his shoulder. "Okay."

"I'll talk to her about my schedule tomorrow," I add. "And I keep what I earn. Plus the repairs on my car."

He nods once. "Deal."

Five days a week. Eight-hour days. That was optimistic of me.

Almost a week later, I still haven't had a day off. And every day gets longer than the last. I was here for almost twelve hours yesterday, but my brother and sister went to a birthday party at a trampoline place with our aunt and cousins, so I didn't feel bad about staying late. There just always seems to be more to do here. Every day. Deliveries need to be unloaded, inventory stocked, someone's sick, someone left early and couldn't clean their stations, the soda's out, a tour bus is coming in, my relief needs to be trained . . . by me. When I just started days ago.

And occasionally, very special customers have the privilege of getting their food delivered to them, which isn't something Mariette's does for everyone.

I even helped in the kitchen before the lunch rush today. Pretty sure she almost kicked me out when I asked, "Aren't key limes just limes?" Twenty minutes later, I left sweating and fully aware that they were absolutely not.

Quite honestly, I love working here, though. I can get a clean fork, refill a drink, remember all the orders for a table of six without writing anything down, carry five plates at a time, and deliver the shrimp bisque to table eight, the beef tips to table one, and the beer to table eleven in one magical and beautiful dance through the room. I'm finally good at something.

"Krisjen!" Mariette shouts through the window between the kitchen and the server station. "I warned you about the roller skates!"

I coast down the aisle, a plate of food in each hand like a pro.

Mariette mutters something in Spanish, and I'm probably glad I don't understand.

"Where does this go?" the new girl, Summer, asks.

I drop the burger in front of Bud Kyler and take the platter from her in my free hand. "Davey always has the crawfish." I set it down in front of him and his friend who have stopped here every day this week on their lunch breaks.

He smiles, and I wink.

"You need a refill?"

He nods. "Coke."

I take his cup, hand it to Summer, and push off, cruising toward the window and skidding left.

"She can move in those skates!" Miguel Padron says.

I race behind the counter, stuff more straws into my apron, and fill a third Coke, grabbing the two others off the soda fountain. "Yeah, they make me faster, Mariette."

"Let her wear 'em, Mariette!" someone else calls out.

"So she can sue me when she breaks her leg?" my boss spits back.

I drop off the Cokes at table three and twirl around, skating backward. "Actually, I'd be suing Macon, since he technically owns the place, and even I'm not that stupid."

Hands suddenly grab my waist, catching me, and I jolt, looking over my shoulder.

Macon looks down at me, and the heat from his body instantly hits me.

I gulp, just as the screen door flaps closed behind him. I almost crashed into him.

Tingles spread under my skin, and a jolt hits low in my belly. I stop breathing for a second.

He's never touched me. Not even a handshake or a brush of his shoulder.

I hold back my nervous laugh and turn around. "I have your lunch," I tell him.

I start for the counter to grab the to-go box under the warmer where I packaged the bun separate from the meat, so it wouldn't get soggy, but he stops me before I get there.

"I'm not hungry," he says. He pulls the mail out of the slot on the wall and starts flipping through. "Reheat it for dinner and drop it off when you leave today."

So he can just throw it away again?

I slip my hands in my pockets. I didn't think much of it when I noticed all the uneaten food in the garage trash can last week, but he's taken his lunch only twice while I've been working here. The other times it's left on the worktable in the garage, untouched. He hasn't joined the guys for dinner, and I haven't been taking him anything then, either. Nor has anyone else from Mariette's that I can tell. No idea if he's eating breakfast. His brothers are big eaters. What's going on with him?

He scans the envelopes, stuffs them back into the holder, and heads for the kitchen door. I slide out of the way, seeing his eyes briefly look down at the skates before he disappears.

Trace and Army stroll in next, the former shouting, "Food!"

"How you doing?" someone asks them from a table as they pass.

"Hey, man." Trace shakes a hand.

A round of shouts goes off.

"Hey!

"What's up?"

"Tomorrow, right?"

"Pregaming all day, baby!" Trace claps the air above his head.

They're having a party tomorrow. Iron's last night. Halloween.

I look toward the door, trying to see if he's with them.

And then he's there. Charging in, jeans and black T-shirt, dark hair covering his temples, and his sun-kissed skin glowing with water that I know isn't sweat. He jumps through the spray of lawn sprinklers everywhere he works to cool down. I smile to myself, picturing it.

He heads for the kitchen, glancing at me and then away. He's been acting like he doesn't notice me, but that's only after he looks to make sure I'm here.

I watch him stroll through the kitchen, toward the back.

"You stay out of there!" Mariette yells at him.

I arch up on my tiptoes, watching him shrug at her in the kitchen. "Just one."

"A whole one!" Trace yells through the warming window.

"Iron Jaeger!" she growls.

"You'll miss me!" He grins at Mariette and dives into the walk-in.

I hesitate, proud of myself for staying out of that house this week.

But he's alone, and he's rarely alone, and I need to know when my car will be ready, and I'm not asking Macon. I don't want to bug him.

I roll through the kitchen, past the grills, and sneak into the cooler, seeing him scan shelves for the key lime cheesecake that's not on the menu.

He doesn't look my way, but he knows I'm here.

He offered a ride along the beach a few nights ago, and I kind of regret turning him down.

But I knew what would happen when we got there. It's safer now. In two days, he'll be gone for three-plus years.

I'll miss him.

Somehow their table out there never seemed like it was missing someone without Macon there, but I'm going to hate only seeing three at that table for dinner very soon.

I step closer to him. The cool air feels good.

"Why doesn't . . . Mariette own this place?" I ask him.

He pulls out a pink box, searching behind it. "She pretty much does. We don't interfere with how she wants to run it."

"But you take a cut."

I slide in front of him, blocking his view. My chest touches his, and he looks down at me, heat filling the space between us.

"What's your point?" he asks.

"I just think it's interesting that she does the work of a business owner but isn't the business owner," I tease. "And then she has to share her profits with people who don't work here. Do you have that kind of arrangement with a lot of businesses in the Bay?"

It's not their style to take from their own people. I'm only half-serious with my underhanded accusations. I just want to spend a minute with him.

But there's a reason the Jaegers insist on maintaining control of this restaurant and the bar next door. The rest make sense. An auto shop. A storage facility. A run-down drive-in up the coast a few miles, and lots of land where they collect rent from people parked on it.

But this place is Mariette's. In every way but the one that counts. Why?

"What aren't you telling me?" I ask him.

"Why should I tell you anything?"

"If you don't set me straight, I'm going to think you all are extorting protection money from that nice woman."

"Like Al Capone?"

He digs in his eyebrows, his air of amusement making him look younger than Trace. I follow the line of his lips as they lift to one side, brushing the stubble on his jaw as something swims in my stomach. His face is more oval. Trace's jaw is more square.

I guess I'm staring too long, because he shifts in a way that makes him seem closer, and he drops his voice. "I would actually love the opportunity to set you straight," he taunts.

The pulse between my legs throbs just once, so hard that I expel the breath I'm holding.

He plants both hands on the rack behind me, walling me in with his nose an inch from mine. "Will Trace mind this?"

I haven't taken my eyes off his mouth. God, I'm hot. My blood is rushing too fast. "Why don't you ask me if I mind it?" I whisper.

A current flows between us, and I know he's going to do it before he does. He takes my jaw in one hand, squeezing it lightly, and I suck in a breath just as he's about to come down, but . . .

He doesn't kiss me.

He stares into my eyes, smelling like grass and vanilla and the beer coming off his breath. "Mariette can't own the restaurant," he says. "Or rather, she doesn't want to risk it. She's off the grid."

Off the grid?

"She would've needed a loan," he explains. "To get a loan, she needs accounts. To get accounts, she needs identification. To get ID she needs a Social Security card. Get it?"

I stare at him. "Yeah."

She's undocumented.

He releases me and looks away. "And I don't know why the fuck I told you all of that."

It still doesn't make sense. Business owners don't need to be full-fledged citizens. "She's been here since she was a child, right?" I press. "How has she not applied for permanent residency at least?"

"Because she would've been deported as soon as she applied, and she wasn't young enough to meet the requirements for DACA."

Right.

And by that time, this was home. She has family here.

Iron continues. "She stayed through several changes in ownership, one of them finally naming the place after her, because her key lime pie was the biggest draw to customers. About six years ago, after she'd worked here for thirty years, the current owner was about to lose it to the bank, so we bought it."

"How'd you get that much money?"

It wouldn't have cost seven figures, but at least in the low sixes.

Iron just sighs. "I have no idea. I was seventeen at the time. Macon took care of it."

The old rumor about Macon and Army selling Oxy and Molly to the college kids back in the day to support their siblings after their parents' deaths surfaces in my brain, but there were so many rumors about them that I never knew what to believe.

Iron states, "Mariette gets to stay in the place she loves, take care of her family, and we make sure she can do that."

Got it. Not that I ever thought that they were taking advantage of her, but it's one of the many reminders that the Jaegers bend and break whatever laws they feel are unjust, and that they are comfortable making that distinction on their own. What people don't know until they spend time over here, though, is that it's always in service to others. Macon could've taken that money and renovated the house. Bought a car. Moved. He stayed.

"You can't tell anybody, Krisjen."

I dart my eyes up to him. "You don't need to say that."

"No, I do," he states plainly. "Because if you turn on us, it'll be my fault, because I trusted you."

He trusts me. His brothers wouldn't. They'd be pissed if they found out that he divulged that information.

But I'll never tell anyone. Mariette's worked hard, and she's lived here longer than anywhere else. This is her home.

"When I come back," he says, "I need this place to still be here, okay?"

I nod, a lump wedging in my throat at the reminder. "I really hate that you're going there. How are you not depressed all the time? I would be."

He laughs quietly, relaxed again, and I look up at him. "Are you going to be okay?" I ask.

But he ignores me, instead asking, "You coming to the party tomorrow night?"

"Who will be there?"

"Me."

I snort, and we both smile at each other, but then he comes in close again, and I know what he's going to want if I come tomorrow. I inhale through my nose, taking in his scent and seeing if I remember it from that night. He smelled like grease and wood and tasted like heat with a whisper of bourbon, but all I smell now is water and sunscreen.

Leaning down, his forehead nearly brushes mine. "Would you mind it?" he whispers.

The front of his jeans brushes mine, and everything feels alive.

"*Do* you mind it?" he teases.

I hear a bell ring outside, and I blink, remembering I have tables. Shit.

I push him away and start to leave. "Y'all are trouble."

"And so are you," he calls back.

I leave the cooler, hurrying back to the front.

I'm not going to go tomorrow night. The last thing I need is another party. Even if it's Iron's last for a while.

Whatever happens there won't make my life better, and I have alcohol at home.

And I really don't want to risk Aracely slashing my tires again. I can't afford it.

At five thirty, I leave, carrying Macon's reheated dinner down the road, but the garage is closed.

I knock on the front door, Aracely answering after a minute as screams go off in the background and Dex peals with laughter.

I hold up the bag. "Dinner for Macon," I say.

I start to take a step in, but she moves in front of me, grabs the bag, and dumps it in the trash can outside, on the side of the porch. "They're barbecuing tonight. You can go. Thank you." Her face lights up with a self-satisfied expression. "Or . . . are you working the 'night shift' tonight?"

I back up, her meaning not lost on me.

I drop my eyes, seeing her long smooth legs in a beautiful line right down to the black ankle boots with silver buckles and a three-inch heel. "Cute shoes."

She arches a brow and walks away, leaving the door open. I smile after her.

We're going to be friends. She just doesn't know it yet.

Trace swoops up, pulling me inside. I spot Army and Dallas, busy in the kitchen, and Iron on the floor, playing with Dex. My smile spreads at how cute they are, but then it falls. He's spending time with his nephew while he can.

"Stay," Trace tells me.

I shake my head. "No. You're having a family thing. Besides, I've got to get home to my brother and sister anyway."

"Bring 'em," he says, excited. "This won't be ready for an hour. Go get them and come back. They can play with Dex."

Paisleigh has talked about Sanoa Bay all week. She's dying to get back.

"Like, seriously," Trace whispers, coming in close and putting his arm around me. "Macon is on a short fuse lately. We could use as many buffers as possible."

Mmm, tempting.

Macon strolls down the stairs, hair wet from his shower and pulls on a T-shirt. He swings past us and into the living room like we aren't even standing here, and I see faint circles under his eyes again. Army and Dallas pause their conversation as he enters the kitchen, and then I hear the clank of beer bottles and the fridge slamming shut.

Army looks over at me, tipping his chin in greeting, while Dallas stares at me like I should leave.

I don't look, but I can feel Iron watching me.

"I have to get home," I finally tell Trace and turn to leave. "You guys have fun."

"Dress up tomorrow night!" he calls after me.

I suck in a huge breath all the way to my dad's car.

# 6

## Krisjen

*Twenty-one to drink, eighteen to sleep over.*

I laugh at the picture on my Instagram feed, a sign hanging on the outside of the Jaeger house tonight.

I look out the window of Mariette's, seeing the bedsheet with the blocky black letters billow in the light breeze. Trace can be clever when he wants to be. And I have no doubt that sign was *all* his doing.

My phone rings, and I see Clay's name. I swipe, answering it. "Hey," I singsong, clearing the dirty plates from an empty table. "Having fun?"

"Oh my God, it's fucking freezing up here." I can hear the shiver in her laugh. "But New England is super pretty, and I should've known Liv wouldn't have dodgy friends. I like them. But I'd like them better in Florida."

Part of me wishes she'd decide to transfer up to Liv's school. I'd miss her, but I'd love to live vicariously. Olivia Jaeger and Clay Collins are most beautiful when they're together.

"What are you dressed as?" I ask.

"Look at IG. We win Halloween. And you?"

I pull my phone away from my ear to check the picture she

must've posted, but then I remember I'm still talking to her. "I'm not dressed as anything," I tell her. "I'm going home."

"No, you have to go to the party."

"Why?"

"Because I need more dirt."

I exhale hard, dumping the dishes next to the dishwasher. "Yeah, at my expense. Jesus, you're priceless."

"Oh, just go for it," she says. "I would."

"Easy to say now from the comfort of a committed relationship when you don't have to suffer any of the consequences for careless behavior."

"Whatever."

Damn right, and I open my mouth to tell her that, but she cuts me off.

"So hear me out," she says in my ear. "I told Liv your situation—"

"Oh, Clay! You didn't."

"Hold up." She rushes to defend herself. "She agrees with me. She says it has to be Iron."

"She's going to think I'm treating her brother's bedrooms like musical chairs."

Why would Clay tell her? Liv is my friend, but she's their family first.

But Clay kind of mumbles. "That's actually nothing she's not used to, growing up in a house full of bachelors."

"But I'm her friend. It's different." I rip off my apron and throw it in the laundry bag by the back door. "I'm not telling you anything ever again."

She seems not to hear me. "She says Dallas wouldn't touch you with a ten-foot pole . . ."

I stop. "But he touched Amy last spring—"

"And she says it's possible that it's Army, but on the couch doesn't sound like him. He prefers privacy."

That's probably true. I've never seen him go upstairs or come down with a woman. He always goes to their places. He shares a room with his infant son, so that's understandable.

So, likely it was Iron, then. "Okay, so . . . what?" I ask her, grabbing my bag and heading out the door. "He surrenders at the jail in the morning. What am I supposed to do? Fall in love with him?"

"No. You go to that house, go up to Liv's room, and pull out the Mad Hatter costume from her closet that she made in high school. Then you go up to him and pick a fight. Let him ravage the granddaughter of the man who's sending him to prison."

*Jesus.*

But I slow as I walk, feeling the breeze on my legs and hearing the sway of the fronds on the palms. We might get a storm tonight.

I want to see him one more time. How could he fuck up so badly? How could he be leaving? Macon is right to be angry.

*Macon . . .*

I raise my eyes, seeing light glowing from inside the garage down the street, a shadow passing in front of one of the windows.

"Krisjen?" Clay says when I don't reply.

I take a second, but then I ask. "What did she say about Macon?"

My voice comes out smaller than it was.

She says nothing, but I hear something brush over the phone and muffled words in the background. After a few seconds, she comes back on.

"You don't want it to be him."

But it's not Clay's voice in my ear. It's Liv's.

"If you think it was," Liv says, "I wouldn't pursue it."

Why?

"Besides," she adds, "he would never screw my friends. It's Iron or Army."

But wouldn't they have mentioned it? Or been more obvious?

"Keep the costume," she tells me. "I'm guessing it'll hold some memories for you after tonight."

"Oh, it'll get dirty," I tease.

She expels some kind of disgusted sound, and I laugh as I continue walking. "Bye."

We hang up, and I pause mid-step next to my dad's car before I veer left again and keep walking to the Jaeger house. *Screw it.* I can say goodbye to him. This could be it, right?

I pass the garage. Macon isn't there, but the hood of my car is up, a drop light hanging from inside it and tools propped around the edge.

The sign Trace painted on a sheet billows from the windows above as more cars pull up and music pours onto the overgrown lawn from the open front door. Without looking at anyone, I dive into the house and jog up the stairs, walking straight for Liv's room. Once inside, I drop my bag and dig in her closet.

Liv worked behind the scenes of our high school's theater department for four years, and she never threw anything away. She'd take discards from costume designs and make them into something she could wear. There was a tweed vest cropped indecently that I fell in love with the last time I was in here, but I don't see it now. She probably took it to college.

Finding the Mad Hatter costume, I take it out and start undressing. It's a spectacular outfit. She always made the costumes without approval. She thought if she could show the theater teacher her new idea rather than describe it to her, it would go over better. It rarely did.

But she tried.

Liv was always trying to get roles that weren't traditionally played by women. For the longest time, I didn't understand why. The audience doesn't want to see a female Captain Jack Sparrow or Hannibal Lecter played by a girl. They won't show up for a woman performing as Darth Vader, Vito Corleone, or John McClane.

Norman Bates, Han Solo, Neo, and Freddy Krueger are men, and the world doesn't want to imagine that it could be different.

But . . . they're great roles, and if I were an actor like her, I could see the allure of playing them. They're complex. Males in a story always get the great scenes. The great lines. The epic fights and battles and power plays. They can be loners and villains, criminals and crazies, and no one really worries about why they're doing what they do. Motive isn't important. They can murder, fight, blow things up . . . No one thinks less of Sherlock Holmes because he was never married or never had children. If a woman wants to be a spy, we wonder why. What happened in her past to make her reject a home and a family?

Liv didn't want to be Ophelia, Desdemona, or Juliet's nurse, because they were either manipulated, victimized, or subservient. And how often do we find ourselves still playing that shit every day? It's not a challenge.

Sometimes I want to blow something up, and I don't even care why.

I finish donning the patchwork skirt that falls mid-thigh, button up the sleeveless waistcoat with nothing underneath, and slip on the red velvet fitted jacket. I tease up my hair, add some blue and green eye shadow, and then finish it off with a bow tie around my naked neck, a top hat, and some lipstick.

I gaze in the mirror before realizing I'm barefoot and dig in Liv's closet for the boots, one purple and one green.

A crash sounds downstairs followed by a muffled shout as someone passes by on the other side of Liv's door.

Grabbing my phone, I head down.

The floor vibrates under my feet, the music banging against the walls, and I hear laughter behind me. Two guys I don't know slam the door to Iron and Dallas's room and race past me. I jump out of the way.

"Sorry," the brunette one says, smiling and still laughing with his friend as they jog down the stairs. A fresh bruise sits on his neck, similar to the one I had a week ago.

The door behind me opens again, and Dallas steps out, pulling on a T-shirt. His hair falls in his eyes, but then he slicks it back over the top of his head, the dark strands threaded through his fingers.

His green eyes bore into me as he passes, and I'm pretty sure Dallas wishes I were a man. He could hurt me then.

Chromatics' "Whispers in the Hall" starts as the lights suddenly dim, and only a blue glow fills the downstairs. People howl with excitement as I come to the bottom of the steps, and I look right, seeing couples dance in what I think used to be the dining room. But I've only ever seen a pool table in there. They hold each other close, bodies moving into each other, and I can make out a zombie nurse, a cat, a Camp Crystal Lake counselor in short-shorts and tube socks, and a ghost with an erection tenting his sheet. Clever.

I start to look for Iron, but then I remember Clay saying she posted pictures of her and Liv's costumes. I check Instagram, tapping on her latest pic and enlarging it.

Clay is dressed as James Bond, complete with fitted tuxedo and bow tie. Her blond hair, in loose waves, is teased and big, while Liv—interestingly enough—is dressed like a Bond girl. Tight, sleek red gown, the shiny silk showing every curve, the slit in the fabric teasing all the way up her thigh. I laugh to myself. She puts up a fight over what role she's told she has to play, but for her girlfriend, she's happy to be dominated.

"Is that Liv and Clay?" someone asks over my shoulder.

I glance at Trace as he peers at the pic on my phone, his chin practically resting on my shoulder.

"Yeah."

He smiles. "That's cool."

A guy wearing skull face paint passes by us with a young

woman's hand in his. My gaze immediately drops to her chest, unable to not notice.

*Holy shit.*

They walk up the stairs, other heads turning as they go.

I tuck my phone away, turning to Trace. "Was she seriously just dressed as a wet T-shirt contest winner?" I snort. "That's awesome."

He hooks an arm around my neck, grinning. "You're not at a high school party, honey. Or a St. Carmen one." He leans into my ear. "There are *men* here."

Yeah. I know. *I've been to some parties here, thanks.*

I look back up at him. Black pants, black belt, no shirt. The word *SAUCE* is written on his abs in blocky black letters. Then there's an arrow pointing down toward his groin.

"What are you—?" But then I stop, realization dawning. *Hot sauce.* I roll my eyes.

He chuckles. "What are you supposed to be?"

I open my mouth to answer, but someone else does instead. "Welcome to the mad tea party, Hatter."

I glance up, seeing Iron approach, his John Wick costume looking entirely too good not to be a daily thing. Black suit, white shirt, and black tie all chic and fitting like the outfit was especially made for him, but I know Iron wouldn't have wasted money getting a costume specifically tailored. His black hair is pushed back, but a little to the side, and while he doesn't have a beard like Keanu, he might look better, because the Jaeger boys' green eyes are something else when they wear black.

"You'll fit right in," he teases, paraphrasing a quote from *Alice in Wonderland.*

He takes my hand, and Trace releases me, walking on my other side as Iron leads me.

"Please tell me you are actually serving minors?" I ask them.

Trace arches a brow. "You sleeping over?"

"If she drinks, she stays," Iron says, holding out his other hand. "Give me your keys."

I look up at him.

And I take out my car key, dropping it into his hand.

Sliding it into his pocket, he takes my hand again and leads us to the kitchen, where the L-shaped counter is full of food and the shorter section has been turned into a bar. Iron takes a cup, uses it to scoop ice out of a cooler, and then lifts the bottle of rum, looking to me before he pours it.

I nod, and the next thing I know, liquor is sloshing over the cubes, damn near filling the glass. My eyes go wide, but I don't say anything as he adds some ginger ale to whatever space is left in the cup.

He hands it to me, and I can't help but laugh. "Thanks."

They're whiskey and beer guys. I'll make my own mixed drinks next time.

I sip, instantly feeling that anticipation that the promise of alcohol brings as the spice burns my throat. Iron pours some Macallan over ice, while Trace pops the top on a beer and the song changes to something harder. A cup drops, its contents spilling. I look up, seeing the garage, outside the kitchen window, full of people, too. Macon sits on a brown leather couch.

He's burrowed into the sofa, slouching with his head resting against the back of it, staring off.

Turin Wilcott is at his side, sitting on her legs and trying to get his attention. Her hand is on his thigh.

"Does Macon know her?" I ask, taking a sip of my drink.

She's a Saint. Several years ahead of me in school. She must be twenty-five or so by now. Curvier, blond, and she has a hell of a lot more money, which she's been spending like crazy since she broke up with her fiancé.

Iron replies, "I don't know."

I watch her lean in closer and slide her hand up his shirt, touching his stomach. His eyelids drop as the bottle in his hand tilts. Jim Beam. It's already more than half-gone.

He raises it to his mouth and swallows, closing his eyes as the liquor goes down his throat.

I frown. "He doesn't look right."

Iron scoffs, dropping a few more cubes into his cup. "He's having some fuckin' fun for once."

"And he's out of our hair," Trace adds.

I look between them, both of them busy moving on with having a good time, and it bugs me. I glance at Macon again, knowing that he'd probably subject them to verbal abuse if they tried to interfere. Or tell him he's drinking too much lately.

They know him better than I do, I guess.

I take the shot Iron holds up in front of me, all of us tapping our drinks in a cheers before we shoot them. Peppermint burns my throat, and I close my eyes, feeling the music under my skin. I lean back into a body I know is Iron's.

He reaches around me with one arm and picks up his drink, his other hand on my hip. "Go," he tells Trace. "She's with me tonight."

I look over at Trace, his eyes flashing to me and then his older brother. I turn around, facing Iron. "I'm with you? When was that decided?"

"In the cooler yesterday." He cocks his head. "I could've had you then."

Trace passes by, leaving us to it. I'm not with him, either.

Iron watches me with those eyes, and my cheeks warm like he's touching my face, but he's not.

I raise my chin a little higher.

"If you're not interested . . ." He starts to back away. "You better tell me now. I have to be at the police station in ten hours, and I plan on getting laid one last time. I'd like it if it were you."

My eyes catch on fire, and the laughter bubbling up is about to pop out of my pores. Is he serious?

"Sure, absolutely," I taunt. "Let's do it now. Upstairs or in your car? I'll just climb on and start bouncing." I start to walk and pull him along. "If we do it quickly, you might have time to fit in another girl. Or two. Come on. We can be back before the beer runs out."

I drop his hand and keep walking, leaving this fucking party. What a mistake. *Asshole.*

But he grabs me.

I pull against his grip as he yanks me in. "I'd like it . . ." he grits out, "if it were you."

Why?

Because he liked it last time?

I jerk free as people around us turn to look. Maybe I want him with me tonight. Maybe it would've been easy to seduce me into staying. In a dark hallway. Up against a quiet wall. As he kissed me and slid into me nice and slow, over and over for an hour, and then took my smell with him tomorrow.

It wouldn't have been hard to get me to stay. I knew that when I walked in here tonight. That doesn't mean I don't enjoy being seduced.

I tip my chin at him. "Truth or dare?"

His mouth twitches with a smile as he remains quiet for a moment. Then he replies, "Truth."

"How would you fuck me?"

His eyebrows twitch in surprise, and I see a guy next to me falter in his dancing and look at me.

Iron squares his shoulders. "I want you to ride me. On the pool chair outside."

Someone close by laughs, and others around us stop, taking notice of our confrontation.

Iron takes one step toward me. "Truth or dare?"

"Dare."

"Open your vest," he tells me.

Not "take off your jacket" or "remove your hat." He's going straight for skin.

I undo the three buttons holding the vest closed over my bare chest, watching him the whole time.

But he's not looking at my eyes. He stares at the open sliver, an inch wide, appearing from sternum to stomach and revealing only a tease of the mounds still covered.

The hair on my arms rises, and I can't hear the music anymore. All I feel are his eyes like a tongue running up that slice of skin.

"Truth or dare?" I ask him.

"Truth."

"Are you big?"

People laugh, Iron smiles. "Ask your friend," he tells me. "What was her name again?"

*Amy.*

I fist my right hand. He's going for broke tonight. Seeing how far he can push me.

"Truth or dare?" he says.

"Dare."

"Take off your hat."

I do, tossing it behind the recliner in the corner.

I steel my spine. "Truth or dare?"

"Truth."

"Will I come with you?"

A snort goes off, and a few more people have stopped to watch us.

Iron steps, closing the distance between us and looking down at my open vest. Sweat dampens my skin, and my nipples harden against the fabric.

"You're almost coming right now," he says.

I arch a brow.

"Truth or dare?" he asks.

"Dare."

"Drop your jacket."

But it's a whisper, and heat pools between my legs.

Holding his gaze, I pull the Mad Hatter's fitted red jacket off my shoulders and let it slide down my arms to the floor.

"Truth or dare?"

"Truth," he replies.

"Do you go down?"

A woman behind me expels a breath.

Iron grins. "I always return a favor."

More laughter.

"Truth or dare?" he challenges.

My heart skips a beat. I'm taking off something important now.

But I get in his face anyway. "Dare."

He stares at me, something playing behind his eyes. Probably the knowledge that this won't end how he wants it to if he asks me to get naked in the middle of this party.

But he doesn't. Instead, he squats down in front of me, slides his hands up my thighs, underneath my skirt, and I let him pull my panties down.

It feels like no one in the room is breathing. I step out of my lacy black underwear, while he looks up at me and slips them into his pocket.

"Truth or dare?" I ask.

He smiles. "Truth."

I reach down where he still squats in front of me and touch his face. I want to memorize it, because he won't have the color from all the work in the sun on his skin when he gets out of prison. "Are they going to be okay without you?" I ask.

His smile falls.

I faintly register the whispers, and I can feel Trace off to my right, clearing his throat.

Iron rises, the fun over, and he's not amused now because he wants to get laid. It's his own fault that it has to be tonight or nothing.

"Tryst Six . . ." I muse, pushing him some more. "Tryst Five when Liv left. Now it's Tryst Four, I guess, without you."

"Ohhhh," someone goes off.

People shift nervously. They can tell Iron's pissed.

"Dare," he grits out, changing his answer.

"Fine. What do you want to do?"

"Tape your mouth shut," he growls.

I smile, my chest bubbling with excitement. I look up, toying with him. "If you had bothered to seduce me instead of taking for granted that I was a sure thing, I would've let you tape up my wrists, too." I bite my bottom lip, watching his eyes drop to my mouth. "Because, Iron, my favorite part isn't the fucking. Color me shocked that you're the one who understands that the least. What a disappointment."

Laughter and howls go off. Iron cocks an eyebrow. At least Trace indulged some foreplay.

"Or is that why you go after teenage girls?" I ask Iron. "Because we're just that easy."

A woman laughs quietly next to Trace, and I look over to see him and Aracely smiling, amused.

Iron tosses him a glare, his younger brother throwing up his hands in defense.

"I love you. I'm on your side," Trace says.

Iron turns back to me, and I notice his hand is still in his pocket with my panties.

"Hey, Army?" he calls out, but his eyes don't leave mine.

"Yeah?" Army replies from somewhere behind me.

"We still got any red paint?" Iron asks him.

Excited laughter and chatter erupt around the room as if that means something. I shoot my eyes left and then right.

Then back to Iron. The corner of his lips tilts up. "I think it's time for a few rounds of Red Right Hand."

Everyone starts moving, someone's hands shooting into the air while a woman lets out a squeal.

*Red Right Hand?*

Army passes me, coming up to his brother. "That is the best idea I've heard in a while."

I look at him, and he looks at his brother.

"Are you sure?" he asks Iron. "She's young."

Iron raises his drink to his mouth. "Old enough to be doing our brother all night long for the past six months."

"Oh, I know," Army mumbles. "We could all hear it."

*Ugh.* Liars.

Snickers go off, Dallas chuckling as he walks by, and I watch Iron throw the rest of his drink back and swallow it.

"Outside!" Army announces.

People move, shouts and laughter beginning again as they make for the nearest exit. Some out the kitchen door that leads straight into the garage, while others pile out the front door in a steady stream down the steps.

I don't wait. Twisting on my heel, I grab my hat and coat and follow everyone outside, joining the river flowing to the side of the house and to the open garage.

I step through the crowd of costumes. Everyone else appears to know what's going on. Army, Trace, Iron, and Dallas take up positions in front of the onlookers, my car that Macon was working on today sitting behind them.

Army uses a key on his chain to pry up the lid on the can of paint that looks like it's been opened a dozen other times. The sides of the can are lined with streams of red, the label long since faded and worn.

I pull on my coat again and replace my hat as I watch Iron

plunge a brush into the paint, bringing it up and then down on Trace's hand—his right one—slathering it.

He does the same to Dallas and Iron, and I look to Macon, but he's not moving from the couch. Turin Wilcott's hand is still up his shirt.

"Celli," Iron calls.

I jerk my gaze, seeing Aracely head over, joining Iron and his family.

"Is this going to mess up my clothes?" some girl asks.

"Oh, yeah," another mumbles.

I lean closer to the guy next to me. "What is this?"

"Red Right Hand," he tells me. "Like tag with a twist."

People start to head into the street.

"Ten rounds," the guy explains. "When the music starts, you run into one of four garages." And he points over our shoulders to the buildings side by side. "One—two." And then he gestures to the Jaeger garage we're standing in and the fire station next door. "Three—four. You're safe once you're inside. When the music starts again, you run again. When it stops, you better be back in one of them."

I check all four safe houses, seeing all the garages are open. One is being set up with a table of liquor. Great. Everyone will be rushing to that one in between rounds.

"You can come back to the same garages multiple times," he says, "but you can't stay in the same one for two consecutive rounds."

Meaning, you can't just hide out. Everyone runs.

"And the paint?"

He points to the Jaegers—and Aracely. "They'll be in the street. As you run, that's when you're not safe. They'll tag you with the paint. Every handprint costs you a piece of clothing."

I button up my vest.

"The object of the game is not to get tagged," he states.

*Obviously.*

I can leave. This isn't how he's going to get me naked.

I charge over to Iron and dig in his pocket, scowling up at him as I search for my keys. Is he trying to be a jerk? If we fuck, it has to be insane. Not because I'm his prize.

I shove my hand in his other pocket and feel my keys but also something else. My underwear.

Iron looks down at me, his chest pressing against mine, but something catches my attention.

I shift my eyes to the right. Macon stares at me.

Again.

A banner hangs on the wall above his head, the hourglass emblem billowing in the breeze. He doesn't blink and barely breathes, and Turin notices, following his gaze.

But mine doesn't leave his.

And for a second, something somewhere inside of me hurts.

I slip my panties out of his brother's pocket and step into them, careful as I pull them up underneath the skirt. I try not to look back at him, but I can't help it.

Macon's attention isn't on me anymore, though. It's on the street and the bottle nearly empty at his side.

"Love your costume, Krisjen," Dallas coos. "We'll have no problem finding you in a crowd."

Yeah, a lot of people are wearing black. Won't be hard to pick out all my green and purple and orange.

"Did they explain it to you, newbie?" Iron strolls behind me as I head to the street with the others. "You had a good education. What's the Red Right Hand?"

"It's from *Paradise Lost*," I reply, joining the crowd in the middle of the road. "Divine vengeance."

Maybe not a good education, but definitely a Catholic one.

He tips his head at me. "You know where you're going?"

"I'll protect her." Trace wiggles his eyebrows. "If she wants me being the only one to see her naked tonight, that is."

I sneer. "You're such a gentleman."

He plants a kiss on my forehead, and I jerk away.

I face them, the night breeze calm but thick, something heavy in the air. I'm already sweating.

I face them as they stand in the middle of the road, digging my heels into the ground and ready for the music to start.

Iron grins at me, but then he pulls off his jacket and rips open his shirt, tossing both on the ground. He gestures his brothers over and tells them something I can't hear, the whole time stealing glances over at me.

"Shit," I murmur.

"Hey, why can't I be a Red Right Hand?" a man shouts off to my right. "How many times you guys want to see me naked?"

"It's for everyone else, Chon," Iron shouts. "They've heard how big you are. As hosts, we have to accommodate."

Everyone laughs. When was the last time they played this?

Macon had to have at least once. Maybe a long time ago?

A drop lands on my hand. I tilt my eyes up, seeing a flash of lightning cut through the sky.

"Are you ready?" Army calls out.

The whole crowd howls. "Whoo!"

The wind picks up, and a distant roll of thunder follows.

"I think it's about to rain," I say.

But Dallas just smirks. "It's a water sport, princess. You're gonna get wet."

Snorts go off around me. *God, I hate him.*

"Where the River Flows" starts over the speakers, lightning flashes, and Iron rubs his red thumb across the rest of his dripping fingers.

"Run!" someone shouts.

My heart leaps into my throat, and I can't help my smile, nearly choking on my laugh as I race off.

I barrel for the garage across the street, every step taking me closer to the bright lights inside, and the nineties black sedan sitting up on cinder blocks in the center.

Commotion fills the small street, feet pound the wet dirt, and bodies fall to the ground.

Iron's naked chest appears out of the corner of my eye.

But a guy crashes into my shoulder, making me whip around, and I suck in a breath as I plummet to the ground. My palms hit hard, breaking my fall. "Ow!"

*Shit.*

I look around, searching for Iron. *Fuck.* Where is he?

"There you are," I hear instead.

My heart stops, and I jerk my eyes to the left, seeing Aracely walk slowly toward me while everyone runs around like the world is ending.

*Oh no.*

She dives down, reaching for me, and I yelp, quickly rolling away as fast as I can.

Scrambling to my feet, I catch sight of Trace leaving a red handprint on someone's back, while Dallas grabs a girl by the back of the neck and pulls her in for a kiss, smearing paint all over her skin like her throat's been cut.

Iron stands beyond, slowly stalking as he watches. Amusement laces his stare, but something else, too.

Why isn't he chasing me? He's not chasing anyone else.

Running, I cross the threshold into the opposite garage, the music stops, and I halt, everyone laughing as they discard clothes, one woman going for it and taking off her entire one-piece catsuit. Another pulls down the top of her maid dress to sit at her waist, her red lacy bra covering her breasts. I lock eyes with her, both of us starting to laugh.

Rain kicks up dirt as I look across to the Jaeger garage, seeing all the boys coat their hands in paint again, and then come to stand back in the middle of the road.

Turin Wilcott slides a leg over Macon's, straddling him and bowing her forehead to his. She takes his hands and places them on her hips for him, like he can't make his own damn decisions.

I shout out to his brothers. "So how do I win this game?"

Army whips his hand around, throwing off the excess paint. "Oh, she's confident, isn't she?"

He smiles, and I wink.

"I have a judge in my back pocket. What do you have in yours?"

His smile falls, Dallas shakes his head, and Trace leans down, planting his hands on his knees and getting paint all over his jeans as he pants and zones in on me.

"She just fucking asked for it, didn't she?" he says.

Oh, yes, I did.

Iron stalks back and forth, the music starts, and we all dash into the rain.

"Ah!" someone shouts next to me, followed by a woman squealing.

The rain falls harder, dousing my hair, and people slosh through puddles, whipping to and fro as they're grabbed by red right hands.

Aracely comes for me, and I'm not sure why she's bent on getting me naked, but it's probably to humiliate me.

I grab the back of a guy's shirt, whirl him around, and block her advance, pushing him at her. She tags his shirt, and I run, hearing her yell, "Bitch!"

Followed by him. "Brat!"

I laugh and see Iron as I pass, but I keep running as screams fill the air.

I leap into the garage across the street—the firehouse next door to the Jaegers—and check myself for any marks.

Others forfeit more items of clothing, taking shots off the makeshift bars set up in every shop, and Iron stands in the rain tipping his chin at me. "You're fast."

I dig in the ball of my foot, getting ready again.

"Round three!" Army shouts. "Ready?"

"Whooooooo!"

The music starts, everyone runs, but I step out, one slow step after another. Iron matches me, walking for the other side, through the throngs of people, his eyes only on me.

Army goes after Chon, Dallas after that girl again, and Trace plants his hand on the naked back of a young woman over and over again as she laughs hysterically, losing every item of clothing.

My heart races. The chaos whirls around us. Iron and I move clockwise in a circle. He could pounce any second.

I call out. "Run!"

He smirks. "I don't chase."

"Then I'm afraid you'll never catch me."

Spinning around, I race for the other side, but Army is suddenly there, in front of me. I halt, rearing back, but he catches me by the neck, a wicked smile curling his lips.

The paint from his hand is ice on my neck.

He peels my jacket off my shoulders, and I let it drop down my arms, catching it in my hand.

"You're too old to see me naked," I taunt him.

He arches an eyebrow. "Assuming I haven't already . . ."

What?

He runs, and I stand frozen for a second as naked people rush around me.

*What did he say?*

I shake my head and run for the safe spot.

He didn't mean anything. It doesn't mean he's talking about that night. It simply means he saw me naked once. Maybe he saw me on the couch the morning after. I was on my stomach, and the blanket was mostly covering me.

Mostly.

Or there was that time in June when Trace and I were in the pool alone. Really late, and we were caught up in the moment. Maybe everyone wasn't asleep.

I land in the Jaeger garage, toss the jacket down, and check the vest for paint. Nothing is dripping through. Good. I know Liv said I could keep the outfit, but she put a lot of work into it. I'd feel bad ruining it.

A woman passes in front of me, shirtless and with her bra strap hanging down her arm, and nearly every guy is without a shirt.

The Jaegers plus Aracely stand out in the rain, ready, the music kicks on again, and some guy next to me holds up his arms.

"Go!" he shouts.

We all run. Trace tags me. I lose the hat. *Dammit.*

Music stops and starts again, and I run, laughing as I leap over someone on the ground, and almost make it to the other side before Aracely almost catches me on the stomach.

Three more rounds, and I lose both shoes and one sock as Dallas, Army, and Trace stalk me and I struggle to stretch this out as long as possible while everyone around me is damn near naked.

Most quit once they're down to their underwear, only about four of us left.

Iron watches me the whole time.

"Go!" they shout again.

Music starts, we rush, more Jaegers than runners now, and it's only a matter of time.

I splash through the puddles in the road, rain streaming down my face. Army sees me, stops, and looks like he's about to give chase. I stumble.

Right into Trace's arms.

He laughs, squeezing my ass in both hands.

I push, squirming out of his hold until he lets me go.

"You don't get to touch me there anymore!" I fire back at him.

"Yeah, let's keep pretending like *you* made that decision."

*Asshole.*

He veers around me, holding my eyes. "I want that skirt, Krisjen."

I yank off my last sock, throwing it at him instead.

He tosses his head back, laughing up into the night sky as he runs off. "Coward!"

I shoot off for the safe zone; the music stops, and I pace in front of the opening of the garage, alone. The last three players are in the garage next to mine, and I'm guessing the nearly naked couple behind me making out behind the tool bench are done for the night.

Iron watches me, and there's no way in hell I'm taking off any more clothes.

So why don't I just quit?

The music blasts loud over the rain; I run, and Trace swoops toward me. I laugh so hard I almost choke, but I dive, rolling underneath him and away.

I don't have time to see where he went before I'm locked between two legs towering over me.

Dallas stares down, holding his fist out. He squeezes, and I see red paint start to drip. I close my eyes just in time, feeling warm drops—one after another—land over the side of my mouth.

I open my eyes and glare up at him through the rain. "You should be nice to people who handle your food," I growl.

I climb to my feet, starting to run, but all of a sudden, everyone is here.

Aracely hits my legs.

I scream.

Army splashes my back.

I suck in a breath.

Trace pinches my nose.

I rage. "What the fuck, y'all?"

I whip around.

And find myself in Iron's arms, his painted hands gripping my waist.

That's five. That's more than the rest of my clothes.

Five hits. Everything else I'm wearing. More than everything, actually, as I only have three items left. Skirt, vest, and underwear.

The music plays, and Iron bites the corner of his mouth. I stare up at his lips.

"You want all these people to see me naked?" I ask him.

"You want just me to see you?"

Maybe.

If I like him, then I'll want more, right? What will he be like when he gets out in three years?

Where will I even be?

I don't want to wait for another man, thinking it will magically get better. I did that with Milo.

And I don't want to just have fun. I did that with Trace.

I start to pull away. "You should find someone else tonight."

"Nah, we're way past that," he growls, yanking me back.

"I can't sleep with you."

His eyes soften, and he almost whispers, "Then just stay with me."

A knife cuts my heart.

But I also know better. If he gets me in his bed, he knows what will happen.

"What do you think you're going to get if you get my clothes off?" I ask.

"A pretty picture in my head to take with me."

"You have plenty of those."

A bell pierces the air, and I look over to see Trace ringing the brass dinner bell on Mariette's patio. Someone dumps a bucket of shrimp and mollusks on the newspaper-lined table as people crowd around, grabbing beers out of an ice-filled bin.

Iron takes my face. "I want to get in the car with you and drive to a different fucking view tonight. I want to drive fast enough that the sun never comes up."

My throat is so tight. "I . . . I can't."

"Smile at me," he says.

I shake my head, and I don't smile.

If all he wants is to feel good, he can easily get that from anyone. I'm not going to feel sorry for him.

"Why me?" I ask him.

"Because you're beautiful," he tells me. "And cute. And I want you to fuck me so I can stockpile all these memories for when I'm older. So I can think back to when I was young and had a pretty girl in my arms before she saw me get old and ragged and realized she could do better."

His jaw flexes, but I stay rooted. Rain courses down my legs, my feet sinking into the mud.

"I want you naked in the back seat," he tells me. "I want to hold you and kiss the rain on your mouth and make the most out of the next few hours."

He wants to forget. He wants to not think. He just wants to feel.

He doesn't want *me*.

"Maybe another time," I say.

He narrows his eyes, but then Trace comes up and grabs him. "Iron, come on. Let's eat. Last meal for—"

Iron pushes him away.

Trace stumbles, bracing himself as Iron charges him.

But I jet in front of him, pushing him away from Trace before he can get to him. "Stop it!" I yell at Iron. "Why do you always have to do that?"

"Because I'm fucking stupid!" He glares down at me. "Didn't you know?"

Trace disappears from my peripheral, but I don't care if we have an audience. Iron doesn't need to get laid. He needs a fucking kick in the head.

I get in his face. "You knew you were going to be sent away if you screwed up again. Why didn't you listen?"

"Look around you, Krisjen!" He throws his arms out. "Nothing to do in this shithole but drink, fuck, and fight." He backs away. "What the hell do you care? What do you want from me?"

"I want you to stop blowing it off!" I shout, rain spilling over my lips. "Stop acting like you don't care, because if you don't, then there's no reason for you to come back!"

He falls silent, a pained look in his eyes.

I continue. "Because if you're not going to come home stronger, then you're just going to be a burden. Because I don't want you to leave, and I know it's going to break your heart when you do tomorrow, and I want to fucking acknowledge it!"

His eyes water, but he doesn't blink. Every inch of him looks like a wall.

I lower my voice just a little, so no one hears but him. "It's not a shithole," I tell him. "And Sanoa Bay will be less without you. You should feel bad about leaving them less protected so you don't do it again."

He drops his eyes to the ground.

"And because I'll miss you," I say.

Slowly, he raises his eyes to Mariette's and then over to his house as if it's the first time he's realizing this is his home, and leaving is one thing, but leaving for prison is a waste. And for what? A stupid bar fight where he attacked a connected frat boy and then resisted arrest on top of it?

He looks like he's not really in his body as he takes a step back, and then another. He turns and walks to his house.

I feel his brothers' eyes on me as Iron disappears inside, and I can't help the guilt that suddenly hits me.

I wasn't wrong. He needed someone to say it.

But what's done is done. I don't want him to leave in the morning feeling worse. Or forgetting the good things he's going to come back to, either.

"Krisjen!" I hear Trace call out.

But it's time for me to go home. No idea if I'll be back tomorrow. I probably just lost my job.

I pat my pockets for my car key, but then I sigh when I remember that Iron still has it.

I walk for the Jaeger garage, seeing Macon's still there with the blonde. Her back is against the wall, her hands climbing his chest as he leans on his forearm and bows his head toward her.

I squat down to pick up my clothes and shoes, watching him sway to the right and stepping out to stop himself.

I rise back up. She whispers in his ear and then slips out from under his arm, running for the kitchen door and throwing him a smile.

I stuff my socks in the boots and fold the jacket over my arm. Water drips from everything.

Macon turns, locking eyes with me, and I feel something in my stomach flip.

He grabs the bottle of Jim Beam from the edge of the car he's working on, and I start to walk for the kitchen. I need to get my key.

But I turn to Macon, speaking softly. "You should get rid of that girl."

"Don't speak."

He doesn't even look at me.

I don't know why I care. I've never seen him go to bed with anyone. Maybe he should.

I climb the three steps to the door. "You're wasted," I blurt out, turning the handle. "You're not going to make any decisions tonight that you're proud of."

And I walk inside, slamming the door before he can spit anything back.

I wish I could say that Macon's declining mood is Iron's fault, but I noticed it at the beginning of summer. He was drinking more, staying up late, and increasingly angry.

And when Liv left for college in August, it got worse. With Iron leaving now, I don't know what's going to happen.

Like I'm one to fix him or anyone else, right?

I search the house, knocking on Iron's bedroom door. I hear a girl in the bathroom and head back downstairs, the house quiet and dark.

Entering the kitchen, I look out the other window leading to the pool deck. I spot Iron's right leg hanging over a chaise lounge, the rest of his body sprawled out. His foot is bare, and a giant umbrella hovers over him.

Setting down my clothes, I walk outside, coming up behind him. Rounding the chair, I see he has his hands locked on top of his head, rain dotting his body and dripping over his tattoos.

He chews the corner of his mouth, but I see the tears in his red eyes that he doesn't try to hide.

I feel my own burn. I'm scared for him.

God, I should've just fucking backed off. He only wanted one last night. I could've left. I didn't have to yell at him.

"You're covered," he says, his voice gentle.

I see him staring at my clothes, and I look down at all the handprints I can see, still feeling the ones I can't. "Yeah," I say, laughing a little. "I think you sent out a group text."

They definitely had a plan with that attack. Maybe we'll play again when he comes home.

"I don't want you to leave," I tell him, gently this time.

Tomorrow morning will come no matter what we say or do, but I want him to know we all love him. I just want him to take *that* with him.

He sits up, swinging his other leg over the side of the pool chair. He shakes his head, and I see his shoulders shake with a silent sob.

"It hurts in here." He touches his chest over his heart. "And it's fucking hurt for weeks, and I just want to smash my head into a wall, because it feels like I'm five years old again." He breathes hard and shallow. "When I would cry at school because I missed my mom and just wanted to go home to her."

I used to do that, too. When your body is forced to be somewhere your heart isn't, it's a constant feeling of homesickness.

"I hate that feeling," he whispers. "I don't want to go there." And then he looks up at me. "Macon's right. Why don't I listen?"

Yeah, Macon doesn't know everything, either. And neither do I.

It's three and a half years. Not life. Iron will be back.

I step up to him, threading my fingers through his hair, and feel his shoulders slowly relax. His forehead falls against my stomach.

I don't want my key anymore.

"I didn't want sex," he says, his breath warm on my skin. "I wanted a woman who gives a shit about me to look at me tonight."

He inhales and exhales several times, and I know he's trying not to lose control of his emotions.

I stroke his scalp, dragging my nails gently as his breath grows hot. "You mean a friend?" I ask.

He keeps his eyes downcast.

"Are we friends?" I whisper.

Tilting his head up, he looks at me. "Friends."

My face relaxes, and I soften my strokes in his hair, watching his eyelids start to close with how good it feels.

I like this Iron. He's better when he's serious.

And I want to be the one who looks at him tonight, because tomorrow night no one will.

"Eleven," I murmur.

He cocks his head, peering up at me.

"I'm not so fast after all," I tell him, looking down at my clothes. "I got handed eleven times."

He holds my gaze.

"Shoes." I hold up two fingers. "Socks, hat, coat . . ." I count off everything I've lost so far, moving to the other hand. "That's six," I say.

He watches me, and for a moment, he stops breathing when I slip a button out of the loop on the vest.

He waits.

I undo the buttons one by one, seeing a lump move up and down his throat and fire light in his eyes.

Peeling off the vest, I drop it to the ground, his gaze falling to my naked top half. The cool rain makes the flesh of my nipples harden into points, and my insides warm in anticipation.

"That's seven," he says so quietly.

*Two more.*

Reaching behind me, I unzip the skirt, holding his gaze as I push it down my hips. It falls to the wet deck. "Eight."

He can remove the last piece himself.

But he doesn't.

He whips me around, my breath lodging in my throat as he pulls me down into his lap.

I drop my head back against his shoulder as he slips a hand inside the front of my panties, teasing my entrance with two fingers.

"Krisjen," he pants into my neck. "Good friends?"

I turn my head, searching for his mouth as I bring his palm to my breast. I flick my tongue over his lips. "Really good friends."

I spread my thighs wide, putting my hand over his and pushing his fingers inside of me.

He slides in deep, jerking me back into him and growling.

I kiss his cheek and the corner of his mouth, brushing my lips over his skin. "Don't stay away," I tell him, rolling my hips into his fingers, sliding him in and out of me.

He groans, his groin hard and swollen underneath me.

He kneads my breast, bringing the fingers of his other hand out and swirling my wetness over my clit again and again. "I want you, Conroy." He layers his lips with mine, rain spilling down our bodies. "Can I have you?"

His pushes his fingers back inside of me, and I gasp.

I moan, turning my head into his mouth and surrendering. I open my mouth, and he captures my tongue, both of us melting as our mouths come back for more and more.

I thrust into his hand, but I need him deeper.

Pulling away, I stand up and push my panties down my legs. I peer over my shoulder, through the trees, still seeing the far-off crowd at Mariette's partying.

I hear a wrapper tear, and I turn around, pushing him back on the chair as I climb on top of him.

His eyes look up at me with fire, both of us hot and frantic. God, I'm so wet. I can feel it.

He rips at his belt, unfastening it, and then opens his pants. He slips his cock out, and I watch as he reaches between us, rolling on the condom.

I kiss him long and deep, feeling him crown me. Slowly, I work my body down on him, taking him inside me and feeling the length sink deep.

Breathing hard, I kiss him again and again. "You don't listen or do what you're told," I whisper as I move on him, "because there's something inside you, and it's good, and someday, you're going to know what it's for. I promise."

I pull his head up, holding him to me as I fuck him. His fingers claw down my back as he sucks and bites my nipples hard.

I bounce, taking him in deeper and harder, feeling the walls inside of me contract.

"Oh God, Iron," I whimper.

I'm gonna come already.

Leaning back, I roll faster and harder as he grips my hips, sucking in air through his clenched jaw and watching my body move.

Heat grows low in my belly, tingles spreading, and I gasp, sweat covering my skin as it builds.

The orgasm explodes, rocking through me, and I tip my head back, starting to cry out just as he puts a hand over my mouth.

I jerk, sliding down his cock a few more times until my whole body goes weak.

He brings me back up to him, his tongue sinking into my mouth.

I just let him kiss me. I need a second . . .

He squeezes my hips, breathing over my lips. "You're not done, are you?"

I smile, finally opening my eyes. "I might like a few more of those."

He smiles back, and I let out a little laugh, happy.

I hug him to me, rolling my hips and starting to work him again, his hands roaming my body. He's so warm.

But then I raise my eyes and see it. The dark shadow through the window. Someone standing in the kitchen.

My heart skips a beat.

They take a drag of a cigarette, the end burning bright as they watch us, and I open my mouth to tell Iron we need to stop, but . . .

I close it again.

I go slow with Iron, feeling his tongue and both men's eyes on me as I tilt my face up to the sky and rain glides down my body.

# 7

## Krisjen

Dallas's back rises and falls in the next bed.

He sleeps on his stomach, his mouth half-buried in his sheets, and I'm actually surprised.

He has sheets.

Milo's were barely ever on his bed, and Trace learned quickly that I wouldn't sleep over on just a mattress.

But Iron has sheets. And now Dallas? There must be some evolutionary leap for men beyond twenty years old. Can't say for sure unless I see Army's and Macon's, too.

Dallas's arm hangs over the side of the bed, his black hair nearly covering his eyelids, and I let my gaze glide down his naked back to where the gray sheet drapes just low enough past his hips for me to tell that he's not wearing anything underneath. He literally came to bed after Iron put me in his and stripped himself naked with me in the room. I was already asleep, but . . . he wouldn't sleep naked normally, would he? Not while sharing a room with his brother.

At least I'm dressed in Iron's white T-shirt. He put me in a pair of his boxers, too, but then he woke up a couple of hours later and took them off again. He must not have gone back to sleep afterward, though, because I woke up alone a few minutes ago.

I pull the shirt, making sure it's down, and then slide my hands between my legs, over my underwear. I close my fingers around myself, wincing. I feel like I'm bruised down there. It hurts a little.

Trace is a little bigger, but somehow, I'm sorer after Iron. I was sore after the couch, too. Iron goes harder. Deeper, maybe. I guess it was him after all.

The scent of coffee fills the room, drifting in from downstairs, and I close my eyes, rubbing myself just a little like it'll soothe the ache. But I also don't want the ache to go away, because it'll be the one place he remains once he's gone.

I open my eyes, about to get up, but there's Dallas. Staring straight at me.

I freeze for a second. How long has he been awake?

I jerk my hands out from under the covers.

"You're in pain," he whispers. "It makes you prettier."

*What?*

Then he turns his head, facing the wall and going back to sleep.

This house, I now realize, is about to get a lot less friendly without Iron around.

Pulling off the sheet, I pull on Iron's boxer shorts and leave the room. Macon's door, across from Liv's, is still closed, as are Trace's and Army's. Soft blue light spills through windows, and I shiver as I head down the stairs. It's probably about 6:00 a.m. By nine, I won't be cold. The temperature outside always warms up quickly.

I hear water run in the pipes around me and feel my nostrils tingle as I inhale the frying bacon and the faint scent of butter. I take a left into the dark, empty living room, and stop at the entrance to the kitchen. Iron works at the stove, and I start to speak, but I stop, watching him.

The muscles in his back stretch and tense as he cooks, but his shoulders have relaxed, and every movement is fluid. Reaching for the salt, putting it back. Stirring something in the pan. The toast pops up, he grabs it. Everything one fluid pace. *Calm, tranquil, serene.*

*Quiescent.*

Stormless.

Fuck.

My mouth opens a little, feeling the lump of nausea rise. So many times I wished he would've calmed down, but now all I want is to see him fight. I want to know the spark in him is still there, undefeated.

He turns and sees me, smiling a little, and I plop down on a chair at the island. It hurts to breathe. Removing the glass lid of the cake dish, I swipe some chocolate frosting off one of the two pieces that remain from the dessert Mariette had me send over for Iron yesterday. I lick my finger, my mouth watering at the taste of the sugar.

I do it again, but a fork appears in front of my nose, and I laugh under my breath, taking it. He's making breakfast for everyone, but I don't want his breakfast. He doesn't make breakfast. Army does. Iron making everyone a meal feels like an apology and a goodbye and defeat. He can make breakfast when he comes home.

I dig in, stuffing as much chocolate in my mouth as I can, and watch him wait about three seconds before he yanks open the drawer, pulls out another fork, and joins me.

We laugh, and I meet his eyes as he takes the seat across from me, both of us devouring the rest of the cake.

We start racing for the finish, seeing who's going to get the last bite, and I giggle as we're both shoving in more than we can chew and swallow. He stabs the last bit with his fork, and I can feel the crumbs around my mouth as he looks at me and chews.

"We need more," he says.

I nod, hopping off the stool and running for the freezer as he runs for the cabinets. He pulls out mugs and spoons, while I grab all the ice cream I can find. There's a gallon of vanilla, some cherry chocolate chunk, cookies and cream, and a whole container of untouched strawberry.

We set the table, scouring the fridge and cabinets for every topping imaginable. Whipped cream, nuts, and some fresh blueberries and kiwi already cut up from last night. We also find M&M'S, hot fudge, marshmallows, and some Christmas sprinkles, but I can't imagine anyone in this house has been making cookies for Dex, so I won't think about how they're probably still around from when Liv and Trace were little.

"What the hell?" I hear somewhere behind me.

I look up, seeing Trace run his hand through his bed-head hair as he scans the breakfast table. Remnants of the black writing from his Halloween costume are still dried on his stomach.

He shakes his head, flips on some music, and takes a seat, immediately digging in as I uncover the ice creams and stick fresh spoons in them.

Filter's rendition of "Happy Together" plays as Army enters with Dex. Dallas follows, and I take a seat next to Iron as Macon steps in, his back already covered in sweat from being in the garage.

Everyone fills their mugs, toppings being passed around, and Dex sees all the candy and starts kicking his legs.

Macon looms, washing his hands, and I toss a marshmallow in the air and catch it in my mouth in front of the baby. He giggles.

"It's easy to catch shit with a big mouth," Dallas gripes.

"Even easier when some shit isn't as big as others." I drop my eyes to the direction of his dick, chewing my marshmallow.

Trace laughs under his breath; Dallas throws us both a look. I can't hold back my grin. I guess Trace is bigger than him, too. Not sure why that pleases me so much. No, wait. I do know.

Something moves in the corner of my vision, and everyone shifts or quiets just for a moment as Macon takes a seat at the head of the table. Army glances, and I start to look but don't. Trace, Dallas, and Iron don't make eye contact as he begins loading ice cream into a mug, too.

I drop a few marshmallows on the table in front of Dex and take a bite of my ice cream as I grip the handle.

"So . . ." I take another bite. "Why do you all put ice cream in mugs?"

Trace jerks his chin to his brother. "Macon," he tells me. "He always did it."

Army holds his up by the handle. "Easy to transport without freezing your hand."

"Or having your body heat melt the ice cream too fast," Iron adds.

"It's also easier to scoop off the high sides of a mug," Army explains.

"And when it does melt," Trace chimes in again, "then you can just drink it."

And he tips it back, demonstrating for me as he catches a glob of ice cream in his mouth.

I close my fingers around my handle again, too aware of Macon's presence at the table.

They're right. Whenever I eat ice cream, it's not usually at a table. It's on the couch in front of the TV. Having a handle is great. "Got to wonder why bowls even exist now."

Iron chuckles, and I watch as Macon squirts some whipped cream into his mug, quickly shooting out and leaving a dollop on Dex's nose. The boy jerks, stunned, and then pats his hands up and down in excitement as he grins wide at his uncle, who winks at him so covertly, I don't think anyone else sees.

My heart starts beating harder, watching them. I've never seen Macon playful. His interactions soften with Dex.

Army dives down and sucks it off his son's nose, making the kid giggle.

"We couldn't keep Oreo ice cream in the house when I was little," Iron muses. "It was my favorite, but it was also Dad's."

"Mom would buy it; Dad would eat it all before the next morning," Army tells me. "Iron would be so disappointed."

Trace stares off. "I don't remember that."

"We were too young," Dallas reminds him.

His eyes remain on his mug as he eats and tries hard to look like it doesn't bother him that he remembers so little.

"He didn't do it forever," Army points out to me. "Dad would go in phases. Eat the shit out of something he liked until he got tired of it. Iron soon got all of his favorite ice cream to himself again."

"Only because Macon started hiding it from him," Iron points out.

I look over at Macon. He eats, staring straight ahead as if we're not all sitting here.

"When Mom got sicker," Iron continues, "and Macon had to do the shopping, he would stuff it underneath the frozen pizzas in the deep freezer for me."

The table quiets, only Macon still lifting the spoon to his mouth, and for the first time I feel like I actually belong at the Jaeger table. I'm not the only one silenced by the reminder that their older brother thinks of them. Always.

Iron steals glances at Macon like he's waiting for any recognition or word from him.

But Macon inhales a deep breath and tosses his spoon down, rising to his feet. "It's a full day," he tells everyone. "Make time."

He pours a cup of coffee and leaves the room, disappearing into the garage again.

No one says anything, but the mood has shifted, the smiles and joking from a minute ago quiet now.

The grandfather clock in the living room chimes, and reality steps back in as they all shove a few last spoonfuls into their mouths and get up. Trace sets his mug in the sink and then bends to retrieve a few garbage bags from the cabinet underneath. He starts cleaning up the trash from the party, while Dallas heads upstairs, the shower starting within seconds.

I watch all of them go about their business, not speaking, and it's not because of Iron and what's about to happen. The house and everyone's moods are always at the mercy of their oldest brother.

And I don't think it will get better with Iron out of the house.

An hour later, we're all standing inside the jail.

"Feel free to pack away my shit," Iron tells Dallas. "Maybe get yourself a bigger bed."

His younger brother flexes his jaw to cover up the shake. "Everything stays at it is," he says quietly.

Iron reaches out and hugs him, Dallas's arms staying at his side for only a couple of seconds before he embraces him back.

Iron moves to his youngest brother, holding him tight. "Stay sharp," he tells him, pulling back. "Be better than me, okay? It wasn't worth it."

Trace nods and looks away, blinking the water from his eyes.

Army takes his turn, Iron having said his goodbyes to Dex at home.

Macon isn't here. He didn't come out of the garage, and I know Iron waited, but eventually we had to leave.

"He hates me," Iron says to Army, his chin trembling a little.

But Army shakes his head. "He loves you. That's why he's not here."

I bite my tongue. *Bullshit. "This could be it," my ass.* What if Iron fucking dies in there? What if he makes dangerous connections and comes out ruined? All he needs is his brother to tell him he'll miss him.

And to tell him that he can come home again.

"Do your time and get back to us," Army says.

Iron gives him one last hug, and I stand there, not sure if I should move in. I'm not even sure why he wanted me here. I'm not his girlfriend.

But he stops in front of me. "Thanks for . . . your friendship."

I let out a small laugh, shaking my head.

"I mean it," he tells me.

I reach out and hug him, feeling his arms around me and his kiss on my cheek.

I joke in his ear, "Just don't ask me to wait for you, okay?"

"Not me," he says, letting me go. "But . . . you will be a Jaeger someday."

I look at him.

"You feel it, don't you, Krisjen?" His eyes light up. "You belong in that house."

I swallow. Maybe I feel it. Maybe I feel it because I have nothing else and I'm too scared to try. Hiding in the Bay for the rest of my life would be easy. I love it there.

He looks over at his brothers and then back to me. "Dallas, you think?"

"Oh, fuck you," I breathe out.

He laughs and hugs me again.

"Get home," I tell him.

They lead Iron away, the cop at the front desk buzzing the officer and Iron through, and I can't help myself. "Call as soon as you can," I tell him.

He disappears behind the door, and we all move, watching him through the window. In moments, his black T-shirt is gone from our sight line, and I feel like my heart is being ripped out. Where are they taking him? Will he be okay? I just want to follow—

"We gotta get to work," Dallas says, interrupting my thoughts. "Come on."

They leave, and slowly, I follow them out, wishing I could at least see where Iron will be sleeping. As if it's a summer camp and I get to approve it before I let him stay.

I walk next to Army, trying to hold back, but I can't. Someone needs to say it. "Look, I know Iron kind of asked for this," I say to him, "but it doesn't change the fact that he's scared shitless."

Outside, clouds are covering the sky and Trace and Dallas head through the parking lot.

"He looks up to Macon," I bite out, "and Macon doesn't show up for anyone. I never saw him at any of Liv's games. He didn't even put in an appearance at Dex's birthday party. All Iron needed was a kind word from him, and Macon—"

But Army turns, glaring down at me, and I lose my train of thought. "Once," he states, "when we needed Macon, he was there for all of us."

"Well, not anymore."

"You don't get it." He searches my eyes. "I love Iron, but all he did was think about himself. It's our turn, dammit. Macon needs *us* now."

I watch him walk off, realizing he's just as angry at Iron as Macon is.

Army hides a lot.

Order up!"

I cock my head, using my shoulder to rub behind my ear to catch the sweat trickling down. I grab the plate, and then another, taking a second glance and tossing it back under the warmer. "This was supposed to be rice!"

I'm not yelling. It's just loud. There are fifteen conversations going on in the restaurant, not to mention Aracely carrying on her conversations as she moves plates about the room, even if it means shouting.

I'm glad it's busy, though. It helps to keep me from thinking about Iron and what he's doing right now. It feels like we dropped him off a year ago, instead of just yesterday.

The cook grabs the plate. "Give me three minutes."

"I don't have three!" I blurt out, and snatch Summer's plate from her, spooning the rice from her dish onto mine.

"Krisjen!"

"My order was first," I tell her. "My rice."

I carry the food off, swiping a ketchup bottle and pinching it between my elbow and hip as I go.

"I'm considering this payback for that onion ring incident!" Summer yells. "We're even now!"

"Affirmative."

I set the plates down in front of the two ladies, one of them so beet red, they have to be tourists.

I drop the ketchup at table eleven and grab the Coke I left at the bar, setting it in front of Sam Martinez, who comes in only when his wife puts tuna sandwiches in his lunch, which he hates but doesn't have the heart to tell her.

"Here you go," I tell him, dropping a fresh straw next to the drink.

"Thanks, hon." He cuts into his steak. "Keep 'em coming."

"Will do."

My phone rings in my back pocket, and I pull it out, seeing Bateman's name on my screen. I answer it, holding it to my ear as I start clearing the dirty dishes at table twelve. "Hey, what's up?"

"Krisjen . . ."

He's breathless. I pause.

"I'm sorry about this," he says. "But you have to come home."

I stop, standing up straight. "What's wrong?"

"Your mother is two hours late from her lunch appointment," he tells me. "And I told her I could stay only so long today."

But I tear off my apron, leaving the dishes as I ask, "Why are you even there? The kids are at school. My mom dropped them off this morning."

"No," he retorts. "It's some staff-development thing that I've had on my calendar since August. The kids are off today, and I have my own errands to run. Your mom assured me she'd be back by two."

I dart my eyes up to the clock above the breakfast bar. It's after four.

"Can you please stay?" I ask him. "I'm really sorry, I just—"

"And your mom also hasn't paid me in five weeks, either."

I hesitate. "What?"

Bateman doesn't say anything for a moment, and while I'm grateful he's continued to come, I can't imagine anyone else would've. What the hell is going on with my parents?

"I'm sorry. This isn't your problem," he tells me, "but I can't get ahold of her, and I've had it. I need to leave."

For today or for good? I exhale hard. "Oh—okay. I'm on my way."

"Thanks, babe."

I hang up and swing around the counter, taking out my bag.

"Order up!" Mariette calls.

I dial my mother. I'm not worried, but if she's on her way home, then I can stay and finish my shift at least. The call goes to voicemail, and I hang up, immediately dialing my father, who I know won't answer.

"Krisjen! Order up!"

I wait for his voicemail and clench the phone in my hand, turning away from the customers at the counter. "I promise," I grit out over my father's voicemail, "you won't be able to walk out of your fucking house someday without hearing my name. You are going to be sorry I was ever born."

I hang up, slide my phone into my pocket, and take my backpack. I don't blame my mother. She always paid Bateman, and if she can't, it's because of what my dad has done to us.

I don't like the way she's handling a lot of this. She has things to sell. The house. Her jewelry. She has options.

And yeah, trying to pimp me out is a whole other discussion, but if nothing else, my mother is a survivor, and none of this would be happening if my father hadn't ditched us without a cent.

I toss my apron into the laundry basket as Summer stops next to me. "Are you okay?"

"I have to go." I don't even look at her. "I'm really sorry. I'll try to make it up another time."

"You're supposed to cover the bar tonight," Aracely snaps.

"Can I get some napkins, please?" someone calls out.

Followed by the bell. "Order up!"

"Seriously?" Summer begs me. "Not now. It's busy."

"I have to," I tell the new girl. "It's an emergency. I know I suck. I'm sorry."

"Go," Mariette tells me. "It's okay. We'll see you tomorrow."

I flash her a grateful smile. Then I look back to Summer, ignoring Aracely. "I'll get you back. I promise."

"Yeah, you will."

I laugh a little and spot the to-go bag under the warmer. I grab it. "I'll take this," I tell Mariette.

Macon wasn't home for lunch, but we saw his truck pull in a half hour ago. Mariette probably thought he'd be hungry.

I hurry out of the restaurant and make my way to the Jaegers' house. I didn't tell Mariette that I wasn't sure I'd be back at all, actually. If Bateman isn't paid, he won't return, and I'll have to be home. What the hell would happen if I went to college in January?

I veer right, into the garage, and find Dallas, Macon, Trace, and Army all working on an old Cadillac. A gold one that everyone knows belongs to the mayor of St. Carmen.

It's amazing how long the Jaegers have survived by making themselves useful to the right people. Public enemies but private friends.

"I have to leave early," I tell Macon. He sits at his workbench, inspecting something that looks like it came out from under the hood of the car. "I won't be able to cover the bar tonight."

He twists his screwdriver slowly, the bolt spilling off onto the table.

Seether's "Careless Whisper" plays in the background.

Macon doesn't reply.

"What's wrong?" Army asks me.

Macon takes the screw, rubbing his eyes.

I study him. "N-nothing," I reply to Army.

I inch to the side to see if I can see Macon's eyes. The bags are darker, and I set the food down in front of him so he sees. Is he okay?

My phone rings again, and I pick it up without looking.

"Where are you?" Mars asks.

"I'm coming," I explain. "I'll be home soon."

"Okay."

"'Kay. Bye."

"Will you be back tomorrow?" Army asks me.

I meet his eyes, the concern taking me off guard. I'm easy enough to replace.

I shake my head. "I don't know. I—"

"We need to know," Dallas cuts me off.

I start to back away, out the door. "I'll try."

"Don't," he replies, leaning back underneath the hood. "You're replaceable. By a dozen girls who won't bring me a cold cheeseburger."

Army glares at him. "My cheeseburgers are always fine."

"Probably because she wants to screw you next."

Macon fits the head of the screwdriver into the bolt, not blinking as he twists it slowly.

It spills out of the notch. He puts it back in.

He breathes in.

Then out.

In. Out.

Little turn of the tool.

Another little turn.

Breathing in. Breathing out.

Army goes on. "Stop treating her like shit."

"She knows how to hit back."

Macon's jaw flexes.

"Dallas, shut up," Trace finally chimes in.

Macon squeezes the screwdriver. His knuckles are white. His hand shakes.

My stomach churns. Does he know we're here?

"Come on." Dallas doesn't stop as he saunters up to me. "Where's the fire you had for Iron?"

"Leave her alone," Army growls.

Macon's hand shakes again. It won't stop. My gaze flashes between his hand and his face. Am I the only one seeing this?

But Dallas keeps going. "We'll leave the door open," he taunts me. "I'm sure you'll be back tonight."

I back away from him.

"What the hell is your problem?" Army yells at him.

But a small voice finally pipes up. "Go take care of your family, Krisjen."

I turn, following the direction of the whisper. All eyes turn to Macon as he rubs his own with his thumb and forefinger. I'm probably the only one who sees it. The way they're watering.

"Mariette will have you back whenever you want," he says, his voice gravelly.

His brothers watch him warily as he rises and moves away from the table.

"Do I tell Mariette to turn customers away?" Army asks him.

"Tell her to close the fucking doors for the rest of the day for all I care."

Dallas moves as his brother passes, and Trace comes out from under the hood, watching him. Everyone finally noticing what I did minutes ago.

"Now get out," Macon barks at them. "All of you. Now."

I back toward the bay door, his brothers following and

scramming before Macon hits the button and the door comes falling down. Locking him back in solitude.

Slowly, I walk to my car, while the boys drift out into the street.

"I don't see how we can't find any employees without fucking kids to take care of," Dallas gripes behind me.

Something's wrong. How can they not see it?

Is it Iron? Or . . .

But I just climb in my car and sit there for a second, tears starting to stream, and I don't know why. It's changing.

The Bay can't change, but it is.

He looks like he's dying.

Liv gone. Iron gone.

Macon . . .

# 8

## Trace

I seem to remember Macon having to quit a job to come home and raise you," Army tells Dallas.

Krisjen drives off, and I stare after her car as it disappears around the trees. What the hell is she doing? I didn't start up with her because I thought I would be rid of her when she left for college this fall. I started up with her because she's hot and fun.

But she shouldn't still be here. She has choices. Why does she look like she's treading water?

"Stop being a fucking coward," Army tells him, "and start taking your anger out on whoever really deserves it."

"I can't."

"Leave her alone."

"But I haven't gotten a reaction out of her yet."

I draw in a breath, my shoulders feeling heavier today.

Army moves into Dallas's space. "You're giving her an awful lot of attention for someone who's supposed to hate her."

But Dallas doesn't back up. "You're not scary."

Not like Macon, he means.

"You're draining me," Army nearly whispers, and I can hear the fatigue in his voice as he talks to Dallas. "It's a drag being around you anymore, and if you're not going to tell me what's wrong so I can help, then you just need to shut up. Or else you won't have to worry about Macon, because right now I'm the one who wants to snap your fucking neck."

"Tryst Five, then?" Dallas taunts.

But Army fires back. "No, still Tryst Six. You're assuming you're irreplaceable. There will be more Jaegers."

I can't help but smile a little. None of us can keep up with Dallas, except Macon, and he only accomplishes that because most of us aren't completely certain that Macon won't actually kill him. Looks like Army is finally learning to lead.

Dallas says nothing, simply spits on the ground and jumps into one of the trucks. He takes off the opposite way from Krisjen, into the swamps, and I don't look to see where Army goes.

I pull out my phone, still staring off as Clay picks up.

"Hey," she answers.

"What's going on with Krisjen?" I ask.

"Huh?"

I wait, hearing a horn honk and realize she's in her car.

Krisjen's not one to hide things. Not like my family. If something is wrong, Clay knows.

Finally, she sighs. "Her dad left. Like eight months ago."

I feel like I knew that. She might've hinted at it in passing. I was probably drunk or something.

"He took all the money, including her college fund," Clay tells me. "That's why she didn't participate in the debutante ball with me last spring. She couldn't afford it. He started over, a mile away on Barony Lane, with his sidepiece, and won't front any child support until . . ."

"Until?"

She clears her throat, probably nervous about betraying a confidence, but she knows better with me.

"Until he knows all the kids are his," she explains. "Mars looks . . ."

I nod, finishing for her. "Different from Krisjen and Paisleigh . . ."

*Jesus Christ*. What a fucking dick. He has more money than he will ever need, and at the very least, he knows Krisjen is his daughter.

*I wish you all could have all the money you ever wanted, so you can see that's not the answer.*

That whole fight with Iron makes more sense. What is her mom's plan to take care of her kids?

"He left Mrs. Conroy the house," Clays explains, "the cars, and her jewelry, which she can sell but won't."

Because she's spent a shitload of time accumulating that life.

"And I heard . . ." Clay pauses, and I hear her engine shut off.

"What?" I press.

She hesitates, exhaling. "So Krisjen didn't tell me this, but my dad called this morning, and . . ." she says.

I tense, waiting.

"Some of the men at the club were circulating an old photo of Krisjen." She lowers her voice as if someone can hear her in her car. "One she sent Milo back when they were together in high school probably, and like the asshole he is, he didn't keep it to himself. Jerome Watson is saying that she'll be his. Her mom, apparently, is pushing for it, because he's rich, and . . ."

And she can't sell her jewelry, but she can sell her daughter. *Yeah, fuck*.

"She would've been a minor in that photo, Trace," Clay explains. "My dad called her mom. He called her dad. No one is answering. He waited until Watson hit the parking lot and then gave him a bloody nose."

Really? Heh.

"My dad's known Krisjen since she was a baby, you know? He was really upset."

"Don't worry about anything," I tell her. "Tell your dad not to, either. We got it from here."

"We?"

I hang up, heading for the house. I like Krisjen. I always have. She's sweet to people, and I don't want that ruined, because I think that's why I was drawn to her. Neither of us has grown up, but where it's just pathetic on me, it's hopeful on her.

I step into the kitchen as Army pulls chicken nuggets out of the freezer. I snatch the bag out of his hand and toss it back in. "Get Dex," I tell him. "Let's go."

"Where?"

"You'll see," I say. "This could be it. Come on."

Krisjen and I have screwed at least twenty times, but I've never been inside her house. I know which one it is, and I've passed it a million times, but the Conroys hire elsewhere for their landscaping, and when we hooked up, Krisjen never wanted to do it at her place.

Which made sense. I can be seen with a Saint. Her parents can't see her with Swamp.

Army parks, and I walk up the long driveway to her house, avoiding the door at first. The Spanish revival has characteristics similar to my house—the clay shingles, the stucco exterior, the lead-paned windows and wooden front door. But her house is white, in excellent shape, and I know from her social media that she has a huge T-shaped pool on the back patio, which itself has as much square footage as the damn house. Or at least looks that way on Instagram.

I spot her crossing the room in front of the window, and I step over the flower bed, tapping on the glass. She jerks around, then sees me. I nod once and head for the door.

No idea if her mother is home, but I don't think she usually is. Rather not bump into her, in any case.

Krisjen pulls open the door, and I stroll in, not waiting for an invitation. "Hey," I say, looking around the shiny foyer. There's a mirror on the ceiling. In the foyer. I shake my head.

"What's up?" I hear the surprise in her voice.

I face her, Army stepping in, his kid hanging half off his shoulder. "Kids eat yet?" I ask her.

"About to."

She's studying me like I'm going to piss in her house.

I whirl around and head into the living room—or one of them anyway. "What are you cooking?" I shout.

But I just hear her yell behind me. "Hey!"

It's too late. I already spot the kitchen to my left and head for the doorway. "It smells good in here," I call out.

"It smells like her," Army adds.

Paisleigh and Mars sit at the kitchen island, but we've never formally met.

Krisjen charges after me, her voice on my tail. "What the hell are you guys doing?"

But then I stop, scrunching up my nose as I turn to Army. "Do you smell that?"

He nods, hesitant. "Broccoli."

I pick up the plate in front of the little girl, inspecting that shit that's popular in homes with women. Thank God Macon eighty-sixed that crap the day he took over. The only green things I eat are jalapeños.

"Krisjen, what are you doing to these kids?" I eye the little girl. "You want to eat this?"

But the middle schooler next to her pulls down his headphones instead. "Who are you?" Mars asks.

I like the scowl on his face. It's protective.

I pick up the grilled cheese on Paisleigh's plate and take a bite.

The butter hits my tongue, and my taste buds fucking implode. "It's actually pretty good," I tell Army.

There's ham on it, and the cheese is on the outside of the bread. Weird, but massively edible.

Krisjen sets her hands on her hips. "It's croque monsieur."

"Croque what?" I try to ask, but my mouth is full, and she just rolls her eyes at me.

Army takes it. "Looks like ham and cheese to me." He bites off a hunk, his eyebrows shooting up and nodding at me in approval.

"Haven't we seen enough of each other?" Krisjen asks.

But I look at the kids. "You guys want ice cream for dinner?"

Paisleigh nods so hard her head nearly falls off.

But Mars is skeptical. "You're the Jaegers," he says. Then, he looks to Army. "Are you Macon?"

"That's Army," Krisjen tells her brother and then points to me. "That's Trace."

"Come on." I start to move for the door. "Get your shoes on. We're going to make sundaes."

"Yay!" the girl shouts.

"Trace!" Krisjen yells, but I ignore it.

I grab Dex from my brother and swing the one-year-old around my head, leading the way as the kids jump off their stools and follow.

"Is that your son?" Paisleigh asks as we walk out the door.

"This?" I hold out the baby to her. "I found it outside. It's not yours?"

She throws her head back, giggling. "Nooooo!"

I hear Krisjen growl behind me and finally hear her lock the front door, following.

Army and I strap the kids into the car, and I vaguely hear some grumbling behind me, but Krisjen climbs in, and we take off.

The drive isn't far. We're barely leaving her neighborhood, actually.

We turn right, climb a hill unusual to find in Florida, and then swing left, the gas lanterns on both sides of the street coming into view and all lit.

A buzz spreads under my skin. Like it always does when I come here.

A canopy of trees hangs over the sidewalks, the soft glow of the lamps lighting the mild fog, making me feel like I'm nowhere near Sanoa Bay.

Nowhere near St. Carmen.

I remember the day I first worked on this street, and while it was beautiful, that's nothing compared to how it looks at night. Like every house has a mom, and there's an apple pie cooling on the windowsill.

Army stops in front of a 1930s Tudor-style cottage, white rock with patches of wear that charmingly reveal the natural brown underneath. The second floor has a lone window where the roof meets at the point, and the shutters have clearly been repainted over and over for a hundred years.

A knocker that I know is an owl adorns the green front door, and unlike most homes that have square windows, this one features domed panes.

Trees loom on both sides of the walkway to the front door, but Army pulls the truck into the driveway and toward the back of the house, out of sight.

"What are we doing?" Krisjen asks.

But I don't answer. "Come on," I tell the kids, opening my door.

Paisleigh scrambles, trying to pull off her seat belt. Mars follows me.

I bypass the side door and take the walk to the front of the house, wanting Krisjen to see it this way. Pulling out my keys, I unlock the door and push it open, stepping aside to let everyone else enter.

The kids run, Army following with Dex, and Krisjen rushes after her siblings.

"Stop!" she yells. "No."

But I pull her back and sweep her into my arms.

She kicks, frowning at me. "What are you doing?" she bites out. And then she shouts, "Mars! Paisleigh!"

"They're fine."

"Are you house-sitting?" she asks me. "Why do you have a key?"

I smile and carry her inside, bridal-style, kind of getting turned on by how pissy she is since she stopped sleeping with me.

"Let me down," she whines.

"No."

"Dude," she scolds. "Come on. They're going to break something. I need to get them out of here."

Heavy footfalls pound upstairs as the kids explore the cottage, and I keep the lights off, so we don't alert the neighbors that someone's here when we're not supposed to be.

She squirms in my arms, and I heft her up again, adjusting my hold. Funny. She never felt this heavy on top of me.

"I never really liked your house." I give the door behind me a slight kick, closing it. "Or Clay's, or most of the houses on this side of the tracks."

I head left, down the two steps on the hardwood floor, into the living room that features a brick fireplace. The owner probably only uses it in conjunction with the air-conditioning just so they can stand the heat for a little bit of ambience.

"Your house is too refined," I tell her. "Too cold."

The smell of brick, leather, and a woman's perfume, probably still lingering on the high-back cushioned armchairs from the last time the owners were here, fills my lungs, and I can't imagine that any more than two people should ever live here.

Two people reading in those armchairs. Laughing over a bottle. Eating and taking a bath in the old tub upstairs, and listening to records and never unable to hear each other. Never forced to shout or do more than whisper. No fighting. Nothing breaking.

"But this house . . ." I muse, looking around. "I could live here."

I feel her staring at me, and I'm sure she's wondering if I'm drunk, because she believes I'm not capable of any decor other than beer-can pyramids and Samurai swords. Of course, I do have two Samurai swords in my room at home.

I step farther into the room, and she hooks an arm around my neck to steady herself.

I walk her past the mahogany bookshelves and the antique vase on a pedestal in the corner. "I would love to have my own business someday, too," I tell her. "A place where people come to sit and talk over beer."

"Like a bar?"

"A pub," I retort.

"Is there a difference?"

"Yes, there's a difference." I scowl down at her. "A bar is drinking and drama. A pub is . . ." I pause, looking around the room as if the word I'm searching for is written on the walls. "Community. Somewhere you feel at home."

Hence pub. Public house. It's a gathering place.

"Somewhere comfortable," I go on, "where the music's not too loud and the food is good. The atmosphere feels like you're in a book. A fireplace and wood everywhere—the furniture, the bar, the walls."

I gaze around the living room, her body warm under my fingers. She's soft. More so in the thighs, and I like it. I can feel the ribs in her back. I never noticed that before.

I smile a little, continuing. "The customers are as good as friends, and it's mine. Someplace kind of sleepy except on Saturday nights when there's live music and the floors are shaking as everyone sings along. People to talk to. People happy to be there. Happy to see you. That's a job I would like." I look down at her. "And then I'd come home to someplace quiet. Someplace like this that's mine, too, and I'm alone and . . ."

I hold her blue gaze.

"Someplace I'm alone and . . ."

*And I don't have to smile if I don't want to.*

But I don't say that out loud.

"Macon wouldn't want to hear any of that," I admit. "That sometimes I want to leave. He's nearly killed himself keeping our family together. Dallas would piss all over my dream, and Army and Iron don't need to hear my whining. You're the only one I've told."

She stares at me, and I fall silent.

Did I make it weird?

I'm not sure why I told her.

"I don't think I've ever held you like this before," I tease.

"It wasn't that kind of relationship."

Yeah. We shared meals. Takeout on the way back to my place. Breakfast the morning after sometimes. This is probably one of the longer conversations we've ever had. Talking wasn't what we wanted each other for.

"I'm glad you left my bedroom the other night." I set her on her feet. "I think it takes everyone some time to figure out what they want and what they're worth. Some people spend years settling for something, because it's better than nothing, before one day we finally realize that it's actually not. Nothing is better than the wrong thing."

Wrong things kill our insides.

She stands there, still looking up at me, but her hand hasn't left my neck.

"It's a winter place," I finally explain, gesturing to the house. "Fred Corcoran and his wife come down here from Boston every November before Thanksgiving, but I saw some of the staff here a few days ago, cleaning, laundering sheets, and stocking the fridge in preparation for their arrival."

I move her hand down into mine and pull her along, back into the foyer, toward the kitchen.

"I got a key a couple of years ago to check in on the cat when they took a weekend away," I tell her over my shoulder, "and they never asked for it back, so . . ."

"There's no alarm system?"

"I guess with the security detail cruising the neighborhood they figured they didn't need one."

"And, of course, you have free rein to come and go," she says more to herself than me.

As a landscaper, absolutely. No one looks twice if my truck is on the street. Or in this very driveway.

She stops and turns to me. "Would you really live here alone? Forever?"

It seems so unlike me. I love everyone, right?

I hook my arm around her neck. "I think that's why I liked you so much," I tell her in a low voice. "You seem the same whether you're around people or not. You never put yourself away."

*I do. A lot.*

Her mouth opens like she wants to ask something, but I just laugh, planting a smile on my face. "It's just a fantasy, Krisjen. I won't ever leave the Bay. Except to go to Orlando," I add. "I would love to go to Disney World. Have you been?"

"Huh?"

Of course she has. They probably have a condo.

We walk into the kitchen, the light from the fridge brightening Army's face as he pulls ice cream out of the freezer. The kids sit at the island, and I start pulling toppings out of the cupboard, knowing where everything is.

"Do you live here?" the boy asks. "I thought you all lived in trailers or something."

"Mars . . ." Krisjen chastises.

But I nod. "We do. We're just breaking and entering." Then I lean down to Paisleigh, pressing my finger to my lips. "Shh . . ."

She goes wide-eyed.

"They don't live in a trailer," Krisjen tells her brother, pulling out mugs and spoons.

I pull off the lid off the ice cream and start scooping. "We live in a humongous . . ."

"Amazing . . ." Army adds.

"Incredible . . ." Krisjen points out.

"Dilapidated . . ." I tell Mars.

"And rotting . . ." Army jokes but not really.

"Mansion." I drop a scoop of ice cream into a mug.

Army passes behind me, grabbing his kid, who is climbing across the counter. "There are holes in the walls," he says.

"A leaky roof," I go on.

"But it rains in the kitchen"—Krisjen grins—"which is kind of cool."

"There's no central air-conditioning," I tell the kids, "and the water tastes like mud."

"And there are bones in the backyard," Army says, "because every animal in a ten-mile radius comes to our house to die."

Mars laughs as he eats a spoonful of ice cream.

"The lights go off in thunderstorms," Krisjen tells them, "and it always sounds like a creaky shutter and smells like early-morning fog and old wood."

Army looks at her over his shoulder, Dex trying to climb out of his grip.

"The ceramic tile floors are this beautiful red-orange color, and the stairs are all uneven like a Dr. Seuss house." She smiles to herself as she makes Paisleigh's sundae. "Because they've endured years of all the Jaeger boys, and all the people before them, running and stomping up and down them and moving furniture on them . . ."

The glow on her cheeks brightens with every word, and I meet Army's eyes, both of us going silent.

"And kids learning to climb them," she continues, "and there's a thin hole about three inches long on one step halfway up that I'm always worried will give me a splinter, but I hope it never gets fixed."

I know that step.

She really loves our house, doesn't she?

"Why don't you want them to fix it?" Paisleigh asks.

But Krisjen doesn't answer her sister. Because beauty is in the small things and character is in the flaws, and learning that fact can't be taught or told.

I've never loved my house, but Krisjen sees it as magical.

Army's eyes fall as Dex swats at him, and I finish doling out the ice cream.

"How can you see if the lights go off in a thunderstorm?" the little girl asks Krisjen.

But I drop the scooper, replying, "Like this!"

And I dive down, force my head between her sister's legs, and haul Krisjen up onto my shoulders, high in the air.

"Trace!"

I plant Krisjen's hands over my eyes, and I hear a peal of laughter from the little girl.

"Don't break anything," Army grumbles.

I hold out my hands, blindly feeling for the refrigerator. "No promises."

I open the door and pull out a small plastic container of something I can't see. "Okay, is this the ice cream?"

"N—"

"Yep!" Krisjen laughs. "That's it."

More giggling from the other side of the island.

I uncap it and start dishing out scoops into a mug.

"Krisjen!" Paisleigh shouts.

But all her big sister says is "Shh."

"And some sprinkles," I singsong, grabbing something that feels like olive oil. "Must have sprinkles!"

"Oh no," Paisleigh groans.

I can hear her palm hit her forehead.

"And I need some chocolate sauce." I reach to my right, feeling for a container.

"No, not there," Krisjen tells me, still covering my eyes. "To the left. More. More. There."

I grab what I'm sure is a pepper grinder.

"Krisjen, but . . ."

"Shh, I know what I'm doing, silly," she tells Paisleigh. Then instructs me, "Now twist it."

I smile, happy to hear the light tone in her voice again.

"Mmm, this is going to be so good," I coo. "I can't wait."

I feel for a spoon, dip it into the mug, and scoop up a mouthful.

"Ugh." Mars groans.

Paisleigh giggles, waiting for me to take the bite.

"I can't watch this," Mars finally says, and I hear his stool scrape against the floor.

I take a huge bite of sour cream and gag, acting like I'm going to vomit as the little girl starts laughing hysterically.

I keel over, and Krisjen starts to fall, letting out a laughter-scream combo as her hands leave my eyes.

I try to catch her, but she topples to the side and into my brother's arms. He holds her, both of them staring at each other for a moment.

"There she is," he says, both of us clearly glad to see her smile back again.

We take our sundaes to the table, while Mars disappears upstairs and Paisleigh plays with Dex in the foyer.

"Thanks for this, guys," Krisjen says, setting her mug down on the table. "I just don't want to be a problem for Mariette or Macon. With my parents and their problems—"

But she doesn't need to explain. "That's how the Bay survives, even given all of its struggles and fighting and noise," I tell her. "We never think we have to do anything alone."

And neither does she.

I inhale the cool air, the central air-conditioning alone possibly worth marrying her and moving in. "I like your room."

We lie on top of her bed, fully clothed, the unfamiliar territory making me a little uneasy. Every time she left my bed this summer, I never gave one thought to where she slept. It's kind of hard to picture her in this house. It's all white and gold and clean and cold. Except her room. The walls are baby blue, and she has a canopy over her bed, because Krisjen was always told she was a princess.

I roll over her, half lying on her body as I bury my face in her white comforter that looks blue in the moonlight. "And this bed," I muse. "It smells like jubilation and girl skin."

I dive into her neck, nibbling gently.

She lets out a laugh and pushes me off. "Stop."

I lie back, cradling her head in the crook of my arm and staring down at her. "I can do better."

I'm not sure if I mean sex or something else, but she simply smiles. "I have no doubt. When it's someone you really love."

I wasn't sure if I really wanted sex tonight, but now I do.

She gazes up at me, and I hold her eyes, not at all disappointed, though. I get tired of being fucked sometimes.

Army took Dex home an hour ago, and I stayed with her, only because I didn't want to go home. She didn't ask questions when I laid down on her bed. We need friends. Both of us.

"Are you mad at me?" she asks, not breaking eye contact.

No. I'm actually just grateful she knows I'm not clueless like all of my family and friends assume I am about everything. I knew she was going to bed with Iron as soon as she showed up at the party.

But I whisper, "Do you care?"

"Yeah."

I can't help but smile a little. "Are you mad at me?" I ask her.

"No."

I hold her body tightly, still looking down at her. I'm not sure why I never did this to her sooner. It feels good.

"Do you miss him?" she asks.

I let out a breath and turn my eyes up to the ceiling. "I don't know."

I feel her eyes on me, and I shift, uncomfortable. Macon, Dallas, Army . . . we don't go there. Iron's gone. Talking won't help.

*Do I miss him?*

"I mean, I love him and I hope he's okay, but . . ." I shake my head, searching for my words. "That feeling like I'm waiting for something—or like something is incomplete—has always been there. I don't really feel any different than I did two months ago when Liv left for college, or eight years ago when my mom and dad died." I squeeze her arm in my hand. "It seems I've always been missing someone."

I feel her slowly inch in as far as she can, molding herself to me.

I like her.

I can't be Macon or Army. I can't be Liv. I don't feel like I have time to learn things. Space to stutter. Room to make mistakes. I'm stupid to them. I know I am. I know I'll fail if I ever really try, so I just try to be funny instead. Or fun. If I can make the house brighter, maybe Macon will know I'm alive.

"I'm glad you told me your dream," she says, her breath seeping through my T-shirt. "And you know what's weird? I see it. Not really the 'living in a cottage' part. I'm still working on that."

I chuckle to myself.

"But the forest-green leather seats on the barstools," she goes on. "The candlelight flickering against the walls. The black chesterfield chairs at the tables, and you in a crisp blue button-down behind the bar."

"Not a T-shirt?"

"Nope." She tips her chin up, assertive. "You're a gentleman now. A respectable proprietor with vast knowledge of the history of whiskey and the difference between aging it in American oak barrels versus French oak barrels."

Do I really need to know that?

"And there's a microbrewery on-site," she continues. "Huge copper tanks you can see through the glass wall, and you call your signature beer—"

"It'll be a distillery, thank you," I fire back. "Rum."

She smiles, tucking herself into me again. *Green leather on the barstools* . . . I was thinking black, but green sounds classier.

"It always gets better in my head," I say. "More detailed. It's a good dream."

"It's going to happen."

I close my eyes, ready to sleep with the picture in my mind, but she does that thing where she drapes her leg over mine so the heat between her thighs is on mine, and I start to stir.

"Are you absolutely sure you don't want to have sex?" I ask. "I mean, you could be practice for someone I really love someday."

She kicks my leg, growling, and I shake with a laugh.

# 9

## Krisjen

Trace slept in my bed, and we didn't have sex. I'm still smiling two days later. He was sweet. I've never seen him like that before.

If I'm around, I'll help him set up that pub someday. I'd love to, actually.

I roll the dish rack back into the washer, picturing it in my head.

I'd be proud to see him have that dream. Really proud. Still not sure about the cottage part, though. It's barely big enough for a family. Or his brothers if they visit. Not sure he's thought that through.

I plop down in the chair next to the cook's station, taking Santos's flask as he rolls out dough for pies.

I take a swig, wincing when I taste whiskey. He raises his eyebrows at me, because I'm a bold little minor, aren't I? But he doesn't say it out loud, just goes back to his baking.

"That kind of sucked." I twist the cap back on and set it down. "What a long day."

"But I bet that wad of tips in your apron doesn't suck."

I chuckle. *No, it doesn't.* Bateman returned the next day for Mars and Paisleigh, so my mom must've paid him somehow, but

Army told me if I need to leave at any time, then I need to leave. They'd deal with it.

A few customers remain on the patio, but the restaurant inside is empty, except for Jessica mopping the floor. It's after nine. I should get home. My mom will be on her third vodka tonic by now.

"How's the family?" Santos asks.

"Can't complain." I can, but I won't. "Yours?"

"My oldest wants to be a plumber," he mumbles. "He got accepted to Texas A&M."

That's impressive. But . . . "Not everyone has to go to college," I remind him.

"Easy for you to say when it's someone else's kid."

I pause, thinking about that one. "Fair enough," I tell him. "We'll pick up this conversation again when it's my child."

"Deal."

Although entirely different situations, he's coming from the same place my mother is. They want the best opportunities for their children, but the difference is, my mother is willing to do—or force me to do—whatever it takes to ensure it.

Not sure she would've let me go to college, even if my dad hadn't taken all the money.

And I'm not sure I would've gone either way.

I want to work, but just as a means to enjoy my life. To pay for trips to the drive-in with Mars and Paisleigh, and big meals with family and friends, and cute clothes that keep my husband's eyes all over me.

And helping those around me who need it.

College would be a waste of money. At least right now. I have no desire for a career.

Iris bursts through the back door, breathing hard. "Can someone help me in the bar, please?" she whines, pulling bags of mixed nuts off the rack and piling them in her arms. "The Torreses are coming in with a shitload of people. I'm getting tables together now, but I'll need help taking orders."

Santos looks through the warmer, probably trying to see who else is still here, because I've already worked a double shift.

I debate for a split second, but then I say, "I can stick around for a little while longer."

Guilt hits me, but I push it aside. The kids are fine. My mom raised the three of us so far without any deaths. I'll only be a couple more hours.

Iris smiles, her shoulders relaxing. "Thanks. Please hurry."

I tap out a text to Mars. **Working a little longer. Text if there's a problem.**

And I stand up to follow her, but Santos pushes a brown bag into my chest. "Take this over first."

I grab hold of Macon's dinner, still not having told Mariette that he almost never eats it.

But yet . . . he continues to let her send it.

Tucking my phone in my back pocket, I push up the sleeves of my black hoodie and walk out of the restaurant, seeing the glow of the garage lights down the lane.

I haven't seen Macon all day, and I don't see the boys' trucks out front, either. It's better when Army or Trace is in the garage with him. I hate being alone with him. He doesn't like me.

Everyone else likes me.

But when I veer right, into the garage, I see the hood of my car up, a work light hanging inside, and a Bluetooth speaker on a shelf playing an alternate rendition of Nirvana's "Something in the Way."

But there's no one here.

"Hello?" I inch in, looking around the car for legs. The door to the kitchen is open, and I call out again. "Hello?"

But he's not in earshot. I reach out, setting the bag down on his worktable, but then I hear a cry in the distance.

"Please!"

I stop, some muffled sobs pricking my ears.

"No!" the man wails again.

The voice doesn't sound familiar.

I jerk my eyes to the back door of the garage, seeing that it hangs open just slightly.

Keeping my feet light and quiet, I head for the back of the shop.

"Please, just let me out!"

*What the hell?* I force my feet to keep going, slipping through the back door and looking around the pool, not seeing anyone. It's coming from the woods. I walk across the deck, into the brush, and see a light.

"Please, Macon," a man begs.

Macon comes into view, standing in the doorway of a container. Like the ones they put on the backs of semitrucks, with no windows and a lock on the outside. Has that always been sitting back here? I've never noticed.

He grips a man by the collar, the muscles in Macon's back taut and the veins in his neck visible from here. I step, but foliage crunches under my shoe, and I dart to the left, hiding myself behind a tree.

My pulse races, and I close my mouth, because I'm breathing too hard.

After a moment, I hear Macon growl, "Where's the food we bought your family?"

"F-Fisher had friends over, and um . . ." the guy gasps. "No, Macon, please!"

I peek around the tree, seeing him shove the man's head into an oil drum I hope is filled with just water.

The man struggles, gripping the sides and pushing against Macon's force.

But Macon doesn't let him up until he wants to. Pulling his face out of the water, I study the guy, trying to figure out if I know him.

There are a lot of people living deeper in the swamp who I haven't met yet.

"Look at me," Macon bites out, pulling him up again by the shirt. "Look at me!"

The man breathes hard, his legs limp underneath him.

"You've had your chances," Macon tells him. "I've been nice, then I was firm, but this is it. You have another drink, or spend money on anything that takes food off your kids' table, I'm going to kill you. I'm going to fucking kill you."

The man sobs. "It's not just the alcohol, man. I'm . . . I mean . . . I've got a problem with drugs, too."

"Shut up." Macon pushes him back down into the water.

The man is one of them. Not an enemy. Macon's trying to get him straight. Would he really kill him?

He yanks the man out by the back of his collar, shoves him in the container, and I rush to the next tree and then the next, trying to get a view inside, but all I catch sight of is a futon and some light that must be coming from a lamp or something. Macon slams the door shut and locks it, the guy inside pounding against the other side.

"Please!" he begs. "Please, let me out!"

"Three days," Macon says. "When that shit is out of your system."

"I can't stop." He sobs hard. "Macon, I wasn't always like this. You know me. Please, man. I'm scared."

Macon's hand rests on the metal door, his head slowly falling. His chest rises and falls in heavy breaths.

"Macon . . ." the guy goes on. "It hurts!"

My stomach twists in knots, and I watch Macon Jaeger stand there. His shoulders shake a couple of times, his exterior slowly crumbling as his guard comes down.

Because right now, he doesn't know anyone is watching him.

"Please . . ." the guy pleads.

I blink, a tear spilling over. I quickly wipe it away.

He has to know a detox not done right can kill someone. Do the others know he's keeping this guy back here?

The guy hollers and pounds, and Macon turns, starting to walk away. His eyebrows press together, and his mouth hangs open just slightly, like he can't breathe.

The guy carries on, and Macon closes his eyes again like the only way he's going to see something good is by not seeing anything at all.

Gripping the side of the barrel, he plunges a hand into the water and splashes it across his face and the back of his neck. He walks toward the house, and I slip around the tree, staying out of sight.

But he suddenly stops, and I watch him as he stares at the riding lawn mower left outside with a couple of beer cans sitting in the holders. Trace was supposed to mow the lawn a week ago. I look around at the growth of weeds and grass. If he did, I can't tell.

And he didn't put the mower away. Macon runs his hand through the rainwater that's pooled in the seat.

*Damn Trace.*

Macon stalks for the garage, yanking the rope off the hook near the side of the door, and disappears inside.

Something doesn't sit right. Macon's going to strangle him.

I start after him. I peer into the shop, seeing him hit the switch, closing the garage door, and head up the three steps into the house and into the kitchen. He still carries the rope.

I hesitate.

Trace isn't home. There weren't any trucks in front of the house.

What is he doing?

I shoot off, heading into the house, and immediately hear footfalls upstairs. I start up slowly, listening as I go.

Their mother stares at me from photos as I climb. She hanged herself eight years ago, two months after her husband died.

But from what I understand, it wasn't his death that drove her to finally do it. He was simply what kept her alive until then, and when he was gone, she just couldn't stay. Trysta Jaeger.

Macon's been drinking a lot the past few months. Not eating. Rarely ever leaves the house. I don't care if it seems normal to everyone else. It's not.

Why the hell couldn't Trace finish the lawn? Or put the mower away? He's almost twenty-one now. Macon shouldn't have to stay on his ass over everything.

I reach the top of the landing, seeing steam seep through the crack in the bathroom door, and I hear the shower going.

But he doesn't have the lights on. What's he doing in the dark?

I glance one door down, at his closed bedroom door. His parents' old room.

She did it in there. In the room where he now sleeps every night.

I approach the bathroom.

He's okay. He's always been moody. Kind of scary. He's never been happy. Or smiley. Or conversational.

I lean in, trying to hear a change in the fall of water. Something signaling he's washing or shampooing, but there's no change.

I place my hand against the wooden door, debating if I should push it open enough to see, but just then, it swings open, and I pop up straight. Macon walks out, stalking right up to me.

I back up. "Sorry," I say. "Sorry."

He stares down at me, wearing only a towel around his waist, but he's not wet yet. The shower still runs. *Shit.* Does he know I was following him?

"Just making sure you're here." I try to swallow, but my mouth is like sandpaper. "Your food is—"

I point off somewhere as I look up at him, but I lose my train of thought at his hard gaze. He takes a step closer, and fear grips me. I'm alone in the house with him.

And he has someone he kidnapped locked in the storage container behind his house.

I drop my eyes, his glare hammering me into the ground.

But then . . . the pulse between my thighs thumps hard once, and I expel every ounce of breath in my lungs, nearly groaning.

Spinning around, I run, trying not to stumble down the stairs as his eyes burn my back. I get to the bottom, grab the handle, and yank open the front door, dashing out into the yard.

I take a few steps and glance behind me, relieved he's not on my tail with that rope, ready to strangle me and drag my body back inside, because I've seen too much.

And then I draw in a deep breath, and after a few seconds, roll my eyes.

Jesus. *Seriously, Krisjen? Way to overreact.*

Rumors are rumors. I've never seen evidence that he's done half the things people say, much less killed someone. And he may be doing something wrong by holding that man against his will in the backyard, but he's doing it for the right reasons. Most people in the Bay can't afford rehab.

It's none of my business.

I must've looked like an idiot to him, though. The fear is suddenly gone, now replaced with embarrassment. I shouldn't have gone in the house. That was stupid.

He just looked . . .

Incredible.

In the backyard, he looked vulnerable. Like something was squeezing his insides, and he was alone, and everything hurt him. Like things are hard for him, and why did it never occur to me that they were? No one notices his pain.

After a glance back at the house, where all the lights are off, I walk to the bar, not wanting to leave now.

But I pick up the pace, jogging faster, because Iris told me to hurry and is probably wondering where the hell I am.

As soon as I open the door to the bar, some old Avenged Sevenfold song blasts from the speakers, the party already underway. I leave my small hoodie on, the temperature well below the eighty-five I prefer, and jump behind the bar, grabbing a dish towel and shining up the glasses sitting on the rack to dry. One by one, I stack them on the shelves.

"You can leave, actually," I hear behind me. "I'll help."

I look over my shoulder, seeing Aracely tying an apron around her waist. The crowd of people behind her talks loudly, and I spot Trace and Dallas in the mix. Army walks in the door, minus his kid, wearing a fresh black T-shirt. I can tell because the fold lines are still a little bit visible. His arms are tanner. They've had a full day.

"I'll stick around for a bit," I tell her.

"I don't want to share tips."

"You don't have to."

I'm not staying long enough to make a lot of tips anyway.

I face her, folding the towel and setting it down. She looks unamused that I'm not letting this turn into a fight. We should get drunk together.

"Hey," someone calls out down the bar.

I quickly fill a glass with ice, pour a shot of Jack, and grab the soda hose, topping off the drink with Diet Coke. I stick a straw in and slide the glass across the bar to Aracely. "On me," I tell her.

I don't give her a chance to tell me to go fuck myself.

I head down the bar, looking up to see Trace. I start to smile, remembering his pub with the chesterfield chairs, but then I force it back down, remembering the lawn mower he left out in the rain.

"What'll it be?" I snip.

But he seems not to notice my tone. "Vodka soda, two Land-Sharks, and the bride will have a . . ."

He looks behind him to a woman I can only assume is

Mrs. Torres. She wears tight black leather pants, an animal-print bodice, and a white veil. Her long dark hair falls to just under her arms, and her lipstick is bright red. Dragon Girl by NARS. One of my favorite shades.

But the man next to her answers for her. "Captain and Diet," he calls out to Trace.

She looks at him, adoration all over her blushing cheeks. "Thanks, baby."

That must be the groom. He's wearing jeans and a Hawaiian shirt.

I dole out the drinks, and Trace takes them without paying, so I just mark it all down on paper to keep a running tab.

A few others come up for cocktails, and I pour four pitchers, handing everything with some extra glasses to all the guys coming up. No one pays, so I just continue to mark everything.

"To the bride and groom!" Trace holds up his beer.

Everyone joins him, Army with the vodka soda I made, and Dallas with one of the LandSharks.

"And ten more years of having sex in every single fucking location except your own damn house!"

Roars fill the room, so loud I can't hear the music. I laugh.

The groom pulls his bride into his body, and she laughs with everyone else.

"We love you," Trace tells them. "Macon couldn't be here, but he did give me the credit card, so order what you want. It's on us!"

He holds his bottle up higher, howls filling the air, and all of a sudden, the bar is flooded as a Brandi Carlile song starts on the jukebox.

I lean over, scooping ice into five glasses and adding vodka, Tabasco, Worcestershire, and Bloody Mary mix, while Iris stands at the other end filling all the servers' orders. Someone wants calamari, another wants cheese sticks, and I'm really glad the point-of-sale system is the exact same as Mariette's because otherwise I'd be crying right now.

Slowly, the crowd thins, everyone getting their first round, and Trace runs behind the bar, grabbing another beer.

I mark another line to keep track of his drinking. If the inventory doesn't match up, I'm not getting yelled at.

He uncaps the beer and slaps a kiss on my cheek as I pop the tops on four Coronas. "Aren't they already married?" I ask him as he rounds the bar again.

"They redid their vows," he tells me. "Every ten years, they say."

I watch Mr. Torres as he tries to put a maraschino cherry in his wife's mouth, but she's laughing too hard to let him. He circles her neck with his hand, pulling her back into him and planting a kiss on her mouth instead.

He leaves her and approaches the bar, slapping Trace on the back. "Macon didn't have to do that, you know."

"He wanted to," Trace says, gesturing to me and handing me the credit card to keep. I stick it in an empty glass next to the register. "He appreciates you."

"How is he?" Torres asks. "I haven't seen anything other than glimpses of him in weeks."

But Trace just nods, lifting a bottle to his lips. "He's fine. Busy. Would you like another round?"

I notice the quick way Trace changes the subject, but Mr. Torres doesn't seem to. He rears back, shaking his head.

But Trace pushes Torres's drink up to his mouth, ordering him, "Chug it."

Torres downs the rest of his whiskey neat, and I start to make him another one. I hand him the new glass just as a woman slips her arms around Trace.

His gaze darts to me, but I move down the bar, clearing away the empty glasses and bottles.

I don't care.

He's not mine. I'm not his.

But I avoid looking back in their direction, because I do care a little, and I know I shouldn't.

It's got to be a girl thing, right? Lingering territoriality? Possessiveness? Like I don't want to be forgotten?

I let out a breath. I'll get over it.

He takes her to the small dance floor, and they move, her body plastered to his and her arms around his neck. Dark hair longer than the bride's, the smooth skin on her lower back glowing underneath his hands. The green silk top looks amazing against her tawny skin.

"You'll never look as good with any of us as she does," a familiar voice says.

I hold back my groan as I wipe down the bar. "Oh, we don't know that." I glance over at Dallas, who stands there with an empty beer bottle. "I haven't been through everyone in your house yet."

His eyes dance because he knows I never will and I'm just talking out of my ass. I uncap another beer and hand it to him, walking away before he can say more.

The jukebox goes through every song twice, and I spend a good amount of time trying not to have a meltdown when Aracely needs help cleaning up vomit in the bathroom. She kicks a stall door in anger, and it slaps me in the nose, but after the pain subsides and we're sure I'm not going to bleed, she buys me a shot but still doesn't say she's sorry.

The bride and groom start making out on the dance floor, and I watch as Trace's hand slips up his girl's shirt. Dallas eyeballs me every time I look at Trace. I really feel like I'm going to end up in Dallas's trunk someday.

I finish the dishes, clean up the bar, and take out a load of trash, leaning against the counter as the party goes on and the servers start dancing and chatting.

But every once in a while, I turn my head and look out the window. The house was dark for a while, but the garage door is back open and the light is on. He's awake. *Still there.*

I don't know why I worried. I'm reading too much into his behavior. He's drinking a lot. It affects the appetite. And definitely his moods. That's what his problem is.

I shouldn't have tried to stop him from having sex with Turin on Halloween. Everyone else was having sex. Everyone was drinking. He needs to feel close to someone.

So why didn't he come out tonight? Why doesn't he ever go out?

"You worked a full shift," Army says, approaching the bar. "Two full shifts, actually. You should go home."

I face him, standing up straight. "My brother and sister are in bed, and if I go home, I'm legitimately scared my mom will have invited Jerome Watson over to ambush me."

He breathes out a laugh, but he doesn't ask me to clarify.

Did I tell him about Jerome Watson? I know I told someone.

In any case, he doesn't ask me more.

"I loved how you described our house to your brother and sister." His eyes gleam under his dark brow. "It made me feel pride again. Maybe the grass always looked greener everywhere else, or maybe . . . maybe I just needed to remember how to see the beauty in things. The little things." He stares at me. "You make things pretty, Krisjen."

I do?

He rises up. "We're going to the strip club. You should come with us."

"I'm a minor."

"I know." He grins. "I'll make sure you're safe. It's not really my scene, but I think I might like to see you experience it."

There's a gleam of mischief in his eyes, and for a second, I'm not sure I like it. I'm a legal adult, but he's ten years older than me. Macon would never invite me to a strip club. I'm certain he would consider it inappropriate.

I turn my eyes back out the window, seeing his light still on, something inside of me warming. "I think I'll be jealous if I go," I murmur.

"Seeing Trace watch other women dance?" he asks.

I shake my head, looking at him again. "Seeing all of you watch women dance."

His smile softens, silence stretching between us. After a moment, he lowers his voice. "It's my one night out. Dex is staying over at the sitter's. You should come."

Meaning, he has his room to himself tonight. I glance down at his bracelet like I might be able to tell if that's the one I squeezed in my fist on the couch that night.

I thought it was Iron, but . . .

It wasn't the same.

"May I ask . . ." I hesitate, but then just go for it. "Who is Dex's mom?"

His eyes hood, the beautiful green turning gray. "He doesn't have one."

I open my mouth, about to rephrase my question, but he knows what I'm asking. If he wanted to answer, he would. "Sorry."

"Me, too."

I'm sure I could find out from Liv or Trace, but Army's message is clear. He's not talking about her.

He starts to back away. "You should come tonight."

Everyone starts spilling out of the bar, hopping into cars with their open containers of liquor, and I kind of want to go. All the other women are going.

Removing my apron, I take out my tips from the restaurant and stuff them in my back pocket, following everyone out of the bar.

"I'll see you tomorrow," I call out to Iris, not asking if I can leave. The place is almost empty, and it's her shift to close up.

I walk out into the parking lot, tires sloshing through puddles as people leave, and I catch sight of Army, stopping in his truck and waiting to see what I'm doing. Dallas is in the front seat, Trace and the girl in the back.

But I look away and keep walking, seeing him finally pull away out of the corner of my eye. Off to the strip club without me.

I walk toward the light in the garage. Macon shouldn't be alone so much.

# 10

## Krisjen

Taillights disappear in the distance. As the roar of the cars fades, it leaves the Bay deserted and quiet as I step into Macon's garage. My Rover is up on the lift, about six inches off the ground, and two of my tires are missing.

The car shouldn't be taking this long to fix, but I'm not complaining. He's busy, and I'm lucky to have him at all. And for free.

The speaker on the shelf plays Hozier, and I walk around the car. Sections of paint are sanded off, all places where I had either scratches or maybe a dent or two. I don't know. I didn't keep track of every time someone's car door slammed into mine, or *maybe* the few times I drove over bushes or through trees, sneaking around with my friends and causing havoc like an idiot.

The driver's side door no longer has the two-foot-long line of silver paint that I just suddenly noticed one morning after coming out of my house this past summer. Coincidentally, I'd told Milo off (again) the night before. It's probably related.

Macon steps out of the house, stopping at the top of the stairs. He holds a greasy cloth in one hand, a car part in the other. I clear my throat. "Iron replaced the two tires that were damaged," I say, walking around the car. "What's wrong with the other two?"

I'm not going to be nervous. If he tells me to beat it, I will. Let's see what happens.

But he continues down the stairs, saying instead, "They were bald."

I follow him with my eyes, taking stock of the dark circles under his eyes that are always there now. I would've thought he was going to bed after that shower earlier. I spot the bag of food on the table, still unopened.

I squat down, picking up a piece of sandpaper on the cement floor.

But a hiss hits my ears, and I halt in my tracks, gasping. A snake sits coiled on one side of the garage door, gray with black spots. That's a . . .

That's a . . .

*Oh shit.*

I jerk my eyes to Macon, but he's already there. He leans down, and I open my mouth to scream for him to stop, but he yanks the tail, catches the neck, and I watch as he walks into the street, flinging it into the woods on the other side of the road.

I'm breathing hard, my heart jackhammering, but he turns and heads back to his worktable, not looking at me.

That was a . . .

That was a . . .

*What the fuck?* We have wildlife here, but that was a pit viper. A pygmy rattlesnake. We did a project in sixth grade about the wildlife threats in our area. I remember.

I put my hand over my mouth, ready to vomit.

I swirl my eyes around me, checking for any more. That can't happen often, right? We don't actually see them in St. Carmen.

I glance at Macon. He squats down on the other side of the car, and I start to hear sandpaper grinding against the car like what just happened couldn't have gone bad in a second.

Like going to look for a gator on the loose by himself a couple of weeks ago wasn't careless, too.

He keeps toying with death.

It takes a moment, but I move for the side of the car opposite him and start sanding the small mark he probably didn't know was there. He really doesn't need to fix my paint job, but it's too late to say anything. He has to fix it now.

I work the paper over the small scratch, but after a couple of minutes, my arm already burns. I reposition myself, putting some muscle into it. The tips of my fingers tingle with the friction.

I look at him through my passenger-side windows, but when he glances up, I drop my gaze again. He's not kicking me out. I guess that's a good sign.

But the next thing I know, he's standing over me. I look up, seeing a pair of gloves in his hand.

"I'm okay," I assure him.

"Put them on now," he says. "Women should have soft hands."

I cock an eyebrow. "Why? Because we're dainty?"

*Please . . .*

But he spits out, "Because you're mothers."

I look up at him again, and for the first time ever, he blinks. Then he drops his gaze. "Even when you're not."

I don't know what that means, but I stop in my spot. I'm not a mom. I won't be one anytime soon.

I grind my thumb over my fingertips, taking note that they're still soft, even though I wash them a hundred times a day at the restaurant. Paisleigh likes the smell of the lotion that Mariette puts next to the sink.

I take the gloves, then he taps the car, near the roof, showing me another scratch that I didn't know was there.

I take that as an invitation to stay.

He buffs out the scratch on top of my roof that was from the tree branch I grazed once, and I sand the paint over the five little scratches from the Coke bottle Mars threw straight up in the air that accidentally landed on my hood. Macon starts replacing the two wheels, and I scan the car one last time for any remaining blemishes.

"High Enough" by Damn Yankees comes on, and I can't stop smiling all of a sudden. I work a scratch a little more, lost in my thoughts.

"My dad used to listen to this music," I say. "When I was little."

He squats on the other side of the car, refastening the lug nuts.

"He had an eighties Corvette he bought in college," I go on, "and I wasn't allowed to touch the car, but he bought me one of those motorized kid cars, and I would fix mine while he worked on his." I still see everything in my head. Him in the driveway, my car parked behind his. "It was pink—mine, I mean—and I like pink, but there were like fifteen shades of pink on that car. It was hideous." I laugh out loud, even as the tears well. "He'd have a beer, and I'd have a bottle of strawberry soda. Out in the driveway. Music cranked up. A light breeze."

I swallow over the needles in my throat. It was perfect.

I haven't seen him in months.

"He was different then," I say, my voice softening. "I guess he forgot the things he loved."

His hair bands, his Corvette, his dreams . . .

"I guess I'll forget the things I love, too." I go back to sanding. "Life takes you over like that. You lose yourself. Who you were when you were five was the real you. Before everything started to kill you."

My father couldn't have been obsessed with his stock portfolio when he was a kid. He wanted other things.

I see Clay's mom out in the world now. Buying a seaside cottage. Learning to garden. Wearing jeans and eating ice cream on the sidewalk.

Regressing, my mom says. A midlife crisis, she says.

But it's not. Clay's mom isn't having a midlife crisis. She's remembering herself.

I look at Macon through the windows, seeing him just sit there, his body still.

I don't want to sell any of me to Jerome Watson. I don't want to lose time.

I walk over, and Macon sees me coming and starts on the tire again. He's attached the others, now removing the lug nuts from the fourth. The one Aracely stuck her knife in. He cranks the wrench, loosening the first bolt.

"May I try?" I ask. "To learn? In case I break down on the road by myself sometime?"

He opens his mouth, inhaling something that looks like it's going to be a sigh, and rises without sparing me a glance.

I lean down, grabbing the wrench in both fists, and pull, the bolt spinning easily. I twist and twist until it pops off, and then I fasten the tool to another bolt. Gripping it with both hands, I pull again, but this time it doesn't budge. I yank, putting everything I have into it. He must've loosened the last one. I jerk it again and again, grunting, but then I stop and look up. "Oh, you know what? We should make a TikTok."

But he blurts out, "Get up."

I do and watch as he puts one of his suede work boots on the long bar of the wrench and stands up on it, showing me how to use my weight to loosen it.

The bar budges, and he steps off.

"Cool." I beam up at him. "Thank you."

He doesn't smile back. He walks off, and I crouch down again, twisting the wrench until the nut falls off.

I look over my shoulder. "And thanks for the tires."

He opens the bag of food I left hours ago, sniffs it, and winces, dropping it back down on the tool bench.

I don't know why he doesn't just tell her to make him a steak, or some stew, or even an omelet. Something light if he's tired of burgers. All it takes is a text.

Moving in front of the tire, I kneel down and reach behind it, securing it in both hands. Shifting back and forth, I wiggle it off the axle, but Macon is there before it drops onto my feet.

He tries to take it, but I stop him.

"Just take the other side."

He tightens his lips and grabs the other end, walking backward quickly, and I hurry to keep hold.

"Why didn't you go to the club like everyone else?" I ask as we set the tire on top of the other three. "Do you wanna go?"

He's going to kick me out of here any second if I don't shut up.

I dust off my hands, my eyes on his back as he hits the button next to the garage door, closing it, and switches off the overhead light. The work lamp under my hood still glows. I guess we're done for the day.

I walk over to the sink and squeeze soap into my hands. "I'll go with you if you don't want to walk in alone," I tell him.

But he flips on the water, barking, "I told you to wear the gloves."

He eyes the grease all over my hands and grabs some kind of brush, the bristles grayed and worn. He pours soap all over it.

Taking one of my hands, he scrubs, struggling hard to be gentle, judging from his white knuckles and pursed lips.

"Have you ever been to a strip club?" I ask, looking up at him.

The heat from his body warms me.

I smile. "I can't imagine you at one."

"I was in the fucking military, Krisjen."

My heart thuds hard. He knows my name. That's twice now he's said it.

I don't know why it surprises me, but it does. *I was in the fucking military, Krisjen.*

Krisjen.

He knows me.

"What?" I hear him ask.

I look up, seeing him staring at me, and I realize I'm smiling a little.

I shake it off. "Nothing. So you wanna go?"

"No."

I shrug, mumbling, "I kinda wanna go."

"What the hell for?"

"Why don't you want to?"

"Why do you care?"

Why *do* I care? No idea. Why am I even here right now?

"Goddammit." He tosses the brush into the sink. "I told you to use the damn gloves."

I gaze at his face as he pumps a different soap into his hands and rubs it into mine. There's a tiny scar on the back of his jaw. A groove with a few lines—like a shooting star. I never noticed it before.

But I always noticed everything else.

The constant pinch between his brows. The fatigue in his eyes. The tension in his muscles, and the stress and anger rolling off him in waves more and more every time I see him.

He's not easy, but he's a good man. I know he is. Feeding these people. Helping their families. Giving up his life to come home and raise his siblings.

"I think someone should be making you smile, is all."

My voice is so quiet, because my heart is beating so hard it hurts.

"I'll be happy if the people around me ever do what they're told," he growls, rinsing off our hands. "Y'all don't listen because you think I haven't been alive longer and might know some shit."

His scent drifts into my nose, and I fight not to curl my fingers around his. Tingles spread up my arms from my hands where we touch.

"Someone should be taking care of you," I whisper, dropping my eyes. "At night."

He stops and just stands there, and he can push me away if he wants, because that's what he always does to everyone else. Eventually, they just stopped trying. I don't want to be afraid of him.

"You take care of everyone, all day," I say quietly. "Someone should be loving you."

His chest moves up and down, and I lower my eyes to the brown leather belt around his narrow waist. Against his golden skin.

"Touching you . . ." But I can only mouth the words. I don't think he hears.

He should have a woman. One woman, because he's got a body he can't fuck around with. He's made for something special.

Deep down, so are Army, Trace, and Iron, and maybe Dallas, too, for someone brave enough, but Macon . . . I just want to see him exhale.

He doesn't need tail. He needs her, someone who can take him far away just behind a closed door.

"I can't dance." I turn off the water and dry my hands. "Not like the girls at the club, so I can't bring a lap dance to you, but . . . I can bend in half."

He meets my eyes just in time to see me clutch the basin hip-high and hold on as I bend backward, my ponytail grazing the backs of my ankles.

I immediately pop back up and grab the key chain dangling out of his pocket, waving my hands in front of him like a magician. "I can also make your keys disappear."

Haphazardly, I fling them somewhere behind me, like he totally didn't notice I just threw them.

He cocks a brow.

I hold up my finger, also pointing out, "I can whistle 'Ave Maria.' The *entire* song."

And I proceed to blow the first few notes. *Aaaaaaaa-vaaaaaay Maaaaaariiiiiiaaaaa* . . .

A whisper of amusement crosses his eyes, and there's definitely a smile there now. I know his scowls well enough to know that's not one.

His body towers over me, his broad shoulders boxing me in a room I have no ambition to leave.

Flutters go off in my stomach.

"I can . . ." My cheeks grow hot. "Do something else, too."

I can't look at him all of a sudden. I stare at his stomach and whisper, "Something they don't do at Flamingo Flo's."

He doesn't move, and while it almost makes me nauseous to have his full attention, I'm on fire.

"Please don't get mad, okay?" I know he would never laugh at me, but I also know he doesn't like to be pushed.

Crossing my arms over my waist, I grab the hem of my sweatshirt and pull it up over my head, bringing my T-shirt with it. Eyes still lowered, I let the clothes drop from my arm to the floor. I wait just long enough to see if he's going to stop me, and when he doesn't, I stand there in my pale blue lacy bra and start to unfasten my jeans.

"You don't have to touch me," I tell him. "Just please don't look at my face."

But he does. His gaze burns my cheeks.

"Will you turn on the water?" I ask, gently pushing down my jeans for him. "A little warm, if you can?"

I feel his eyes travel down my body, to the lace of my matching underwear, and up to my bra that doesn't hide the hard points of my nipples.

He leans in, and I hold my breath as he turns on the water behind me. I hear it spill into the sink. "Switch over to the hose," I say.

He pauses, but then . . . he flips the lever, and the water changes over, spilling out of the hose and onto the cement floor. A stream pours out of the garage, carried by the slight slant of the foundation, and I bend over, picking up the hose.

Inching my underwear down my thighs, I twist my leg out, open myself up, and let the dribble of water spill over my clit. I watch it wetting me, teasing the tender skin, and in a moment, the pulse starts to throb and heat floods me down low as I grow wet.

What's the worst that'll happen? He'll yell at me? Make me feel stupid?

Pushing my thumb into the mouth of the hose, the water shoots hard, spraying against my nub, and it feels so good, I close my eyes.

I move into it, breathing harder as I rock my body just a little and roll the spray in slow circles over my clit again and again.

I wish he'd touch me. I would let him.

I try not to, but I raise my eyes and meet his, locked on my face. My heart punches my chest. He's not watching the show. He's watching me. I told him not to.

But he's not stopping me.

Water spills down my legs, drenching my clothes. I lean back into the sink, watching the water cascade over my body. "I tried my fingers," I tell him. "And a vibrator, but I like this the best. Sometimes I'm in the shower for a while, lying in the tub with the showerhead, and . . . doing it to myself again and again."

A wave of pleasure courses through my body, and I sigh, my chest caving.

"I'm scared of you," I whisper to him. "I'm scared of what they said about you in whispers all while I was in high school, and even more scared of how I thought about you when I didn't even know you." My mind would drift to an idea of Macon Jaeger, and how even though he had a houseful of family and a whole tribe on his side, I still always thought of him as on his own against the world.

"But mostly . . ." I gasp, "I'm scared when you look at me, which you've only done five times since I first walked into your house." I wet my lips, looking at his and hating how those stories I heard left out so much about how he works so hard that he doesn't sleep. I remember every time our eyes have met. "And I'm scared of why I would have gone to that club with your brothers tonight only if you were going to be there, too."

I wanted to go. I just didn't want to leave without him.

"This isn't the first time you've seen my body, is it?" I ask, but I can't look at him. "Did you watch me by the pool the other night?"

Army, Trace, and Dallas were at Mariette's after Red Right Hand.

"I think about you," I murmur. "Do you ever think about me? Do you even know I exist most of the time?"

I lean in, the top of my head just under his chin.

"Hold it," I tell him, guiding his hand to the hose.

He takes it, and I pull my hair out of the ponytail, watching his chest rise and fall faster as I unhook my bra and drop it to the ground.

I start to take the hose back, but he drops it to the ground, the water feeding a whole river down the garage. He presses his forehead into mine just before he grabs something on the wall, flips a switch, and I hear a machine start.

I suck in a breath, staring up into his eyes and knowing what's about to happen. My heart races as he switches the water back to the faucet, rinses off the end of the vacuum hose, and then presses the end of the long gray tube to my clit.

It sucks, I jolt, and he grabs my hip with his other hand, holding me to it.

"Ah," I whimper, gripping the sink behind me on both sides and letting my head fall back. My flesh gets tugged, and I squirm, but all the time trying to get closer. I buck, my hair falling over my face and the suction making my head spin. *Oh God. Fuck.*

This is so much better than the water.

I wrap my arms around him, one clutching the back of his neck, the other holding his waist as I rest my head on his collarbone and thrust my hips into him, the orgasm building and fucking coming.

I whimper, the heat swirling low in my belly until . . . it's there. I hold my breath, stiffen, and clutch him harder, crying out as it explodes all over me. My stomach flips, my head drops back, and I hang on.

I close my eyes and ride it out, loving the feel of his eyes on my body.

He drops the vacuum tube, and I lean into his chest, clutching his belt in front of me. Everything is light. Dizzy.

And when he hugs me back, everything is warm. Like a blanket. Like a shower. Heaven.

I want to look at him so badly. Tell him to put me in the back seat of my car right here in the garage and drive into me. I open my mouth to speak, but then he starts pulling up my underwear instead.

"That was relaxing," he breathes over my temple. "Thank you."

Our chests match in rhythm as he reaches into his pocket, and I look down to see him slip a twenty into the strap of my panties. My stomach knots.

"You're a good girl," he says.

And then he presses a kiss to my forehead and walks back into the kitchen, closing the door behind him. Leaving me alone with my jeans around my knees and not another look at my face or uttering my name from his lips.

I clench my teeth to stop my chin from shaking.

# 11

## Krisjen

I'm not upset. Days later, I'm still thinking about it, but I'm not upset. Macon hasn't looked at me one time since, or said my name. He hasn't smiled or given any impression that what happened relaxed him at all, in fact. You could hear him yelling at Trace this morning when I got out of my car for work, and Mariette is in a tizzy after he called about something and stressed her out more. She's given me his meals to take every day, which I throw in the garbage that's sitting right outside the front door of the restaurant on the deck as soon as I walk outside.

He hasn't missed the food, because he hasn't called to complain. I don't know what he's been eating.

Okay, I'm a little upset. I humiliated myself. I did it to myself because why? Because I thought I would be the one person he'd finally open up to? Because making Macon Jaeger happy would mean something. Because I'm arrogant and self-important. A rich teenage girl, thirteen years younger than him, who has no idea what real pain is. Or what struggling is.

I thought I was going to be profound or some shit to him, didn't I?

*Jesus Christ.* I chew the corner of my mouth.

*Or maybe he's just a fucking asshole who paid me for my services because I'm meaningless in his life.*

*Twenty bucks* . . . I rub my tired eyes—I'm sleeping worse and worse every night.

"Hey . . ."

Clay walks into the bar and plops down on one of the many empty stools in front of me. She's got beach hair for some reason, which is very unlike Clay. I love it, though.

"Hit me," she says, dropping her Prada onto the seat next to her.

I lift my eyebrows.

"Please?" She pouts. "I'll sleep it off in Liv's bed. I won't drive. Promise."

I inhale a breath and push off the back of the bar, unfolding my arms from my chest. Filling a glass with ice, I grab her favorite vodka, top it with some tonic, and squeeze in a lime. I slide the drink over the bar to my friend who's just as underage as I am.

She moans as she lifts it to her lips, taking three swallows. "I realized today how much I love working with deceased people," she says, setting the drink back down.

I break into a small smile. Clay works in a funeral home while she takes online classes.

"We have a makeup artist, right?" she asks, but it's not really a question. "They do the hair, too. But oh no, the deceased woman's daughter wants to do it herself, so I let her come in. I take her to the room, and she freaks out because her mother is naked."

"She was naked?"

"No, she had a sheet over her, of course!" She scowls at me like she probably did with the poor bereaved. Clay doesn't like to be told how to do anything. "But the daughter wanted her dressed, and I'm trying to explain that I can't put on her funeral clothes until the hair and makeup are done in case she spills powder or drops the lipstick."

It makes sense. But I guess now she'll know to warn the next person who wants to do their own family member's hair and makeup. See? She learned something, even though she's not ready to admit it.

She winces. "I don't think I have the bedside manner for this."

"You do." I lean my elbows down on the bar, coming in closer. "We're just not used to serving others, Clay."

Except when dressed in cute cocktail dresses at thousand-dollar-a-plate charity dinners. That's how we empathize. From afar. With a checkbook.

"You know you're choosing a weird career, right?" I tease, still unable to stomach what she has to see every day. "But there's no one else I'd trust to take care of me if I go before you."

"Oh God." She drops her head back. "Please don't say that. And please don't specifically request me in your will, because I won't be able to deny you your final wish, but I won't be able to handle it, either. Thankfully, Liv said that I can let my boss tend to her body if anything happens." She reaches over and grabs a bar menu. "Which it won't because I'll die."

"You've talked about your deaths?"

"It comes up with what I do." She flips the menu over, reading the other side. "Macon doesn't even want a viewing. Straight to cremation. Sounds like him. No fanfare."

I rise up straight. "He said that?"

"Nah, it's in his will," she tells me. "Liv showed me. He just had it redone this past summer, actually."

I stand there as Clay scans the appetizers, oblivious to my shock. He just had his will redone? Why?

The loss of appetite. The fatigue. The drinking. The mood swings. Is he sick?

Or is he anticipating an early death? Lots of people would love to see him dead. People who want the land and know that while they can't get it away from him, his five siblings won't put up nearly as good a fight. They would never go to the lengths Macon would to keep it.

But then Clay startles me out of my thoughts. "Coconut shrimp!" she shouts, beaming. She meets my eyes, slamming the menu down on the bar. "Psh, please. Two orders."

I sigh. "But then I have to go over to the restaurant and get it."

"Ohhhhh, I know," she mock whines back at me. "You chose a weird career."

I snicker, loving how she throws my words back at me. I turn and punch in the order to the POS system. "I'm just not used to serving others."

"That's not what I hear."

I jerk my eyes back over my shoulder. What did she say?

She smirks, props her knee against the bar and crosses her arms over her chest. "Iron?"

I growl under my breath. "Shit. How did you hear about that?"

"Liv."

"Iron told her?" I blurt out.

"Trace told her."

"Ugh." I finish inputting her order and twist back around, feeling her smug smile on me.

"So, was it him, then?" she presses. "On the couch? It was Iron?"

I fill a glass with ice and make myself a drink. "Could've been. I never asked him, and it was good, but . . . I don't think it was, honestly."

A blush warms my cheeks after admitting that to her. I don't want to feel ashamed, but Clay's only slept with one person. I don't know why it matters that I've slept with more, but it matters to some people, and that matters to me. What's Liv thinking about all this?

"I don't know." I take a drink, leaning down onto the bar again. "I'm getting more confused. Maybe I'm remembering a feeling or a scent that night that wasn't really there to begin with. Maybe I'm remembering it as more than it was."

I was in such a hard mood that night, and maybe it felt better than it otherwise would have.

But it wasn't just about what I was feeling. It was what he was doing.

"Whoever it was," I tell her, lowering my voice, "it was like he was talking to me without saying anything."

It was fucking. But he was intimate.

"Shit." Clay breathes out.

I nod. "Yeah."

*Exactly.*

"Well, then," she says. "You have to find him."

I smile, and she smiles back, and I make another round of drinks.

Marymount Academy dismissed at noon today, but there are students still lingering in the parking lot. A few drift through the halls. Thanksgiving is in two days, and has always been my favorite holiday, a sentiment no one around me ever shared. There's no stress to look a certain way, like on Halloween, or pressure to shop, like on Christmas. It's just staying at home with a houseful of people and some really good food. This year will be a shitshow with my family falling apart, but I'll try to make sure the kids can't tell. We're supposed to go to my grandparents' house, but the invitation wasn't extended to my mother. I'm sure my father will stay away so he doesn't have to face us.

"Krisjen, hey!" someone calls out.

I look up, spotting Cate Laurel, Emaline Truax, and Antoinette Viega, juniors last year when I was a senior. They walk toward me, down the hallway.

Cate comes in for a hug. "What've you been doing? We miss you."

*We never hung out.*

I glance at the girls' locker room behind them, hoping my former coach is still in there.

"Oh, just working." I smile, thankful I put on some lipstick. My clothes look like shit, though. "Waitressing."

Toni's face falls. "Why?"

I chuckle to myself. "What are you all up to?" I ask instead.

They're out of uniform, with fresh makeup on. Definitely not going home.

But Cate cocks her head. "Are you still hooking up with Trace Jaeger?"

I lift my eyebrows.

"Where will they be tonight?" she pries.

I hesitate, feeling the wind blow through the corridor from the open double doors at the entrance. "At home, I guess. There's a storm coming."

She grins, the two others' faces lighting up.

*Oh no.*

I mean, I get it. I invaded the Bay last year, too, but . . .

I let my eyes fall to Emaline's exposed stomach, Cate's short-shorts.

I know the Bay now. It's different.

"Don't cross the tracks," I warn them.

"Can't make any promises." Cate starts to back up, the others following. "We're bored. You understand."

"We'll stay away from Trace," Emaline says. "But the rest are fair game."

"Which one's the single father?" Antoinette asks her friends. "I want him."

She doesn't even know his name.

Laughter fills the hall as they spin around and rush out the door.

Shaking my head, I walk to the locker room door and yank it open.

Let them come if they want. The guys can take care of themselves. I'm not even going over there tonight. I finished my shift.

I step inside the locker room, the smell of basketball leather permeating the air, which is still thick from the showers the students took today. There's no one around, the rows empty except for the odd towel or shoe left lying around.

I kind of miss it here. In high school. There was no pressure to be anyone yet.

But that's about all I miss.

I head down to the coach's office, because even though I wasn't a great lacrosse player, I was reliable. I showed up, gave it my all, and Reva Coomer agreed to write me a recommendation for college if I ever needed one. I emailed last week to take her up on that offer. I'm still not feeling much interest in school, but it might be my only means of escape. It can even be somewhere semi-local so I can still be close to Paisleigh and Mars.

But as I approach the coach's office and look through the window, I see it's empty. Turning the knob, I open the door. It's not locked. She must still be here. I'd texted to tell her I'd pick up the letter by three.

She could've emailed it, but I wanted to say hi. I'd hated her lessons the least.

Crossing the office, I open the door on the opposite side, peering into the corridor that only the coaches use. Across it lie the head coaches' offices for the boys' sports, and their locker room beyond.

Milo sits in Coach Davenport's office, Ana Moreno straddling his lap. She's a junior.

I watch as they lock hands and she moves over his mouth, deep and slow. Gross.

How old is she? Sixteen? I pull out my phone and hold it up, walking to the window and zooming in like I'm filming. Which I'm not because she's a minor.

Milo's dumb, though.

Ana sees me and quickly hops off him, backing up with her fists balled at her side.

Milo looks back at me and says something to her, sending her out the opposite door. I try to hold back my smile as I slip my phone in my pocket.

He rounds the desk and opens the door to the corridor, and I hold my hand behind me, ready to grab the knob to Coomer's office and bolt if I have to.

He stops, leaning into the doorframe and folding his arms over his chest. "What are you up to?"

"Why are you here?" I blurt out.

"I've been helping the football and basketball coaches."

"They're letting you around high school girls?"

He literally finished his senior year from home last spring, and while no formal charges were brought, everyone knew why.

But his smile spreads behind his closed lips. "Mmm." He nods. "And nothing's really changed with them, either." He looks me up and down, because once upon a time I was that naïve, too. "Other than that, there are no Bay kids like last year," he points out.

Liv Jaeger was the only Bay kid who ever went here.

"You know half the parents here have interests in seeing that shithole torn down," Milo tells me. "They're all wondering how the Jaegers are able to keep the developers off their backs."

"Do they know?"

He grins. "They do now."

What does that mean? I haven't told anyone about the cameras at Fox Hill. Did they find some?

And then it hits me. Cate, Emaline, and Antoinette aren't the only ones heading for the Bay tonight.

"It'll be lockdown," I remind him. "The cops will pull those little shits over even before they get across the tracks."

The canals flood in a big storm. Curfew will be in effect.

"Those little shits," he replies, "used to be your classmates. You think you're a Jaeger now?"

If Macon has cameras on our turf, is it possible that Saints have cameras in the Bay? St. Carmen wants trouble there tonight. They're coming over to cause trouble. On purpose.

"The local news should be entertaining tomorrow," Milo says.

"Why are you warning me that there's something going down tonight? You know I'll tell them."

He backs into the office. "The more the merrier." And he shuts the door, heading into the men's locker room.

*Son of a bitch.*

Whipping around, I dig out my phone, forgetting all about Coomer.

Clay picks up, but I'm already speaking before she has a chance to say hi.

"Is Liv in town?"

Clay takes a second, but then replies. "Just got in. Why?"

*Fuck*. I'd rather she wasn't here for this, but it's almost the holiday. Of course she was coming back.

"I need your help tonight," I say. "And I need you both to trust me."

# 12

## Army

God, I don't want to go home.

He's there. He's always fucking there, and he never leaves anymore. It's like being in a room that's on fire. You're constantly aware of it. Never not aware of how much time you have until it reaches you.

I pull off my shirt, using it to wipe off the sweat on my back and forehead before tossing it into the cab of the truck. Clouds block out the sun, while the wind cools my skin.

"I think she'd pay me," Trace pipes up.

I follow his gaze, seeing Elaine Bertrand and her perfect timing as she walks to her pool that we just cleaned, behind hedges we just trimmed, in her white bikini. She casts us a glance that lingers just long enough that there's no mistake what she wants. Daniel Bertrand's young wife wouldn't be a chore.

I tighten the strap, securing the equipment. "I'd get more."

"Is that a bet?"

He stares down at me from where he stands in the bed of the truck, his eyebrows raised.

"Oh, shut the fuck up." I shake my head. "If you do anything like that for money, we're both dead."

Macon will kill me, too.

Dallas throws trash bags filled with clippings into the truck as Trace jumps down, sweat matting his hair to his temples. "But you have already, haven't you?"

I stop, gaping at him. "How many rumors are flying around about Macon and me exactly?"

"No, that one's just about you."

I grumble, "Great."

I grab the cooler off the driveway and slide it onto the floor in the back seat.

Trace follows me. "You know, I wouldn't care," he tells me. "You were my age when you and Macon had a houseful of kids to take care of. And that doesn't even count the people you guys took care of in the Bay. If you did what you had to, then . . ."

I don't look at him, every muscle inside of me tensing. "Then what?"

"Then I'm glad," he says. "I mean, not *glad* glad. I would wish you didn't have to do it, but I'm grateful. I never would've been able to do whatever it took to take care of us."

I didn't do whatever it took. I never had to.

I draw in a breath. "When you're tested, you find out exactly what you're capable of." I drop my voice to a whisper. "And what you're not."

"So, then you did—"

"I didn't fuck for money," I blurt out. "Dipshit."

He smiles, and I roll my eyes. Trace never asks questions. Usually.

I know they all know the rumors about what Macon and I did to pay bills. Some of it's true, some of it's not, but none of it I care to relive. Iron's old enough to remember some things, so he knows better than to ask. Dallas doesn't get personal, and Liv doesn't want to know, because it would hurt her to learn how much we put ourselves through for them. What's done is done.

Who knew Trace would be the brave one?

"Well, I know what I'm capable of," Dallas chimes in, walking up. "I might be able to put up with getting paid to get laid."

I throw him a look. "Macon is looking for a reason to kill you."

But he just scoffs, cupping his hand under the spout of the cooler and filling it with water. Throwing his head back, he splashes the water over his hair, smoothing it back. "He can barely haul his ass off that stool in the garage. You seen him? He looks like shit lately."

He's looked like shit before; they're just too young to remember. I close the tailgate, ignoring Elaine's eyes, which I know are still on us.

Macon wouldn't kill Dallas if he screwed for money that we no longer need. He would just realize it was all for nothing.

Trace looks at me. "Is something going on with him?" he asks.

"No."

"Would you tell us if there were?"

"No."

He hits me over the head, and I laugh and jog backward around the truck as he pursues me.

"But just think!" I point out. "If he killed Dallas, it would be one less mouth to feed. And with Iron gone, it would be an extra bedroom. We could move Krisjen in."

Trace comes at me, but I plant my hand on his head, pushing him away.

"Can't you just fuck her already," Dallas yells at me, "so she can move on to Macon, and then she'll finally leave after she's made the rounds?"

Trace stops, looking over at Dallas. "Leave her alone."

"She's a good kid," I add, heading back to the driver's side. "And I'm not going to have sex with her."

"But you look at her."

I glance at Trace even though it was Dallas who said it. Iron already went after Krisjen. I raised Trace like a father. It's different.

"She's beautiful" is all I say. "I'm a visual person."

Trace laughs, throwing open the door and dropping into the seat next to me. Dallas climbs in the back.

"It's okay," Trace tells me. "I couldn't take my eyes off her there for a while, either. And she's a Saint. Something about them is a little more exciting because we can't have them. Feels forbidden." He looks over at me. "As you remember."

I pause, my hand clutching the key in the ignition. "What the fuck's your problem?"

He knows better than to bring that up.

"She's good," he says, not grinning anymore. "Really fucking good. Sorry to say, the best I've ever had."

Sorry because he doesn't love her and wishes he did.

"When you're not fucking her," he goes on, "you're thinking about fucking her."

"Don't talk about her like that." I turn on the car, hoping that shuts him up.

She works hard; she's reliable, trustworthy, and cute as hell. And she's perceptive. More than I like sometimes.

I have no intentions toward Krisjen. She's a kid. But she's somebody, and she's his friend. He shouldn't be acting like she's something to use to blow off steam.

"I think you need another Saint," he says. Before I can tell him to shut up, he looks back at Dallas. "And maybe you need one, too." He smiles at his brother. "She's a biter."

*Jesus Christ.* "Give me a beer," I bark back at Dallas.

Trace laughs, diving into his phone as Dallas reaches into the cooler, handing a can to me over the seat. I pop the top and take a gulp, setting it in the drink holder in the console and shifting into *Drive.*

But then Trace growls, "Ah, son of a bitch!"

And I hit the brakes.

"Goddammit!" he yells, and I look over to see him pull on his seat belt, which he never does.

"What's wrong?" I ask.

"That little shit!" He scowls. "A constant pain in my ass!"

"Who?"

"Krisjen!" he says, like he wasn't just singing her praises. "We gotta go to her damn house."

"But we're expecting a storm."

He holds up his phone, and I'm not sure what I'm seeing, but I know it's Milo, and I know it's our sister. Liv and Milo. In the same photo. At Krisjen's house.

I floor it, not even checking traffic before we skid onto the road, hooking an immediate left.

I tell Trace to text Macon, letting him know we'll be home later. It's already getting dark, and Dex needs to be picked up at the sitter's and fed dinner.

I don't know what Liv—or Krisjen—is thinking right now.

When we pull up to the house, the gate is wide open, the driveway filled with cars.

Trace sighs. "Fuck . . ."

*Yeah.* Something is wrong. Krisjen has never had a party at her house. In the time I've known her, anyway.

And I can understand if Milo heard about it and showed up, but she was taking a shot of something with him. In the photo posted two hours ago. Two fucking hours. Who knows what's happened since then?

Liv was there, too—with Clay—after what he did last spring? It doesn't make sense.

Krisjen also didn't invite us. She comes to all of our parties.

I pull around the well-manicured trees in the middle of the

driveway and park alongside a black BMW, not caring that I'm blocking them in. We jump out and head to the house, but I veer for the backyard. A couple makes out in the back seat of a convertible, and I do a quick glance around for cops or parents.

Rounding the corner of the house, we slip between two cypresses that make up part of a privacy wall and step onto the back patio.

If you can call it that.

It's damn near half a football field. Beautiful light-colored stone tile with a pool that almost looks like a Tetris pattern. A square, attached to a rectangle, attached to another square. Trees shade three different seating areas, two of them with firepits. A swarm of partygoers dance and loiter, talking and drinking.

I recognize some faces. Some who graduated with Liv who are back from college for the holiday. Some are even older, and some . . . way younger.

Krisjen stands waist-deep in the pool, dressed in a yellow bikini, talking to my sister, who leans back into Clay's arms.

I scan the deck. No Milo.

Trace starts for her, but I shoot out my arm, stopping him. I head over instead, he and Dallas following closely behind.

I approach the edge of the pool, seeing Liv's eyes dart up first, and Krisjen turning to follow her gaze.

I lock on her face. "What are you doing?" I ask.

She parts her lips, but all she can manage is "Hi."

Flyaways from the bun on top of her head dance in front of her blue eyes—which are huge as she looks at me right now. A little scared.

Squatting down, I crook my finger, bidding her to come.

She does, slowly, because she knows she's in trouble.

"I can't believe they came," I hear someone say in the pool, but I keep my eyes fixed on Krisjen.

"Is Callum here, too?" Dallas asks.

But Clay chimes in. "Don't worry about Callum. I don't think he's coming back for Thanksgiving."

Dallas falls silent, and I lower my voice, so only Krisjen can hear. "Did you invite Milo?"

"Not exactly."

"But you let him in?"

She hesitates. "You didn't have to come," she says instead. "I just wanted Trace and Dallas."

I cock an eyebrow. So she posted that photo on purpose. She did want a few Jaegers here. Just not me?

I let my eyes fall down her body. Having Milo here. Dressed how she is. Why?

I'm pissed enough at Liv for being here, but my sister can protect herself. Krisjen can't. Not in a way where she'll win.

She's soft. And I like that about her.

I flex my jaw. "Why are you partying with him?"

"I don't think I should tell you."

Her eyebrows are pinched together in concern, and I reach down, grabbing her under the arms and hefting her out of the pool. She yelps a little, Liv and Clay rushing up to stop me, but I already have Krisjen's feet planted on the deck. I glare down at her. "Then let's go somewhere private where you can make me mad."

I take her hand and pull her behind me, gazes following us as we pass a firepit and then a crowd of people outside the back patio doors.

She follows, holding my hand just as tightly as I hold hers, and a jolt hits my heart.

As soon as we're inside her house, though, I stop. What the fuck?

Neon glows everywhere in the otherwise dark space. On people's stomachs, their bare legs, their backs . . .

Most of the lights are off, and I spot a black light under the chandelier in the kitchen. Taking a step, I continue past the stairs and into the crowded foyer, as naked, sweaty bodies painted in yellow, purple, and pink move with the music. Some people are in bathing suits, others in their underwear.

I stop again, the dim glow of light making the wallpaper look blue as it climbs the stairs. "Your Woman" plays over the speakers, and I'm surprised she can hear me when I ask, "What the hell is this?"

"It's a black light party," she replies. She comes to my side, looking around, a little pleased with herself. "I told everyone to come scantily clad and I'd supply the highlighters."

Some chick is topless as others draw all over her, some guy signing her ass while a girl colors in her nipples. There are vulgar drawings and asinine words on some people, while others have exotic designs and flowers and "Class of . . ." labels.

"Some of it's kind of pretty, huh?" she asks.

I turn to face her and see that she, too, is covered. I hadn't seen it out at the pool.

There's a heart on her cheek, hand-drawn abs on her stomach, and I smile at the Wonder Woman symbol on her chest. Words are written up and down her arms, and I make out a few. *Beautiful. Smells good. Happy. Sweet. Kind. Safe place. I wish I'd kissed you.*

"Some guy I graduated with wrote all this." She looks up and down her right arm. "He was pretty quiet back then, but I guess I was nice to him and he remembered."

I look at her face, taking her chin in my hand and rubbing my thumb over the spill marks at the corner of her mouth. "Did Milo draw that?"

I have to fight not to rub her too hard as I try to wipe it off.

"Why? What does it say?" she asks.

Why didn't she check what he drew?

I lean in, the pink marker slowly coming off, but it's smearing. She looks up at me, I look down at her, and an urge hits me. I don't think. I dive in and lightly suck the corner of her mouth.

She plants her hands on my stomach, her breath hitching, but she doesn't push me away.

I'm gentle, licking her skin, and my mouth just barely touching hers.

*God.* I haven't touched a Saint in a long time.

Rising back up, I hold her eyes as I wipe her mouth clean with my thumb and pluck a fresh highlighter out of the bowl on my right. I draw a thick line down the middle of her forehead, five daisy petals under her left eye, and a string of triangles from her nose to her upper lip, down her chin and neck. I stand back and recap the marker.

"What did you draw?" she asks.

"No idea."

Some kind of war paint, maybe? She looks good.

Taking the marker out of my hand, she pulls a chair in front of me and hops up on it. Uncapping a marker, she rolls it on like lipstick, holds me in her stare, and I almost raise my hands to glide them up the backs of her thighs.

But I don't. I just watch.

Tossing the marker off somewhere, she wraps her arms around my neck, and I catch her as she circles my waist with her legs and hangs on to me.

She kisses my shoulder, leaving a print of her lips as my sole evidence that I was here and only she touched me.

Tightening her arms around me, she leans into my ear. "Milo is locked in a storage room in the pantry," she tells me.

She's not whispering, but no one else can hear over the music.

"All of these people were heading to the Bay tonight. Into the cemetery." Then she pulls back and looks me in the eye, giving me a chance to respond.

The cemetery. Our cemetery.

"Why didn't you tell us?" I ask her.

"Because you would've protected your property," she says into my ear again. "And who knows what would've happened."

"So you lured them here with a party?"

"Just about." She nods, looking kind of proud of herself. "I also promised the Jaegers would be here, and that ensured the females would come and stay out of the Bay, too."

So, she did need us here after all.

"That's why you posted," I say, more to myself. "You knew Trace would see it."

"And he'd come and bring at least Dallas, and the two biggest reactionaries aside from Iron would be here, and not in the Bay, in case Milo and his friends went anyway."

So when she said "You didn't have to come," she wasn't worried about me. She knows I don't come out swinging if Saints invade the Bay.

But she wouldn't want Trace and Dallas here if Milo were here, would she? There would definitely be a fight.

And then it clicks. *The pantry.*

"But you had to get rid of Milo before Trace actually showed up," I think out loud.

She smiles like a parent proud that her kid finally got the point. "Milo doesn't care where it happens. He'll strike wherever will get a Jaeger arrested. So now, Milo is pounding away in the pantry, you're here like I promised everyone, and the Bay is safe. Seriously, it was like rocket science, putting all this together."

I shake with a laugh, pulling her in tighter. "I'm glad someone else thinks like I do. We'd make a good team."

I could use the help babysitting Iron, Dallas, and Trace.

"But . . ." I point out, "if someone is coming to dig up graves, I need to know in the future."

I know exactly what they would've been after in the cemetery.

She fires back, "No, you don't. You know how it'll go bad if you try to stop them. Saints don't always win, but they never pay. You bide your time."

I hold her, never liking it when a Saint thinks it's their place to handle me or my family.

But she can handle me anytime. She cares about us.

"Besides . . ." She starts swaying to the music as I hold her. "Saints? Digging? Six feet of anything? In the rain? Yeah, no."

I laugh.

"They would've just resorted to destroying headstones," she says, but rushes on when I try to interject. "Which I understand are old and sacred, but the bodies would never have been disturbed."

They won't be deterred forever, though. They've been fucking with us since their ship landed.

"Thank you." I inhale her fruity body spray, and stare at her neon purple lips. "You're good at this."

"At what?"

I shake my head, trying to find the words. "At . . . being a friend."

She smiles, a gorgeous light hitting her eyes. "Thank you."

Sweet and sincere, she says it as if it's the best compliment she's ever gotten. She circles her arms around my neck, hugging me tight.

"But I still don't want you to do it again," I say as she holds me. "Milo, I mean. He will hurt you. Every time."

"Okay," she agrees, and I like how quickly she does it. "I won't do it again."

Not sure if I believe her, but I hope she involves me quicker the next time she decides to take matters into her own hands.

I keep holding her, people passing by, the music pumping, and there's no way in hell I'm dancing, but there's no way I'm leaving her here, either. Not with him.

"I'm too old for this party," I say.

I have to be the oldest person here.

She pulls back, her smile softening. "Me, too."

She keeps one arm around me and pulls out her bun with the other.

"But if I tell them to get out," she states, "Trace and Dallas will hear Milo beating the walls of the pantry. And you know what happens then."

Her chestnut-brown hair spills down around her, but I can barely focus with the heat between her legs pressed against my stomach.

"So how long should we wait?" I play along.

"Until the rain starts."

The cops won't let anyone in the Bay who doesn't belong there after that point.

"So what should we do?" I ask.

"I think it looks like we're doing something now."

I tighten my grip on her thighs, Krisjen pressing her body into mine, and déjà vu floods my head, and I'm warm all over. God, she feels good.

"Why doesn't Dallas like me?" she asks.

I narrow my eyes. "Do you want him to?"

"Of course."

The quickness of her reply surprises me almost as much as the answer.

"I mean, I'll live if he doesn't," she's quick to point out, "but I hope I know you forever. It'll make it a lot easier if he stops trying to pick fights. What's his problem?"

"It's not you," I tell her. "He's been like that for a long time."

Albeit worse the past year or so. He's been intolerant, short-tempered, and pissy for years, but I'll admit, he's pretty fucking awful to Krisjen. I'm not sure why.

"Our parents died at the wrong age for Dallas," I tell her. "He was fourteen—too young to be treated like a man, and too old to be protected like a kid. Macon didn't know what to do with him. Neither did I. He just . . . He wanted to be alone a lot, and we let him." I pause. "We shouldn't have."

We had other things to worry about. It was easier to be lazy about it and hope that whatever was eating him sorted itself out.

"I don't think Macon would know what to do differently even if he could go back," I admit.

"And you?" She cocks her head. "How were you doing then? You were only what, twenty?"

I hesitate. I don't like these questions.

But it's nice to be asked. Liv, Dallas, and Trace were too young, and I never wanted Macon to worry about me. He had enough.

"When you're tested," I tell her, "you find out exactly what you're capable of, and what you're not." Those are the same words I said to Trace not even an hour ago, but I didn't explain what I meant, and he didn't ask. I clear my throat. "A few months after it all happened, Macon and I were struggling to keep everything going. People in the Bay needed help, and we could barely feed the kids in our own house. Customers had taken their business elsewhere when my father died, and St. Carmen was breathing down our necks. We were going to lose the land any day." I hold her eyes. "They were hitting us while we were down."

Her eyes search mine, and I can see the concern etched on her brow. She knows this story isn't going anywhere good.

"We were finishing up at this house," I continue, "doing their landscaping shit. It was late. And I remember wondering why they had asked us to come so late in the day. That house was usually early in our rotation on the first of every month."

Someone squeals, but I don't look. I don't even see the party anymore.

"The husband called us inside," I tell her, "made small talk. Macon just wanted to leave." I breathe out a weak laugh, realizing how he hasn't changed. "Then he asked us."

She goes still, waiting for me to say it.

"He wanted us to go up to the bedroom with his wife." I pause. "Both of us. And he wanted to watch."

Her face falls. "You didn't . . ."

"Maybe I should have. It was thousands of dollars," I explain. "But that's the thing, Krisjen. I found out what I wasn't capable of, but maybe I had that luxury, because I had Macon. And he always took care of us. He found money somewhere. And then more. And then more. And I honestly don't know if he was stealing it or killing for it, I was just grateful he never allowed me to be subjected to people like that again."

It wasn't even about the sex. Maybe I could've fucked her. Maybe I could've been paid to do it, and maybe even with her husband watching.

It was the embarrassment of them always thinking we could be bought and sold, and the shame of living just across the tracks. Of having to see them over the years and be constantly reminded that they could do that to us. I was twenty. I almost threw up in the driveway on my way out.

I'll never let Dex find himself in a situation like that.

I look down into her eyes, glaring now at those blue pools and gripping that soft skin that I like more than I'll ever admit, because Saints all feel the same. Like they've never worked a day or broken their backs under the hot sun. "You assume Dallas is the only one who doesn't like rich little bitches who dangle us on a string." I get in her face, my nose nearly brushing hers. "But as sweet as you are, I think you'll be one of them in ten years, won't you?"

She draws in a short, shallow breath, her fingers curling and her nails digging into my skin. She shakes her head, and I shake her.

"You're not different," I state. "You're not. We can pretend for as long as we want, but we know where this story goes."

I squeeze the backs of her thighs, hearing her whimper, and I don't know why I'm taking it out on her.

But it feels good. I'm not twenty anymore, and I want to fuck one of this town's daughters, even though I told Trace I wouldn't touch her. She was bred to be desirable. This is what they're for.

I'm hard in my jeans.

But she speaks, touching my face. "Look at me," she says.

I do.

"I'm only looking at you," she whispers.

The party swirls around us, but we may as well be alone, because nothing else exists. I'm the only one in her eyes, her voice is steady, and she's mine until I put her down.

"You want to pay for me?" I hear the smile in her taunt. "You have more money than I do. You can play with *us* now."

She comes in, brushing her lips over my cheek, and I wrap my arms around her like a steel band.

*Fuck yes.*

I slip us behind the potted tree, press her into the wall as the grandfather clock next to us goes off. I lose track of the chimes as I reach up and run my thumb up and down her throat.

"I would let you pay for me." I rub my mouth up the nape of her neck. "But you wouldn't have to."

I heft her high and bring her back down, rubbing myself hard between her legs. She gasps, holds me tighter, and then she covers my mouth with hers, moaning. I start to rip her bikini top down, but she stops me, holding it in place.

*God, I need to touch her.*

Rolling her hips, she grinds on me, and I take her ass in my hands, situating myself between her legs as I pin her to the wall. I open my mouth, sinking my tongue inside hers. I jolt. *Jesus.* Something electric courses over my lips, down my jaw, and sinks straight into my stomach as I lose myself in her wet heat.

Releasing her mouth, I press my forehead to hers, staring into her eyes as I rub my thumb over one of her nipples poking through her top. The flesh hardens, and I want it in my mouth. Lifting her higher, I nibble it with my teeth, biting and licking over the fabric.

She whimpers and squirms. "Army . . ."

It sounds like a protest, but she's dry-humping me.

We pant and moan, sweat covering my back, my cock straining against my jeans. I kiss her, reeling as she bites my bottom lip.

I reach down, unfastening my belt and opening my jeans.

"No," she finally says. She pulls away from my mouth, looking down to see my bulge between us.

I gently press her into the wall. "No?" I taunt.

I flick my tongue over her bottom lip, but I'm just fucking with her. I'm not mad. Just frustrated.

I dip my hand down, rubbing her pussy through the fabric and feeling her hard little nub.

I groan. God, she's fucking hot.

"You're not going to let me have fun, are you?" I tease.

She shakes her head. "Isn't this fun?"

And she covers my mouth again, molding her chest to mine, and resumes grinding herself on me, the only things separating us are her bottoms and my briefs.

My hands roam everywhere, her ass, her breasts, her face . . .

She's right. This is fun. I would want a bed if we were going to do more anyway.

She pulls away from my mouth, her face pained as she moans, and I swear I feel her wetness through our clothes.

"Slower," I whisper, not daring to look behind me. "Or they're gonna know we're fucking."

We're still dressed, and we're hidden behind the potted tree, but not completely.

I hold her tight, trying to set the pace and slow her down, but I keep needing to go harder. I press into her so hard I feel bone.

"I can't stop," she says, kissing me again and again.

"Slow." I grip her hips, trying to control her. "Move small."

But she doesn't. She rides me, tilting her head back as I go at her neck, kissing and biting.

"I won't go inside, okay?" I pull her bottoms to the side, baring her cunt and soaking up her heat as she pumps her hips again and again.

My orgasm rises, blood pulsing hot through my stomach and between my thighs.

"Oh God," she whimpers in short, stuttered bursts. "It feels . . . so good."

"Hold on to me." I bite her jaw. "Hold hard."

She cries out, and I don't even look to see if anyone is on to us. I slam my hand into the wall, sucking in a breath and trying not to come. But she jerks and gasps, her tits shaking with each thrust as she rides hers out, and I can't hold it back.

"Goddammit," I breathe out. *Fuck.*

I pull myself away, stroking down my length as I spill onto her stomach. She whimpers, looking down between us and watching me come.

Sweat dampens my forehead, and I drop my head down to her shoulder, feeling her hand slip around the back of my neck.

"Sorry," I pant. "I was trying not to."

"I wanted you to," she whispers.

Reaching behind me, I pull my T-shirt out of my back pocket and wipe it off her. She keeps kissing me, and I can't stop smiling.

I haven't felt anything that good in a long time.

I tuck the shirt back into my pocket, holding her as she holds me. The party still rages around us, unfazed.

"Come home with me tonight," I say. "We don't have to do anything else. Just come home with me."

But she shakes her head. "If I come home with you tonight, something is happening."

"Yeah, we can hit breakfast early," I joke, rising up and looking down into her eyes as I let her feet touch the floor again. "And I don't have to come all the way over here to pick you up. I mean, I have standards. At least one date before I sleep with you."

She smiles, but it's brief. Her breathing steadies, and she starts to check her swimsuit, making sure everything is still on.

We're done. She doesn't want more.

"You're not interested," I say.

*In me.*

I was fun, like Trace. Or a pity fuck, like Iron.

But her eyes pop up. "No," she retorts. "I mean, yes. I'm interested. It's not that. I just, um . . ." She swallows and suddenly looks way too young for me again. "I feel like I'm free-falling, Army," she admits. "Trace, then Iron . . . I need to stop for a minute."

I take her face in my hand. "Then grab on to something."

Her eyes soften, and she leans into my touch. I don't know what it is about her, but I don't even need to sleep with her. I just really like seeing her in the morning.

"You want to take me to breakfast before we sleep together . . ." she says, but it sounds like she's saying it to herself. She lowers her voice, and I almost don't hear. "We haven't slept together yet . . ."

I study the far-off look on her face. What is she talking about?

She looks up at me. "It wasn't my parents, was it?"

"What?"

"The man who offered to pay you to have sex with his wife?"

*Oh.* "No."

"It wasn't Clay's?"

"God, no."

She nods once, satisfied.

She fixes her hair and starts to leave. "I'll be at Mariette's early. Come over and eat."

I stop her. "I want you in my bed tonight."

"No."

"Why?"

She turns fully, facing me. "Because I wanted it easy, and Trace wanted it easy, so it was easy. And I knew before I even touched Iron that it would be once, because he was going away, so I was prepared to say goodbye. But you?" She hesitates and then kisses the corner of my mouth. "I think you're easy for people to fall for. I need a minute."

Okay. That's not a terrible thing to hear. It's kind of annoying, though, that she's too young for me but somehow a lot wiser.

She steps away. "I need to get out of this swimsuit."

I cock an eyebrow, and she laughs, realizing how enticing that sounded to me. She leaves, heading up the stairs, and I watch her disappear into her room.

*What the hell am I doing?*

I comb my hand through my hair, staring after her.

Is it because she's just a little bit forbidden and I want to feel it all over again?

Or maybe I just want to be happy, because it'll piss Macon off for me to have something of my own.

Or maybe she's kind.

Maybe she's someone you keep, and she'd never hurt me.

I'd like a date to find out.

I glance out of the window at my side, watching Dallas smoke in the driveway and Trace under the hood of some girl's car, laughing and talking to her.

I shake my head, making my way to the kitchen. He's probably using the "Can I pop your hood?" routine. Within days, she'll be calling him over to check "this weird sound" she heard while driving. It's amazing how often this works out for him.

I walk around teenagers as I step through the kitchen, desperate to put my T-shirt back on, but it has cum all over it.

Moving past the stove, I open the only door I can find and step inside. I reach up for a chain to the light but find nothing. I pat the wall on both sides of the door, finally finding the switch. Flicking it on, I don't see Milo, but I hear pounding and muffled shouting.

"Get me outta here!"

I spot another door straight ahead and close the one behind me.

Picking up the padlock, I yank on it for good measure, but yeah, it's secure. Looking up and around, I quickly find the key sitting on a shelf in front of some jars of pesto sauce. Krisjen wouldn't have been able to keep it on her in a swimsuit.

I pick it up.

Milo Price is ten years younger than me, too. The responsible thing to do with him six months ago would have been to press charges over how he tried to assault my sister. What I wanted to do was kill him.

I could have. A lot more easily than having sex for money. It's a question I often ponder. What would I be like if I weren't worried about going to prison?

Dallas, Trace, Iron . . . they all think I'm boring. I know they do.

I'm not boring. I'm just worried. All the time. Afraid. All the time. About them. About Macon. About Dex. Someone has to be the cautious one. The reliable one.

I slip the key in, twist it, and pull off the lock, stepping back as the door bursts open. Milo rushes out, sweating like a pig and sucking in air like he was in a fucking coffin.

"You son of a bitch," he growls.

But he stops just short of getting in my face.

He shifts on his feet, his dark hair wet with perspiration and his shirt nearly soaked. I'm sure he thinks I helped lock him up.

"You gonna hit a kid?" he challenges me. "Huh?"

Gotta hand it to him. He knows I'd kick his ass, but he still talks like he'd kick mine.

"Clay's here if you'd rather she do it." I plant my hand on his face, brushing the scar down the side of it before I push him away. "She made you prettier."

Turned out, my sister didn't need her brothers to protect her. That Saint of hers was only too happy to take care of business herself. And being as connected as she is, she knew she wouldn't get in trouble for spilling his blood.

But Milo isn't scared. "You know where I'll go." He closes in, a few inches from my face. "*Please* stop me."

I smile at his dare. *Why does he think I let him out of the pantry to begin with?*

"You better hurry." I step out of the way. "The rain is starting."

He remains in place for another few seconds and then walks past me, never turning his back until he's out the pantry door. "Don't be long," he says.

"I'm right behind you."

He leaves, and I follow, weaving through the crowd until I make it to the foyer. The music pumps, the black lights showing off all the artwork over all the naked skin, and I look around for Krisjen.

But I don't find her, thankfully.

I spot her brother instead, the twelve-year-old huddled in conversation with Santos's son, JC. Mars is shirtless, some kind of anime character drawn on his arm.

I charge over, yanking JC's arm. "Hey!" I glare down at the kid. "What are you doing here?"

His eyes go wide, and he straightens, clearly shocked to see me. "What? Um . . ." He struggles to find his words. "Well, they sneak over to our side all the time," he says, as if that's an excuse to come here.

He lowers his hands, trying to hide the beer, but I grab it.

"Give me that."

"It's dark in here," he argues. "No one knows I'm Swamp."

But I turn my scowl on Mars. "And where the hell are you supposed to be?"

He swallows. "My grandma's."

I grab his beer, too. "Y'all get out of here. Goddammit." I wouldn't let them come to any of our parties, either. "Get home!"

They scram, running out of the front door, and I start to tell

Mars to get his ass upstairs, but it's too loud for him to sleep here anyway. Best that he heads back to his grandmother's, where Krisjen probably still thinks he is.

I set the beers down and take off outside, just in time to see a dark silver Audi speed out of the driveway. And if it's Milo, he's not alone. There are two others in the car with him.

I glance over at Dallas. "Let's go!"

He throws his cigarette down and starts for me, Trace rising from underneath the girl's hood.

"Hey, what's going on?" Trace asks.

"Stay," I tell him. "Help Krisjen get these people out of here."

Dallas climbs into the truck, and I open the driver's side door.

But I hear Trace call out, "Don't do anything stupid."

I haul my body into the seat and slam the door. I meet Trace's eyes through Dallas's window. "Me?"

I'm legit asking, and he knows it. He laughs, and I start the engine, racing out of the driveway.

I'll be a grandfather before Trace is ever married. I'm not the immature one.

I speed onto the street and stop, seeing Milo's taillights glow bright red to my left down the lane. He turns, disappearing, and I jerk the wheel, racing after him.

Fat raindrops land like darts on the windshield, and I kick on the wipers, trying to find him in the distance.

There are several cars ahead of me.

"So, what's going on?" Dallas asks.

"Just a little deterrence."

I had to get him out of her house. If I'd stayed the night, I would've let him stew, but since I was leaving, he had to, as well.

Dallas points ahead. "There he is."

I change lanes, going around an SUV, and stop at the light, Milo in the next lane, two cars head.

"They see us," he says.

Milo adjusts his sideview mirror until he meets my eyes.

"They're gonna speed," I warn Dallas.

I can't. Not on this side of the tracks.

"If we're lucky, they'll get into an accident," I say.

He chuckles. "These kinds of games aren't like you."

"Yeah, she's driving me nuts."

I say it before I can stop myself.

I've been thinking about her for a while. I shouldn't have asked her to go to the strip club. It's somewhere you go with a woman you've been with for a while for a fun night out, maybe. Not someone you want to fall in love with you. Someone you want to impress.

The light turns green, and Milo shoots off, speeding like his parents sit on the town council.

I punch the gas pedal, keeping my eyes peeled and accelerating faster and faster.

The rain is like rivers pouring down the windshield, and I speed up the wipers and tighten my fist on the wheel. Milo's headlights blur through the rain.

"Just stay next to me," I tell Dallas, "and don't cause any bullshit."

"He deserves to disappear," he fires back.

Yeah, but I'm not orphaning my son by going to jail for this asshole.

I squint, trying to see through the windshield in the dark and the storm. "Fuck, it's thick," I gripe.

He halts at a stop sign, I'm two cars behind, and I watch him turn left.

I smile as the car between us follows him, and I approach the sign, getting ready to stop.

But Dallas yells, "Go!"

I bolt through the stop sign, but I don't turn left, following

Milo. Instead, I spin the wheel right and hit the gas, firing down the street, the pavement going from smooth to broken in an instant. Water splashes up as I race through puddles, Dallas and I bouncing inside the truck.

There's one road into Sanoa Bay, two converging into that one. Saints usually stick to the freshly paved street that takes them past the tourist-ridden wetlands and the airboat and fishing recreation bullshit, avoiding this nearly abandoned street altogether.

We hit a pothole, Dallas grabbing the handle above his door as he catches air, and I press my back into the seat to stabilize myself.

But I hear a squeal from the seats behind us, and I jerk my eyes to Dallas.

He looks at me, and we both do a double take toward the back seat. Keeping my eyes on the road, I stick my hand back there and feel two bodies.

"What the hell?" I yell.

JC and Mars pop up, JC folding his lips between his teeth, trying not to laugh, while Mars looks more contrite.

"Ah, shit," Dallas grumbles.

"Dammit!" I bark. "You little shits."

"Just keep going!" Dallas shouts. "Hurry!"

Tall trees and heavy brush surround us, and we bounce over the tracks, into Sanoa Bay. Taking a left and then a right, I don't see any taillights ahead of us.

A small fork lies up the road, and I charge as fast as I can, swerving as low-hanging branches hit my windshield.

"Gotta get there before he makes the turn!" Dallas shouts.

"I know that! I can't see."

Ben Calderon's driveway appears, and I jerk the wheel right, speeding up a small incline and slamming on the brakes. A thick row of trees blocks the view of the street from the driveway, and I yank my door open, glancing in the back seat before I jump out.

"I'll deal with you two later," I grit out. "Stay here!"

"Yeah, right," JC replies, but I'm in too much of a hurry to fight with him.

Hopping out of the truck, I move to the tailgate, pulling it down. Sliding one of the many containers toward me, I flip open the lid and find the spikes.

I grab them.

"Hurry!" Dallas yells.

I hand him one side and take the handle of the other, leading the way through the trees and looking both ways. *No cars coming.* I walk to the other side, Dallas remaining where he is as we stretch the chain link of spikes across the road.

"This isn't gonna kill them, is it?" I shout.

Iron had a lot of fun with these things back in the day. As long as they're not going fast, it should be fine, right?

But Dallas yells at me, "He attacked our sister! And likes to beat up on women!"

"Right."

I mean, it can't be that unsafe. They sell them on Amazon.

I drop the chain, making sure it's straight.

"They're coming!" he shouts, running back for the brush.

I follow, both of us situating ourselves out of sight as Mars and JC come up to watch.

I grab them and pull them back.

The Audi gets closer and closer, rain dancing in front of the headlights. *Almost there, almost there.* I hold my breath, the fear that a stupid prank could turn bad making my stomach churn a little.

The car zooms past, and shots pierce the air. *Pop, pop, pop, pop.*

The car swerves and the tires expel their air, the sound of rain and the deflated rubber hitting the street filling my ears.

The car goes off the road and disappears into a shallow ditch, its taillights sticking up in the air.

Dallas smiles. "Never gets old."

JC will keep his mouth shut. I look down at Mars. "Snitches get stitches."

He nods once, totally on board.

I race to the other side of the street, hearing some girl and guy screaming in a way that sounds mad and not injured, while Milo's seat belt hits his window and he shoves his door open.

I back up before he can see us.

"Who's that?" I hear Dallas ask.

I follow his gaze, seeing another car coming.

"Get the chain!" I whisper-yell.

But he stands his ground. "It's probably more of them."

I watch, realization hitting when I recognize the make and model of the car that owns those headlights.

"It's Conroy!" I tell him. "Pull it back!"

He doesn't. Just shrugs.

"Dallas!"

Goddamn him.

I don't have time to stop her. She flies past, her tires popping instantly.

*Ah, shit.* Macon's going to fucking kill us over more tires down the drain.

*Son of a bitch.*

She swerves left and right, finally skidding to a halt ahead, and I run up to her, pulling her out of the car. Trace jumps out the passenger side.

I hold her by her upper arms. "You okay?"

"Are you serious?" she shouts, scowling. "My tires!"

She looks back at the road and the spikes, and I glance toward the ditch, but Milo and his pals are still down there and can't see us.

Yet.

We have to get out of here.

I take her hand, pulling her into the trees and back toward my truck, leaving her dad's Benz in the road.

"Where's my brother?" she demands. "Why'd you take him? Mars!"

"Shh," I insist.

Milo will hear her.

I drag her back up to my truck in Calderon's driveway with Dallas and Trace following.

I point at Mars. "You sleep at his house," I say, gesturing to JC. "Get home! Both of you. Hurry!"

JC grabs Mars by the elbow, leading him away. We're not far from home.

"Let's go," I say, then to Trace and Dallas, "Take the truck. I'll meet you there, and we'll load up some tires to bring back for her car."

They climb in and shove off, racing down the road the short distance back to the house.

I feel pretty fucking stupid for being that petty with that piece of shit, but I forgot how good it felt to do something that's not work, and end the night with something pretty.

I take her in my arms, then notice the white dress she's wearing. Sleeveless and ending at mid-thigh, it has straps across her chest and back, showing slivers of skin. Her hair is soaking wet now, but she feels just as good.

And slowly, I start to spin, holding her eyes the whole time.

"What are you doing?" she asks, stumbling as she tries to keep up.

"It's our first date."

We're dancing.

I twirl her faster, around and around, again and again, and when I dip her fast and low, she finally smiles. Uncontainable and uncontrollable.

I guess she's sleeping over.

# 13

## Krisjen

I need to get home," I tell Army.

He pulls me by the hand, up to his house. "Just let us fix your car before Macon wakes up and sees we just cost him five hundred more in tires."

Which he'll have to pay for, because it's one of his brothers' fault—again—that they're ruined.

Trace and Dallas hop out of the truck, and Army releases my hand, heading over to them. But I grab his hand again. "I can't crash here tonight."

He stops and looks at me, but I don't know what I'm trying to say.

He squeezes my fingers. "Sleep in Liv's room," he tells me. "Your brother is over with Santos's kid. We'll do your tires now, and you can leave in the morning."

He walks off, and I start to protest, but then he barks at Dallas before he reaches the front door. "Where the hell you going?" Army asks him.

"To bed."

"Help us," he orders him as Trace lifts the door to the garage and they start rolling out fresh tires.

But Dallas just laughs under his breath and disappears into the house.

Army clenches his jaw but lets him go, and I tuck my wet hair behind my ear. Rain kicks up mud on the ground, and I pull off my heels, bare feet in a puddle.

"Army, stop," I call out. "I can afford a tow truck and my own tires. I can't stay here."

"I'm not going to try to fuck you!" he shouts.

Trace stops and turns to me wide-eyed, and I just close mine for a moment.

"Not tonight, anyway," Army adds. "Get out of my hair and go to sleep."

Embarrassment washes over me, and I can feel myself sweating. A tickle of a smile curls Trace's lips.

I hold up my middle finger, mouthing, "Fuck you."

He pouts, using his own dialect of sign language while mouthing, "But I love you."

*Asshole.*

I spin around and head inside, throwing my shoes into the living room as I search for a phone. Mine is still in my car, but one of them always seems to leave one behind in the house. I rummage through the living room, checking chargers, and then into the kitchen, but the light over the stove and the one in the hallway bathroom suddenly go out. I look around for any other sign of light.

The electricity has died. I look outside the living room window, seeing that the lights on the street and the ones across the road are dark, as well.

"Krisjen!" Army shouts. "Check the breakers!"

*Nope.* I don't live here.

I find a lighter and flick it to life as I head around the pot of water on the kitchen table that's filling up from the leak in the roof.

I walk upstairs instead, going for Iron's phone, which is probably still in his room. He couldn't take it to prison.

I stalk down the hall, his door dead ahead, but a sound hits my ears, and then I notice something under my feet.

I lower the flame and see water on the floor.

What the hell?

I hold the flame above my head, but I don't see any leakage from above.

And then I hear the sound again. The crying.

*Dex.*

Peeking my head into Army's room, I see Dex standing in his crib and walk over, making sure he's okay. I touch his head full of straight brown hair and feel his pajamas, making sure everything is dry.

I caress his little cheek. "I'll get you something to drink, buddy."

Leaving his door open, I grab towels from the closet in the hallway and lay them over the water.

Then I notice where it's coming from. I walk toward the bathroom, my feet stepping on the stream that flows out from under the door.

I hesitate a moment, knowing something's not right.

I push it open.

Macon sits on the floor, his back against the tub, and the sink is lying on the tile. Water from the broken main gushes out of the pipe, and I can smell the vomit. My stomach coils. What happened?

He has one knee propped up, his arm resting over it, and his head turned away. I drop down in front of him, checking for blood or any sign of a broken bone.

He just sits there, though. Eyes open. Calm breathing.

"Krisjen!" Army calls for me.

I don't move.

A cup from the sink rolls over the water, and I pick it up, holding it under the stream spilling from the pipe. I fill it and then twist the valve, shutting off the water. I set the cup and a clean hand towel on the little table next to the tub.

I breathe hard, taking his face and trying to turn it toward me, but he gently jerks away.

I lean in, smelling him. I don't think he's been drinking.

What the hell happened? Did he do this?

I feel him watching me, and I look up. "What happened?" I ask in a whisper. "Are you hurt?"

He doesn't reply.

"What can I do?"

"Leave."

I shudder inside. I don't want to leave. Did he get sick? Maybe he leaned on the sink too hard? Or fell into it?

Or . . . he got angry and ripped it off the wall.

I hold his eyes while his soften on me. "You look pretty," he whispers.

And I study the drop streaming down his wet face, telling myself it's just water from the broken pipe. I want to touch him. I want to help.

I hold back.

Rising, I walk away and start to close the door. "I'll take care of Dex," I tell him. "I'm right downstairs."

And I twist the lock on the inside of the door, leaving him alone.

I set the glass on the breakfast table the next morning, listening for Macon's footsteps on the floor above me. He's usually up by now.

I cleaned up the water in the hallway, fixed the breaker, and got Dex a snack and a drink, and put him back to sleep before the boys even got done with my car last night.

Then, I slipped into Liv's room before they came upstairs.

Once Trace and Army were in bed, though, I still couldn't sleep. I left the room three times over the course of the night to gently try the bathroom door, still finding it locked every time. I almost woke up Army, because I started to get scared. Something was definitely wrong, and maybe leaving Macon alone wasn't the best idea.

But the fourth time, about three thirty in the morning, the door was finally open and the bathroom empty. The water on the floor had been cleaned up.

I stare at the icy, yellow drink I just placed on the table, but then I grab it again and pour the smoothie into a black mug. I set it at Macon's seat.

I'm still in my dress, I haven't slept, and I probably wasted my time, making him something for breakfast, but it's only 6:00 a.m. and Mars is still asleep. I already called, and he told me to leave him alone.

Sounds like he had fun with his new friend in the Bay, at least. He didn't want to rush home. Not sure why that makes me happy.

Army and Trace drift into the kitchen, Aracely busy cleaning up the mess the boys made when they got back last night.

"What the hell happened to the sink?" Dallas shouts, heading to the moka pot.

No one answers him, and I busy myself, wetting a dish towel before I sit down at the table to clean the mud still on my feet.

A long pair of legs walks past, and I instantly recognize Macon's work boots.

"It's on the goddamn floor," Dallas keeps going. "One of you fucking her on it or something?"

I flit my gaze up, seeing Dallas throw me a look. Macon pours coffee, Trace pours cereal, and Army busies himself making Dex's breakfast.

"Dallas, knock it off," Army tells him.

But I go back to cleaning my legs. "We were on your bed, actually."

"Good, you can wash my sheets."

"You're just a fuckboy, Dallas. I'm not auditioning to be your wife."

Trace pours milk and grabs a spoon; Macon sits.

Dallas scoops some sugar into his mug. "Oh, I wouldn't marry a slut."

"You couldn't keep a Saint anyway," I mumble. "We're hard to impress."

"That hasn't been my experience."

I look at him, smiling as I rest my chin on my hand. "Oh, tell me about it."

*Please. Tell me everything.* I'd love to know who he's had.

Amy, obviously. That doesn't mean he knows us.

"Bitch." But he says it nice and soft, and I almost smile. It's good to be back to normal.

But Army slams a piece of silverware down on the counter. "Shut up!" he yells at Dallas. "Just stop!"

"Or what?" Dallas taunts.

But it's me who answers. "Or I'm going to stay forever."

"You're probably pregnant already."

I scoot into the seat next to Trace, resting my head on his shoulder but still looking at Dallas. "Uncle Dallas. I like the sound of that."

"Would you even know who the father is?"

I lift the coffee to my lips. "Well, it's definitely a Jaeger."

Trace snorts, dropping his head and shaking with laughter.

Food hits my forehead, and I jerk, watching scrambled egg spill from my skin onto the table.

"Ohhhh," Trace murmurs.

I kind of want to cry, but I sort of want to laugh, too.

"Goddammit. Are you gonna do something?" I hear Army ask, but I can't see who he's talking to.

And before I even see him coming, Dallas reaches over and grabs me by the neckline of my dress and hauls me onto the table.

"We're going to look back on this and laugh," I squeal.

"We're not sleeping together."

"Can we shower?" I retort.

Trace's laughter fills the room, and I feel a whole container of sugar dump on my head. I cry out, kicking on top of the table. "You're gonna love me! I swear!"

"Fuck off!" Dallas growls.

But I hear a faint voice pierce the commotion, different from the others. "Krisjen . . ."

I turn away from Dallas's onslaught, trying to open my eyes.

Dishes tumble to the floor.

"Krisjen?"

I blink, everything going still as everyone stops.

Macon sits at the head of the table as Army leans halfway over it, one hand on my arm, the other fisting Dallas's hair.

Macon stares at the table, the look in his eyes settling like a hole in my stomach.

I release my grip on Dallas's chest.

"Make me another one?" Macon asks me. He holds the mug with the smoothie, tipping it back and emptying it down his throat as he rises from the table. "And dinner tonight," he says. "Something different than what's on that fucking menu. Please."

He leaves the table and heads for the garage.

"I can get you something from town," Army calls out to him.

But Macon shakes his head, his voice sounding strained. "Just her."

I can't stop stealing glances out the restaurant window. As if I can see Macon a hundred yards down the dirt road inside of his garage.

I've been distracted all day. I borrowed Trace's truck, took Mars home, and cleaned up the house, while Bateman picked up Paisleigh from my grandparents'. He'd stay with the kids until my mom got home, which I'm grateful for, because I don't want to go home right away when I take Macon his food tonight. I keep checking the clock, dropping plates, forgetting flatware—because something is wrong, and I can't see him right now. The door is open, but not even a glimpse.

What was going on last night? Macon loses his temper, but that was . . .

He crumbled. Collapsed on the bathroom floor, and he stayed in there almost all night.

If it were Trace or Army, I could bully them into spitting it out, but Macon is impossible. He bitches about having to do everything on his own, but I doubt even he believes that he doesn't have to. Men like him don't feel like men unless they do it alone.

I shake my head, piling the dishes into the tub, because the busser never showed and neither did Summer. They're probably together.

Macon's voice drifts through my head again. *Just her*, he said. Two little words that made me feel so important. To someone who's important.

The savory scent of soup fills the kitchen, and I lift the lid on a pot simmering over a burner.

Inhaling deep, I almost shiver at the warmth under my skin. It's in the high seventies today. Definitely cold enough. For the tropics.

My phone buzzes, and I reach into my apron, grabbing it as I replace the lid.

*Bateman.*

"Hey, how is everything?" I answer.

"Baby, I have to leave."

I pause. "Please . . ."

"She's late," he tells me. "I have to go."

"Please don't do this."

"And she hasn't paid me."

Jesus Christ. Is this really happening? Again?

"You have to come," he says, "or I'm calling their father."

Yeah, good luck getting ahold of him.

I rip off my apron. "I'm coming."

I hang up, seeing Mariette pause mid-pour as she fills a pie shell.

"I'll be thirty minutes," I tell her, running out the door. "I'll be back, okay?"

She expels kind of a strangled, stressed sound, because she offered to be understanding, but we're busy right now.

"Half an hour!" I shout, pushing through the door. "I'll hurry."

I jump in my dad's car and race out of the Bay. I shouldn't have taken a job. I should've stayed at home with Mars and Paisleigh. I figured Army was right and I needed something to do with my time while they were in school, but it would be nice for them to see a familiar face when they get home. Someone who's not paid to be there.

I just don't want to fucking be there. It doesn't feel like my home anymore.

I cruise down the driveway, screeching to a halt in front of my door, and kill the engine, jumping out. My mother's car isn't here. No surprises there. She's courting a new boyfriend, on the hunt for husband number two. There's not time for kids, I guess.

Bateman opens the door before I even get there, stress etching lines on his forehead. "I'm really sorry about this, honey," he says. "It's not your fault. I know that."

"Go," I tell him, walking into the house. "It's not your fault, either."

It's Thanksgiving tomorrow. I get it. He's got things to do.

Nor should he work for free.

He grabs his bag, walking out the door. "They've had dinner. No homework over break."

I nod. "Happy Thanksgiving." And I help him close the door.

He's gone, and I pause. That might be the last time the kids ever see him.

Did he say goodbye?

Knowing him, probably not. He assumes he'll be back once she straightens her shit out. He's been with Paisleigh since she was two.

"Krisjen!" Paisleigh exclaims, and I turn to see my sister dragging a plastic dinosaur on a leash. "Can we watch a movie?"

Mars is behind her, strolling from the kitchen to the stairs.

"Pack an overnight bag," I call out, loud enough for them both to hear.

Mars pulls off his headphones. "Huh?"

I take Paisleigh's hand. "Pack a bag."

"Why?"

"We're going for a sleepover with the Jaegers," I sing, looking down at my sister.

She gasps, beaming.

My brother twists up his lips, because he wants to go, but he persists in acting like everything about me is annoying.

"Let's go!" I start running up the stairs with the kids. "Leaving in ten minutes!"

They start tossing everything they could possibly ever need into a bag as I dial Army.

He answers on the first ring. "Hey, what's up?"

"Can you come and get me?"

He pauses only a moment. "Where are you?"

"I'm home. I'll explain later."

"Are you okay?"

"No, I'm waiting," I retort. "Hurry."

I hang up, grab a few things myself, and hear a honk outside in less than ten minutes. They must've been working this side of the tracks.

"Let's go!" I yell to the kids.

Mars and Paisleigh spill down the stairs with their gear, and I swing a duffel over my shoulder and pull out a baseball bat from the foyer closet as they pile outside.

I throw my bag and theirs into the back of the truck and open the back door, pushing them in next to Trace.

"What's the bat for?" Army looks over the front seat to me.

"It's a surprise."

I open the front passenger-side front door and haul myself up, forcing Dallas over.

"Gimme a break," he growls.

"Take Lamplight Glen," I tell Army.

I see him staring at me out of the corner of my eye, but I crank up the radio as a song I like comes on.

Shifting into gear, he hits the gas, and I fist the bat as he speeds out of my driveway, takes a right, and jumps onto Lamplight Glen. My palms sweat, but I turn up the music more, and even Dallas just stares at me like he's not sure I won't kill him if he touches the dial.

"Take another right," I order.

Army cuts a sharp turn, and I hear the tires skid as he charges onto Barony Lane.

"Stop," I tell him.

"Wha—"

"Stop right here!" I yell.

He hits the brakes next to a silver Bentley Continental parked in front of a quaint, Spanish-style brick cottage, a beautiful little piece of heaven made for two.

I hop out.

"What are you doing?" Army shouts.

The music pumps, the night air blows through the palms overhead, and I swing the bat back, bringing it down hard onto the driver's side window. It smashes through, the glass shattering, and I hear a bunch of swearing go off inside the truck.

"Oh, son of a bitch," says one.

"We're going to jail."

"Krisjen!"

I grind my fists into the handle of the bat and throw my arms behind my head one more time before swinging hard, crashing the end through the windshield.

Whipping around, I climb back into the truck, everyone staring at me.

Trace speaks first. "Was that . . . ?"

"Mm-hm," I reply.

"Why did you do that?" Paisleigh asks.

I flip the visor down, forcing my breathing to even out as I check the lipstick I don't actually have on. "A friend locked their keys inside. I was helping them get in."

And I flip the visor back up.

"That was Dad's car," Mars says.

"Looked just like it, didn't it?"

Army snorts, drives off, and I see Dallas shake his head.

Trace starts laughing, and I lean my head out the window, closing my eyes and letting the wind blow through my hair.

"Who wants ice cream?" Trace calls out.

"Me!" Paisleigh cries.

I'm not taking them to my relatives tomorrow. My father can send a cop if he wants to deal with me about his windshield, and my mother can send one, too, if she wants the kids back.

The next morning, I open my eyes, feeling a body next to me. Fog clouds my brain, and I roll over the other way to get room, so I can go back to sleep. It's too damn hot in here.

But as soon as I move away, I land on another body.

"What the hell?" I breathe out.

Blinking my eyes open, I lift up off the bed and look down, seeing Clay half-underneath me.

She bats her eyelashes. "You were so good."

The person on my other side laughs, and I turn my head over my shoulder, seeing Liv, smiling wide.

"Y'all . . ." I climb off Clay, and they both crack up.

I crashed in Liv's room with Paisleigh, but I don't see her. I grab my phone, checking the time. It's only seven. I wipe my eyes. "Shit."

They'd been staying at Clay's house. I didn't expect them here.

Liv kicks me. "Get out of our bed."

I climb over her. "Well, I'm not taking Iron's."

"Why not?" She links her hands behind her head as Clay lays hers on Liv's chest. "Dallas really is the softest guy. He just needs love."

I shake out the wrinkles in my hoodie. "He needs a punch in the stomach."

"God, yes," Clay chuckles.

He still hasn't warmed up to her, either.

I pull on the sweatshirt and sweep my hair up into a ponytail. Paisleigh better be in the house. How the hell did she get out without me hearing? Stealthy little shit.

I head for the door, doing a quick sweep of my notifications. Nothing from my father about his broken window.

Good.

"We cleaned up down there when we got in last night," Clay tells me. "Don't let them destroy it."

"Yet, anyway," Liv adds.

It's everyone's day off. Her brothers are definitely going to have some fun.

But I nod anyway, leaving the room.

As soon as I close the door and turn, I smell turkey. I stop, close my eyes, and inhale. Goose bumps spread up my arms. *Ah, yes.*

I didn't think they'd actually cook. Not that they don't know how. Macon and Army, especially, have taken care of their siblings for nearly a decade, but I don't know . . . No one in this house seems in the mood for anything other than alcohol lately.

I check the bathroom and see that the sink has been replaced, no evidence that anything had been wrong. I pull out a new toothbrush from my toiletry bag and swipe toothpaste across the bristles.

I clean my teeth, rinse, and drop my toothbrush in the cup with the others, even though I probably shouldn't keep my toothbrush in here. Dallas will clean the toilet with it.

I open the window before I leave to let in the sweet fall breeze and practically hop down the stairs, feeling delighted with energy. I don't know why, and I'm not going to ask. We deserve some fun.

I look around for my sister, finally finding her in the pool with Army and Dex. She doggy-paddles, her little head bobbing side to side as she smiles.

I squint. She's wearing her swimsuit.

I pull back, laughing. Told her to pack the necessities, and all she probably heard was "we're going to a house that has a pool." She hates ours because there's no deep end and she likes to cannonball.

I check the turkey, really just to get another whiff, and start to make coffee. I pass by the second kitchen window, spotting Macon in the garage—as usual—but then I see my brother and stop. He's sitting in one of their trucks as Macon leans in the driver's side window, telling him something I can't hear.

My twelve-year-old brother scoots up in the seat, fists the steering wheel in both hands, and I straighten, realizing he's about to drive. "What?"

He shifts, the car lurches, and I hurry over to the screen door, looking down into the garage and watching him pull out.

*No.* I dart my gaze to Macon, but before I can shout for Mars to brake, he turns the truck, slams on the gas, and parks along the fence.

He climbs out, headphones around his neck, and looks up just enough to catch the keys Macon tosses him. Without a word, he climbs in our mom's Rover and slowly backs it into the garage, only stopping once to pull forward again to correct himself.

I realize my mouth is hanging open, and I close it. How long have they all been up?

Macon starts to turn back toward me, and I dive back into the house before he sees me.

No one died, I guess. And Mars is doing something that's not on his phone for a change.

I back away, leaving them to it, only sporadically checking over the next few hours to see that they're both still in there. Mars moved on to touching up my paint, in a mask with a spray gun, with Macon watching him. Once in a while, he grabs his mug, and I see the soup container I left him in the fridge during my shift last night on the table behind him. He refills the mug with soup, and I just barely contain my smile when I see him chew. He's eating. That's good.

I make up some cheesy potatoes, while Clay comes down and sticks her seafood stuffing in the oven. It smells awful.

The boys come in and out, one of them sticking something on the grill outside, and Paisleigh puts on dry clothes, staying in the living room with Dex and dancing to music.

I pull on a pair of tight jean shorts and roll them up just above my knee, and then borrow a cropped white blouse from Liv, buttoning it up to my neck. I brush out my hair, put on a little makeup, but can't stop smiling at how I could never show up to my grandmother's looking like this on a holiday.

I walk downstairs in my bare feet, turning off all the lights before I start lighting any candle I can find. Wind blows through the windows, making the flames flicker, and everything smells like flowers and food. I almost feel like my head is floating. Or like heaven is hanging low today, and I can smell it.

"What's this?" Army asks, looking around at the firelight as he enters the living room.

Dallas and Trace set food on the table.

"Kind of a tradition in my family," I say. "We keep the lights off and light candles all day." I pause, searching their faces. "Do you observe Thanksgiving?"

I saw turkey and assumed, but they're part Seminole. I should've asked.

"Don't worry," Army says over his shoulder as he heads into the kitchen. "We cook. It's a good family day. And we are a little English."

"And German," Trace adds.

Followed by Dallas, "And French."

"Definitely Spanish," Liv chimes in, she and Clay walking past me.

There are piles of food on the table, and I look around as I set down my dish. "You guys eat pizza on Thanksgiving?" I ask, noticing one that's half cheese and half old-world pepperoni.

"Everyone is allowed to make their favorites," Trace tells me. "Like a giant potluck."

"Cheese fries," Liv holds up a plate, plucking one from the pile under melted cheddar.

There are burgers and hot dogs, black beans and rice, tamales, some kind of roast pork that I think Mariette made for them, and I know there are plantains somewhere on the table, because I can smell them. There's also street corn, shrimp, and crab cakes. Army carries the turkey to the table.

I look toward the window, knowing Macon and Mars are still in the garage. Going to the freezer, I pull out some ice cream, grab a few toppings, and put it out for him.

The kids' music channel that Paisleigh and Dex are listening to plays a rendition of "Shout," and I start singing along as everyone sits and loads up their plates.

The kids laugh, Mars enters the kitchen and washes his hands, and I can't hold back the smiles as I make Paisleigh's plate.

"Oh," she coos when I serve her an actual hot dog on Thanksgiving.

Army carves up the turkey, and I pause for a second, just enjoying the moment. It won't last forever, just hopefully for today.

I grind my fingers in my fist, feeling the small cut I didn't notice until this morning. Glass from my dad's windshield must've hit me.

I'm a rabble-rouser, it seems.

No matter how Milo treated me and how I fought back, I've never thought of myself as a fighter. Until now.

Luckily, my dad doesn't seem to be pressing charges. I haven't heard anything yet.

Which means he doesn't know it was me or . . . he knows it was me.

"'Shout, shout, let it all out,'" I sing.

The music goes off, and I see Army with the remote in his hand. I fall quiet. They want to talk at the table, of course.

But then Macon strolls up. "Turn it back on," he orders his brother.

Army looks at him but doesn't argue. The music plays again, Macon sits, and I take the only seat left, slowly lowering myself into a chair at the foot of the table. I feel like I shouldn't be sitting there, but I seem to get stuck with this seat a lot.

I lift my eyes over the food, to the other end, but Macon doesn't look at me.

"To the first family of St. Carmen," Clay calls out, holding up her glass. Everyone follows, and I take the Coke I poured myself. She looks around. "The traitors are at your disposal."

Then our eyes meet, and I laugh. "Yeah, we are . . ."

"Woo-hoo!" Trace cheers.

Glasses clank, everyone tips back their glasses—Dallas and Trace with bourbon already—and we dig in, sampling everyone's contributions to the table.

Paisleigh eats two bites of her hot dog and wastes no time in standing up in her chair, leaning over the table, and grabbing a slice of pizza.

"Paisleigh!" I chide, laughing at the same time.

But Trace holds out his plate, stuffing the insides of a tamale into his mouth with the other. "Yeah, pass me one, kid," he mumbles over his food.

She doles him out a slice.

"Pepperoni for me," Liv tells her, holding out her plate, too.

I shake my head and scoop some black beans and rice onto my plate. It's amazing how quickly etiquette disappears around family. True family.

*But she'll remember this Thanksgiving.*

The air outside sweeps through the house, making flames fight to cling to their wicks, and curtains blow like the trains of dresses. Music plays, Mars goes for a second ear of corn, and I find myself watching everyone more than I'm eating, because nothing lasts, no matter how tightly we hold. This table won't look the same next year.

Just like, I'm sure, it doesn't look the same this year with Iron gone. Maybe next year others will be, too. Liv will spend it with Clay's family, or not come home at all, waiting until Christmas.

Maybe Trace will go for it, leave to work at some small inn somewhere that has a pub where he can learn the trade.

I raise my eyes, seeing Macon through the strands of hair blowing in my face. He dips a spoon in and out of his mug, staring at the melted ice cream dripping from its end, and I suddenly feel like my arms are made of steel, and so are his, and if he reaches around and I reach around, we'll hold the table together.

But he doesn't look up at me.

Liv serves me some of her cheese fries, which I dip in ranch, and Clay periodically checks my plate to see if I'm eating her stuffing, and then gives me a quick scowl when I haven't yet touched it.

Finally, I roll my eyes, scoop up a glob, and shove it into my mouth, grabbing Trace's shot of bourbon and washing the mouthful down with the only thing on the table that tastes worse.

Trace laughs, and I cough, swallowing about three more times to get everything down my throat.

Another bottle eventually comes out, and Trace spikes my drink—and Army's when he goes off to put Dex down for a nap.

We talk a little, even Dallas relaxing as the liquor starts to take effect, but then Clay rises and Liv follows.

"Would rather stay, but . . ." She starts to clear their plates. "Mimi is expecting us for pie."

Her grandmother. The one who doesn't like that Clay is a lesbian, but she's old and alone, and Clay knows she and Liv win at the end of the day. She has everything. No one can hurt them.

Within five minutes, they're gone, Dex is asleep, Paisleigh and Mars have gone down the street to the bounce house at the Torreses', and the tapers on the table flicker in the wind, only a few inches left to burn.

My mother hasn't called.

My phone hasn't rung at all.

Paisleigh hasn't noticed.

"You gonna clean up?" Dallas asks.

It takes a minute to register that he's talking to me. I put my phone back face down, looking up.

But Army shakes his head. "Ignore him, Krisjen."

"We fed her and her brother and sister," Dallas points out. "It's the least she can do."

Army rubs his hand over his eyes and up into his hair, looking suddenly exhausted.

He rises, taking his and Liv's empty plates with him to the sink.

"Everything comes at a price." Dallas eyes me. "Saints know that more than anyone."

I pick up a black bean at the edge of my plate. We forgot dinner rolls. I love bread on Thanksgiving. "Yes, we're always willing to pay for a kindness," I murmur.

But I should've shut up. He's looking for an invitation to continue the conversation.

"Everything you do is for money," he spits. "You fuck the right sons—bosses even—as a way to elevate yourselves, because nothing in life is really about skill, talent, or knowledge. It's about who's willing to do *whoever* it takes to get what you want. The house, the club memberships, the board positions . . ."

My throat is tight. I swallow.

"And then, years later," he goes on, "after you're done having Jerome Watson's children—so paternity isn't contested, of course—you can have discreet affairs, right?

I raise my eyes. I guess that's how it's done in some marriages.

"You'll meet him in hotel rooms," Dallas continues, "or maybe his house in the Bay . . ."

Meaning I'll be fucking one of them. Probably in the motel down the road. While wearing Jerome Watson's huge, shiny rock on my finger.

"And you'll let him rail you against a wall, because you like the smell of his workday on him, his dirty nails digging into your ass, and his tongue on your tits. It makes you feel alive."

Dallas's eyes sparkle. He's dying for me to make a move, so he can make one back. I know that feeling. That incessant temptation to poke the bear, so you don't have to feel guilty about channeling your anger onto someone you're not really mad at. They're just there.

"You know why?" he presses.

It's a rhetorical question, but I know the answer. "Because I wish I could love the man I was married to in our home every day just like that."

The problem is, Dallas is right. I want nothing to do with Jerome Watson.

I'd sell my body, but I know as sure as I'm sitting here that he'd be having an affair within weeks of the marriage, and just like Dallas said, I'd seek one out eventually to find even an hour of happiness—or an hour of mere escape—once a week.

And after it was over, I'd climb back into my clean, white Mercedes convertible with his sweat on my skin and the feel of Bay cock still inside me. I'd go home to wipe away the guilt and shame with pills or drinks before the feelings had have a chance to rise to the surface.

I lower my eyes, a memory playing in my head. "You know, I saw your parents in town once," I say, feeling my collar suddenly chafe my neck. I don't undo the buttons, though. "Just once, though. They didn't cross the tracks much."

Army stands at the sink, looking out the window into the garage, but I know he's listening.

"Your dad was on his bike." I glance at Trace. "And he pulled up to the Harbor Point Fishing Boat, stopping at the curb."

It's an old houseboat, sitting on a circle of land right in the median on Main Street.

I smile, remembering. "She'd been waiting for him. She came in close, bowed her head, and kissed him. He slid his hand up the back of her thigh." I glance at Macon, but he still stirs the ice cream in his mug. "You must've been at least twenty or so at the time, because I was old enough to remember."

He still doesn't look up, his chest barely moving as he breathes.

"That long married, and they were still like that. But then when she pulled back, he slapped her on the ass, and she smiled before climbing on behind him." I laugh to myself. "I asked my mom why he hit her and why she liked it."

Dallas is frozen, unblinking. A whisper of a smile curls Trace's mouth.

I tell them, "My mom said, 'Make no mistake, honey. She's the boss of him.' Years later, I understood." I soften my voice. "Women love being owned by a good man."

I wouldn't do anything Jerome Watson told me. But I would for someone.

"Someone I can't keep my hands off," I say more to myself. "Someone who climbs on top of me and pins my arms above my head before we're both fully awake in the morning. Without a word. Slow and quiet. I'm the first thing he wants."

No one moves. Army barely breathes.

"He's late to work all the time," I go on, "because I make the mistake of walking around in my underwear, and now he's hard and needs his wife on her knees."

We can hear the children playing in the distance outside, as the wind kicks up and blows a napkin on the table.

"I used to want to do certain things with my life when I was younger," I tell them, "but now I don't know what the hell I want, except just to be in love with someone and love our family. To be with people I care about and have great days and a football team living in our house, helping other people make memories and making sure we all smile ten times more than we cry."

I don't give a shit about tomorrow. I never did. I just wanted to be good for people.

When I rise, Trace rises with me. I stop, looking at him, but even he doesn't look like he knows why he did it. I take my plate, and he follows my lead, both of us carrying them to the sink.

But Army is there, stopping Trace short and taking his plate. "You guys go. I'll clean up with her."

Macon sits back in his seat, gaze still down, and Trace looks back at Dallas.

"Now," Army orders.

Trace casts a look at me, like he wants to take me with him.

He leaves my side, and after a moment, I hear Dallas's chair move away from the table.

The oldest is still there, because Army doesn't give him orders.

I veer around Army, setting down my plate, but he grabs my face in both hands. I gasp, forced up on my tiptoes as he presses our foreheads together.

"It's going to be one of us," he tells me. "Not Jerome Watson. You'll be ours, or I'll make sure we all fuck you before we give you back, so nothing compares. So you always regret leaving us."

*I can wonder if it's my son he's playing Daddy to . . .*

I look up into his eyes, feeling his hard body against mine. Army?

He presses me into the fridge, hovering over my mouth as his fingers work my shirt.

*What . . .*

In three seconds he's peeling my blouse off my shoulders, the breeze coming through the windows caressing my breasts. I bring my arms up, covering myself.

"We're going to keep you," he whispers. "Will it be Iron? Trace? Who do you want?"

He kisses me, wrapping his arms around my waist, but it only lasts a second before I hear my name.

"Krisjen . . ."

Army goes still, and so do I. I turn my face, seeing Macon at the table not looking at me.

But he speaks. "Come here."

He sits there. I don't move.

"Come here," he tells me again.

My heart drops into my stomach, and I don't even think. Keeping my arms over my breasts, I go to him, Army's hands falling away.

I walk up to Macon's chair at the head of the table, and he

stands, rising above me. He tips up my chin, looking down at me, and I can already feel his arms around me. So tight. His breath on my temple and the warmth of his chest.

He reaches behind his head, pulling off his shirt, and I know he's going to lift me up. He's going to lift me into his arms and look into my eyes and not look away.

But he doesn't do any of that. He slips the shirt over my head, covering me.

Then he looks at his brother. "You know she's not her, right?" he asks him, a stern look in his eyes. "You do realize that?"

I glance back at Army and then up at Macon again.

*Her?* Who are they talking about?

# 14

## Army

I square my shoulders, every muscle in my body going so tight they burn. "Are you fucking kidding me?"

I bare my teeth, seething as I walk around the island, glaring at Macon.

But he just looks away, saying nothing more. Stepping around Krisjen, he heads for the door to the garage, but I shove all the shit off the corner of the island, sending it crashing to the floor.

"You're not leaving," I growl. "Goddamn you."

He turns his head, looking at all the dishes and food on the tile.

"You're not leaving!" I yell. "Not anymore. I always make sure you never have to deal with me, but you're not running off into your garage this time."

He continues for the door. "Clean it up."

A sob lodges in my throat, and I don't know why my fucking eyes are burning. I'm not sad. I want to kill him. *Goddammit.* I grab the kitchen table in both hands and flip it over, everything toppling to the floor as the table crashes to its side. Krisjen backs up toward the sink, and I barely notice Macon pulling her back as he launches forward, getting in my face again.

But I'm way ahead of him. "You bring *her* into this?" I glare at Macon. "Fuck you! Fuck! I have been the only one by your side, protected you like a goddamn brick wall, so they never know how weak you really are! I've always been your brother! And you treat me like I fucking work for you."

"You do."

I rear my arm back and punch him, my fist exploding as it crashes against his jaw. Pain shoots from my knuckles, down the back of my hand, but I clench my teeth to hide the pain.

His head twists to the side, and he stands there for a couple of seconds before he faces me again. I get in his space, refusing to back down anymore as I meet him eye to eye. "I am just as strong as you are," I say in a low voice, Krisjen not making a sound behind him. "I've been quiet, I've swallowed the shit because you're the oldest and I respected you for having the strength to make all the decisions I never wanted to make and do the dirty shit I didn't want to do when we were kids, but that doesn't make you a man."

"Neither does making babies you can't support."

I search his eyes. Brown, like our mother's. Like the person behind them is two hundred feet under the water. Just like hers looked.

Tears well. "Do you love me at all?" I ask him. "Do you love us? Do you feel anything for Liv or Trace or anyone?"

How could he say that to me? He knows I loved her. He knows that my son will be hurt when he realizes his mother left him. He knows what I'm going to face. That I don't deserve this.

But his only response is "You don't have to live here."

"Macon . . ." I hear Trace say behind me. I didn't hear him come back in. Macon walks around me, into the living room.

But I follow. "No one lives here, Macon," I spit back, his spine tensing. "No one really wants to be here."

"Army, don't," Krisjen says.

I turn to where she's standing in the kitchen. Looking so sad with those blue eyes. Blue just like Dex's. Blue just like *hers*. "You want to go for a ride?" I ask.

I need to get out of here.

But Macon moves, and I look to see him snap his gaze to Krisjen. His jaw is still flexed—still tight—but for a split second I catch it. He lingers on her too long. He's paying attention to her. Why?

I look at her and then back to him. "Oh, Jesus," I say, and then shake my head. "How many times did you tell us to stay away from them? And now you want one. You want her."

"I don't want her," he fires back. "I just don't want to have to feed another one of your kids."

*You son of a bitch.*

Everything feels like it's bubbling over. I don't know what I'll do if Macon tries to leave, or what I'll do if he doesn't.

But then my phone rings, and I reach into my pocket, pulling it out and answering it.

"This is Highland State Prison," a recording says. "Will you accept a collect call from Iron Jaeger?"

"Yes."

I stare at Macon, the room gone silent. I know he hears the other line because he waits.

"Hey, man," Iron says, and I almost cry, realizing how much I miss him.

"How are you?" I ask, my voice cracking.

"Still alive." He chuckles. "Tell Dallas I get it. Having a boyfriend has proved useful."

I laugh. There's no need to go to extremes. We have Bay people in there, watching his back. He's safe.

"How are all of you?" he asks.

I stare at Macon, Dallas and Trace staring at me. "Oh, you know us. It's no party without you."

"Yeah . . ." He's quiet for a minute, and I almost ask about Thanksgiving on the inside, but I don't want to know. He continues. "I wish I was there. I don't want to ever come back here. That's for sure."

"Good." I approach Macon. "We really miss you."

"Miss you guys, too," Iron tells me. "You're telling Dex bedtime stories about me, right?"

"Yeah."

"Does Macon want to talk to me yet?"

I pull the phone away from my ear and hold it out to my older brother.

I look at him, and he looks at me, the phone suspended between us, because this is my role, isn't it? The one who cares. Who signed permission slips and went to conferences and took them to the doctor and the dentist and bought their Halloween costumes and what the fuck did he do? Oh yeah. He paid for it, so that absolves him for never showing up.

He doesn't take the phone, and I pull it back, holding it to my ear and taking a second to clear my throat. "He's indisposed in his bedroom," I tell Iron, "with some, um, redhead, I think. You want me to interrupt him?"

"Are you serious?" I can hear the amusement in Iron's voice. "Don't you dare interrupt him. Jesus."

I smile at the brother in my ear as I glare at the one in front of me. "Yeah. Call tomorrow. We can talk more."

"Okay," he says. "Take care. Tell everyone I love them."

"Will do."

I hang up, tossing my phone onto the couch. I look at Macon. "He says to tell you he loves you."

And I rush him.

I slam into his chest, then he falls into the table against the window. Our mother's handblown glass vase topples, and I grab him as he grasps for me, both of us crashing onto the floor with the vase. I throw him underneath me and get in a punch, digging my fingers into his throat.

"He just needed to hear your voice!" I shout. "What the fuck? What if he dies in there?"

He throws me off him, and I slam into the edge of the coffee table, an ache hitting my ribs.

Macon rises, grabbing the back of my head by the hair before I can climb to my feet. He pins me to the floor, my stomach pressing into the rug as he digs a knee into my back.

"Don't," someone says. "They need to do this."

"No," Krisjen cries.

I can't see what she's trying to do, but she needs to stay back.

Macon grips the back of my neck, squeezing hard.

"Fuck you!" I muster every ounce of strength I have and flip over. We roll, throwing punches, and I'm not even sure what I'm hitting, but I feel his fist in my gut and another in my side.

"Stop!" Krisjen cries. "Please!"

I notice her legs at our side, but she's pulled out of the way before I can tell her to get back.

"Don't," Trace tells her. "You're gonna get hurt."

I'm on top, straddling him, but I'm not up there for more than two seconds before my back is bending backward and I'm flying over his body. He flips me over his head, my boots landing on our mom's figurine table, all of her glass crashing to the floor. Some land with a thud, and some have that sound like ice in a grinder.

A fist squeezes my heart, and I tilt my eyes back to see Macon, on one knee, looking at the table and its contents at my feet. He's not breathing.

I rise, feeling the tears coming and one spilling. It takes a minute, but I look down at the blue shards that used to be a vase, and the yellow ones that used to be a pitcher.

Trace and Dallas stare at the floor, Krisjen staring at me and then Macon.

"I'll go," she tells him.

She moves to the kitchen to get her stuff, but I grab her by the back of the shorts and haul her back into me, her back pressed against my chest. Wrapping my arm around her, I taunt Macon as I press my cheek into hers.

She's not what's causing this.

"Dallas?" I say, but don't take my eyes off our oldest brother. "Trace? Go get drunk somewhere."

Macon takes a step toward me.

Trace holds out his hand. "Give me Krisjen," he tells me.

I shake my head.

Macon turns his head to the youngest. "Take her," he commands Trace.

Trace looks at me, and again, I shake my head.

I hear Krisjen's small voice. "Don't leave," she begs Trace.

But they do. Dallas first, and then Trace, albeit hesitantly.

Maybe he figures she'll stop us from killing each other.

The door slams shut, Krisjen's body shakes against mine, and I hold Macon's gaze as I press my nose into her hair.

Everything about her is sweet.

And I know exactly what he needs.

I whisper, "We could share her."

His eyes narrow. Her breaths grow smaller against my body.

"We could go to the boat . . ." I tell him. "Go out to sea tonight where the world doesn't exist, and we could make love to her. On the dark water. Where she can come as loudly as she wants to."

The pinch between his dark brows gets deeper, and I know I'm right.

I slip my hand under her shirt—his shirt that she wears—caressing her stomach.

"It's been a long time since you felt something warm, hasn't it?" I ask.

But I don't need him to answer. I know everything that happens with him. It's been ages since he's been to bed with anyone.

"She wants you," I tell him, feeling Krisjen's breathing hitch. "She looks at you. Did you know that?"

His gaze falls to her, and I honestly don't think he knew. Has he been on another planet?

She doesn't make my food for me.

"She's so warm," I tell him. "Do this with me."

He meets my eyes, steeling his spine. "She's eighteen, you piece of shit."

"Then take her to the boat yourself." I release her. "Take her away tonight. Just you and her. She won't say no."

His jaw hardens.

"Touch her," I beg him.

Please just fucking touch her. Be a fucking man instead of a machine or a piece of furniture.

"Let's go out," I go on. "Me, you, her. No more fucking pain. At least tonight."

Something has to change. I want my brother back. I don't care if he doesn't want me to have her. I hope he doesn't let me touch her. I hope he fucks her, because he can't get enough. I hope he wants to keep her.

But instead, she turns, faces me, and before I know what's happening, her hand is whipping across my face.

I blink, turning back, but she does it again, and then I hear her finally speak. "No."

Sickness rises up my throat.

She starts to walk away, but I pull her back, opening my mouth to apologize, but Macon shoves me away from her. I crash into the window, hearing it splinter and crack but not break.

"I'm getting out of here," I tell him, "and I'm not leaving her alone with you."

I take her hand, but he grabs me by the neck and slams me into the wall this time. The breath is knocked out of me, and my spine feels like it was knocked into my sternum.

A picture comes down, and I hear Krisjen cry out.

"Krisjen, go!" I yell. "Just get out of here."

I don't wait for her to leave, though. Hooking an arm around Macon's neck, I drag him to the floor, both of us tumbling and rolling into furniture. I accidentally kick the TV, and feel hot blood dripping from my nose.

Macon flips me over, but I slam my fist into his jaw, jarring him long enough to throw him off. He lands next to me, and I scramble, getting on all fours, ready for him to come at me again.

But then I see that we're not alone.

I trail my eyes up four black-clad legs, and recognize the two men in full uniform, silver badges shining, and sidearms locked at their hips.

"Macon, what the hell?" the younger cop asks.

The other one steps up. "Man, we just came over to—"

But Macon blurts out, "Take him!"

What?

I stop breathing as Krisjen turns her worried eyes on me.

"What?" one of them asks, looking stunned.

Macon gets up to his knees, wiping the blood from under his nose. "Take Army. Let him cool off in a cell tonight."

My mouth drops open.

"No!" Krisjen cries.

"Jesus Christ," I grit out.

The older cop, Tom Chavez, asks, "Are you sure?"

"Take him now!" Macon bellows.

Every muscle knots, and I struggle to climb to my feet. They move in, but I grab the TV and throw it onto the floor, growling.

Chavez and Marquis, the younger one, grab me, each of them holding an arm and forcing me toward the door.

Krisjen moves. "Macon, don't," she begs him. "I'll leave. I'll go."

"Good idea." He takes her arm, pushing her toward the cops. "Take her home, too."

They grab her as she yells, "I have to get my brother and sister!"

But Macon has lost his goddamn mind. "Get them out of the Bay!"

"What about Dex?" I scream back.

But I'm out the door, being pushed down the steps even as I dig in my heels.

He'll stop them. He'll call them off in a second. He's never kicked me out of the house before.

"Stop, please," she says to the police. Then she calls back to Macon, "Are you serious?"

But he says nothing.

He doesn't stop them. I lock my molars together. "Son of a bitch . . ." I bite out.

Trace comes running to my side. "What the hell's going on?"

"Take care of Dex!" is all I shout.

Dallas appears. "Army?"

Macon will tell them to stop. He wouldn't do this.

But Chavez shoves my head down. "Get in the car or I'll keep you for longer for fighting me."

Trace runs for the house. "Macon!"

I land on the seat, still gripping the door. I look at Dallas. "Take care of the kids."

"Don't worry," he says.

He pinches his brows together. I've never seen Dallas worried. He looks six years old.

Marquis shoves Krisjen, but she shoots out her hands, stopping and flipping around. "I'm not going anywhere!"

"Now!" he shouts.

"Screw you."

In half a second, she's twisted back around, her wrists are being cuffed, and she's stuffed into the car, locked to the handle above the door.

"What?" She yanks at the cuffs over her head. "No!"

"Feel free to tell your grandpa." He pushes her legs inside. "He'll thank us."

He slams the door, both cops climb in the car, and I run my hand through my hair as I stare at the road ahead.

I won't give Macon the satisfaction of seeing me waiting for him to save me. Fuck him to hell and back.

They drive off, taking us away on absolutely no charge or authority other than my brother, who I never thought would use his power against me.

"What just happened?" Krisjen lets out a sob.

I sniff, smelling the blood in my nostrils. "Oh, didn't you know, Krisjen? Swamp has cops on the payroll, too."

And I kick Chavez's seat as he drives.

He eyes me through the rearview mirror. "You shut up. We're doing you a favor, man. We're not getting you away for his sake but for your own. Let him cool off."

Except he wasn't going to kill me.

'Course, I didn't think he'd have me thrown in jail, either. Seems I don't know my brother as well as I thought.

Chavez was born in St. Carmen, and every time I see him over here, he has a phone in his fist. Full of all the information he's gathered for my brother.

The younger one in the passenger seat, Johnston Marquis, grew up in the Bay. He looks over his shoulder at me. "Your kid will be fine."

Krisjen moves forward, pleading through the plastic partition. "I have to get my brother and sister."

"Just leave 'em, Krisjen," I blurt out. "They'll be fine till morning."

"What do you know?" she fires back. "You've always had backup."

I laugh, sniffling again as I swipe my hand under my nose and pull away blood. "Oh, is that what you call that . . ."

She's the fucking oldest. Like Macon.

They have a burden I'll never know, but they are also a burden they will never understand. Something goes wrong with kids who are forced to parent their siblings. In ten years, she could be blaming Mars and Paisleigh for her shitty life, because . . . well, everything would've been fine if they didn't exist.

Right?

I mean, we're the sole reason Macon is a monster, right?

"You do look at him," I say, my voice soft. "I wasn't making that up."

When she doesn't say anything, I turn my gaze on her. "Was he next?"

She glares ahead, refusing to look at me.

I grab her leg under the knee and pull her toward me. She gasps as I fit my knees between her legs.

She yanks against the cuffs, her fists balled above her. I lean my hand on the door behind her head, hovering over her body. "I don't see Dex's mother when I look at you." I gaze at her, her shirt riding up and her stomach showing. "But when I fuck you, Krisjen, it will be for revenge."

"Army, man . . ." I hear Marquis warn.

But he'll have to pull the car over to stop me.

"She's a Saint," I tell Krisjen. "Dex's mother."

Her eyes falter just slightly.

"She gave me my son, and then acted like we didn't exist, because I tainted her clean white sheets and our son was a dirty secret."

She doesn't say a word.

"She destroyed me, Krisjen," I whisper, choking down the shit rising up my throat. "What am I supposed to tell him when he runs into her someday?"

I know the cops are keeping an eye on us, but I don't think they can hear.

"She didn't want me. No one fucking wants me. Why?" I blink a few times to get rid of the burn behind my eyes. "She didn't see me as a man. As strong. Trace and Dallas and Iron don't fear me, and Macon doesn't see me at all. Liv doesn't respect me."

They love me.

They don't seek me.

"People don't walk on me," I say. "They just step over me as if I'm not here."

Everyone. Not a single fucking person needs me, and I can't put that burden on Dex. I can't make him responsible for filling a hole I can't fill anywhere else.

When she finally speaks, her voice is low but still firm. "So what are you going to do?"

"What do you think I should do?"

"I think you should have it out with her," she says, strands of her hair blowing in front of her mouth as she speaks. "Kidnap her, tie her up, yell. Then let her go. You'll get away with it."

"Are you both having this conversation in a cop car right now?" Marquis gripes.

But I smile. "What should I say to her?" I ask Krisjen.

"What do you want to say?"

"Nothing."

It's funny how quickly that answer came.

"I don't want her to know . . ." I whisper, "that she still means anything to me."

She shifts underneath me, and I don't know if it was intentional or a reflex, but our bodies brush against each other, and I grab her hip. I touch her skin, squeezing, and all too aware of how she's tied up right now.

These fucking rich girls. Why do I like knowing I can't have one?

I hover over her mouth, trailing my hand up her torso to just under her breasts.

She pants, jerking away from my mouth and baring her teeth.

But she's not saying no.

I reach down, pulling the thin, light blue strap of her thong out of the top of her jean shorts. "Women wear this stuff when they want someone to see it. Was it for me?" I taunt. "Or him?"

I lower my mouth, ready to kiss her, but she catches my bottom lip between her teeth, biting me hard. The sting hits me, but my cock jerks, too, as I gasp.

She releases me, and I groan, looking down at the fire in her angry eyes.

"He should've taken you," I whisper.

I grip the bottom of Macon's shirt on her body and slowly push it up just a little.

She exhales hard, a whimper escaping her mouth.

"And I promise you," I growl at her, yanking her hips into me. "My brothers were too gentle with you."

I bend down to her stomach, kissing and biting and feeling her squirm under me.

"Dude . . ." Marquis blurts out. "Stop."

But God, I don't fucking care. I'm taking this moment. It won't happen twice if I let it get away.

I bury my nose in her skin, digging my fingers into her body, and she flails, trying to shove me off, but I look up at her, her tits poking through her shirt as her chest rises and falls in quick breaths.

She glowers.

Holding her eyes, I flick my tongue over her stomach. "I bet . . ." I tease her. "That I can get you to come on my tongue."

"Army!" Chavez yells.

Krisjen's mouth falls open, her breath staggered. But then she works up a scowl and tightens her jaw.

"Tell me no," I whisper.

I think I like her all tied up, unable to push me away. But she can still speak if she wants.

I squeeze her breast, and she jerks, hitting my head with hers. "I don't like you."

"I don't care." I kiss her again and again, her lips not moving or opening. "Your grandfather took my brother. There's only one thing I want from you."

Her eyes flash to mine, and for a moment, I tense.

I don't want to be bad. I don't want to say this shit.

But I don't want to stay the same, either.

If she doesn't want me, she's going to know there won't be a second chance. I'm not the one you run to when you're lonely. Not anymore. I'm not going to always stick around.

I don't need anyone. Stay or don't stay. Be here or don't. I don't give a shit.

I reach back and thread my fingers through her hair, kissing her again and trying to stick my tongue in her mouth. I bite and move over her lips, taking what I want.

"I should send you to Iron for a little visit." I kiss her. "He should have another turn with you."

She doesn't kiss back. But she doesn't pull farther away, either.

"But I think you're just going to want more of me." I catch her bottom lip between my teeth. "Someone older who has more experience."

She pulls away, lifting her chin. "And which one are you again?"

I laugh, taking her neck in my hand and touching everywhere I can reach. I grab her ass in my hand and thrust us together.

She grunts, feeling my cock through my jeans. "Look at me," she says.

I don't. I rip open her shorts. She moans.

"Man, you cannot do that here!" Chavez barks, and I feel the cop car veering to the side of the road. "Stop!"

I see Marquis out of the corner of my eye turning in his seat. "Are you guys . . . actually . . ."

Chavez jerks his head, looking as well. "Are they—"

But I don't pay them any attention. "Rich girl, poor girl," I taunt her, kissing and biting her neck. "Y'all look the same when you're naked."

Maybe if I'm an asshole, people will fear me like they do Macon. Or at least see me like they do Dallas.

I should've tried to be a prick a long time ago.

But she urges, "Look at me."

Pain shoots through my heart, and I hover over her lips as I push her shirt up.

"Look at me," she whispers. "Fucking look at me."

I can't stop myself.

I meet her eyes and halt, entranced.

A lock of hair drapes diagonally over her face, her blue eyes filled with heat and something warm. Something that's her and always is.

"Kiss me," she begs.

I sink into her mouth, and she kisses me back this time. Both of us take it deeper, as we press ourselves against the leather of the seat. I reach down, starting to peel off the strap of her panties.

"Oh, Jesus," one of the cops say.

I hear car doors open. I think they're about to pull me off her, but all I hear is "Just hurry up, goddammit!"

I tear my mouth away just long enough to tell them, "Turn off the dash cam."

There's some shuffling, and then the doors close.

I don't look to see where they went, but I've got a girl chained up in the back seat with me, and I'm not hurrying anything.

I come down on her, sinking my teeth into her breast, sucking it into my mouth and gently grazing her skin with my teeth.

"Ah . . ." she mewls, her body undulating, seeking me.

I kiss and suck, tugging her flesh into my mouth and moving from one breast to another.

I want to please her. I want her to want me.

But as soon as the thoughts occur to me, I push them away. I'm going to take this for now—just right now—and feel this with her. That's it.

Feel it and remember it and be grateful. For something of my own for one night.

I rise up, looking down at the sweat glistening across her stomach as I unfasten my belt.

She watches me open my jeans.

"Look at me," I tell her as I move down her body. "Don't close your eyes."

Her eyes watch me lower myself between her legs, and I slowly peel down her panties, savoring every second it takes until she's bare.

"They're not watching, are they?" she asks.

They. The cops.

I cast my eyes up and around, seeing no one and nothing but the blur of trees behind a curtain of rain over the windows.

"They're not watching." My heart rises into my throat, and I can't wait. I cover her with my mouth, sucking her naked skin and finding her clit, nibbling on it.

"Ah," she moans. "Oh God . . ."

She rolls her hips nice and slow, but so fucking strong like she's already dying for it.

"Don't stop," she whimpers. "More."

I lick her pretty cunt in long strokes over and over again, massaging one of her tits. I suck her between my teeth, go back to stroking her with my tongue, and then stick it inside of her.

She struggles for breath, putting one thigh over my shoulder and locking my head to her sweet, fucking heat.

I put my other hand over her mouth, eating her harder and

going faster. Suck and lick, and then I use my tongue, and my thumb to rub her hard nub. She rolls her hips, searching for my mouth again and again, faster and faster.

"Oh God. Army," she pants.

She starts fucking jerking, and I can tell the little one is about to come.

I stop.

I pull up and lean over her, watching her chest rise in short, shallow breaths, and then she blinks her eyes open. She finds me above her, sweat beading her brow.

"Army?" She looks near tears. "Please."

"I said look at me."

She had her eyes closed.

She stares at me and finally nods, understanding.

I want her to watch me do this.

Bowing down, I take another nibble of her breast, and then I sink back to her cunt, starting slow again.

She likes the sucking part best, so I play with her clit, stopping to tongue it more and more and get her going again.

I flick it over and over, hearing her breath go ragged, and look up to see her mouth open as she breathes and watches me eat her.

I bite her, tugging her between my teeth, and press down with my tongue again, rubbing her in circles.

She sucks in—moaning—two times, and then stills. Then . . . she cries out, rocking her pussy into my mouth, and whimpering before she lets her head fall back in exhaustion.

I let her break eye contact for that. She behaved, and I'm almost happy to leave it with that.

There would be something appealing about running into her on the street one day and seeing her remember how I once made her come but wasn't interested in fucking her. She'd always wonder why.

Leaning down, I take her face in my hand and kiss her on the lips. She kisses me back, her breath so warm.

"I like you," I tell her.

Our eyes meet, and she's quiet for a few seconds. "No one's ever said that to me before." She smiles small and sweet. "I like you, too."

My groin is so hard, it's throbbing.

"We're . . ." she starts saying in the sweetest voice I've ever heard. "We're not done, are we?"

I break into a smile.

Leaning back up, I pull out a condom, tear it open with my teeth, and watch her watch me roll the goddamn thing on.

Gripping her hip, I tell her, "Wider."

Excitement gleams in her eyes, and she opens her legs so I can fit myself between her thighs, and I position myself at her entrance. I work the head in—once, twice—and then thrust, sheathing myself in her slick, warm pussy.

"Army," she groans, letting her head fall back.

I pump, not taking anything slow anymore. Withdrawing, I push deep again and again, frantic to feel it all.

I moan, kissing her and biting her mouth, licking her tits and her neck, lost in her mouth and her arms.

"Krisjen," I gasp, thrusting harder. "Our beautiful girl. Ours."

"Yeah," she says.

My chest sticks to hers, and I kiss her everywhere I can reach, pumping between her thighs.

But it's too tight back here. Fucking car. I need to get deeper.

I rise up, and she looks stricken until I flip her over, and she realizes what I want. Wrapping her fingers around the handle to hold herself so the cuffs don't chafe her wrists, she braces, hanging on as I yank her hips back and sink inside of her again.

"Oh," she whispers, matching me thrust for thrust.

I pull her into me again and again, Krisjen arching her spine and backing up into me.

I reach around, palming her breast and smelling her hair as we grind as fast as we can, because we can't go slow anymore.

"Army," she cries out. "Don't stop."

The night outside the car is pitch black, the only sounds are our skin and her moans. She slams back into me, my cock sinking deep inside of her, and I glide my tongue up her back.

"I'm coming," she cries.

I squeeze her body, trying to hold myself, but as soon as she goes off, her flesh tightening around me, I growl, letting myself explode.

Fire courses through my stomach and thighs, and I release, spilling. "Fuck!" I shout.

Her pussy contracts around me as she rides out her orgasm, and I flex every muscle, burying myself as deep as I can as I finish.

*Jesus.*

I fucking hate condoms, but she's so tight I can't even tell.

She drops, hanging more limply from the cuffs. "God," she whispers.

I smile, knowing she came. I can tell when they do. They're like boa constrictors on the inside when they're coming. I taught myself what to do to make sure they do every time.

Spots fill my vision, the cop car tilting around me, but I clear, seeing the windows all fogged up.

I kiss her back through her shirt, grabbing the handlebar and pulling her up to ease the weight.

I'm about to turn her over and get her back to sitting so I can check her wrists to make sure she's not hurt, but before I can, the car door is whipping open.

"All right, go," Chavez snaps at us. "Jesus, y'all are crazy. What the hell?"

I look up, and there's an arm reaching inside the car and holding out a ring of keys to me. He has one pinched between his fingers.

I take it, uncuffing Krisjen and handing them back.

Krisjen scrambles to dress as I pull up my jeans, condom still on.

"You owe me," the cop says. "Get her into a real bed, and you better not have gotten anything on my seat."

I smile, both of us jumping out of the car as fast as we can.

Once outside, the officers take off, and she and I are left to walk back to the house, but she's just standing there, looking at me.

And as if on cue, we both start laughing.

She buries her head in her hands, and I hook an arm around her neck, kissing her hair.

"It's okay."

She brings her hands away, blushing. I think we can trust those two cops in particular not to tell stories, but even if not, it was worth it. For me anyway.

It was fucking amazing.

We make our way back to the house, and he can kick me out again, but I'm taking my kid this time.

I open the door for her, holding it wide and letting her go in first.

I see the small end table in the living room still lying on its side, and I stop her when we're in the foyer. Pulling her to me, I kiss her forehead, feeling like I've grown new muscles in just the last hour. My body feels like it weighs ten pounds instead of a hundred and eighty.

"Go to bed." I look down into her eyes. "If you want it again, then get into mine."

She flexes her jaw, but the sudden rise in her chest and excitement in her eyes tells me exactly where I'll find her when I go upstairs.

I watch her walk up, smelling the smoke before I see him.

Turning right, I find Macon in the chair in the corner next to the window. I can barely see his eyes in the dark as he pinches a cigarette between his thumb and forefinger, bringing it to his lips.

He's an inch taller than I am and his shoulders a lot wider, his time in the Marines sticking with him after all these years.

But I feel bigger than him now.

"This isn't your house," I say, stepping up to the frame between the living room and foyer. "This was our parents' home. And all that dirty money you used to build our family's presence was money I helped you make."

I'm valuable.

"I work, and I talk to our customers," I continue, "because you can't deal with people, and they sure as shit can't deal with you. All of this is as much mine as it is yours."

I gesture to the house, but I mean Sanoa-fucking-Bay, as well.

I pause for a moment, thinking. "But I also know I would've lost the Bay years ago without you," I tell him. "I can't do what you do. I don't have the stomach."

Tryst Six is a blessing to some and a target to others, but it's always respected, and it wouldn't exist without him.

But I do play a part.

I take another step, not blinking. "I'm going to have another kid. Maybe a few more, and maybe it'll be with Krisjen, or another Saint, or maybe someone else, but I want a family in this house again, and you're going to shut up about it." I grind my teeth. "Because you know Dallas and Trace will follow me if I leave you, because they can't deal with you, either."

He stares at me, and I wait for something from him.

But he says nothing.

I shake my head, turning, and head out of the room.

I stop at the stairs and look at him once more. "You know . . ."

I force down the lump in my throat.

"I hate what we had to do to put food on the table back then." My breathing shakes a little. "But those are honestly my favorite memories because we were together. It was just you and me, barely adults ourselves, and Liv, Iron, Dallas, and Trace could be kids.

They'll never know what we went through and how close we came to getting killed or arrested so many times. And I never wanted them to, because it was *our* secret. Yours and mine." I feel my eyes burn with the tears I won't let fall. "Something you and I had, just between us. We were brothers, and you used to talk to me."

The dark figure in the chair doesn't move, and I'm no longer budging. I'm not leaving my house.

I walk up the stairs, Krisjen coming out of the bathroom and wrapping an arm around my waist from behind as she follows me into my bedroom.

# 15

## Krisjen

Army Jaeger has a dark side.

*Jesus.* I bite back my smile. *He's good at faking docile, isn't he?* Maybe Macon should loosen the leash on him. Or maybe that's why he doesn't.

November wind blows into his room, billowing his curtains, and I feel Army's body molded to my back. But I feel him everywhere else, too. The marks his teeth left. His grip.

I clench my legs, the skin raw deep inside.

He nestles into my neck, and I arch my ass into his groin as I reach back and caress his neck. Both of us moan.

Last night was aggressive. Just like on the couch. It had to be him or Iron. I should just ask, but I'm embarrassed that I don't know, and I'm not sure how I'll feel if I find out.

Macon wouldn't have pushed me away in the garage if he'd already had me, and I don't want it to be Dallas.

But guilt makes me go still as I stare at the curtains blowing.

Last night felt special. By the pool felt special, too.

But I still would've rather loved them. Iron, Army, *and* Trace.

I flip over, nestling into Army's chest and looking up at his sleeping face.

He's the only one who kept hold of me. Even when it was over. Even counting Milo. Who knows what made Dex's mom do what she did—there are two sides to every story—but I know Army loved her. And he loved her right.

Dex's wail lights up the baby monitor, Army having moved him into Liv's room last night for some privacy.

Army jerks, groaning as his head crashes back onto the pillow. I turn down the volume on his nightstand and start to rise. "I'll check on him."

"No." He pulls me back. "I got it."

"I left my phone downstairs anyway." I need it in case my brother or sister calls. "I'll check on him. If he's messy, I'm waking you up, though."

He chuckles into the pillow. "Thank you."

I know he's exhausted, and I'm sure it's as much emotional as physical. What Macon did to him last night might've been the most Army has ever been hurt, not counting his parents' deaths.

I find a pair of his boxers in a drawer and pull them on, and then I grab his gray hoodie off the chair, slipping it over my head. Walking for the door, I tie my hair up into a ponytail, seeing Army roll over onto his stomach and hug one of his pillows.

I close the door behind me and tiptoe next door to Liv's room. Cracking open the door, I see Dex standing up in a Pack 'n Play, looking at me over the top.

I reach down and pick him up. "You're over a year old, man," I whisper, holding him in my arms. "You should be sleeping through the night."

But then, he's also a Jaeger. He was born restless.

He stares up at me, and I feel his diaper, remembering what a full one feels like with Paisleigh. Not that I ever changed one.

He's dry, though. Just wide-eyed and staring at me.

"Don't look at me like that, or I'll be wrapped around your finger, too."

He gurgles some baby noises, and I start to rock him. "'Shout, shout,'" I sing. "'Let it all out.'"

I keep going, gently murmuring the lyrics I know, and humming the tune for the parts I don't. His head falls to my chest as I sway back and forth, probably smelling his dad on the hoodie. I smooth his dark hair at the back of his head, my heart swelling at the feel of his little body against my chest. I smooth his dark strands through my fingers, feeling him grow heavy and surrender to sleep, but I sing the song again, holding him a bit longer.

Laying him face up, I find his pacifier and give it to him. His eyes are still open but only a little. I cover him with the blanket and rub his chest.

Leaving the room as quietly as I can, I head down the stairs, still feeling his hair, as soft as water, between my fingers.

*Mothers. Even when you're not*, Macon had said.

I shake my head and enter the living room, looking for my backpack. My phone is probably dead.

Grabbing it from the pocket, I veer into the kitchen and pour myself a glass of water.

I gaze out the window at the pitch-black night, finding yellow eyes peering back from somewhere beyond the pool, as the palm trees, dark blue in the moonlight, dance in the breeze. Snoring hits my ears, and I look up at the ceiling, legit hearing Trace all the way down here.

Whispers of a wind whirl about the house, shaking shutters, like we're in a vortex around which storms always brew, and I close my eyes—I love it here at night the best. Everything talks. Even the floorboards.

A draft sends a lock of my hair floating in front of my face, and I feel him. Behind me.

"In the Marines . . ." he says, his breath on my ear.

But it's not Army.

"We'd call you a barracks rat," Macon tells me. "A girl who just moves from room to room to room."

My chest caves, and I open my eyes to see him reach around me and set a bottle of Jim Beam on the counter. He grips the neck with his hand as he hovers at my back.

Drawing in a breath, I lift my gaze back out the window and take another drink of water. "In my world," I tell him, "men call women names, too. I can't say that I'm shocked that there's little difference between you and Milo Price. Or you and Callum Ames. Or you and my father."

I don't want to piss him off, because then he'll make everyone miserable, but I'm not family. I don't have to love him no matter what.

I turn around, taking inventory of the shadows beneath his eyes, getting darker every day, but I pause, noticing the sallow color to his cheeks. There was anger in his voice, but his expression falters, like he's just trying hard to be angry. Like it's the last emotion he can muster, and I'm the only one who's left.

I blink, glancing at the bottle and then back to him. "That shit isn't doing you a bit of good."

He sneers. "Every single brother of mine you've fucked drinks."

"They drink for fun. You don't."

"See, that's where you're wrong." He backs off me and drops into a chair at the table, still fisting the bottle. "Right now, I'm hungry for food," he tells me. "I want to eat, and that feels really good."

I listen. He's talking, and I want him to talk.

"Little things please me," he says, his voice gravelly. "The scent coming in through the windows. The cooler temperature tonight. The slight humidity weighing on my skin." He swallows, and I watch the lump move down his throat. "The sound of the wind outside, and how it always felt like this house grew out of the land just like the trees."

I grip the edge of the sink behind me.

"I don't want to be anywhere else right now." He almost smiles. "In this chair on this floor that's still stained with coffee grounds caked in the cracks from when Liv broke the pot when she was four while wrestling with Army."

He drops his eyes, his long jean-clad legs spread in front of him as he leans back in his seat.

"Next to the stove my father cooked at," he whispers, "and always made sure I watched and learned, because he knew I'd need to know someday."

He goes on. "I'm not worried about the Bay and how a year from now Trace will be a fucking greenskeeper at the country club they'll build on the land his ancestors settled. Army will be living in a trailer. We'll never see Dallas again, and Iron will be perpetually in and out of prison for the rest of his life, because no matter what I did"—he pauses, and I hear the strain in his voice—"I failed at making any kind of a difference."

My eyes sting.

None of that will happen. It can't.

"I love them a little more tonight, and dislike you a little less." He raises the bottle, takes a swig, and sets it back on the table, letting his eyes fall down my body. "And maybe I can almost see what they like about you."

The heat of his gaze warms my skin.

"And where will you be?" I ask him.

He meets my eyes again.

"You said Army will be in a trailer," I remind him. "Iron in prison. Dallas will leave . . . Where are you during all of this?"

He goes still, like a statue. Then he picks up the bottle again. "Oh, I don't think I'll stick around here much longer, either."

My stomach knots. If he leaves, everything will end.

He rises, heading out of the kitchen, and I stand there as his footfalls hit the stairs. There's a moment of silence, and then his bedroom door finally closes.

I lock my jaw, closing my eyes. *What the hell did that mean?*

What does he mean?

I walk, drifting up the stairs, and stop, taking a look at the pictures on the wall. Family photos, not one of them professionally done or in a studio.

In the swamp. On boats. At the beach. In the living room. First cars. Birthday parties.

Not one of them taken in the past eight years, though. None of them with Liv or Trace as teenagers. Dallas had long hair at about ten years old, it looks like.

Macon and Army are in so many, because they were completely raised by their parents, who took pictures.

Army with his beautiful green eyes.

Macon with his mother's brown ones.

Their mother. I find her in one of the pictures. Long dark hair just like Liv, and a smile that doesn't reach her eyes. Eyes that are still beautiful, despite the dark circles.

*Just like Macon's.*

I scan the photographs, noticing fewer with her in them as the kids grew up, but in each one, she's losing more and more weight.

A tear spills down my cheek, and I walk to Army's room, but I don't go in. Instead, I cross the hall to Macon's.

Leaning back into the wall next to his door, I slide to the floor and listen for him in the room where she died.

# 16

## Dallas

The first thing I ever was in life was a poet. Since I was a kid. Before the drinking. The sex. Before I dabbled in coke, started grinding my teeth more than I smiled, and constantly began looking for the next fight.

And the next one.

And the next one.

Without ever writing a word, I was a poet. I saw beauty in the unlikely places that scared my parents. In abandoned train tracks. The foster home hells where my friends lived. In house fires, motorcycle crashes, and the destruction in the wake of a storm. In living too hard and dying too young.

In tears. In bruises. In abandonment.

I didn't hate these things, because these things are profound.

Horrible.

Tragic.

But profound.

And profound is beautiful, because it changes us.

The things I hated were the things that were lazy. Things that lacked pride. Things like . . . Keurigs. And punch cards and restaurants that considered potato chips an acceptable side dish.

My parents never got it. Why I wanted to peer over the edge of my grandpa's grave to watch the dirt piling on top of his casket. Why I stole the car when I was twelve to drive out and meet the hurricane as it hit the coast. Why I liked smeared lipstick, skinned knees, messy morning hair, and the sting of my mouth being raw from a night of being used. It was all so beautiful.

There's even beauty in knowing that my mother wished she never would've had me. Knowing a part of her thought she should've stopped after Iron. There's beauty in knowing she was the beginning of Trace, Liv, and me, and we, in return, were her end.

The world is full of beautiful things, but almost no one sees it.

No one except Krisjen Conroy.

She's one of the most beautiful things I've ever encountered. Beauty in motion. In everything she does.

She's slow, considerate in her movements. Artful.

I love the flyaways of her ponytails and buns. Her sneakers with no socks. How kind her eyes are, and how she looks at you like you alone are precisely the person she was just waiting to see. I love how she skips the last couple of steps to a counter or the fridge, how she dances in the kitchen when she thinks she's alone, and the way she takes more than one bite to eat a grape. She's always appreciating the view, and I imagine she'd be as happy at a gas station as she would be a castle.

She's in love with being alive.

And that's also why I despise her. She can be what I can only see. She's the breath others breathe. I'll never be beautiful like that.

I jostle the girl in my bed. "Hey," I bark, pulling on my jeans and ripping off the towel around my waist.

She stirs, the other one on Iron's bed to my left moaning in her sleep.

"Get up," I tell them.

I fasten the belt around my waist and grab the towel, rubbing it over my head to dry my hair.

"Tizz." I shake her again.

That's not her real name, but that's all anyone has ever called her since we were kids.

"What?" she mumbles, turning over.

"Get out of my bed." I toss the towel down. "Both of you, get out."

It's fucking eleven o'clock.

The brunette on Iron's bed rises, her eyes still half-closed as she holds the pillow to her naked body and searches around for her clothes. Tizz throws off my covers and swipes her shit off my floor. "Asshole."

*Yeah, yeah. Until next time when you're drunk and horny.*

She dresses and whips open my door so the handle crashes into the wall. Both of them stumble out into the hallway, hair in their eyes and each other's hickeys on their necks, looking beautiful but not exactly profound yet. That will come in about a half an hour as they cry in their showers and own up to their responsibility and self-loathing over what no one but themselves made them do with me in my room last night.

I'll be drunk again before my own self-loathing hits. Fuck, I hate sex.

Opening my drawer, I see it's empty, and dig into one of Iron's, finding a clean black sleeveless T-shirt with the sides cut out. Slipping it on, I leave the room, but as soon as I step foot into the hallway, I hear the commotion downstairs and catch Krisjen rushing past me with a picnic basket. It takes a second, but I recognize it as ours. I wasn't aware we still had it. She must've found it in the attic.

"What's going on?"

She turns her head, her face lighting up, but she doesn't stop. "Can you help?"

"With what?"

I watch her scurry down the stairs, but then Trace coasts past me, holding an old Yeti cooler I didn't realize we still owned, either. "Forty-First Annual Bug Jam!" he answers for her.

"What?"

"You know what he's talking about," Krisjen calls back. "I need you all. It'll be fun. Come on!"

I follow them down, the heat in my chest expanding, but the rising anger warms my stomach, too. I don't even want to stop myself. "I don't give a shit about St. Carmen's reindeer games," I growl, rounding the wrought iron banister.

Army stuffs a backpack with Dex's shit, tossing in some sunscreen and diapers. His son sits on the couch, digging his hand in a cup and then stuffing little crackers into his mouth.

"Why is she in our house?" I snap.

No one answers me. Trace sifts through keys, deciding which truck to take. His baseball cap sits backward on his head, his greasy hair slicked back underneath.

Krisjen folds a picnic blanket.

Army turns, arching an eyebrow at me. "Just give us a break, will you? For once? It sounds fun. A nice break from the same shit we do every day."

"Like Krisjen Conroy?" I throw back, turning my eyes on the girl who thinks she lives here. "You fuckin' me next, honey?"

"If you want," she chirps, unfazed. "I'd be excited to see if I have to fake my orgasm. Or if you can tell."

Trace loses it, a chuckle erupting from deep in his stomach. He doesn't dare look at me.

"There are children here," Army tells us, but I head over to the kitchen and squat down, opening a low cabinet. I can't be sober for this.

But when I look, the cabinet is empty. All the bottles are gone.

I pop up, looking over the counter at them. "Where's the liquor?"

"I dumped it," Krisjen replies.

I whip my arm, slamming the cabinets closed and zoning in on Army. "Her or me?" I grit out through my teeth as I walk back into the living room. "I'm not living in this bullshit anymore." I turn to her. "Who the hell do you think you are?"

Running around here, sticking her nose in our business like some self-proclaimed matriarch.

"Just stay home," Army tells me. "Cool off."

But Krisjen chimes in. "He's going with us."

"Fuck you, slut!" I shout. *Where does she get off?*

Army grabs the front of my shirt and shoves me, but I twist and slam his arms away, pushing him in the chest.

Hooking the back of my neck, he whips me around, but I grip the back of his just in time, taking him with me as we smash into the entryway table. Stuff crashes to the floor, Dex erupts in wails, and I hear Krisjen.

"Stop. Please stop!"

I plant my hand on my older brother's face and shove him away, watching him fall into the front door.

I suck blood off my tongue and spit on the floor, all three of them staring at me.

A lump moves down Krisjen's throat. The corner of my mouth tilts up in a grin.

She dashes past me. "I have to get something from upstairs. Dallas, help."

And I do as I'm told, following her.

"Dallas!" Army yells.

But I hear Trace mumble something to him. I don't hear what he says.

They don't get it. Just like our parents. No one gets it.

The pain I cause because pain distracts me, but love does so much more damage, and they don't see that. I would respect Krisjen only if she were aware of it. If she knew what she was going to do to us when she leaves, I would smile. I would be satisfied if she knew that it would end but that she just couldn't stop herself.

But she doesn't, so that makes her simple.

Krisjen veers to the left, into my sister's room, and I follow her in, slamming the door shut behind me.

"This is my family," I grit out. "And we have been through more shit than you would ever be able to handle. They listen to every split tail who comes through here, because having a woman around reminds them of our mother, even though not a single one of us understood that fucking woman."

Krisjen picks up her black hoodie, pulling it on.

"In a few months, you'll realize you were made for better," I go on, "and we were good for a ride. You'll leave, and we'll still be here, trying to hold our shit together. Please just fuck off. You know this isn't home."

She walks to the window and stares out as she sweeps her hair up into a ponytail. A brown lock falls down her temple, nearly touching her eyebrow as she lowers her chin to study something outside. Her bottom lip twitches just barely.

In a way only I would notice.

I love staring at her, but I hate her all the same. I want to be her some days, and make her cry most others. I want her to hit me.

And sometimes I want her to feel me in the dark.

I'm not beautiful in anything I do, but I will change her.

I open my mouth, but she speaks first. "Do you remember your mom well?" she asks, still looking out the window.

I close my mouth.

A car hood drops closed outside, and I hear the heavy creak of a door that only a car from the seventies can make.

"Do you remember what she was like when she was sad?" she presses. "How she behaved?"

I narrow my eyes. How is any of that her business?

"Was she self-isolating?" she goes on.

I walk slowly toward her.

"Loss of appetite?" she asks.

I approach, standing next to her as she watches Macon outside.

The old Dodge he's working on is parked half in the street, the driver's door open as he tries to turn over the ignition.

"Insomnia?" Krisjen asks. "Mood swings?"

I freeze, staring at my brother. Krisjen cocks her head, gazing at him. My hands ice over.

"Macon shouldn't drink anymore," she tells me. "You want to drink, you go to the bar."

Macon steps out of the car, but then he stops and just stands there. Staring at the ground. His chest rising and falling like every breath weighs too much.

I clench my teeth.

We watch as he twists his head, cracking his neck, and gets back to work.

*He's fine.* Why is she saying all of this?

Krisjen turns, looking me in the eyes. "He needs help around here, he needs healthier food, and he *must* get some sleep," she states. "And he needs to wake up with more to think about than just problems. Everyone needs things to look forward to. Even just a day of fun."

*Self-isolating*, she said.

He's . . . he's always had moods. That's nothing new.

Did he eat much at Thanksgiving? Anything? I don't watch people eat. What do I care? I . . .

Macon can take care of himself. He always has.

"At some point we're going to address that chip on your shoulder," she tells me, "but right now, if you're not in that car in ten minutes, you're a piece of shit."

Whatever I was going to say to her is lost, and she leaves, closing Liv's door behind her. Walking to the window, I peer out again, watching him move around the car. He doesn't look up. Ever. Not at the car that passes on the road. Not at the kids playing across the street. Not at Trace carrying shit out the front door and loading up the truck.

I shake my head. She's overreacting. She's just trying to make up shit. Insert herself by creating a problem that doesn't exist. Macon is fine. He should get laid a lot more, maybe even get a girlfriend, sure. Maybe he should have kids by now, I don't know. He's ten years older than me. I guess I assumed I'd have my own place by that age. Why doesn't he have anyone?

Why doesn't he fucking leave us? I would've. Why is he still taking care of us? *Why—*

I punch the wall, the fire in my gut blazing, and I don't know where it's coming from. I back away from the window, running my hand through my hair.

Why didn't he just leave?! Why didn't he just fucking leave and live his life? He didn't need to stay. I wouldn't have stayed!

My eyes burn.

He isn't yelling at me anymore.

He doesn't yell at me at all. He doesn't eat with us. He's in the garage all the time. Alone. All the time.

This isn't my fault. I didn't ask anything of him. He didn't have to stay.

He's okay. He's always okay.

I go to the window again, watching him head back into the garage, dressed in jeans and a gray T-shirt. Just like my first memory of him.

Needles prick my throat. Macon is my first memory ever. Not my mother or my dad.

Macon.

*Something crashes, and I jump, looking away from the TV. Trace screams behind me, because the noise scared him. He's little. Just learned to walk.*

*"You keep fucking knocking her up!" Macon yells as our dad holds him by the collar against the wall. "You just leave her alone!"*

*"Stop it!" Dad pleads with him. "Stop!"*

*He shakes Macon, but my brother is almost as tall as our dad. Dad isn't hurting him, but they're fighting a lot, and Macon messed up the table. It's upside down in the kitchen.*

*He shakes his head as Dad tries to hold him. "There are too many of us," Macon tells him. He cries.*

*Army picks up Trace. He tries to hold him in one arm and take my hand, but I pull away.*

*"I hate it here," Macon shouts. "I hate her like this! Why can't you leave her alone?"*

*Dad stands there, his black hair gone white at his temples. I stare at the tears in the plaid shirt tied around his waist.*

*Macon loves Mom more than he loves Dad. He's always mad at him.*

*The ceiling creaks, Mom in her room. She's there a lot. Alone. A lot.*

*"She can't have another kid," Macon chokes out.*

*He and Dad look at each other, but my dad doesn't say anything. He leaves out the back, the screen door flapping shut behind him.*

*Looking back at Macon, I see the wet spots on his T-shirt, and he wipes his face dry. He doesn't look at us, just runs out the front door.*

*"Dallas, come on," I hear Army say.*

*Instead of following him, I go to the window in the dining room and climb out to the wing of the house that used to be here. Big columns still stick out of the ground, and there's lots of boards everywhere. Iron sits up on a platform nailed onto the old rafters that my dad built for the older boys, and only they're allowed to go up. He lets me climb up there sometimes, though. Iron is six.*

*The light shines down, and I stand under the treehouse, seeing him through the cracks. He's lying down, his arms under his head. There's music somewhere. It smells good out here. Flowers.*

*I almost call up to him to help me up, but I don't. I don't want him to move. It's nice to look up. I love Iron. He's nice to me.*

She can't have another kid.

*I hold my fingers, looking back at the house and up at the rafters. I don't know where to go.*

*My throat hurts. I want to cry.*

*The sun goes down while I'm out there.*

*And then . . . someone picks me up. I'm in the air, flipping around, and I'm on Macon's back, holding tight as he climbs up to the treehouse. I smile at the feeling in my stomach, suddenly feeling better.*

*We sit on the landing. Army follows with a bag. Iron pops up, seeing us, and Army takes out ice cream and cups and spoons and chocolate sauce. I grab the bottle because I can do it myself.*

*"Is Mom okay?" Iron looks at Macon.*

*"Mom's fine," he mumbles, scooping ice cream into the mugs. "Trace is in bed. Ice cream for dinner."*

*We all get our cups, and I squeeze the syrup into mine. Lots and lots.*

*"Stop yelling at Dad," Army whispers to Macon.*

*"Fuck him."*

*Macon doesn't look at him, but he looks at me, and I get scared. Then, he holds out his cup, and I smile, squeezing the syrup into his as hard as I can.*

*He smiles a little at me, and it makes me feel good. I like it when he does that.*

*Army takes a drink out of one of my dad's bottles, but Macon takes it away and finishes the whole thing. Army doesn't get mad because Macon is scarier than Dad.*

My mom was pregnant with Liv in that memory. I came to understand later what had really happened that day. How it finally dawned on me that there were a few years between Macon and Army, and almost five between Army and Iron, but there was little time between me and Trace, and Trace and Liv. My father's ignorant attempt to give my mother a reason to live turned out to be a burden that just made it worse.

It's a whole new experience to remember things as an adult. How Macon was only thirteen that day, but I saw him as a man when it happened. I feared and revered him more than either of my parents because he was stronger than they were. A rock. Constant.

And how incredible he was at that age to send my father running from the house. How he was often the one who made sure we bathed and brushed our teeth, and had clean dishes and clean sheets. Dad worked a lot and Mom just . . .

*Self-isolating*, Krisjen had said.

*Mood swings.*

*Loss of appetite.*

*Insomnia.*

It was gradual and quiet. Her withdrawal from us. Hiding away behind closed doors. Only Macon could tell what was going to happen eventually.

And now only Krisjen has noticed what the rest of us have been too close to see.

I step toward the door but see a jacket folded over Liv's desk chair. An old leather motorcycle jacket Macon grew out of in high school that Liv found years later. I roll the soft, smooth leather between my fingers. The faded ribbed padding on the elbows and shoulders. The standing collar missing a button. He wore this a lot. On a bike. With no helmet. Because needlessly toying with death just might be worth the feel of the wind.

I drop it back to the chair, head to my room, and push my hangers aside. I dig in the back for Iron's clothes and pull out his identical jacket. I slip it on, tie my boots, and grab my wallet.

I head down the stairs and into the garage, grabbing Iron's keys off the ring on the wall.

"I want you to come," I hear Army say.

I glance over, seeing Macon under the hood, Trace, Krisjen, and Army standing around him.

"With Iron gone, the Jaegers look weaker," Trace adds. "You're the only one who intimidates them more than him."

Macon says nothing. I was wondering how they were going to get him to go have some fun.

"Please?" Army asks, his mood light despite their brawl the night before.

I move Iron's bike, flipping up the kickstand as Krisjen dabs sunscreen on her nose and cheeks.

"I don't know why y'all think he's afraid to come," she chirps, looking at her reflection in a hub cap hanging on the wall. "St. Carmen is your land, too, isn't it?"

"Was," Trace tells her.

But I chime in. "Is." They all look at me, like they didn't expect me to really come. "I know what to do," I inform them.

Macon rises, his attention piqued. "And what's that exactly?"

I roll the bike out of the garage. "Remind them that we're still here."

It's all our turf. We forgot that. "Krisjen, you coming?" I call back.

She hesitates for a second, but she doesn't ask questions. She climbs on behind me. I hand her a helmet, but she tosses it back on the couch in the garage. I smile.

In no time, Trace and Army follow with Dex, all of them climbing into the truck, and I start up the bike, Krisjen wrapping her arms around my waist. I rev the engine, seeing Trace smiling at me, and I catch movement in my rearview mirror, watching Macon pull on a faded leather jacket. He stares after us, looking reluctant for a moment.

But then he turns and grabs his keys.

The wind flies at me, hitting my sunglasses, but I only go faster, gripping the handlebars tighter. Krisjen's arms constrict like a snake.

I race down dirt roads, through puddles, and bounce over the tracks. I watch her in my rearview mirror, looking off to the side, her hair flying. We lost my brothers behind us a few minutes ago.

I kick it into the next gear, lurch forward, and charge way over the speed limit, the bike rumbling underneath us. She laughs. I go faster. She holds tighter.

I lean to the right, her body following mine as we round a soft turn too fast, but she doesn't tell me to stop. I race and race farther and farther, homes and palm trees and people zooming past. We rush past cars, my heart lodging in my throat, and I laugh to myself.

It's been a long time since I've been on a bike.

I don't think I've ever had a girl on one. It's scarier. I love how she holds me, lets me carry her. She's trusting. Why?

Before I know it, we arrive at Garden Isle, the pristine white beach the Saints love to keep for themselves even when they prefer to invade ours because we have a lighthouse and no rules. I skid to a halt, hearing screams and laughter from the carnival a hundred yards away on the other side of the parking lot. I don't realize how fast my heart is beating until I feel the ache in my chest.

She starts to climb off, but I reach back and grab her leg, stopping her.

The sun beats down as a breeze carries the scent of their bake sale. Bake sales are beautiful. Not at all lazy.

I look ahead but keep holding her leg. "Aren't you afraid of anything?"

Army is probably angry at how fast I was going. Macon, too. Liv would've yelled at me to slow down. I put Krisjen in danger, but she didn't seem to notice.

"Pain," she finally says. "I'm afraid of dying in pain."

We're all afraid of that.

"You can't think straight when something hurts," she tells me, "and I want to be there in my last minutes."

I dig under my fingernail with my thumb.

"What are you afraid of?" she asks.

I pause just a moment. "You."

She sits there.

I swallow the lump in my throat. "The last woman to live in our house, other than our sister, was our mom."

We've been like this a long time. Liv was never one to fuss with the house the way my mom did. Baking, decorating . . .

Krisjen's not like Liv, though. Krisjen is someone they'll start to depend on, but she's not family. She can ditch us anytime.

"She knew I was in the house that day," I say, and then clarify. "My mom. She knew I was the only one in the house. She didn't even lock her door."

I was thirteen. The same age Macon was when he confronted our father about continuing to get her pregnant. I was alone with her that day. I heard something fall on the floor upstairs. I knew. I didn't go upstairs.

"I want you to leave," I tell Krisjen.

The longer she stays, the harder it will be when she goes.

I expect her to argue, but she doesn't. She simply says, "Okay."

My stomach sinks. She moves to climb off again, but I curl my fingers around her thigh tighter. "You're not afraid of anything else?"

I feel her looking around me, trying to meet my eyes, but I can't let her.

"My second-grade teacher had a sister," she tells me. "She was shot in a parking lot coming out of a store one night. The killer didn't know her. She was sixteen."

I listen.

"Life isn't about what happens to us, Dallas, because things are going to happen. Rich, poor, good parents, bad parents, no matter what, we can't predict other people. If I can't change it or prevent it, then I don't think about it. Just adapt when it happens, and remember how lucky I am to breathe at all."

I blink, my eyes burning. That's what I fear. A world where so much is at the mercy of chance. "And if I can control what's going to happen?"

"Then please don't get arrested," she says.

And to my surprise, I start laughing. A woman who just might understand me.

I release her, letting her climb off, but I stay on the bike. "I still want you to leave." I meet her eyes. "For your sake as much as ours. Macon doesn't let us love Saints. And he's right. You'll never want a life in the Bay. Money always wins over the heart."

"But you have money," she says. "Don't you?"

I turn my gaze away, feeling another smile pull at the corners of my mouth. "Probably more than I know about."

Macon doesn't tell us everything.

So, no. She wouldn't be giving up much security if she was with one of us, but she'd be giving up status. Luxury. We have money, but we'll never have servants. Or fancy dinners. Or world travel.

"Clay and Liv are together," she points out, taking off her hoodie and tying it around her waist. "He's fine with Liv being with a Saint."

I dig a pack of cigarettes out of my breast pocket. "Is he?" I light one, blowing out the smoke. "Why do you think he changed his mind about letting Liv go to Dartmouth? Sending her off and even helping pay for it, so she can't use debt as an excuse to come home to a state school to be near Clay?"

Her brows pinch together, and I see the wheels turning in her head. She straightens, staring down at me. "He thinks the distance will kill the relationship."

I nod. "We had to mop Army up off the floor after his girl destroyed him. Macon's tired of cleaning up problems that should never have been problems."

"Did he ever have to clean up after you?"

I snap my gaze to hers.

But before I can answer, she's walking away and throwing me a sly smile over her shoulder.

I wasn't going to tell her, but she knows there's something she doesn't know. She's not stupid, is she?

I take another drag. By the time the full measure of the consequences of fucking the one Saint I should never have fucked hits the Bay, she'll be gone anyway. Probably.

Macon will be cleaning up after me for years.

The truck pulls up to my right, and I hear the rumble of another bike somewhere farther in the distance. I spot Aracely at the carnival entrance adding tequila from her flask into a frozen lemonade she just bought, and Krisjen finds Liv and Clay where everybody is dancing to a DJ playing music. I could buy them all a drink. Liv has to go back to school in a couple of days. She'd appreciate it.

I *could* buy them all a drink to be nice. I'm not going to. I've grown enough for one day.

I turn my face up to the sky, just as thunderclouds roll in, and the warm wind blows the tent flaps. I smoke the last of the cigarette, the breeze caressing my hair, and the smell of hot tar drifting through my nose. Reminds me of kites. I don't know why.

"We're all going to be wet in an hour," I hear Trace call out.

He walks over to me, smoothing back his dark hair and refitting his baseball cap over it.

"Yeah."

No one cares, though.

He sees my cigarette and reaches into my breast pocket, stealing the pack. He lights one up, and we both gaze at the crowd of people, taking in the view. Army circles his arms around Krisjen, and she laughs. I look at Trace watching them.

"You still want her at all?" I ask him.

He shrugs. "Sometimes."

His answer surprises me. I thought he'd lie, act like he doesn't care.

"She's good at loving," he tells me. "She was pretty hot on Iron that night."

He saw them through the trees. I'd only heard about it.

By the pool. On a lawn chair. In the rain.

Iron's the only person I ever really feel comfortable with. Of course he'd make love to a girl outside, in the night air. If someone wants to look, that's on them. Not him. That's why I love him.

With Krisjen, though, I hated her more. *Of course she would fuck another one of my brothers, making a spectacle of herself for everyone to see. Sluts spread for anyone.*

Yeah, double standard. Boo-fucking-hoo.

But really . . . She was going to hurt him. She's going to hurt Army. Women bring pain. Wives make everything worse. I would've been fine without a mom.

I watch her dance as she smiles with my sister and her girlfriend out on the dance floor.

But honestly, I'm glad Iron had something that felt good before he went away. I'm really glad.

"She'd be a sight with all four of us," I say before I can stop myself.

Trace turns, looking at me.

I inhale a deep breath and flick the cigarette butt off. "I've been trying to get rid of her, but I've been completely ignoring how useful she could be."

"What the hell are you talking about?"

I hold his eyes for a moment. "She'd do anything for us, Trace. For the Bay." I look back out at her as she pulls her hair out of her ponytail, looking like such a tomboy in her jeans and T-shirt, no makeup. Makes me dream about stripping her down. "Krisjen Conroy on camera would buy us our land and anything else we wanted for good. Her grandfather would pay whatever it took to keep a video quiet."

He immediately squares his shoulders. "No."

"You and Army have already fucked her," I tell him. "I can do what needs to be done. We'd be good to her. Gentle. Take her somewhere private and quiet. On the boat, maybe?" I don't blink. "She'll have the night of her life, Trace."

It doesn't have to be a bad thing. We'd make sure she enjoyed it.

"Don't tell me the idea of your older brothers having something you got to have first doesn't turn you on," I taunt him.

He stares at her as she dances, but then starts to walk away. "You're a son of a bitch."

He doesn't look back at me, and I just smile. "Think about it," I call out.

He keeps walking until he's lost in the crowd.

I know Trace. He's usually up for anything, and everything else he just needs time to warm up to.

I scan the crowd once more, spotting lots of Bay people and lots of Saints. Milo Price texts on his phone, and I take note of the cameras on the light posts and the drones flying around, catching footage that typically broadcasts on the town's social media pages. Phone cameras are taking video, and the live cam at the top of the visitor's center has a 360-degree lens I know is in full working order.

Anyone, no matter where they are in the world, can see us right now.

My body warms. Taking out my phone, I tap out a text.

**I know you're watching.**

The message reads **Delivered**, then **Read**.

I smile, putting my phone away.

# 17

## Krisjen

If only Iron were here, it would be a perfect day. I should go see him. Keep him connected, so he remembers why he has to come back. I sent off a care package yesterday with some food, a card filled with pictures of our roasted oyster night at Mariette's and everyone's signatures, and some magazines. I want to see his face, though. Make sure he's not fighting.

"Thank you." I take the bowl of chili and grab a plastic spoon, giving Mrs. Chadwick one last smile before walking away.

This is my favorite part of the Annual Bug Jam. The chili cook-off. There are at least a dozen tents filled with the scent of spices, some of the booths belonging to families with their secret recipes, and some businesses trying to connect with the community. The cotton candy booth is next. They have twenty-one flavors.

I stroll, seeing Dallas still sitting on his bike out in the parking lot, three women standing around him. I shake my head. Dude doesn't even have to get up to get what he wants.

Trace has Dex on his shoulders, and I don't see Army right now, but he mentioned wanting to go look at the cars on display.

I'm going back on Dallas's motorcycle, though. That was fun. He was trying so hard to scare me, but I didn't mind, because he wouldn't purposely hurt himself just to hurt me. Like he wouldn't deliberately crash the bike with us both on it.

But I hesitate, chewing on that thought for a second.

"Look at them, huh?"

I pop my head up, seeing Jerome Watson. My face falls. It didn't even occur to me I'd see him today.

He half sits on the edge of his chili booth's table, looking different in jeans. His flannel is tan, blue, and green, making him look more handsome than I like. A white apron is tied around his slim waist.

"There's something admirable about how they've held on to the land this long."

He doesn't look at me, and I turn my head, following his gaze. Trace and Dex dance with Liv and Clay. Aracely gets in Dallas's face, while he smokes another cigarette and is clearly trying not to laugh.

"I like survivors," Jerome tells me. "No one can say the Jaegers aren't resilient."

I look back at him, the heat from the chili seeping through the bowl to my hand.

"But every year is the same for them, isn't it?" he asks me. "Nothing changes. The battles, the turmoil, the same faces, the same bullshit, the same dirt roads and dilapidated houses . . . Things live in the Bay; nothing grows."

I lock my jaw, breathing heavier. That's not true. Jerome stands up, and I don't back up as he slowly closes the distance between us.

He lowers his voice. "What will you do when you tire of their bodies and realize you didn't know you'd miss having possibilities in life? Hmm?" He stares down at me. "A beautiful home? Being able to send your children to college and give them a future? Maybe opening your own business?" He cocks his head. "A children's boutique," he finally says. "I can see you running something like that. It's cute, like you."

I start to back away, but he grabs my hand and puts it on his chest.

"And I have a body, too," he whispers.

I don't have a chance to rip my hand away before someone takes it away from him and encloses me in his arms. I tense but look down and see the Tryst Six emblem on a leather bracelet. He locks me against his chest, his jaw resting against my head.

I relax. *Army.*

Jerome looks at him over my head, and I see people out of the corner of my eyes, taking notice of all of us.

"It's good to see you," Jerome tells him. "Been a long time."

Heather Lynch and A. K. Weathers stare at me, holding their frozen lemonades. They must be back from Florida State for the holiday.

"I don't know why"—Jerome grins—"but I'm lamenting all the times we made each other bleed in high school."

High school? Army would've been like fifteen when Jerome was eighteen.

"That was good times," Jerome goes on. "But a woman is one thing we still haven't fought over."

Jerome's eyes drop to me as he steps up. Army's arms barely move, but I feel the slight tightening of the muscles around me. Jerome's gaze rises to his, his expression stern and void of emotion. "I once promised you I'd have everything that was yours," he tells Army. "I will."

I clutch Army's wrist, feeling the bracelet under my hand.

"You won't" comes the strong, deep voice behind me.

But it's not Army.

My heart hammers against my chest. I look down to my fingers wrapped around the wrist with the bracelet, my pinky brushing against the long bones in the back of Macon's hand.

Jerome turns and walks away, back to his booth, and the arms around me fall away as I twist around and look up at Macon. His head is turned, watching Jerome, his eyebrows lowered as he stares. Army, Dallas, and Trace linger out of the corner of my eye, the pulse in my neck throbbing as my back and my arms still buzz under the skin everywhere he touched.

Without looking back down at me, he leaves, and I hesitate until Army finally arrives and takes my hand. My fingers gone limp in his, I barely hear him ask, "Are you okay?"

All I can do is nod. Thoughts creep in that I don't want to face.

It felt like him. Exactly like him.

The couch . . .

But I shake my head clear. It wasn't him. A part of me just wants it to be.

When I heard his voice, my heart wound up and started going nuts like one of those windup toys that bounce up and down, up and down, up and down. I was just surprised. He doesn't normally do things like that.

He did it for Jerome, unable to resist carrying on their high school pissing contest. Not for me.

"All right, everyone!" someone calls over a loudspeaker. "If you have a team, please make your way to the east parking lot! The Forty-First Annual Bug Jam will kick off in ten minutes!"

Army starts leading me away, and I see Trace tip back and empty his bottle of beer.

The pads of my fingers still vibrate, feeling his bracelet.

Déjà vu washes over me.

Macon is just still a mystery I'm trying to crack, so my imagination is going wild. I know it wasn't him.

"Participants must be eighteen years or older, spectators—"

"So what did he say to you?" Army asks.

I shake my head. "Nothing."

Macon rarely speaks to me.

But then I realize Army is asking about Jerome. "Oh, um . . ."

I look up and shake my head clear. "Just some nonsense about how real chili has beans."

It serves no purpose to repeat Jerome's bullshit. Today is about fun.

"Dumb motherfucker," he mumbles under his breath. "If it's got beans, it's not chili."

I shake my head. "It's just a stew."

The announcer goes on as we approach the crowd, pushing our way through to the light green VW Beetle that I only know was made in 1969 because I watched Trace and his buddies restoring it one night last summer.

"The record is thirteen people," the woman calls over the speaker. "Held by the Hurricane Ladies Book Club."

"Named for all the hurricanes they drink while they pretend to talk about books they don't read!" Baylor Kane, a senior at Marymount and the son of one of the moms in the Hurricane Ladies Book Club, teases nice and loud.

Everyone laughs, and I look around at who we have on our team. Aracely, Army, Trace, and Dallas. Liv and Clay walk up to join us. Someone must be watching Dex for a few minutes while we do this.

I arch up on my tiptoes, scanning the people behind me. Did Macon go home?

"And that's not fair, either!" another guy shouts. "Women are smaller."

"You're pretty small," another woman fires back.

"Ohhhhh" come taunts from the crowd, followed by some laughter and a chide: "There are children here!"

Army pulls me along. "Let's do this."

The teams start approaching their cars, wind kicking up as I pull my hair back into a ponytail and pull on my hoodie again. I look back at Dallas. "You joining in?"

His mouth twists to the side, but I can see the amusement in his eyes. He whips off his jacket as all of them pile their leathers next to the rear tire.

"Boys in first," Clay instructs. "I'm not getting crushed."

Macon probably went home. I don't know if it did any good to get him out today. I probably just solidified in his mind why Saints are frivolous and foolish.

The MC announces all the teams, and as soon as they call out Sanoa Bay, I spit out, "Eyes up."

The boys raise their chins, taking the hint. Don't avoid eye contact. Let them see you. Clay and I cheer extra hard—Liv too cool for that—until the speaker moves on to the next team.

"Staff will be walking around to ensure everyone is safe," she says, "and to offer help if you need. Are you ready?"

Everyone shouts and howls, and there are a few rushed instructions about the rules for arms and legs that I don't hear, but then the air horn slices through the air, splitting my ears at the same time everyone starts leaping into the cars.

It starts too fast for me to tell what's going on, but the men go first, sliding into seats and hopping into the back.

"Krisjen!" Army calls. I dart my eyes to him in the passenger-side seat as he gestures for me to hop up to the sunroof. "Slide in. Come down in my lap."

Trace scoots his seat up on the driver's side, squeezing his legs into as tight a space as possible as Aracely throws her weight into Army's door to get it closed. Stepping up onto his open window, I hop up to the roof of the car, about to swing my legs in first, but someone pulls me down into the back seat. I squeal.

"Hey!" I laugh, getting caught up in the fun. Dallas shifts underneath me, and Army throws him a look from the front seat.

"We got to puzzle this shit together," Dallas barks. "Little people on the floor."

He shoves me down between his legs, but I end up in some weird position on my side, my left leg unable to fit enough for me to sit.

"We're gonna need to lay someone this way!" I hear Trace instruct. He shifts his seat in front of me, and I pull my hands back, checking that my hair isn't in his tracks. I wince. This feels unsafe.

"She's not gonna be able to breathe!" Army yells, and I hope he's talking about me. I need more room.

I try to shift my legs, but they run into more legs, and I see Aracely coming down feetfirst above me. I flinch. "Watch my head!"

Cheering starts outside, I try to turn my gaze, but all I see is Dallas's crotch. I try to inhale deeply, but this is ridiculous. Why do I have to be on the floor?

"Aracely over here!" Dallas shouts. "We have to use every inch of space. Krisjen, move!"

Something knocks into my head, and I finally growl. "I'm going to die down here!" Clutching Dallas's thigh, I haul myself back up.

"Don't be a baby," he shoots back. "Just sit on me, then."

"Sit on you?" Army blurts out. "She's not sitting on anything of you."

"I'll sit on his ex," I offer, watching Aracely slide through the roof.

Someone laughs, and Dallas grabs me by the waist, trying to move me over onto his lap as he digs his fingers into my stomach. I try to hold back my laugh because his fingers tickle. "Let me go!" I shout.

"No—"

But then I'm out of his arms, his words cut off as I'm flipped over, straddling someone else's lap in the seat next to him. My smile fades, and I don't blink as I stare at Macon and he stares back. Aracely descends, pushing against my back and shoving me into Macon.

"Yeah, yeah, exactly like that," I hear Trace say. "Aracely, get in Dallas's lap like Krisjen's in Macon's. Your puzzle pieces fit together once before."

"Shut up!" I hear her snap.

Puzzle pieces.

Someone pushes into me again, and then again until I'm almost nose to nose with Macon.

His eyes don't leave mine.

Holding me, he takes my arms and guides them around his neck, pulling me flush with his chest. Tight.

His hand covers the back of my head, protecting it, and it only takes a moment for me to get a handle on what we're doing and to follow his lead. Hugging him close, I circle his neck with both of my arms and bury my face in his neck as the car jostles underneath us, more bodies piling in.

"Ara, damn," Dallas groans. "You gain weight or something?"

"Dallas?" she says with a heavy accent, and I can tell she's about to say something in Spanish. "Yo pretendi mis orgasmos contigo."

I recognize Army's laughter, because he, Macon, and Iron are the only ones who are bilingual. For some reason, their parents raised Liv, Trace, and Dallas with only English.

Macon's fingers curl into my skin. Goose bumps spread down my arms. I close my eyes. *This could be it.*

Dallas goes on, "What the hell did she say?"

"You don't want to know," Army replies.

Jerome is nowhere in sight. Macon holds me, and when his arms tighten, so do mine. Someone knocks into me again, but I don't get hurt. Macon's got me.

The space inside the car is getting tight.

I can't breathe.

It's hot.

I never want to leave.

"Clay, you need to shave!" someone shouts.

"I shaved!"

"Get your foot out of my face."

Voices, grunts, an insult about someone's breath . . .

His neck is warm. I can feel the creases in the skin of his neck on my mouth. I shift, trying to press my stomach to his, but I rub against him. I stop breathing, he holds me.

"Are we done?" someone asks.

*No.* I close my eyes.

"Someone shout! Tell them we're done!"

"Done!" I hear Army and Dallas shout.

"Done!" comes someone else.

"Oh my God, hurry," Dallas bites out. "I can't breathe."

I inhale him, I . . .

The air horn goes off, and I squeeze my eyes shut tighter . . . before I finally open them.

Cheering fills the air, car doors flying open and everyone starting to fall out. There's laughter outside, but as the car empties, I pull back, lingering, though I can't meet his eyes.

I don't know what's going on here. What does he want? He's confusing. I hate that.

But my attention keeps drifting to him.

"We fucking lost," Trace gripes.

"Did those old bags win again?"

"Be nice," Liv says. "Like we were going to win with you four taking up space in here."

"God, it's hot," Clay complains.

Everyone climbs out, and hesitantly, I follow. I join everyone else outside, Army pulling me to his side. The Hurricane Ladies Book Club, pealing with laughter and having a hell of a time, collect their trophy and gift basket.

"Beer tent," Trace calls out.

Army follows, pulling me.

But I dig in my heels. "You go," I tell him.

He opens his mouth to argue, but I assure him, "It's okay. I have to get my brother and sister anyway. They're at the bounce houses with friends. My mom is away for the weekend." I pop up and kiss him on the lips. "I'll see you tomorrow."

I turn to leave, but he pulls me back. "Hey." He pauses, looking into my eyes and knowing something is wrong. "Let me give you a ride."

"It's a short walk. We're good." I keep my tone light, smiling for him. "Go. Have fun."

He looks at me like he has more to say, but I turn and leave before he can.

Guilt nips at me, but I wouldn't even know what to say if I wanted to explain.

I wasn't lying. My brother and sister are at the bounce houses, and I do need to watch them tonight, but I could've taken them in Trace's truck to the Bay. They like it there.

I just . . .

I need to be alone.

I walk through the crowd, but then someone pops up in front of me, blocking my way. "I have a key to the truck. Let me take you home instead."

I raise my eyes, see Dallas standing there. He cocks his head, but the look in his eyes isn't playful.

"It's no trouble," he tells me, holding up the keys.

I look back to see if Army is still there, but he's gone.

"I thought we were becoming friends," Dallas teases.

I study him. "And what does that word mean to you?"

He chuckles, and I take my leave as quickly as possible.

"See you tomorrow," I tell him.

I'm not sure Dallas does much of anything out of the goodness of his heart. And while I'm glad he's talking to me—and doing it pleasantly—I know he always has a motive, or he expects to be paid for going out of his way.

He's not complicated in the way Macon is. With Dallas, once you know what he doesn't want you to know, I'm guessing a lot about him makes sense.

But also, unlike Macon, Dallas will pull you under to save himself. He may have good moments, but I'm not sure he's good.

I slip in between a game booth and the visitor's center, heading toward the bounce houses, but as soon as I'm out of site of the Bug Jam, hands shove me in the back, sending me flying to the ground.

What the hell? I gasp, catching myself with my hands, and hurry to flip over, looking up at my attacker.

Milo stands there, then squats down. "You okay?"

Three girls flank him, all four of them looking down at me.

Oh shit.

# 18

## Krisjen

I stare up at Milo, Cate Laurel, Emaline Truax, and Antoinette Viega—the seniors from Marymount—standing behind him.

My fingers dig into the dirt behind me. "You want to do this here?"

His grin is in his eyes, mouth set in a straight line. "I'll be quick."

He grabs me by the front of my hoodie and hauls me off the ground, twists me around, and grips my ponytail at the scalp. I grunt at the burn.

"Milo . . ." one of the girls chides.

But he throws me into the wall of the restroom, and I stop myself before my face hits.

"Swamp slut," he growls, flipping me back around. "His cum still inside you?" He grabs me between the legs. "Which one has his smell all over you?"

I breathe hard. "Um . . ." I search my brain. "I don't know. I didn't shower between the one last night and the one this morning."

He throws me into the lime-green wall again, and I see his hand fly with only enough time to brace myself before it lands. Fire spreads across my cheek, and he squeezes a fistful of skin from my stomach so hard a cry crawls up my throat.

But before I can let it out, he throws me to the ground.

I land on my stomach, a sharp pebble digging into my palm.

"Enough!" the same voice says. I recognize it as Toni Viega now.

"She can take a man's hands on her," Milo tells the girl. "Haven't you heard?"

I raise my eyes to look for the Jaegers. I see Trace. Beyond the game booths, in the crowd. I don't want any of them to see. Not here. Not in St. Carmen.

Turning over, I keep my eyes locked on Milo as I rise to my feet.

I used to hit him back. He liked that, because it made him angrier.

But he doesn't matter enough anymore. Let's see if he can make me scream.

"Should we be gentler?" he asks me.

He comes in close, Cate and Emaline following as he grabs me by the collar again.

But Toni shoves off. "I'm out of here."

She leaves, and I smile through the pain in my face, the skin feeling like it's ripping.

"Should we take her somewhere?" Milo asks them.

Cate grins. "We should."

My chest rises and falls with quick breaths. "Yeah, so you can do what men do to women to show what men they are, right?" I feel the fire in my eyes as I goad my ex. "Trace's tongue between my legs. Iron's hands squeezing my hips as I rocked on top of him. Army's mouth sucking me so hard," I taunt. "They have me coming when called and doing what I'm told, and all they do when they raise a hand to me is crook their finger."

His eyes flare.

I smile wide. "It's just sad for me that I can't fit all five at the same time."

In one quick movement, he has me by the hair, slaps me, then grabs my neck and shoves me to the ground.

I land hard, feeling a sharp pain shooting through my back as all the air leaves my lungs. Leaning down, he hauls me up again, and I don't have time to push him away. His hand whips across my face, the force sending my head spinning and an ache flaring up my neck. Warm blood spills from the inside of my cheek.

He drops me back to the ground, and I lie there, trying to remember what I'm supposed to do. Instinct wants to kick in. I should run. I should yell, call for help. Fight back.

Tears fill my eyes.

But Milo backs away, telling them, "Don't stop until something breaks."

I look over my shoulder, struggling to get my feet under me.

When I rise and turn around, Milo is gone, Cate and Emaline remaining to finish me off.

I swallow, blood going down my throat. "Are we done?"

Emaline rushes me, taking hold of my arms behind me as Cate grabs my shoulders and plants her knee in my stomach.

Bile lurches up my throat, and they throw me down again. Their feet circle me, ready for my move.

But I just laugh weakly, feeling like I'm going to throw up at the same time. I struggle to my feet only to have another hand whip across my face. I fall to my knees, no idea who hit me that time, but I rise again.

And again and again.

I feel a drop of blood fall down my cheekbone—or maybe it's a tear. My eyes are watering, my vision is blurry. I feel sick.

They shove me to the ground, one kicking me in the back, the other in the stomach. They back away, wait for me, and shift on their toes, ready. My arms shake under me as I try to stand up, but I cough, feeling the vomit rise.

I blow out three hard breaths, steel my muscles, and force myself up.

I stare at them through the hair that's fallen in my eyes, and I feel the fire spreading across my stomach and over my face.

"Fight back," Cate demands.

I sniffle. "Nah, I'm good."

A hand flies across my face. Emaline, I think. "Fight back!"

I groan, a few tears streaming that I can't stop. The corner of my mouth stings. My knees shake.

Cate pushes me to the ground, both of them coming in, and I hold my stomach to protect myself, but then . . . nothing comes.

Cate whips backward, grabbed by the hair, and Aracely is there, slapping Emaline to the ground.

I breathe a sigh of relief, dropping my head back to the ground, and for a moment, all the pain is gone. God, yes. I don't think I'm going to be able to take more.

Yelps and growls go off around me, and I don't even look to know Aracely doesn't need any help. None what . . . so . . . ever.

Using every muscle I can muster, I roll onto my stomach and start to pry myself off the ground.

"We could have you arrested!" Cate screams, blood dripping from her nose.

But Aracely just flashes her white teeth, gesturing to the live cam on top of the visitor's center. "And you'd even be able to prove it."

They see the camera, which would've caught Aracely beating them up, but it also would've caught them jumping me. Milo jumping me.

Emaline stares at the cam, frozen. "Shit."

I chuckle, wiping the blood under my nose. They'll get the town's recording deleted, for sure. They're connected like that. But it's live. Not that many people will be watching, but a few will be, and at least one will be recording. They leave in a hurry, turning and disappearing back to the festival.

"Thanks," I breathe out to Aracely.

She studies me. "Why didn't you fight back?"

I pull down my sleeve, using it to dab at my cheekbone and mouth. "I'm a Saint, Aracely. The only way to beat us is to keep getting up."

A smile peeks out, but she covers it by rolling her eyes. It was four against one. How else did she think I was going to win?

"Why'd you help me?" I ask her.

I would think she'd enjoy letting me get my ass kicked.

"Well . . ." She shrugs. "I did watch for a little while."

I snort. *I'm sure.*

I'm not mad, though.

"But then you just kept rising back up like some kind of hero," she goes on. "You cunty little bitch."

I laugh as she brushes the grass and dirt off my knees, and I'm about to invite her back to my house for some margaritas, but I don't feel so good. Everything sways in my vision, and I faintly hear a shout. "What the hell?"

I look behind Aracely, seeing Trace rushing over. Army follows.

I meet Aracely's eyes. "Don't tell them. Please. You know what'll happen."

This isn't about me. Milo's baiting them, and if they're going to risk themselves, it won't be for this.

"Oh my God, are you okay?" Clay runs over.

Everyone crowds around, but my forehead feels like it's on fire, and I need to get my sweatshirt off. I'm burning up all of a sudden. "I'm fine, I just . . . I . . ."

The world swirls around me, and I let my mouth fall open, feeling sick. I'm going to throw up.

"Krisjen," I hear Army say. I think he touches me.

"Who the fuck did this to you?" Dallas charges.

My knees start to give out. "I don't feel so good." I drop. "I need to sit—"

Someone's arms scoop me up before I hit the ground, and I let my head fall into him as I close my eyes.

"Go get her brother and sister at the bounce house." Macon's voice vibrates against my ear.

"What?"

"Now!" he shouts at someone.

Sweat covers my forehead, my stomach roiling as I let him carry me away.

"Aracely, who did this?" Liv asks as we leave.

"I didn't see."

Thatta girl.

No more Jaegers in jail.

A half hour later, I'm sitting on the sink in Macon's bathroom, sucking on a fruit punch Capri-Sun. He said I needed something cold in my stomach.

My legs dangle over the side as he dabs a pad with some saline solution on the corner of my lip and cleans up my nose. The guys and kids are making a ruckus downstairs, and I can't tell who's being louder.

"So did you have fun?" I ask, swinging my legs as I look up at him.

He holds my face, dabbing ointment on the cut on my cheek. "You got the shit kicked out of you, and you're smiling?"

"I'm still breathing."

He meets my eyes, looking unamused before returning his attention to my face.

I can't explain it. I'm injured, but I'm not in pain. All I can feel right now are his hands.

"You still feel nauseous?" he asks me.

I shake my head, drinking the rest of the juice.

"Who was it?" he demands.

I drop the juice pouch in the garbage can. "Just some girls. Aracely and I took care of it." And then I add, "Mostly Aracely."

"Krisjen . . ."

"Did you have fun?" I press again and try to get him to look at me. "It was pretty amazing to see you stand up to Jerome. I don't usually get to see you in action. I liked it."

He goes still, breathing a little harder.

"Is he an old rival?" I say in a quiet voice.

He throws the bloody pads away and cracks an ice pack, activating it. "Saint versus Swamp isn't anything new."

He places the pack along my jaw and takes my hand, planting it there to hold it in place.

"He'll want you more now," he says, almost whispering. "Because he thinks you're mine."

My heart thuds hard.

"Maybe I should've fought back," I tell him. "All Bay women are fighters, right?"

"My woman won't need a steel jaw." He puts away the supplies. "Just a steel stomach."

I watch him as he avoids my gaze, doing everything he can not to look at me. God, I want to know her. The woman who will belong to him.

He peels off some thin strips of tape, bandaging the cut on my cheek. He's pretty good at this. My parents would just pay someone to do it.

"Sometimes I wonder how much of your military training you're willing to use to keep the Bay safe," I think out loud, listing on my fingers. "You seem to know computers, mechanics, and you're definitely skilled at strategy . . . What did you do in the Marines?"

"I was a combat medic."

I laugh, feeling the sting as he puts the final piece of tape over my cut. *Of course.* I should've seen that coming.

"Did you ever see combat?"

He nods.

"Must've been hard." I start to lean into his fingertips as they brush my skin, but I stop myself. "Especially seeing that aspect of it. But still . . . do you miss being out in the world?"

He swallows, turning away to get another piece of tape and then coming back to me. "The more I got a glimpse of how big the world is, the smaller I wanted mine to be," he says. "I saw a lot, traveled . . . And I learned that the only things that brought me joy were the things that were familiar."

I hold my breath. *Keep going.*

"People I knew," he continues, "muddy roads with memories, key lime pie, the couch I first made out with a girl on . . ."

"You still have the couch?"

"It's in the garage."

*That's awesome.* I want to ask him if that's where he lost his virginity, too. Or if it was in a bed, and if the bed is still in the house.

I can't picture him in a bed, though. My mind wanders, and I see it in my head. In a shower. It was in a shower. He picks her up. She wraps her arms and legs around him, and he holds her close as they do it against the wall.

"What?" I hear him ask.

I blink, realizing the look that must be on my face. I drop my eyes.

"Um . . ." I pause, trying to find my voice. "Thank you for helping me."

I hop off the counter and head out of his bedroom, but he catches me in the hallway, taking me by the elbow.

I turn.

"Liv's room," he instructs. "You need rest. Mars will make sure Paisleigh gets her bath, and I'll send her up when it's time for bed. Mars can sleep in Iron's."

He heads down the stairs, and I drift toward his sister's bedroom door, barely noticing the ache settling in my body. He thought I was heading to Army's room. I'm not sure where I was going, but yeah, I need sleep.

Closing myself away in Liv's room, I pull off my jeans and take off my bra, then slip my arms back into my T-shirt, and uncover the bed. I hope Liv is sleeping at Clay's tonight.

My phone rings. I drop the blankets and pick up my jeans, digging out my phone. Clay's name flashes on the caller ID.

"Hey, I'm okay," I assure her before she can ask.

"Good." It's quiet wherever she is, so she must be home now. "If it was Milo—"

"I can handle myself," I tell her, but I'm smiling. She's worried. At least one Saint still loves me. "You just worry about spending time with Ms. Jaeger."

"Speaking of Jaegers," she teases. "Army?"

Great.

I stroll to the window, looking out onto the derelict wing, a wild garden of flowers and weeds and ivy climbing and reclaiming.

"And who told you that, now?"

But she just replies, "Please."

Just then, a figure moves into my line of sight. Macon walks into the dark, abandoned skeleton of the house that his ancestors built. He moves alone, stopping in the middle of the garden, and stands there, looking down. Looking at nothing.

I can see the leather bracelet from here, the hourglass glimmering as it catches the moonlight.

When he had his arms around me today . . . My hand was on his wrist. On the bracelet.

It felt the same as that night.

It takes a moment to work up the courage. "Could it have been Macon?" I ask her.

She's quiet.

"That night on the couch," I explain. "Can you see it being him?"

She hesitates but then states, "You want it to be."

Is that an observation or an accusation?

"Is there a spark?" she asks me.

I almost laugh. *A spark . . .*

"Bright and big and warm and lodged in my chest every time I'm alone with him," I tell her, my voice cracking. I don't know why I want to cry. I'm not sad.

*Jesus.* I'm eighteen. He's thirty-one. What am I thinking? I thought Jerome was too old for me, but Macon is about the same age. And I don't think I would even care if he was older than that.

But Clay replies, "I know that feeling."

Yeah. These damn Jaegers. It was over for her the moment she first kissed Liv.

But Macon will want someone more mature. I'll never grow up. I'll always want balloons on my birthday.

"You did say it was the best you ever had," Clay points out. "It would make sense, I guess. He's the oldest, more experienced . . ."

I watch him, his beautiful body dressed in black pants and no shirt. I try to imagine him on me. Has he been on me already?

"It couldn't have been him." I shake my head. "Macon keeps everything pent up."

"No one does all the time."

By Monday, I'm still thinking about Clay's words.

Macon is a man. Even though the bulk of my experience with him is intimidating and far from warm, he's not the machine he presents himself to be. He's not. He can laugh. Play. Be over-taken with desire.

She's right. He may resist those feelings as much as possible, but they do burst forth at some point or another. In his hand around someone's neck. His kiss on their temple. His thumb brushing a breast.

And around the time I get off work in the early afternoon, I let myself admit silently in my head that if it wasn't him on the couch that night, I don't want to know. Even if nothing ever happens between us again, I like the allure of thinking it *might've* been him. And that he wanted me.

I climb the stairs to Liv's room to change my clothes before running to get the kids from Bateman, but when I reach the top, I see Army and Dallas moving boxes out of the room next to Dallas and Iron's. They pile them in the hallway, the boxes overflowing with clothes, decor, fake flowers, and old board games. Mixed into the mess are an easel, a drafting table, and a large mason jar, cloudy with paint splatter and filled with brushes.

"You all are home early. What are you doing?" I ask, trying to see into the room. This door was always closed. I never had a reason to open it.

Army heaves another box to the top of the pile. "Macon said to clear it out."

"What is this room?" I spot a window with sheer pink curtains and the foot of a twin bed. A pile of canvases lays on top of it.

"It was Mom's art studio," he tells me.

Dallas opens the window, and I spot Trace behind the door, tossing out an old vacuum.

Their mom painted? There's no art displayed on the walls in the house.

Then I see the glassware on a shelf. I draw in a breath, holding it for a second. She was a glassmaker, too.

Macon and Army's fight on Thanksgiving . . .

That's why they looked devasted when they broke everything on the tables.

Shit.

Army comes up to me, gently taking my face in his hands. "You okay?"

I hesitate, turning my attention back to him. The swelling has gone down a lot, but the cut on the corner of my mouth stings. It reopened every time I tried to eat today. But I nod. "I'm okay."

He smiles. "Should we send Aracely and her crew after them again?"

"Oh, she made her point," I say. "Don't worry."

He holds my eyes. "I've missed you at night."

I place my hand on his as he holds my cheek. I don't know what to say. He's the one I should want. Out of all of them, he's the one who's ready for forever.

I take a deep breath, looking around at all the things cluttering the hallway. "There's some cool stuff here." I peek into boxes. "What does he want with the room?"

"Hopefully it's for Dex." Army pulls away, back to taking boxes Dallas and Trace hand him. "So I can have some privacy again."

And he smiles at me like we both know why he wants his room to himself.

"Why didn't you just tell him you needed it a year ago when he was born?"

"I did."

I start to shake my head, but then I stop. It would be just like Macon to punish Army for having a kid, but if it was their mother's studio, Macon might've had other reasons for keeping the room off-limits.

I start to back away. "I need to get the kids from the nanny."

Bateman has been paid up, but I don't want to be late like my mom.

But Trace calls out, "They're already here."

"What?"

"Mars is making dinner," Army tells me, "and Paisleigh is doing her homework in the garage."

"Bateman just gave the kids to you?" I blurt out.

"We're persuasive," Dallas mumbles.

*Yeah, right.* I should probably call the poor guy and make sure he hasn't called the police to report the kids being kidnapped.

I head downstairs, but then halt as Army's words finally hit me. Mars is making dinner?

I peek into the kitchen, seeing my twelve-year-old brother rolling balls of ground beef between his hands as a pot steams on the stove. I get weepy. Aw. *Spaghetti and meatballs.* I taught him to make that.

All I say is "Hey" as I walk to the door to the garage. Twelve-year-olds are tricky. If I hover, try to help, or gush about how much I love him, he'll stop and never cook again.

"Hey," he says back.

I walk into the garage, seeing Paisleigh sitting on a stool at the worktable. Her legs dangle as she swings her feet in her pink Chucks. "Hey." I smooth her ponytail as I look to see what she's working on. "Good day?"

She nods. "Trace got us from home. Mars went in the truck with the others, but I got to go on Trace's motorcycle!"

I freeze, thankful she's busy coloring instead of seeing my snarl. "I'll be talking to him about that."

I look around. The garage door is up, the hood of a car that looks like it's from the eighties is propped open with tools discarded nearby. "Why are you in here by yourself?" I ask her.

She changes out her crayon for an orange one. "The mean one was here, but he left."

The mean one. *Macon?*

"He was mean to you?"

"No. He gave me ice cream." She starts coloring the title of her

Rosa Parks Day worksheet. "But he was mean to the people who came over."

I peer outside, but I don't see any unfamiliar cars or trucks. "What did they say to him?" I ask her.

"I dunno. He left with them."

"In a car?"

"No." She points diagonally, in the direction of the firehouse. "Over there."

I walk around her. "Stay here."

I should stay out of it. If Macon wanted help, he would've asked for it. His brothers are home.

It wouldn't have been Milo, would it? Or Jerome Watson?

Walking across the street, I try the door of the firehouse, but it's locked, and I don't see any lights on inside. It's just a volunteer station. No staff. I'm sure all the Jaegers are on call when needed.

"Ah!" some cries in the distance.

I dart my head around the corner of the building, seeing the forest of trees and the long planks of wet wood creating a path over the shallow water and moss. There are houses through it—where Aracely lives—but I've never been in there.

The insects buzz, filling my ears as I start along the narrow, low bridge toward the cries. The cypresses and oaks rise high, casting the swamp in a perpetual twilight, and I keep my eyes open for alligators.

Despite all of the creatures designed to kill you in here, I move slower than I probably should. Why did I never come in here before? It's green and dark, and it smells like nothing does on my side of the tracks. Like a library with no roof.

I step off the bridge, onto the moss-covered ground that only gets mossy when the land hasn't been covered in water long enough for something to grow. The little floods will come, though.

I approach a small collection of houses, seeing stilts underneath them to keep them dry during heavy rains. The sound of dishes crashing comes from the purple one.

There are also two white houses, a green one, and a yellow one, but I start up the steps of the one with all the noise.

I stop short of knocking on the door, though. It's a Bay house. Bay business.

"Macon, please!" a woman screams. "Please, don't!"

What the hell? I pry open the screen door.

I peek inside, placing one foot over the threshold, and spots cover my vision as I adjust to the low light.

A woman I've seen around but haven't talked to yet stands in the middle of the living room sobbing, her eyes staring in the direction of the hallway to the loft, at something I can't see. A baby, less than a year old, cries in the swing, and to my right sits the kitchen. Aracely and Summer move around, one searching the cabinets, and the other doing the dishes.

I meet Aracely's eyes. "Just leave," she tells me. "We don't need help."

"Macon!" the woman screams, but for some reason she doesn't go down the hall toward him. "He can't help it! Please!"

Her cries make my stomach curdle. What the hell is going on?

Summer slams the cabinets closed. "There's nothing here."

Aracely reaches down and picks up another little boy hidden behind the counter, maybe three years old.

"He told you to buy food!" Aracely scolds the woman.

A thud and a muffled cry carry from somewhere in the back of the house, and the woman looks terrified. What is Macon doing?

I reach into the apron at my waist, taking out the baggie of cut-up grapes I prepared for Paisleigh for after school. I don't want Aracely to think I'm inserting myself, so I just set it on the counter in case she wants it.

"Please," the woman whimpers.

Someone chokes out a cough over and over again in one of the back rooms.

"You know him!" she yells. "He just needs help."

I glance at Aracely, concern etching her brow, but something else, too.

Worry.

I flex my jaw, she shakes her head at me, and I shoot off, rushing down the hallway. They're afraid to stand up to him. I don't live here.

I glance in bedrooms as I pass, finally finding Macon in the bathroom. I stop, watching as he holds a man under the shower, and I can feel the ice-cold spray that's filling the small space.

The man sputters and coughs as the water covers his face, letting in little air.

I pause, recognizing him. It's the same guy Macon had locked in the container in the woods behind the house. A bottle of Wild Turkey lies in the sink, only a couple of swallows left.

He's drinking again. Instead of using his money to take care of his family. I understood that much from what they said in the living room.

The guy coughs and vomits, spilling all over himself. Macon's knuckles are white as he holds him under the water.

I murmur, "Macon . . ."

He's not helping him. He's punishing him.

But Macon just bellows, "Aracely! Get the kids out of here!"

"Please, man," the guy spits out.

"Macon, he's hurting!" I hear his wife cry.

But Macon doesn't stop. I don't even think he knows I'm here.

Ripping the man from the shower, he drags him out of the bathroom, and I jump out of the way just in time as he shoves him down the hallway, back to the living room. The man lands on the floor, his wife falling to his side and trying to hold him.

Aracely stuffs diapers into a bag, getting ready to remove the kids from the house.

I grab Macon's arm. "Stop!" I whisper to him.

He turns his head, looking right at me, but his eyes are bright with anger.

"You can't just tell addicts to quit," I tell him quietly. "He could be a danger to himself and his kids just as much if he's not using. That shit is a symptom."

"It's the disease," he bites out, hauling the man back up off the floor.

His wife's guttural sob makes me wince.

"Not always!" I bark, my voice louder now. "It's how people cope with real fucking problems that aren't just going to go away with tough love! You can't do it like this!"

"So what do you think he needs?" he fires back. "Medicine? Therapy? Rehab?"

I don't even have to think about it to know that none of those are options for people in the Bay. These men don't talk about their problems, and rehab takes people away from their jobs when they can't afford to miss a paycheck.

My eyes flit over to Aracely, catching her shaking her head at me.

"Don't," she mouths.

"I want to die," the man says, shaking.

"Do you?" Macon replies, but it sounds more like a challenge.

His eyes gleam, and I stop breathing for a second.

In one fell swoop, he throws the man over his shoulder and takes him out the front door, the wife screaming behind him.

"Goddammit, Krisjen!" Aracely growls. "Stop him!"

My mouth drops open, and I stand there, paralyzed as Macon descends the steps and keeps walking. Why? What is he going to do?

The woman runs after Macon and her husband, and Summer grabs the baby, Aracely taking the toddler.

I shoot off, running after Macon.

He crosses the bridge pathway, and I run alongside, my shoes soaked in mud and water. "What are you doing?" I yell as he hauls the man back to the center of the Bay. "Where are you going?"

"He said he wanted to die," Macon says all too calmly. "His family is better off."

"No!" his wife begs. "You care about him. I know you do. He needs you. Please. You've always been there for him. Don't do this."

I follow in horror as Macon walks onto the main road. The Jaeger house stands tall across the street, and I spot Paisleigh still doing her homework in the garage. She doesn't seem to see us.

Macon takes the man into the small junkyard behind Mariette's, and a lump lodges in my throat as I watch him throw the guy into a car, lock the door, and grab the control from Santos standing nearby.

I shake my head, my heart racing a mile a minute. Screams fill the air as Macon presses the button and the compressor starts up, coming down on top of the car, slowly flattening it.

Men filter in, watching, but not a single person races to help him.

"Macon!" the guy cries from inside the car.

His wife only sobs quietly now.

I come to Macon's side. "Stop," I order him.

"He's a drain on my time and Bay resources."

"You can't kill him."

He doesn't reply, simply watching the crusher come down. The windows blow out, and I jump. Fuck this. I start after the guy. I have to get him out of the car.

But Macon yanks me back into him. I fight, but he holds me tightly, forcing me to watch.

I don't know what I was going to do to help the guy, but no one else is moving.

"Your pretty little ass wants to go to bed with us," Macon growls in my ear, "but you don't want to wake up with us. *This* is the Bay." He shakes me. "Fun, isn't it?"

The hammers close, flattening the car more and more, the ear-splitting screech of metal all we can hear over the man's screams. I shake, nearly in tears as the guy disappears to the floor of the car, forced down.

"People say they want to die all the time, Krisjen," Macon says. "Most don't."

His arm around my waist tightens.

"They're just tired of fighting to live. They're tired of problems. Tired of nothing ever changing . . ." He pauses, his voice softening as his chest rises against my back. "Tired of money. People. Themselves. *So* tired of themselves and being in their own heads."

I shake my head as the car gets smashed.

"Right now he's remembering the color of the wrapping paper at his fifth birthday," Macon tells me. "How good a cheeseburger tastes. How he wanted to have a store of his own someday, learn how to surf, and see some redwoods. The time he laughed so hard while watching a movie with his mom one night, how it felt to wake up to the smell of good food cooking, and how it felt to kiss a beautiful girl for the first time." His voice drifts off as if the memories are his, too. "And that one time the night air smelled like flowers, the top was down, and his song came on. The wind was a perfect temperature . . ."

A tear spills down my face. It's like he sees it. As if he's remembering it himself.

His voice is a whisper. "Right now he's remembering everything he's forgotten."

He releases me and the compressor stops, the man still crying out from inside the car.

While I exhale in relief, the men move over and rip off the door, pulling him out by his feet.

He falls onto the ground, wet with sweat and red from the panic, but otherwise uninjured.

They don't help him up, though.

Macon walks over, peels him up off the ground, and I know he's about to hit him. Or threaten him.

But that's not what happens.

He hugs him.

I see him whisper something in the man's ear as the guy cries and his wife climbs to her feet. Then he wraps his arms around Macon again, sobbing.

"Don't ever do that again," Aracely suddenly says at my side.

But I don't care. "He's a hypocrite," I bite out. "He drinks."

"Yeah." She turns to face me. "Because he cares more about their lives than he ever did his own."

# 19

## Krisjen

If Macon's way of doing things for that guy works, then everyone will believe it's right.

Knowledge, skill, talent, hard work—they help, but how much of the outcome just ends up being the luck of the draw? A fifty-fifty shot? That man could sober up, find inner peace, grow stronger . . .

He could also hurt himself. Macon is constantly playing the odds. Do any of the people here know how brittle that game is?

No.

They trust him.

They put all their security into one man because he's the reason they eat when they lose their jobs and stay in their houses when medical care takes all their paycheck.

I crane my neck under the shower spray, my hair pinned on top of my head as I let the hot water spill down my back and legs. What do I know about anything, right? I didn't grow up here, with these challenges. There's a reason he doesn't look at me or talk to me.

The shower curtain slides open, and I pop my head up, seeing Trace step into the shower with me, naked.

I go wide-eyed. "Get out!"

He pulls the curtain closed again, holding his arms out around me to feel the water.

"Trace," I grit through my teeth. "Get out!"

"I got a date," he grumbles.

"Right now!"

He pushes me aside and leans back under the water, wetting his hair. "I won't be long."

I cock an eyebrow, moving as far away from him as I can. My eyes fall to his flaccid dick. "You never are."

"Ouch."

His nonchalance as he closes his eyes and smooths back his hair under the water makes me feel . . . I don't know.

Like we're four, best friends, and our moms are bathing us together.

He starts shampooing his hair, and I grab my loofah, lathering it with soap. I hurriedly wash my arms, the back of my neck, my stomach, and my breasts, and I look up to see him watching that part. He grins, and I drop my eyes again to see he's hardening.

I turn away.

"You can look," he teases. "I know I'm bigger than Army. Iron, too."

*Whatever.*

"I am, aren't I?" he coos.

*Ugh.*

I face the other way, placing my foot on the edge of the tub and soaping my leg before doing the same with the other one. We switch places, and I rinse, taking the showerhead and washing off my back. He reaches around me to rinse off his hands.

And he stays there, at my back. "I love you, you know?" he says.

I go still.

"You were really good to me." He takes the showerhead and rinses my spine and the backs of my arms. "I loved how your face would light up and you smiled all the time, and I really needed someone to smile at me. I acted like it was nothing, but you're irreplaceable."

My heart warms, my chin trembling a little.

"I'm glad it's him," he sighs, planting a peck on my temple. "Army is good. He's not stupid enough to let you go."

I hang the loofah from a hook, and he replaces the showerhead.

I smile to myself, joking, "Well, he knew I'd be a good waitress. I bet you're glad he had the bright idea to offer me a job. Now you get to see me every day."

He chuckles, sliding open the shower curtain again.

I turn off the water.

"That was Macon, actually," he says.

I pause, and he steps out, grabbing a towel and wrapping it around his waist.

"What?" I whisper.

He nods. "Yeah, he was the one who sent Army after you that night. He told him to bring you back."

He tosses me a towel, and I catch it, but I'm staring at the floor. Why didn't Army tell me that?

"And I am so glad he always does what our big brother tells him to do."

I faintly hear him laugh, and then he's gone.

Lost in thought, I leave the bathroom in my towel, get in my pajamas, and take the pins out of my hair, letting the locks fall down my back.

I stand at the window, watching Macon outside in the darkness as he moves through the ruins of the old wing.

There are a dozen reasons why he could've wanted me here. None of them have to be because he likes me. The one thing I do know is that he's a mystery to everyone, especially to the people who know him.

I follow him from Liv's window to the one in Army's room as

he wanders, the moonlight making the overgrown weeds and palms look blue around him.

I haven't seen him since the compressor earlier today.

He stands under a rafter, on an old section of flooring made of broken clay that reveals patches of wood and cement underneath. Still and quiet, he stares off like he does all the time.

But then I notice how he cocks his head.

Like he sees something in the darkness.

I follow his gaze, but I see nothing from here. He takes a step, and then another, slow and soft, and then . . . in one quick whirl, Army rushes up with a stick or a branch and sweeps it across the ground. A snake jumps two feet from where Macon stands, and I suck in a breath, hearing Army yell, even through the glass.

"Jesus Christ, man!" he bellows at his brother. "What the fuck?"

Macon stands there.

"Macon?" Army shakes his shoulder. "You okay? What are you doing?"

Army's worried expression searches his brother's face, and I can see how hard he's breathing. I don't think Macon's pulse has changed.

I swallow hard. I can't move.

*He cares more about their lives than he ever did his own.*

The guys think I went to work. I wait in Liv's room until I see all the trucks make their way down the road, in the direction of St. Carmen, and then wait at the door with my hand on the knob.

I listen for him.

Something slams downstairs, and I feel the garage door vibrate through the house. Another door closes. Maybe the kitchen door. He probably needed a drink.

Then, there's no more noise. I wait another minute or so, confident Macon's in the garage, beginning his day's work.

Slipping out of Liv's room, I head over to his bedroom. I don't know why I tiptoe. Stopping short, I pluck a few clean, folded towels out of the hallway closet. If he catches me, I'll just tell him I was stocking his bathroom.

Stepping into his room, I quickly close the door behind me. And I look around, feeling immediately stupid.

Am I really afraid he's going to do something to himself? I could be way off. His brothers don't seem worried enough to intervene, and they've known him a lot longer.

But his mother suffered from depression, and it can be hereditary.

If I'm right, what then? He won't accept help.

I look around, knowing the signs won't be obvious. There won't be a pile of crumbled-up drafts of a suicide note, but I am looking for signs that he's drinking and hiding it. *Empty liquor bottles. Pills. Drugs.*

My throat tightens. *Or objects to cause himself harm.* I've never seen deadly weapons in the house, though.

I look in his bathroom first, seeing clothes on the floor and a pile of towels. I inspect them for blood, and then I check his sink and shower, looking for anything that raises alarm.

Heading into his bedroom, I find unmarked boxes on the top shelf of his closet. I reach up to look inside one, finding it full of pictures. I smile a little, immediately recognizing the Jaegers long before I knew them. A very young Army, his arm around Macon, who's dressed in camouflage pants and a T-shirt, his hair so short.

More pics of the family, but I force myself to put the lid back on and stack it back on the shelf. I'm only invading his privacy for his safety.

I open his dresser drawers, feeling around just enough for

anything hidden, and then look under the bed and pillows. I whip open the drawer of his bedside table, spotting some money, a watch, and a . . .

My heart pumps hard, seeing it and knowing what it is without even pulling the drawer all the way out. I reach in and take the handgun by the grip, holding it up.

My hand shakes, looking down at it and curling my finger around the trigger but not pressing. I don't even know how to check for bullets, much less take them out. I swallow hard.

This is the Bay. I guess I should've known they'd have weapons. It's not uncalled for and no reason to worry. Especially given how many people Macon pisses off. I would probably think it odd if he didn't have one. Careless, even.

And also, he was in the Marines. He was trained how to use it. I don't think they're allowed to keep their service weapons, but it's entirely possible he's had his own for years.

But the mess in the room . . .

I look around at all the clothes, the shit piled on his dresser. Macon's not like this.

Keeping the gun in my hand, I close the drawer and turn to walk out, but I see the rafter in the corner of the room, posted between the two walls. A small, thin groove dents the wood, the color stain worn away to reveal the natural tone underneath. That's where the rope was. From his mom.

I flex my jaw. My God, why does he sleep in here? I run from the room, scanning the hallway as I dash into Liv's room and stash the weapon in the back of her closet.

But I pause, my hand still wrapped around the grip. What if the gun really is for self-defense? Should I be hiding it? What if he needs it?

I hide it anyway, just for now. Just a day or two until I know he's okay.

I put the towels back where I got them and head downstairs. I don't bother getting dressed, still in my sleep shorts and T-shirt as I enter the kitchen.

Breathing in and out, I force my heart rate to slow down, and lift the window to my left. I draw in the fresh air. The curtains blow, and I push the images from my mind, and all the questions I can't answer, or that he won't answer if I ask. He sleeps in that room where she did it. He sees that rafter every day.

I open all the windows downstairs, letting in the warm breeze and the smell of the trees as I put on some music. "Take the World" plays on low volume. Moving around the house, I decide to pitch in on a few things, not really because I want to but because it'll give me an excuse to be in the house.

Like throwing out the slimy green onions in the fridge.

But then I find expired milk, green sausage (that's not green because it contains spinach), and three opened bottles of ketchup that should be bled into one. Before I know it, I'm tearing the whole refrigerator apart and cleaning it. Then I move on to the freezer and toss out the expired food in the pantry.

I arrange an extra disposal can for recycling, which they've just started to take part in. I'll break that news to them tonight. Then I vacuum out all the spilled rice from the kitchen drawers and cabinets.

I find some candles and set them around, lighting them, because candle flames are pretty, and then I start an early dinner to simmer on the stove before I finish the dishes.

I'm not sure how much time passes, but I finally finish up by starting the dishwasher and hand-washing the pan from breakfast when the door to the garage swings open. Macon steps in, stopping when he sees me.

He stares, and my eyes drop momentarily to his sweaty chest and olive skin, and the way his jeans hang off his hips with no belt. He's losing weight. I jerk my gaze back down to the pan in the sink.

"What are you doing?" he asks. "Why aren't you at work?"

There's a bite to his tone, but not like when he's talking to his brothers. More like he's just unpleasantly surprised.

"I, um . . ." My vision fogs as my heartbeat picks up pace again. "I just wanted a quiet day." I meet his eyes. "Aracely's sister is filling in for me."

He pinches his brows together, looking down at the dishes. "You're cleaning."

Now his tone sounds like he's confused.

"Well, I *can* do it," I joke. "When I want to."

He gives me a look, and I swear, there's almost a smile there.

He's in and out several times over the next couple of hours, getting something to drink, washing his hands, pulling his phone off the charger.

I clean the living room and get started on the floors, lifting the corner of the couch to roll up the area rug and take it outside.

I heave it up, but I'll never get it on my shoulders. Dragging it across the floor, I stop short when I realize someone is pulling it. Looking back, I see Macon lift up one end and put it on top of his right shoulder, and I do the same with my end. "Thanks."

We take it outside, hanging it on the fence to air out, and I go back in to sweep and mop.

He goes upstairs, and I start sweating the moment he goes into his room. He's going to notice his gun missing.

I think every muscle in my body is tensed for ten whole minutes as I wait for my head to roll from his wrath.

But when he comes back down, his hair is wet from the shower, and he's wearing clean jeans, not even making eye contact with me.

I exhale.

I empty the dust pan into the garbage, and he walks to the stove, lifting the lid of the pot.

He inspects it for a moment, finally asking, "What are you cooking?"

Well, if he can't tell, that's not a good sign.

"I found it in a box of recipes." I set the dustpan down and grab the notecard, showing it to him. "Ropa vieja." I try again, properly. "Ropa . . . vieja?"

He eyes the card, a look passing behind his eyes, and then lifts the spoon.

"Pork?" he asks, studying the ingredients.

I nod.

"My mother used beef."

"Oh." I read the card again as he takes a taste. "It said any meat was fine."

"It is."

I watch him replace the spoon and lid, telling him, "It probably needs more salt. I've noticed I have blander taste buds than *everyone* else on this side of the tracks."

"It's not bad," he mumbles, turning to the fridge. "If they want more salt, they can add it themselves."

He grabs a soda and sets it on the counter, turning to me. I jump when he takes my face in his hands, and I watch him with wide eyes as he comes in close. But then he turns my face side to side, and I realize he's checking my bruises. "If this ever happens again, I'm going to make an assumption about who was responsible and deal with it, you understand?"

So, if I don't tell him, he'll guess. I don't want them risking anything for my sake.

I pull away and grab a plate, doling out rice and stew, handing it to Macon.

But he shakes his head. "I'm not hungry."

He grabs his soda, moving for the garage door, and I sit down with the plate, grabbing a fork out of the basket to eat by myself.

The next thing I know, he slams the door and walks to the stove, making himself a plate.

I smile to myself. He sits at the head of the table, and I look down from the foot, watching him as he eats.

He takes up the whole room. The whole house. I've seen him angry. I've seen him quiet. I've never seen him happy. Or in love. Or scared.

Where does he hide it?

He bleeds apathy. Dispassion. Indifference. Control. Nothing else gets out. No wonder he's sick.

"What?"

I shift in my seat, realizing I'm still staring. He doesn't look at me as he chews, but he knows I'm watching him.

I stick my finger in my dish and lick it, tasting the gravy. "I remember hearing about you as a kid," I start to tell him. "A man over here hit his wife, and you forced his hand into the spinning wheel of a motorcycle. Is that true?"

He doesn't reply. Or look at me.

The house sounds peaceful for once. Quiet.

I breathe slowly. "You and Army sold drugs in order to pay the bills after your parents died?" I repeat another story I heard.

Still, nothing.

"You keep the alligators well fed?"

His mouth twitches, and I see it. The smile as he stares at his food, taking another bite.

A shot of pride hits me.

I continue. "In the tall grass field just before the bay, overlooking Del Mia Island, you allow duels," I press on with another rumor.

He shakes his head, amused.

I dip my fork in and out of my dish. "There's treasure concealed in some of the graves at Santa Maria Cemetery."

Still no comment.

"You cut yourself and make people drink your blood to prove their loyalty," I tell him.

His chest shakes. I think it's a laugh, but not a sound escapes. He takes another bite.

"You have a harem of wives?" I question.

He cocks a brow, and I can feel the eye roll even though he doesn't let it out.

"And every girl," I tell him, "on her eighteenth birthday, has to be submitted to you for first refusal."

"Jesus fucking Christ . . ." he whispers to himself.

"And they also say you secretly own parts of St. Carmen."

Finally, he looks at me. "Like real estate?"

"Like people. Some of the children are yours, they say. You have a plan to breed us out."

He can't stop himself. He laughs, bowing his head, still holding his fork. Then he looks at me, disbelieving. "What the fuck?" He scoops up another bite. "I sound like the devil."

I'm glad he's smiling. I'm sure he was aware of some of what people say about him, and he was probably never offended by it. Macon knows people are stupid. He always knows that when you make yourself rarely accessible, they'll make up stories about you. That worked in his favor. An air of mystery feeds fear, and fear is power.

I fill my fork. "No matter what I heard, I never thought you were a monster," I say. "It's nice for Clay to have a father willing to pay whatever it takes to protect her, but I was always fascinated with Liv, having you willing to do anything to feed her. Without even meeting you, I knew you'd bleed for her."

He looks at me, and a nerve shoots from my heart down to my stomach.

"And I only ever believed the first three things," I tell him, smiling.

He grabs the salt and douses his dish with it. "Just keep your ass out of the cemetery, okay?"

I laugh, seeing his half smile and light eyes. Lighter than I've ever seen them.

And I know then and there that I won't give this family up until I know that someone is loving him. Until he's in her arms.

# 20

## Krisjen

I brush my teeth, rubbing the steam off the mirror. The shower runs, and I'm running late. I quickly spit toothpaste into the sink, and then brush some more. A hickey colors the skin just above my collarbone, and my tank top is stretched out from Army's hands underneath it. I smile to myself as I spit again. It's nice to be with someone who's kind. Affectionate in public. Gentle.

Trace stumbles through the door, his eyes half-hooded, and his dark hair sticking up in every direction. He flips up the toilet seat, his abs flexing as he fumbles with his zipper and starts pissing right in front of me.

I stop brushing mid-stroke. "Seriously?"

He opens one eye, peering over at me. "Nothing you haven't seen before," he mumbles.

Ugh. I spit. "Bet you say that to all the girls."

Dallas chuckles, walking in and grabbing his toothbrush. Squeezing on some toothpaste, he scrubs his teeth next to me, both of us alternating using the faucet and rinsing out our mouths.

I set my toothbrush in the cup. "I have to get the kids to school."

"Already covered," Trace says, fastening his jeans and flushing. He squeezes the back of my neck in some kind of endearing little hug without washing his damn hands.

"Are you sure?" I ask him.

"Don't worry about it."

He's heading into St. Carmen anyway, I guess.

"Thank you," I call out as he leaves, stretching his arms over his head and yawning.

"I'll be back for dinner," Dallas says, sticking his toothbrush in the cup. "Can you make that sandwich I like?"

"I'll tell Mariette." I twist off the cap of the mouthwash. "I'll be out."

"Where are you going?"

But I take a swig right out of the bottle before I can answer.

The shower shuts off as I swish, and the curtain flies open. Macon fastens a towel around his waist.

I glance over, only long enough for the mouthwash to dribble out of my mouth a little. The cuts of the muscles in his arms and shoulders glide in smooth lines, and his long torso, narrow waist, and tawny skin are a couple of shades darker than mine. His dark wet hair drapes to a point between his eyes and down his nose, and his eyebrows make him look amazing when he's angry. I kind of want to piss him off right now.

I'm not sure why he's not using his own shower, but I'm not complaining.

"Get out," he says, stepping out of the tub.

Dallas wipes off his mouth and throws down the towel as he goes. I whip around to spit out the mouthwash and follow him, but Macon takes my arm and pulls me back before I have a chance. "Not you."

He takes my face in his hands, inspecting the cuts and bruises as I stand there wide-eyed, my mouth ballooning with mouthwash that's starting to burn my tongue.

He turns me side to side. "It's healing."

I nod.

But then he says, "You didn't put ointment on last night."

Like he instructed me to . . .

How the hell can he tell?

Spinning around, I dive down and spit out the mouthwash, wiping off my mouth. "Do you want a smoothie?" I ask him.

I see the shape of him through the steam on the mirror as he hovers at my back. "No," he says.

I don't move, watching him as he stands there, nearly a head taller. He doesn't tell me to move—or leave—and I go still as he cocks his head, the heat of his body so close it warms me.

Something vibrates under my skin, and I want to feel something that's not gentle or kind, and all of it hidden away in a dark room.

"Where's Army?" Macon whispers.

His breath sends tingles across my neck. He knows Army is still asleep.

"Get his fucking ass up," he tells me.

And then he leaves.

*These goddamn men . . .*

I never realized how my school skirt chafed my thighs until I left high school. I run my hands over the pleats and tuck in the black Polo shirt of my old school uniform as I hike up the driveway of Fox Hill.

Kent Sharpe, the security guard, steps out of his guardhouse.

"Hey," I chirp.

"Hi, hon." He pulls the toothpick out of his mouth. "All your classmates already left for the day."

He doesn't know I already graduated.

"Oh, I know." I pass him, turning to maintain eye contact as I walk backward. "I forgot my phone on the patio."

"Uh-oh."

"Exactly," I state. "Do you mind if I . . ."

"Of course not." He waves me off. "Talk to the host, and he'll take you back."

"Thanks."

Spinning around, I keep walking, super glad he didn't ask why I'm not driving. I left my car parked along the highway. I don't want it seen up here.

Crickets buzz beyond the green, in the trees, and a few frogs croak at a nearby pond. I love my town at night. So many nocturnal creatures, and they're loud. A reminder that a whole other party starts after the sun sets.

I glance to my right, seeing my father's Bentley Continental, the windshield all repaired, and face forward again. I smile at Rafe as he opens the door to the clubhouse for me. His eyes take in my uniform. He doesn't ask questions.

Stepping inside, I keep my eyes forward and head straight for the stairs. I try to look like I know where I'm going and what I'm doing, but not so fast that I look like I'm trying to hide it.

I swing around the newel post and head behind the stairs, not up them.

"Still here?" someone calls out.

I look over my shoulder, seeing Louis Fine, the host who works the restaurant, as he crosses the foyer into the bar.

I turn back around and keep going. "A few of us, yeah!"

"Good kids," he coos. "Working hard."

I keep going, rounding a corner and disappearing from view as I walk down a long hallway. Marymount Academy, my alma mater, schedules three service days a year as part of our civic credit requirement for graduation. We pick up a little trash off the streets, or mow an elderly person's lawn, or walk some sick people's dogs, so our parents and teachers can take pictures and say, "Look what good humans we're putting into the world."

But basically it amounts to a day off school where you half-ass it, hang out with your friends, and then cut out early when no one is looking to go party at someone's pool.

Except me. I was a little shit about a lot things in high school, but I liked service days. No one wanted to go to the assisted living centers, because the old people always wanted to talk to you, but I love to talk.

A lot of students opt for spending the day at Fox Hill, though. There are always famous pros around, lots of hiding places, and the food is excellent. If you're lucky, you get a cart girl willing to serve you if you tip right. It looks like all the current Marymount students have already left after their service day today, so I won't run into anyone calling me out, but . . . it's also why no one working here is batting an eyelash that a uniformed minor is walking around alone.

I open a door and step through, closing it behind me. I walk past three racquetball courts on my right, the rubber balls like thunder as they bang against the walls.

Without a hitch in my step, I slip through another door, then down a hallway, and quietly twist the handle of the last door on the left.

I peer inside.

Rows of long and short lockers rise high in the room, towels strewn on the counters and on the floor, because rich men do not pick up after themselves. The women's locker room is much cleaner.

A shower runs in the back, but at this hour, I don't see anyone walking around. I slink in, closing the door behind me.

Stepping between two benches, I slide down a row, my back to the lockers as I come to the end of the aisle. Waiting, I slowly peek around the corner, but I don't see anyone, so I hurry on to the next row. Stopping at 17-b, I punch in the code. *One-two-seven-eight-key.* Same code my father uses for his debit cards, the auto start on his cars, and—I open the locker and smile, seeing what I'm after—his cell phone. Snatching it, I close the door, cross the aisle, and hide away in a bathroom stall.

Quickly, I pull out my phone, turn off the volume, and slip it back in my skirt before opening up my dad's cell. Going to texts first, I see a thread from Blake Tyson, his girlfriend, and scroll through messages until I reach those dated last year.

While he was still living at home.

Florida is a no-fault state, and I'm sure my mother was unfaithful many times, so I'm not sure I'll use this, but just in case. Proving infidelity could guarantee custody of the kids and alimony.

I start screenshotting and texting to my phone, feeling it buzz with every notification in my pocket. I see emails from his lawyer, but I bypass those, spotting bank statements instead. I don't look. I don't have time. I forward documents to myself, careful to delete any record of the texts and emails, as well as the screenshots.

Peering out into the locker room, I stuff his phone back with the rest of his stuff and close the locker up.

I blow out a breath, sweat covering my back. I'm not sure that I'm nervous. What's he going to do if he finds me? But I don't want him to know what I'm up to and give him a chance to cover his tracks.

I start to walk out, but I stop and look down in the direction of the shower where he's no doubt washing off his Wednesday night racquetball game before he goes home to her.

For a while after he split, I thought he wasn't seeing us because he was in Atlanta. Settling into his new office. New house.

Then I found out he never left town.

He must've known I'd see him eventually. He didn't even try to prepare me. As if my reaction wouldn't faze him.

As if I no longer mattered.

That's how quickly things can change.

It's amazing how people smile at you and kiss you on the forehead and they never wanted to be there. I can't say much surprises me anymore.

At least now I know a little more about myself because of my parents' actions. I will be fierce about my family someday.

I slip through the door to the racquetball court and make my way for the clubhouse entrance again.

Clay's dad shakes off his long coat, letting the host take it while his dinner party laughs and moves into the dining room ahead of him. My father cheated on my mother, and I can't stand him. Clay's dad cheated on her mom, and still, I don't think he's a bad guy. The tragedy they endured—the loss of Clay's little brother—is something I hope never to experience, and I wouldn't have the audacity to judge.

I pluck a stuffed mushroom off the tray heading in after them and lock eyes with my best friend's dad, smiling. "Thanks for defending my honor, Mr. Collins."

And I pop the mushroom into my mouth, not stopping to chat as he turns toward me.

My own dad is undoubtedly aware that Jerome Watson is circulating a picture of me. I don't think he punched him like Mr. Collins did.

I hurry down the driveway, but someone grabs my hand. "What are you doing here?" Army asks.

I spin around, but he presses his finger to my lips before I can speak.

He pulls me across the green, around the clubhouse, to an unmarked door underneath the patio porch overhead.

I know the door.

The Wolfe Room.

He yanks me inside, and we head down a nearly pitch-black stairwell.

I step into a room, seeing Dallas and Trace standing next to a table full of beer bottles.

Army releases me. "Why are you here?" he asks again.

Why shouldn't I be?

Instead, I ask, "Why are you here?"

"We work here, remember?"

Trace and Dallas remain quiet.

They shouldn't be in here. Not in this room. I've never even been in here before. I glance around, taking note of a few leather chairs and some nice landscape art on the walls.

But very dark and moody. And very little to do. From what I can see anyway. No TV, no bar, not even bookshelves. As if the entertainment is brought in. I look up, seeing several compartments in the roof. I drop my eyes, shifting in my Converse.

"I had something to do," I finally admit.

I've been here a hundred times. Did they forget I'm from St. Carmen?

Army approaches me. "Why are you keeping secrets?"

"It's fun." I grin. "I'm feeling very Harley Quinn. I just completed a covert operation all by myself."

"There's nothing covert about Harley Quinn."

True. "How about I just did something naughty?"

"And didn't get caught?" he presses. "Catwoman."

"Eh." I fold my arms over my chest. "I don't look good in black."

It completely washes me out.

"Is this going to come back and bite us in the ass?" Army looks ready to scold me.

I shake my head. "If it bites anyone's ass, it'll be mine."

He steps up to me, looking down into my eyes like I'm so adorable.

"My father is here," I tell him. "I broke into his locker and texted myself screenshots from his phone. His email, his credit card charges, his texts . . ."

"Did you erase the screenshots you took?"

"Yes."

"And emptied the trash?" Dallas chimes in.

"I'm not an idiot."

"Did you erase the texts you sent yourself?" Trace questions.

I widen my eyes in shock, covering my mouth with my hand.

When Trace cocks his head and opens his mouth, ready to chastise me, I drop my hand and scowl. "Yes, you moron."

I'm a child of the digital age.

Army blinks his long eyelashes over those beautiful eyes. "You did it for your mother."

I shrug. "My mom is my mom, but she deserves her cut. And so do my siblings."

"And you?"

I don't reply.

I guess I could squeeze my college fund back out of my father, but I didn't think about it. I'm not sure I can demand anything yet. I need to study the information I just got.

But Trace steps closer. "She has us," he tells his brother.

"And we have her," Dallas adds.

They both move closer, standing with Army, and the room suddenly feels a lot smaller.

I turn around and grab the door handle, but a hand covers mine on the knob. I stare at the leather straps around his right wrist.

"I want her," I hear Dallas say behind me. "It's my turn."

I freeze.

"Dallas, that's enough," Army tells him.

I turn around and move away from Dallas, toward the other side of the room.

He pulls off his T-shirt and tosses it aside.

I shake my head. "Knock it off."

But before I know what's happening, he catches me in his arms.

Not roughly, though. The hold is soft, gentle.

The pinch between his brows makes his eyes look pained, his green darker than Army's. Like camouflage.

"Dallas, let her go," Army bites out.

But Dallas's eyes don't leave mine. "I want her."

He doesn't.

He wants to feel powerful.

He wants his turn, because he thinks I didn't care who Iron was. Or who Trace or Army are.

But he whispers, so only I can hear. "Stay with us."

The hair on the back of my neck rises.

He brushes his thumb across my cheek, bringing it up to look at it, and I see a thin drop of blood from the cut on my face. He sticks it in his mouth, and my mouth falls open long enough for him to grab the back of my hair and cover my lips with his.

My growl is muffled in his mouth, and I shove at his chest, but he doesn't budge. Lifting me by the backs of my thighs, he hefts me up.

"Let's take you back to your house," he says. "We'll take care of you, and you take care of us."

"Dallas . . ."

I think it was Trace that time, but I'm too stunned to concentrate.

What the hell is Dallas doing? What does . . .

And then I realize.

*You take care of us*, he said.

"You want pictures of me?" I ask.

He smiles, Army and Trace slowly moving in.

"For a start," Dallas says.

"No," Trace tells him.

Followed by Army. "Enough. Let's go."

"Let her make her own decisions," Dallas snaps.

I barely breathe.

I've been with Army and Trace already. *Why not help them in the one way I can?*

That's what Dallas is thinking anyway.

He'd humiliate me as a means to an end.

But for some reason, I haven't said no yet. I know Dallas isn't asking me to do anything he wouldn't be willing to do himself.

He would do it.

"Will it help?" I ask quietly. "Will a Conroy on camera get you what you want?"

He lowers me to my feet, takes out his phone, and tosses it to one of his brothers, but I don't see who.

He touches my face. "We'll forget the camera is even there. I promise."

He drops down in front of me, holding my eyes as he starts to slide his hands up my skirt.

I reach down and grab his hands, but I don't pull them off.

"Start the camera, Trace," he says. And then to his other brother, "Army, take off her shirt."

Oh my God.

I can't get enough air. I'm suffocating.

Army moves, Dallas starts to slide my underwear down, and I suck in a breath and freeze.

*Shit.*

I start to push him away, but then . . . a throat clears loudly, and I dart my eyes up.

Santos stands in the open doorway, so big he takes up the entire frame.

I suck in a breath, yanking away from Dallas and fixing my underwear.

*What the hell? What was I doing?*

Trace and Army twist around, and Dallas stands up tall. I adjust my clothes, pushing hair out of my face that fell from my ponytail.

"Santos?" Army blurts out. "What the hell are you doing here?"

I swallow through my parched mouth, my face hot.

"Macon says to bring her home," Santos says.

Army moves forward. "What?"

"How did . . . ?" Dallas starts but stops.

Then . . . they all glance at the corner of the room behind them. I follow their gaze, not seeing anything.

But as I step to the side, the light from a lamp catches a small piece of glass on the corner, near the ceiling, above a deer antler.

A lens. Army had said they have cameras here.

My chin trembles. Macon just saw all of that?

"How did you get here so fast?" Army asks him.

Santos looks down at his shoes, deliberately not answering.

Army laughs bitterly, shaking his head.

"What?" I ask him. What's so funny?

"He has a guard on you," Army tells me.

What?

I gape at Santos, not remembering if I've seen him anywhere near me other than the restaurant. Why would Macon have a guard following me?

"Since when?" I ask Santos.

"Since you got jumped at the Bug Jam."

Jesus.

Well, that explains how he got to us so fast. He was already here. All Macon had to do was call him.

"We'll take her home," Army says, taking my hand.

But when we move toward the door, Santos doesn't move out of the way.

"To the Bay," he commands Army. "He wants her home now."

"That's not her home."

"To the Bay," Santos repeats.

Army squeezes my hand like he's gauging whether the three of them can take Santos.

I look up at Army. "He doesn't want this," I say. "Which means he wouldn't use it."

Even if I went through with it.

I pry my hand out of his and step forward. "I'm going home," I tell the guy. "To my house."

"Macon says to bring you to him."

And then he sweeps me up, knocking the wind out of me as he throws me over his shoulder like a wet sheet.

I scream. "Are you kidding me?"

"Motherfucker," Army bites out.

But no one tries to stop him, Dallas and Trace saying absolutely nothing as I'm carted toward the field house where their trucks are parked.

We pull up in front of the house, all the windows dark and the garage door closed. The boys jump out of the truck, and I step out of my mom's Rover, Santos in my driver's seat. He didn't trust me to drive here, and even though I bitched a little, he was right not to. There's no way in hell I actually want to look in Macon's eyes right now.

We walk through the front door, the shutter hanging above flapping against the house in the wind as Trace and Dallas scan left and right, because they're just as nervous as I am. We turn into the living room and see Macon sitting in the chair, a stream of smoke from a cigarette rising from his fingers.

Army steps forward. "Macon—"

"Leave her here" is all he says.

I look to Trace, and he darts forward. "Macon—"

"Get the fuck out of my sight."

I can't swallow. *Shit.*

An image of the container he keeps out back flashes in my head.

I look to Army, frozen for a second, but then I nod. *I'll be okay.*

Army hesitates, but he backs away. Dallas and Trace follow him up the stairs.

Snuffing out his cigarette, Macon rises and approaches me. His black pants hang too low, his arms looking like dead weights.

I back up. "Don't hurt me."

He stops in front of me, the glare in his eyes making the brown look a little red.

But still, he says nothing. Like he doesn't want to talk at all. He wants to strangle me.

My voice is barely above a whisper as I stare at his stomach, not really seeing it, though. "I wasn't going to do it," I say. "I just knew it would solve everything."

"And when your little brother and sister see what you did?"

I jerk my eyes up. "They would never have known," I state. "My grandfather would never have let that video see the light of day."

He cocks his head, the pinch between his brows replaced with condescension. "You are the stupidest person I've ever met."

What does that mean?

"I wasn't going to do it," I tell him.

He pulls his phone out of his pocket and taps a few times before my own phone dings with a notification. I reach inside my skirt, pulling it out. Opening the notification, I play the video he sent.

His brother starts to remove my clothes in the back seat of that cop car on Thanksgiving, Army's teeth tugging at my mouth as my hands stay cuffed to the handle above the door.

The window shutter outside slams against the house hard, and I jump, about to cry. Macon watched this?

The fucking dash cam. I thought they turned it off.

He must've gotten the footage from the cops. Why? To protect me?

He's already had a video of me for days.

"Why haven't you used this?" I ask.

But he doesn't reply.

I clench my jaw with realization. *He watched this.*

My chin trembles. "What if I'm not strong enough?" I ask quietly but don't expect him to answer. "What if I give up and go home for Mars and Paisleigh? Jerome Watson is willing to pay a lot for me. What if . . ."

But I can't continue.

Jerome Watson is promising a nice house and nice clothes and nice servants, and my family can keep living how they're used to. What if I give in?

I try to find my words. "I thought . . . for a minute maybe it would be a good idea to use the only thing I have if it would win the Bay for you before I go. Before I let someone I hate do those things to me for the rest of my life just for lousy money."

People screw all the time, every day. For worse reasons. I wasn't in love with Trace or Iron. I don't think I love Army yet. No one was going to get hurt.

But I wouldn't have done it. I know that. I would've stopped if Santos hadn't come in. I didn't want it, and it would've changed the way I felt about the brothers. And the Bay.

Macon walks back to his chair, falling into it, his arms draped over the armrests.

I look at him, his eyes on the floor, deflated. No longer angry. I go to him and drop to the floor at his feet, sitting between his legs.

When he doesn't move or push me away, I lay my head against his knee, feeling his hand come down on my hair.

I close my eyes, an electric current running through my chest.

"I'll never do anything like that," I tell him. "I promise."

"If you do . . ." He strokes my hair. "I'm going to lock you in your room."

A smile spreads across my face as tears spring to my eyes. I wrap my arms around his leg, and I don't know if I'm happy he doesn't want to see me do those things to help his family, or how he just insinuated Liv's old room is now mine. I don't know what I am to him, but I know he's keeping me.

His hand shakes in my hair, and I hold him tighter, but he pulls away. "I need sleep," he says. "I wish I could sleep."

I look up at him, watching as he rubs his eyes. He looks so tired.

"That fucking shutter, Krisjen." He breathes out, and I realize it's still blowing in the wind outside. "Just go." His voice is strained. "Go to bed."

"I don't want to go."

"Now."

"Please just let me stay for a little while," I whisper.

"Krisjen . . ."

"I just want to be near you."

"Now!" he barks.

I startle and hurry to my feet. I want to stay. Nothing will happen, I just don't want to leave him alone.

I want to be where he is.

But I'm not someone he needs. I can't even get my own act together.

The Jaegers will be fine. They survived—flourished—long before me.

And they'll still be here long after.

# 21

## Krisjen

The next morning, I don't think Macon has gotten any sleep.

"Macon!" Dallas yells. "I need a shower! Come on!"

I stop, hearing the commotion inside Macon's bedroom. Dallas stands to the right, dressed only in a gray towel as he bangs on his brother's closed bathroom door. Army slips in around me, heading toward him. "Macon!" he calls out.

"What the hell is he doing?" Dallas gripes.

Army pounds his fist on the door three times. "Macon! Answer me!"

But there's no reply.

I drop my work apron on the floor and enter the room, hearing the shower inside. "How long's he been in there?" I ask.

"The shower's been running since I got up." Dallas pounds on the door again. "At least an hour."

"Macon!" Army joins him, knocking hard.

My stomach coils. I jet over to his closet, rip a shirt off a wire hanger, and straighten the hook at the end, pushing the guys aside.

If everything was fine, Macon would've answered. Goddammit. I knew he didn't sound right last night. When's the last time I saw him eat?

"Use the other bathroom," I tell Dallas.

"Trace and some girl are in there."

"Then use the downstairs one!"

"But it doesn't have a shower . . ."

"Just . . ." I bite out, giving him a look.

And I don't need to say more. He twists his lips to the side and spins around, pouting his way out of the bedroom.

"Macon!" Army shouts again.

I fit the end of the wire hanger in the little hole, feeling for the pin, and I push. The handle twists, giving way, and I open the door, immediately seeing him.

"Get out!" he yells.

Army stands behind me, but he doesn't try to push past to see.

Macon sits in the claw-foot tub, his back against the wall and his legs bent up with his arms hanging over his knees. His head is down as the spray pours over his body, a stream gliding down his nose.

I close the door, Army stumbling back a few steps.

I look at him. "Go to work."

"But—"

"I'll be here," I tell him. "I'll call if something's wrong."

"Krisjen—"

"He won't want you here."

He won't want me, either, but I'm not family. It's different. He cares what they think.

Army's next words are lost as he stares at me, his eyes filled with pain. I can't tell if I hurt his feelings, or if he's just worried, but he's smart enough to know Macon won't want anyone to see him like this. Especially another man.

Army struggles for a minute, trying to decide what's right. He was twenty when his mother took her life. He knows something is wrong.

He takes my face, kissing my forehead. "I'll get the kids to school."

"Thanks."

He leaves, and I slip inside the bathroom, closing the door and locking it before heading over to the tub.

Water spills off Macon's forehead and mouth as he bows his head, and I lean close to his lips, trying to smell if there's alcohol.

But he jerks away as if suddenly realizing I'm there. "Don't."

I press a hand to the back of his neck and then to his forehead, both burning under the hot water.

"Stop," he growls, pulling away from me and leaning back against the tile. "Just leave. Get out."

I turn the faucet, making it a little cooler.

"I said get out!" he shouts up at me.

I startle.

He clutches his head in his hands. "Please. Get the fuck out."

My eyes pool with tears, and I clench my teeth to keep them from falling. I don't know how to help him.

I look up at the blinds drawn over what little light streams in through the small window near the ceiling.

And the lights are off.

The same way his room is always dark now, and how he only ever wants to be alone.

I don't think it's to shield him from the world, because if it were, then it would be helping. It's to pretend that he doesn't exist.

If no one sees him, he's not really here. Not alive.

It's how he's fantasizing death.

I reach out, touching the side of his head, my fingers on his hair.

But he shoves my hand away, and I gasp as he bites his words at me. "Get out!"

And then he slams the back of his head into the wall, and I cry out, grabbing him before he can do it again. I climb into the tub, crouch over his lap, and wrap my arms around him, my hand at the back of his head.

He wrestles, trying to shake me off, but I just hold him, burying my face in his neck.

"I don't want anybody!" he snaps. "I just want . . . Please, I just want to be gone. I just want to be gone."

He tries to push me off, but I hold tight, trembling.

"Don't see me," he says. "Please don't see me. You have to go."

He pushes a few more times, but every time gets weaker before he finally gives up. His hands fall away, and he just shakes in my arms.

"Please . . . don't . . ." He bows his head, turning it left and right, shielding me from seeing him, but I take him and come up close to his ear, so he can hear me over the shower. I whisper, "You can let one person see you like this. Just one."

Tears stream down my face, and I reach behind me, pulling the shower curtain, closing us in, away from the world. Hard breaths rack his body, but he doesn't fight me. Molding my chest to his, I touch his face and bow my head next to his, inhaling and exhaling. Over and over until I feel his chest rise with mine and both of ours fall in sync.

"One person," I breathe out.

His body slowly calms, and I run my thumb over his face as I hold it, feeling the difference between hot water and warm tears.

His stares at his stomach. "Don't make me leave here."

Water spills down my face. He can stay here forever if he wants.

"Keep me with you" is my own only request.

I sit on him, one leg bent up and my foot planted on the bottom of the tub as I press my mouth to his temple.

He's too warm. "I need to cool you down," I tell him.

Reaching over, I twist the faucet right, adding cold water. He jerks a little but doesn't say anything.

I feel his jaw flex under my hand, and I don't know how long we sit there, but long enough for doors to slam shut downstairs. The house empties as his brothers leave for work, and the kids go to the sitter and school, and then I hear engines fade down the street.

I add more cold water and then some more.

When he speaks again, his voice is soft and quiet.

"I just want to stop sometimes, Krisjen," he tells me, still not meeting my eyes. "It wasn't always this bad, but when it is, I can't remember when it was good. I don't like it here."

I stroke his cheek with my thumb. Here as in Sanoa Bay? Or here as in life?

I don't ask. I wouldn't know what to say.

All I know is that I feel it, too, sometimes. People make life hard. Even the ones who love us bring pressure and obligation, and I'm no exception. We're all culprits of making someone else's life difficult.

But he's felt it for too long. And he feels it more than other people. Some do.

A distant knock hits a door. "Krisjen?" I hear someone call in a muffled voice. "You home?"

Aracely. I think she's knocking on Liv's bedroom door.

Macon startles. "Don't . . ." he says. "Don't let her see me."

"I locked it," I assure him.

I raise my voice. "I'm here," I tell Aracely. "I'll be out in a bit."

She's quiet, and I don't waste my time imagining what she's thinking about why my voice is coming from Macon's shower.

"No rush," she finally says, closer. "I dropped off your paycheck."

"Thanks."

After a moment, I hear the door downstairs close, and I probably should've told her to tell Mariette I was going to be late.

"Can you make it colder, please?" he asks me.

I do. I feel him draw in a big breath as I close my eyes. It's like a waterfall in my hair.

"That feels better," he says.

His shoulders relax. I climb off, sitting down next to him in the tub.

Finally, he opens his eyes again. "Don't tell them."

I want to promise him that I won't, but I'm not sure what's right. He's falling fast. What if he ends it and I regret not trying everything?

"I don't want you to leave," I say.

It's all I know for sure.

Licking the water off his lips, he looks like he's about to talk, but it takes a few seconds to say the words. "I . . ." He takes a breath. "I don't know why I feel like this. I never did." His tone grows a little stronger. "And that's what shakes you, because you don't know how to fix it."

I know there are no magic words.

"It's just this black cloud that hangs over you and follows," he tells me, and I see more tears pool in his eyes. "If you're hungry, you eat. If you're injured, you go to a doctor. If you're running late, you drive faster. I have a house, a healthy family, a little money in the bank, my own business, a means of supporting myself and those around me, so why do I feel like this? How do I stop it?"

*Tired of fighting. Tired of problems. Tired of nothing ever changing . . . Tired of money. People. Themselves.* He was talking about himself that day.

"And in those moments," he continues, "I know exactly why she couldn't hold on until Monday when she could see another doctor. She couldn't feel like that for one more second. She just wanted it to stop. She was done.

"I want a woman. I want kids," he tells me. "I see her in my head, Krisjen. My baby inside of her that will look just like her, and I know it as I look down into her eyes in the shower. I want it. I want it all."

He swallows, his head bobbing a little.

"But that's why she did it," he says. "I know now why my mother did it. She loved us too much to let us see her weak for one more minute. She stopped being there for us long before her body died, and she just couldn't stand being aware of that anymore. My woman is out there somewhere, and I'm going to let her find another man, because it will kill me when I fail her. I don't want her to see this. I don't want any of them to see this." Tears fall, and he squeezes his eyes shut, turning away. "Just go. Please just go."

I wipe the water from my eyes. I won't say anything to Army or the others. Yet. He's talking, and that's more than he was doing fifteen minutes ago.

"My maternal grandmother killed herself, too," I tell him. "Pills. Around the same time your mom did, now that I think of it."

That's when things started going downhill with my mom and my parents' marriage.

"I was only ten, so I don't remember much," I say, "but what I do remember is that the family was close before she did it. My mother and her siblings saw each other all the time, spent holidays together, their children—my cousins—were all best friends. We were a family."

He breathes normally now, the cool water hopefully helping.

"We've rarely seen each other since," I tell him. "As heartbroken as she was, and desperate to be at peace from what she was going through, she was the glue. Maybe she thought the same thing you did—what your mom did—that she was saving all of us the pain. Saving us from dealing with her. Saving us the heartache of her heartache, but . . . her life was more important than she knew." I don't cry about it anymore, but it's hard not to imagine what life would be like—what my mom would be like—if my grandmother knew how much she was loved. "Our family fell apart after she was gone. She wasn't a burden or weak. She was so important to us."

I look over at him. "No one can tell you that you have to stay." I can't help the tears that fall. "No one knows how it feels, and you're not alive just to save everyone else from themselves."

It takes a minute to calm myself, because I want to tell him that he has to stay. *What will we do without you? You have to take care of them.*

That's all that's kept him here this far, and it's not working anymore.

All I can say is what I know for sure. "There will be hard days, Macon. There will be more days like this. When it really hurts to stand up. To face people."

I want to touch him—his hand, something—but I hold back.

"But there will be days that no one can touch," I whisper. "There will be days when you'll be the strongest one in the room, and they wouldn't have made it through without you. There will be kids and road trips and hunkering down for hurricanes with our beer and movies and food fights and babies and ice cream in coffee cups."

His head turns just a little, and I can see his eyes.

"And early mornings in warm beds," I say, "when the rain and wind chimes are going and you're holding her, and these feelings right now are so far away and you can't stop kissing her. You'll love being alive."

His eyes close, like it's a memory and she's real and he wants her.

I hold the inside of his elbow, and finally, he looks down at me. His brown eyes shimmer, the whites now red, but God, he looks younger than Trace in this moment.

"I hate you seeing me like this," he says barely above a whisper.

I give him a half smile and tell him again, "You can let one person see you like this." And I rest my cheek against his shoulder. "I have a steel stomach."

Time passes, the tiny bit of sunlight in the room moves across the floor, and I get him out of the shower and into some jeans. I block out light, turn on a fan to drown out noise, and change into one of his T-shirts and a pair of his sweatpants before lying on the bed with him. Hugging the pillow to my body, I face him and he faces me, and I watch him long after he falls asleep. The guys come home, kids' laughter drifts up the stairs and through the door along with the smell of pizza, and I want him to eat, but I'm not going to wake him up. He needs to sleep for a week.

Water runs, bath time, kids in bed, no one disturbs Macon's room, and I wake again, turning over to see that it's after eleven at night. The house is quiet. I lean in close, the warmth of his body lighting a buzz under my skin. He sleeps, and I climb out of bed as gently as possible, leaving the room.

Downstairs, I find the rooms empty, and when I step into the kitchen I see only Army sitting at the table in the dark. He nurses a glass of whiskey.

I pull out a chair and sit down, looking at him even though he won't look at me.

"That story you told me," I ask, "about the man who wanted to pay you and Macon to have sex with his wife . . ."

He doesn't move.

"Macon did it, didn't he?"

Army turns the glass on the table, his jaw flexing as he stares at it.

"You couldn't. You left," I say. "He stayed."

The fact that he's not saying anything is enough of an answer. So much makes sense now.

"That's why he barely steps foot in the Bay." My mind whirls. "Why he never attended Liv's games."

I knew she tried to act like she understood, but she didn't. How could she? She had no idea the shit he was carrying around.

Army takes a sip of his drink. "Doing what you have to in order to survive isn't noble if your soul can't survive you," he states. "Macon knows that now."

I stand up. "He had no choice but to be capable of everything, Army." I gaze down at him. "And you banked on that with every step you took away from that house when you left him behind."

# 22

## Macon

For a long time, I was happy I was born first. Not because being the oldest gave me more power, or because I didn't have to share my shit and always got to have my own room, but because I got to leave first. It was the ultimate screw-you to my father, who thought being his son meant I'd help him raise his kids, cook the meals, change the diapers, do the laundry . . .

As soon as I turned eighteen and graduated, I bolted. I joined the military and got far away with barely much thought to my mother, because over the years and the constant threat hanging over our heads, I stopped believing she was ever going to do it. I didn't want her to. I just couldn't stay anymore. It would be fine. Life was getting easier for her. The kids were growing up. It would work itself out.

Joke was on me, though. Five years later I was called home for a funeral and two months later, another one. At twenty-three, I was the sole guardian and provider of four minors, and my parents had left us nothing but this house.

I regretted ever leaving, though. Not because I thought staying would've done my mother any good, but because the burden of being the oldest fell to Army when I left. And he didn't deserve it. I was already angry, fighting the fog in my head every day. But he's kind and calm, patient and warm. He didn't deserve the stress. He deserved a brother who wouldn't abandon him.

And he deserves Krisjen.

I trace the lock of her hair falling down her cheek and across her neck, the end lying over one of my pillows, and drift my eyes back up to her closed ones. My arm is folded under my head, facing her as she faces me, the curtains billowing with the early-morning breeze. She opened my windows last night. Must've done it while I was asleep, but the fresh air feels good. The scent of flowers and fresh earth blows in, the sounds of palm fronds rustling in the wind.

But I smell her, too. That perfume in her shampoo and the coconut on her lips, and I want her to wrap her arms around me again, so I can close my eyes and pretend the sun will never come up.

He deserves her. I don't want to tell her to go, though.

Just then, she blinks, her eyes opening more and more, and I watch as her gaze focuses, and she realizes that I'm staring at her.

We stay like that, and I know she wants to ask me if I'm okay. If I need anything. But thankfully, she doesn't. I'm so tired.

Propping herself up, she checks the time on her phone and then looks at me again. "I need to get the kids up," she says softly.

I stay silent as she turns over to climb out of bed, but then . . . she comes back around, dives in, and leaves a kiss on my cheek.

All of the adrenaline in my body rushes to that one spot.

She flips around, jumps out of bed, and leaves the room, closing the door behind her.

I sit up, a wave of nausea and an ache in my head hitting me. I look over, seeing she left me a glass of water. Grabbing it, I drink it down and plant my feet on the floor, slowly standing. The walls close in, and I don't know if it's because I haven't eaten since before yesterday, or because I've been sleeping for nearly a day, but I force myself into the bathroom. Refilling the glass, I drink it and refill it again, drinking until I'm not thirsty anymore.

The sickness rises, though, and I rush to the toilet, vomiting everything I just drank. There's no food in my stomach, but I lurch and lurch, spilling everything I have until it's gone.

I rinse out my mouth and drop my ass to the edge of the tub, trying to get my stomach to stop churning.

The house starts to wake. Laughter. Kids. Doors creaking open and slamming shut. I miss my sister in the house. She would keep that shit in check.

I stare at the floor, trying to feel my feet under me. Trying to stand.

*Get up. Go. Get up.*

Another day. Same as yesterday.

*Stand. Don't think. Stand. Get up. Work. Don't think. Do a job. Fix something. Build something. A car. A bike. The broken shutter. The door to the backyard. Turn it off. Move.*

*Fucking move.*

Another day. Same as yesterday.

I can't leave the room. I can't get my muscles under me.

I squeeze my eyes shut, feeling the wetness under my lids.

I don't want to see people. I can't talk. I can't stomach the conversations. It feels like everyone is on a carousel around me, swirling and laughing, and I'm losing my balance. I sway. I'm going to fall.

How can they just go through their days not feeling how cold everything is? I can't just act like I'm not cold.

I rub my hands over my face. What the fuck am I talking about? They don't feel it, because they don't feel it. Because it's not happening. Why do I feel this?

*Fuck.*

Music drifts up the stairs. Krisjen's dance music. I picture her in the kitchen, dancing. My heart beats.

My feet are under me.

I rise and push down my sleep pants. Pulling on some jeans and a T-shirt, I yank open my bedroom door. I don't pass anyone as I head down the stairs, slip on some shoes, and leave out the front door. I stand in the street for a few seconds before I veer left, toward the restaurant.

Opening the back door, I head inside the nearly empty place, finding Mariette at the kitchen counter. She's always here early. Like me, she prefers to work in peace.

She hears me and turns, a paring knife in her hand. Then, she relaxes and returns to her work. I sit on the crates next to the freezer, my head still pounding.

I love her. Blood or not, she's family.

She was my mom when I needed one. Not when I was five or ten or fifteen. When I was twenty-three and twenty-seven and thirty. When I realized that life only gets harder and we're all works in progress till the day we die.

Walking over, she grabs my chin and raises it, inspecting my face.

Going back to the counter, she grabs a mug and pours in tea from a nearby kettle.

She carries it to me. "Drink it."

I nod, taking the cup.

I sip slowly, my gulps getting bigger and bigger and thankfully, I'm keeping it down. To be honest, I never liked tea, but the warmth is soothing.

I set the empty cup down while she preps vegetables for the day.

"How often are you thinking about it?" she asks.

When I don't answer, she looks at me, and I look at her.

"Have you tried anything yet?" she presses.

I shake my head, at least giving her that.

If I'd tried anything, I wouldn't be here.

She scoops the chopped celery into a container and places a lid on it, taking the washed carrots out of the strainer and placing them on the cutting board.

"You should talk—"

"No," I snap.

I went to a doctor a few times, but I said more to Krisjen last night than I told that guy in three visits. He was smug and entitled, and once I made the mistake of telling him I'd been in the military, that was it. That was the easy answer to what was wrong with me, even though I admitted to feeling bad since I was a kid.

I knew there was other help out there—other doctors—but I never considered it again. I'm too busy, money is too precious, and no one in the Bay would ever trust me again if they found out. Especially the men.

So I pushed it down. I turned off my brain. Some days it wasn't even an effort. The feelings came and went just as quickly.

Other days were hard. Now, in recent months, they're always hard. Noise hurts my ears. Rooms feel too tight. Food tastes like sand.

"The last time I saw your mom," Mariette tells me, "she was smiling and hugging people, and she had put on makeup and looked so good." She smiles to herself, but then it fades. "That's when I got scared because I knew she'd decided." She chops one carrot after another. "She was happy because she knew it was going to be over soon."

I wasn't here. Army never told me that. I'd never asked what the days before were like.

"My head is a hellhole all the time." My eyes burn, exhausted. "Maybe she thought she'd be a burden if she stayed."

"And yet, no one is happy she's gone."

People might be happy if I am. Maybe not.

Maybe Dallas and Trace would be happier if they didn't feel obligated to stay. Maybe Army would feel like he had a life of his own. Maybe I fucked up Iron.

"You were always different," Mariette muses. "Even as a kid, you were quieter. You turned inward. You thought about things more than other people. Aware of the darkness and always spotting it first. Sensitive to the world."

She looks down at me. "But that's the part of you that saved us. We're still here only because of you."

I stare at my lap, shaking my head just slightly.

"My family and I get to stay because of you," she continues. "People have food in the fridge and are protected because of you. You planned, anticipated, and turned your head inside out in one move after another in order to protect what was ours. You overthink and keep yourself hidden, so no one really knows you. That makes you intimidating and unpredictable. No one can do what you do. Army doesn't have the stomach. Trace and Iron want other things, and Dallas wants to burn everything he sees. You're the one we know will always be there."

I can't look at her.

"Your weaknesses are your strengths," she tells me. "What would I have done without you?"

I clench my fists, feeling the muscles in my arms tightening over and over again.

Mariette scoops some soup into a disposable container and hands it to me. I take it, the warmth seeping through to my hand. "Eat it soon," she orders.

I take a sip and then another, eating bits of chicken and some noodles and getting hungrier the more I eat.

I smile a little. "I like your soup," I whisper.

She goes back to work. "That's Krisjen's recipe," she says. "She makes all of your food."

My body warms.

I finish the soup and head back to the house, seeing Trace take the garbage cans out to the road while Dallas loads the truck. Army gets Dex buckled up to go to the sitter, and Mars comes running out of the house with his lunch and backpack.

And I didn't have to yell at anyone to do any of it.

Army stops and looks at me. I turn away and walk toward the garage, twisting on the hose. Pulling off my shirt, I set it aside and lean over, letting the cold water run over the back of my neck.

It helps. I run it for a minute until I'm so cold, I couldn't think if I tried, and my body feels a surge of energy under my skin. I turn it off and pull my shirt back on.

I walk to the trucks as they start to climb in. I hesitate for a moment, but I force it out. "I'll come in with you."

Army stops just before closing his door. "Huh?"

"I'll take Fox Hill with Trace."

I move toward the other truck, jerking my chin at Trace to toss me the keys.

He sighs, walking to the passenger side. "Well, how am I supposed to drink on the job now?" he grumbles. "Shit."

Army casts me one long, last look before turning on the engine. He drives off, toward the sitter, and I start to climb into the driver's side, but I hear music. Looking over, I glimpse Paisleigh and Krisjen bouncing around the pool deck to some Olivia Newton-John song.

*Pink.* She reminds me of things that are flamingo pink. And water guns and treehouses and fresh-cut grass. I can smell sunscreen, all of it reminding me of being a kid.

She's like it's summer all the time.

I climb in the truck, excited to go, because she'll be here when we come home.

She's sleeping in my room tonight.

Not forever.

Just one more night.

# 23

## Krisjen

I head out to the patio, my arms full with plates as I push open the door with my butt. I set down the meals at table fifteen, grab the empty glasses at sixteen, and look out to the road, seeing Paisleigh . . . riding a bike.

My mouth drops open. What . . . ?

I almost drop the glasses.

She races past, sitting on someone's blue bike and trying to catch up to another group of kids.

I smile and laugh at the same time, about to call her over, but I don't want to distract her and make her fall. When did she learn to ride a bike?

I guess the extended stay in the Bay is good for her. My mom is away for the week, so she's none the wiser that I let Bateman take off—with pay—while the guys and I keep the kids. Mars hasn't complained, and Paisleigh's ready to move into the Jaeger house.

I watch her as I head back into the restaurant, smiling, but then I hear a rumble behind me and look over my shoulder. Two trucks fly in, filling the remaining parking spaces in front of the restaurant. Army, Dallas, and Trace jump out, and I search the cabs for Macon's outline but don't see him. I thought he went with them again today.

I glance over at the house. The garage is closed.

Walking back into the restaurant, I clutch the glasses in my hands, but then I spot him. Leaning on the lunch bar, sipping a glass of soda like he was there the whole time. The worry that started to wind its way into my chest and head melts.

He stands there, his gray T-shirt smudged with grease and dirt, and the sun has certainly worked its magic the past week, putting a tan on his body and color back into his face. The bags under his eyes are still there, but he's sleeping at least. He looks over at me, and I give him a smile he doesn't return, but that's okay. I can read his eyes well enough now to know he had a good day.

It's a little better since he started getting out of the house more. He refused my offer to make an appointment for him to talk to someone, even though I told him he could do it over the phone, and talking to someone is the best way for him to manage this. But Macon's instincts tell him he can rely on only himself. I'll keep trying, though.

Trace and Dallas walk past, whipping off their shirts, and Army circles my waist, bringing me in.

"Miss me?" he asks.

I laugh, drawing my hands back from his chest. "You're all wet."

He leans into my ear. "Clean your tables, and then come into the shower and clean me."

I chew the corner of my mouth, and he waits.

"Seventeen! Order up!"

I jump and pry his hands off.

"Saved by the bell," he teases as I walk away.

I slip behind the bar, refilling the glasses, and leave them there as I grab my order. I don't know if Macon is looking at me, but I'm barely aware of anything other than him standing right there as I drop the plates at the table and make my way back for the drinks.

Someone touches my arm. "Can I get rice and beans instead?"

I nod. "Sure."

I take the drinks to the table outside, come back in and get the rice and beans, and sweep through the room, clearing dishes and getting more napkins.

Army and the guys sit at a table, waiting, and people say things to me but I'm too distracted. I feel Macon's eyes.

On my stomach, on my hair draping down my arms, on my chest through my white tank top. On my face.

Lost in thought, I'm in Army's lap before I even know what's happening.

He smiles, holding me tight.

"Seriously?" I ask.

He needs the whole world to know he's horny.

Paisleigh rushes in. "¿Puedo tomar algo?"

"Huh?"

"¿Puedo tomar algo?" she says again.

I look at Army in confusion.

He chuckles, looking at my sister. "Yes, you can have something to drink," he tells her. "Go in the kitchen and ask Mariette. She'll get you some juice."

But I grab Paisleigh before she runs off. "You're learning Spanish?"

"Jasmine only speaks to us in Spanish," she informs me.

"Traeme una limonada," Army tells her.

She salutes him. "Bueno." And then she runs off, behind the counter and into the kitchen.

First, riding a bike. Now a new language.

"Seriously?" I say again. "She's spent less time over here than me, and she speaks the language already?"

"Kids are sponges," Trace adds.

"You don't know Spanish."

"Talking will never be what I'm best at," he taunts, his double meaning clear with the gleam in his eyes.

Army and Dallas chuckle at his comeback, and I struggle not to roll my eyes.

Glancing over at Macon, I see a couple of women at the counter, one of them swiveling her chair in his direction and smiling. He doesn't smile back, but he's talking to her. He nods, his expression calm, his breathing relaxed. Tranquil.

"What's going on with him?" I hear Army ask.

I tear my eyes away.

I don't have to ask to know he's talking about Macon. "Have you asked him that?"

I don't want to talk about Macon behind his back, even though his family should be involved.

He's talking to me, though, and I don't want to ruin that.

"I mean with you and him," Army clarifies.

"Nothing." I shrug it off. "He just needs sleep."

"You've slept in his room all week."

Goose bumps spread up my arms at the reminder of how I can't wait for the days to end now. How he just looks at me and doesn't have to say that he doesn't want to be alone, and I get my pillow and follow him.

Nothing has happened, but I wake up with his arms wrapped around me.

I stare at him talking to the girl. She taps something on her phone and hands it to him. He slips it into his pocket.

Wait . . . That was his phone. What was she typing into *his* phone?

Is he going to kick me out of his bed tonight?

"We're just sleeping," I murmur to Army. "Nothing else."

"He keeps looking at you," he states. "I don't like it."

The hair on my arms rises, hearing the jealousy in his tone.

I lift my eyes again, seeing that Macon is looking at me. She talks, but he stares at me now.

I stand up, turning to the guys. "Ready to order?" I ask,

changing the subject. I don't know what to say to Army about Macon, but I know it's going to take me more than two seconds to figure out. I don't have time to think right now.

"We already did," Dallas tells me. "We're getting it to go and taking it into the bar."

The bar . . .

I blink and twist away, grabbing someone's empty glass and making my way to the counter.

I stop next to Macon as I reach over the counter and pull up the soda gun. I start to refill the drink.

"I don't think you should drink tonight," I say as quietly as possible. "Or be having relations with women right now."

He leans down on the counter again, lifting his cup to his mouth. His jaw flexes. "Relations . . ."

"You know what I mean."

I'm not even sure what I mean. Do I mean a relationship, or just sex? I think about it for a second, picturing him on a date. Or taking someone to bed. I don't like either.

I try to soften my tone. "I just mean that instant gratification behavior does more harm than good. It's just a Band-Aid over the real problem."

"I wasn't going to fuck her, Krisjen."

My stomach drops a little, like it does every time he says my name.

"Tonight anyway," he adds, turning to me. "And I'll be thirty-two in January. I don't need relationship advice from a teenager."

I lock my jaw, a lump stuck in my throat. My eyes burn.

*A teenager?* Is that how he sees me?

I care about him. Does that mean anything to him?

"Just fucking relax," he says under his breath. "I'm not hanging myself today."

My chest caves, my face cracking, and I don't want him to see.

I bolt, walking as fast as I can into the kitchen, behind the dishwasher, and press my hands into the cool steel of the countertop. Mariette and the guys work up front, unfazed.

Macon charges into my secluded nook, and I whip around, facing him.

"Don't fucking do that," he says. "You're mad? Then hit me. I'm not made of glass. You can hit me!"

I glimpse the cooks through the small space between the ovens, seeing them look over, but Macon doesn't seem to care who hears.

"I don't want to hit you," I say.

He closes the distance between us, and I suck in a breath as he grabs me underneath my arms and plops my ass down on the counter. He comes in close, one hand on the microwave behind my head.

"You want to take care of me?" he taunts. "Bring me soup and let me cry on your shoulder like someone who's not a man?"

"That doesn't make you less of a man!" I whisper-yell. "I just don't want . . ."

I trail off. I don't know how to say it.

"I don't want . . ."

"What?" he barks.

"I don't . . . I . . ." I stammer.

"What?" He bares his teeth, pushing away from me. "I don't know how to do this. What do you want from me?"

"I just don't want you to leave," I burst out.

He's trying to act in a way he thinks normal people do. Drinking, working, sex, because he still can't let them know that he's in pain.

"I don't want you to do anything you don't want to do." I search his eyes. "You don't want her. You don't want to fuck around in that bar all night."

Maybe ten years ago, but not anymore.

He inches toward me again, his expression pained. "You don't know what I want," he whispers, swallowing hard. "Krisjen, I can't tell you the things I think about sometimes."

My chin trembles. I'm scared.

But I do know him.

Taking him by the back of the neck, I draw him in, his eyes cast down and refusing to look at me.

"There are so many people who I don't see," I tell him. "My mom and dad. Milo. Trace. No matter how I try to slow down and see them, I can't." I take a washcloth off the rack and run the cold water over it, wringing out the excess. "I keep reaching for something I know is there, but I can't grab it. Like they're not real. No different than any stranger passing me by, and I just keep walking."

I place the ice-cold cloth on the back of his neck, feeling him exhale.

"But I see you. Even when I close my eyes, I see you."

He looks up at me, and I jerk my chin to the restaurant and Bay beyond us. "You take care of them," I tell him. "I take care of you. End of story."

He holds my gaze for several seconds, finally closing his eyes and leaning in. Pressing a hand into the microwave behind me again, and the other on the counter at my side, he almost brushes my nose with his. His warm breath falls across my lips.

I press the cloth into his skin, running my other hand over his neck and face.

And everything else in the world quiets as he leans into it. All I can see is him, and all he can see is me.

"Until someone else comes along . . ." I tell him.

He nods.

# 24

## Macon

Army's going to want her back. He's been quiet about her sleeping in my room because he knows something's going on with me, but he still wants her. He makes sure I see every time she lets him touch her.

I blow out a breath, bowing my head under the hot spray of the shower. The scent of the candle burning on the sink fills the bathroom, mixing with magnolias breezing in through the window above my head. An image of me racing my first motorcycle down the coast hits me, the sun shining on my face. Girls in swimsuits on the beach. A red sail far out on the water.

I forgot about that.

The scent reminds me of it, though. I'm not sure why.

That was a good day. I was seventeen, I think. Freedom.

Krisjen says she just likes firelight, but I know something that smells like eucalyptus is something people use for stress, and she's doing it for my benefit. She burns other things that smell like spearmint and citrus, and she plays music a lot and keeps the windows open, so fresh air can travel through the house. Aromatherapy bullshit like it's going to fix me, but . . .

It stirs up memories, all of them nice. At any moment, I feel twelve, sneaking out with Army and Iron to climb trees at midnight.

And the house does feel better. It breathes again. I like coming home, and even my brothers seem happier. They're taking care of shit—Trace finally put the lawn mower away—but I don't know if I'm happy that they're stepping up. They're doing it because they're worried about me.

I don't want them to act like I'm not strong.

I inhale the scent, drawing it in again and again, the memory of that day in the sun, next to the sea as I raced through the wind. A great summer day.

Fisting the shower handle, I brace myself, jerking it right. I hold my breath as it only takes about two seconds for the water to go from hot to cold. Forcing my neck under the spray, I let the icy water coat my back, and then I raise my head, dousing my face. I exhale, my head clearing. Jesus, that helps. I do it every shower now.

She's smart. And yeah, I like her ridiculous candles.

I plant my hands on the wall, letting the water spill down my chest. I like her girly music, and how she sings to Dex, and the way her body looks in my sweatpants. And how her feet were curled into mine when I woke up this morning.

I look down, seeing my dick hard.

I slam my hand down on the handle, cutting off the water and grabbing my towel. Quickly drying, I dress, pulling on jeans and taking out a T-shirt. I swing it over my shoulder as I dry off my hair. Crossing the room, I stop and look at the bed, sheets crumpled and the dent of our heads still in the pillows.

I hesitate for only a moment. Walking over, I pull up the bedding, smoothing it out, and fluff the pillows. It's not military-style, but it's better than yesterday.

I draw in a deep breath. *Okay.*

Heading downstairs, I stop about halfway, looking around and listening. The house is silent.

There's nothing.

I keep walking, checking the grandfather clock in the foyer as I pass. *Ten after seven.*

They're not usually gone yet.

I step into the kitchen, seeing Krisjen pull a pan out of the oven. The hair on my arms rises, and I'm not sure if it's because it smells like steak, or because I'm looking at her.

She smiles at me and takes the tongs, placing a rib eye on a plate.

I pour a cup of coffee. "Where is everybody?"

She sighs. "They were rushing off when I got up," she tells me. "It's supposed to rain later, so they wanted to get all the jobs done before it starts."

*They wanted to get all the jobs done . . .*

Jesus fucking Christ. Are they all trying to make me proud or something?

She hands me the plate, and I look down at it, replying, "I'm not . . ."

But then I stop, shutting my mouth. Staring at the meat and the juices pooling around it, I force myself to let go. To follow her lead.

"Thank you," I whisper.

She says nothing, simply turning back to the dishes, and I take my food to the table, sitting down as she sets a knife and fork next to the plate.

I stick the steak with my fork, my stomach grumbling at the feel of how tender the meat is. My mouth waters.

I take a bite, the taste and the char making me nearly fucking groan. Jesus. I hurry, slicing into the meat again as I chew and swallow the first bite.

She sets down a glass in front of me, starting to walk away, but I call her back. "Can you put it in a coffee cup or something? I can't have people seeing me drink a pink smoothie."

She snorts, trying to contain her laughter as she picks up the glass and carries it back to the kitchen. Digging out a mug, she transfers the fruity drink.

I take another bite and stuff in another, while she disappears into the pantry. I gulp down half the smoothie, the breeze blowing the curtains at my side.

I take another bite, looking up to see Army half-dressed and frozen in the entryway between the kitchen and the living room.

I swallow. "You're still here?"

He opens his mouth, then closes it, glancing toward the pantry as Krisjen sifts through cans and boxes.

"I'm going in a few," he says.

I cut the last piece of meat, the pulse in my neck throbbing. He was hoping to find her alone. She doesn't work today, so he stayed behind to get laid.

"I thought you were heading to the marina," he says.

"I am."

Krisjen strolls out, carrying a few cans and setting them on the counter. "Hey," she singsongs to Army.

He looks at her.

I look at him.

He looks at me.

She dives back into the pantry, and I swallow my last bite.

"She's coming with me today," I say without thinking. "Ames will like something pretty to look at."

I rise, taking my plate to the sink, and then pick up the drink.

I don't want her home without me, and I don't have time to ponder why. I'll think about it later.

I head over to him. "Did you eat?" I ask.

He shakes his head.

I hand him the smoothie. "Finish this. She's sneaking kale in there or some shit and thinks I don't notice."

He takes it, the whisper of a smile crossing his lips.

He should fight me for her attention. He has every right, but

I'm glad he almost never pushes back. There was a time that lasted far longer than it should when I just needed one person who did what I told them to do. One person I knew would get it done.

Army is the longest relationship I've ever had. And I know I owe him.

I'll give her back tomorrow. Just one more night.

I pull on my T-shirt, grab my keys, and walk into the garage, yanking the canvas off my motorcycle.

Two hours later, we're cruising up to the marina.

She pulls off her helmet and throws her head back, her hair flying over her shoulders like a blanket. With a huge-ass smile on her face, she giggles. "I've always wanted to do that."

I don't react, but inside, I'm smiling more than I want to admit. She's so innocent. In a way that's sweet, pure, and endearing, and for some reason, a little annoying, too. I wish anything made me as happy as she is reenacting a shampoo commercial.

I take her helmet, hang it on the handlebar, and unzip my leather jacket. "We probably have enough spare parts to make another bike," I say. "If you want to learn how to drive."

"No," she replies right away, walking around the motorcycle to me. "I like riding with you."

I clench my jaw, trying to shield the way I suddenly can't breathe. She stands at my side, wearing a short, tight white dress, held up with one strap over her left shoulder, the other bare, and her lips painted pink.

She clutches the inside of my upper arm and looks at me. I ache everywhere.

I lead her down the dock, fishing boats rocking and yachts anchored in the distance. Light dims as a cloud passes in front of the sun, and I see Garrett Ames step off the deck of his fifty-seven-foot motor yacht, walking toward us as he slips his cell phone into his breast pocket.

"I honestly expected the other one," he says. "Army, was it?"

His blue eyes gleam like I'm so amusing.

"Ms. Conroy." He turns his attention to Krisjen. "You've grown up."

He looks her up and down, and I take her hand off my arm and put it in my hand instead.

Jerome Watson walks up behind him, and I feel Krisjen's fingers tighten around mine.

"We should sit down," Ames says, gesturing to the restaurant up the stairs. Diners sit around walls of windows at tables with linen that make me uncomfortable.

"No," I reply.

Ames studies me. "It looks suspicious, meeting on the docks and all."

"My boat." I point to the forty-four-foot cabin cruiser to the right. "Nothing to brag about, but we could motor out a little. Away from eyes."

"So they can find my body washed up on shore in a week?" he fires back.

I cock my head. "I didn't come here with an army. Just one little girl."

I know she's far from that, but Garrett Ames thinks all women are deaf, dumb, and blind. Pretty sure that she's of no consequence to him.

But still, Krisjen teases, "Are you saying I don't know how to handle a single guy? I can handle lots of guys."

I laugh, surprising myself. Jerome's gaze darts from her to me, and I squeeze her hand. "I know how deadly you are," I tell her.

Wiping the smile off my face, I zone in on Ames. "You want two hundred acres," I tell him, cutting to the chase. I don't want to be here any longer than necessary.

"Give or take," he says. "In exchange, you get approvals from the city council for your permits. Plus, you get to put out a contract for construction."

All of which I could have anytime I wanted. Sanoa Bay is going to have streets. Proper paved streets. Finally.

But I'd rather not strong-arm anyone on this, so I'll let him think he can get for me what I can't get for myself.

"What do you want the acreage for?" I ask.

"A solar field. Why do you want the permits?"

"Infrastructure."

He gives me one of those "Bless your heart" smiles. "Kind of like making beds in a burning house, isn't it?"

I grind my teeth together. They've been saying that shit for years. And we're still there. I haven't given up the land. I haven't even given up a single acre.

Jerome steps forward, eyeing me. "Allying yourself with the Collinses might buy you some room, but allying yourself with her . . ." He gestures to Krisjen. "Buys you nothing with the Conroys."

I almost whisper. "That's not why we like her," I taunt.

My sister has Clay, and Clay's father has been generous with help and pulling some strings, but I never asked for it. And while I appreciate anything that makes my life easier, I would've been fine on my own.

Garrett Ames holds my eyes, and I know he's about to threaten me or readjust my reality as if I don't know that everything that I have will be his if I'm just suddenly gone one day.

But before anyone can say anything, Krisjen speaks up. "Doesn't the state offer tax rebates for land dedicated to solar energy?"

*Yes, but* . . . And then I realize where she's going with this.

"That's true." I gaze at Ames. "An acre is roughly . . . forty-three thousand square feet. That equals over four hundred kilowatts of solar panels multiplied by two hundred acres. You're talking a utility scale project."

"You could just rent the land instead," Krisjen chirps, oh so innocently. "It would eventually pay you more than they will."

I smile. "Very true."

Ames's eyes turn hard on her, then he steps up to me. "I'm only interested in what I can own. I don't need a landlord," he bites out. "You have something I need. I have something you need. Think about it. You have a week. And then I stop acting like you're of any consequence in all of this."

For the first time in a long time, my arms feel strong. Fire and heat course under my skin, and I hope he tries.

He takes the last step up to me, lowering his voice. "And I know Dallas liked to fuck my son," he tells me.

Krisjen jerks her gaze to me. "Callum?" she murmurs.

Yep. Callum Ames. Her classmate in high school and an arrogant, predatory piece of shit.

I don't answer out loud, though. It's not my place to air Dallas's business. I'm just glad it lasted only a month, and that Garrett Ames doesn't want anyone to know about it any more than I do.

Callum, his all-American, frat boy dickhead of a son wanted everyone to think he screwed girls, but it was my brother he really wanted.

But he was also only seventeen when he hooked up with Dallas. I don't know if I would've been able to get Dallas out of that if Callum's father decided to pursue action.

Thankfully, Callum is off at college, and hopefully, he never comes back. If he does, it won't be good. He wasn't happy when my brother ended it.

"If they ever touch each other again," Ames warns, "the Bay will be visited by people who get paid in cash and know how to make even bones disappear. And then it'll be visited by bulldozers next. You know what's better than two hundred acres? Two thousand."

He backs away, telling me again, "You have a week."

He turns and heads for the stairs, Jerome slowly following. "You can't survive," he tells us. "Everyone knows it but you."

He spins around, both of them climbing the stairs to the restaurant.

Still holding Krisjen's hand, I walk hard, back to the bike.

I want him to choke on every grain of sand in the Bay.

And I want it now. I can't battle this guy for ten more years. We've held on to the land, but nothing is getting better, and it has to or otherwise I have no idea what it was all for.

I need to change something.

"A solar field?" Krisjen says.

"Yeah, it's bullshit."

Men like him own oil rigs, not clean energy. He wants it for something else.

We reach the bike, and I hand her the helmet.

"You could get permits in a heartbeat." She holds the helmet with one hand, twisting up her hair to fit inside. "You have everyone in power wired."

How does she know that? Did someone tell her about the cameras?

Nevertheless . . . "But they don't all know that," I point out. "When they do . . ."

"They're going to be more aggressive."

"Exactly. They won't wait around for me to strike."

Concern hits her eyes. "They would kill you?"

I don't answer, just climb on the bike.

"Don't let them," she says.

Don't *let* them? "You think I would—"

"You know what I mean."

I stop, staring at her. *Don't make it easy*, she means. Like I have a death wish.

"I know what you mean," I tell her, making my voice gentle.

Sprinkles of rain have started to fall, and her skin in the white dress almost sparkles with the drops.

I give her a small smile. "You look pretty."

She pulls on the helmet, fastening it, and then hikes up her dress just enough to climb on behind me.

She wraps her arms around me tight.

"Don't worry, Krisjen." I start up the motorcycle. "Men like that won't be the end of me."

I push the kickstand out of the way, looking over my shoulder.

"And you don't leave the Bay without protection from now on," I demand. "You're a target now, just like the rest of us, and there's no telling what they'll do."

"You let Liv, Clay, and Aracely come and go as they please."

Fuck.

"You think I can't defend myself," she goes on. "I can when I want to."

But I'm not arguing about this. "You don't leave the Bay without a male."

The rain falls, the drops darting to the ground faster and faster, and I tip my head back, feeling the cool water and the beautiful, welcome weight of her body around mine.

Like an anchor.

"Do you mind if we just drive around for a while?" I ask her. "In the rain?"

She'll get soaked, but somehow, I know just what she likes.

And true to form, she replies, "All night if you want."

I take off, not wanting to be anywhere else for the first time in a long time.

# 25

## Krisjen

He pulls into the garage and hits the brakes. My body lurches into him as I hold him tight, the smile on my face constant ever since we left the docks.

He kills the engine, and I savor the feel of him in my arms one last time before I let him go. Hopping off the bike, I unfasten the helmet and shiver, laughing at how the rain drips off both of us. We're soaked.

Leading the way up the steps, he hits the button to close the garage door, and my teeth chatter as we pour into the dark kitchen.

I rush to the island and dig out a clean dish towel from a drawer, using it to squeeze the water out of my hair. No lights drift in from the living room, the house silent all around us.

I slip off my shoes and hold the towel to my chest. "Where is everybody?"

He whips off his jacket and hangs it on the back of the chair. "Close, I'm sure."

He lifts his arms, pulling his T-shirt with him, and I gaze at his taut, tan stomach, the cut of the muscles there flexing, and his ribs cutting through his skin.

In a moment, he's in front of me, taking the towel and drying off his face and neck. "Why didn't you tell me you were cold?" he asks.

I grab the towel back, like it's any substitute for a blanket, and breathe out a laugh. "I didn't want you to stop."

He looks down at me. "Yeah, me either."

It was fun. We went everywhere. A hundred miles down the coast, all day, in and out of neighborhoods and busy shopping districts along the shore. In and out of rain and sun until we turned around and started getting pummeled on the way back home. I almost told him to keep going. I've never been to Cape Canaveral. We could've gotten a room. He should get out of town for a night once in a while.

"Are your brother and sister here?"

"With my grandparents tonight." I set the towel down. "Are you hungry?"

When he doesn't answer, I look up. He stares down at me, his warm eyes burning into me.

I don't blink. The house is so quiet.

I'm cold. I want my dress off.

"You should get into a warm shower," he says just above a whisper.

For a moment, there's an invisible cord pulling at me, pulling him to me. He's going to touch me. He never really saw me as a kid, did he? I'm not too young for him.

But he grabs his wet T-shirt and leaves, the pain low in my belly almost unnoticeable compared to the cold I feel everywhere else.

Jesus, what's wrong with me?

*We could've gotten a room?* Did I actually just think that after everything he's going through?

I head upstairs, seeing him close his door just as I dive through Liv's. I drop my dress to the floor and peel off my wet underwear. Pulling on a black cropped T-shirt and some sleep shorts, I pick up my dress and head to the bathroom.

Throwing it over the shower rod to dry, I grab my brush from a shelf and start smoothing out the wet strands as I work the hair dryer over them.

Chills break out over my legs, still cold. The temperature was in the seventies all day, but add the rain, the wind, and the bare minimum attire, and I felt it more than Macon, who at least had on jeans and a jacket.

I think he enjoyed himself today, though. He just kept going and going, looking around once in a while and taking in the view, same as me. Trace rarely had me on his bike. He preferred to ride alone.

And Dallas was trying to scare me, going fast and testing me on the way to the Bug Jam.

Does Army have a bike? Iron does. It's all he drives.

They're not a gang, but they kind of are. I should get them all patches to put on their jackets as a joke. The idea makes me smile.

But then Macon walks in, and I lose the smile, finishing my hair and turning off the dryer.

I set it down and comb out my hair as he comes to the sink and wets his toothbrush. I glance at him, dropping my gaze to his sleep pants, and then turn away again. I stow the hairbrush and get my own toothbrush ready.

The room fills with the sound of brushing and water running, but he finishes quickly, rinsing out his mouth.

"I told you to get warmed up," he says, cleaning his toothbrush.

I spit. "I'm tired," I say in a low voice.

I rinse my mouth, and he slips his toothbrush back into the holder. "Get your pillow."

I watch him in the mirror as he leaves behind me. I don't know when it became a thing that I sleep with him all the time, but sleeping is now my favorite thing.

I wipe my mouth with the back of my hand and walk out, shutting off the light. Diving into Liv's room, I grab my pillow.

But his words come back to me from that day in the shower. *My woman is out there . . .*

I think about that a lot. How he wants things and refrains from taking them because he thinks the cycle will end with him.

But he wants me in his bed because he remembers how good warm things feel. He doesn't want to be alone.

*I'm going to let another man have her . . .*

I drop the pillow back to the bed and pull my T-shirt over my head. Slipping my shorts down my legs, I pick up my pillow again and hug it to my naked chest. Underwear still on, I try to slow my breathing as I see his room through the hair hanging in my left eye as I cross the hall.

Stepping inside, I watch him stand at his bedside table, his back to me as he sets his alarm.

I almost can't talk for a second. "You're . . . you're warm," I say in a soft voice.

He turns, his gaze dropping to the pillow over my naked skin.

"Right?" I swallow. "Like a shower?"

*He can warm me.* My heart pounds in my ears.

The slight pinch between his brows digs deeper, and I'm not sure what that means. He doesn't look as if he likes what he sees.

"You're bold," he says, arching an eyebrow. "For a teenager."

Yeah. He's pissed. He thinks I'm spoon-feeding him. Pitying him.

I whip around to leave, but he's on my back and shoving the door out of my hand as soon as I start to open it.

"The last Saint on my bed got off without punishment."

*Clay.* I breathe hard.

We broke into their house last spring, and she lay on his bed while Callum Ames took her picture.

As a joke.

She was fully dressed, of course. And Macon wasn't here.

I wet my lips. "I never want to leave your bed," I whisper.

"And I want you to take that woman's number out of your phone, too."

His fingers play with locks of my hair at my back. "You want to do for me what she wants to do?"

I nod.

A hard breath hits my ear, and he lifts me up, back against his body, burying his face in my neck. I drop the pillow, moaning as I tilt my head back, close my eyes, and reach my hand around to touch his face.

"Macon . . ."

His hands slide up my body, covering my breasts, and I shift on my tiptoes, trying to keep contact as his mouth moves over my neck—touching, brushing, biting, breathing . . .

He rises up straight, taking me with him so my feet leave the floor. "How are you so powerful?" he growls, sliding a hand down the front of my panties. "Goddammit, you make everything worse."

I smile. My skin fires under the surface, and I feel like everything is vibrating. "I know," I groan.

His mouth leaves my neck, and I catch his lips with mine, cutting off his breath.

Twisting around in his arms, I let him slip his hands down the back of my underwear, cupping my ass and pressing me into him. His hard ridge digs into me, and my belly floods with heat.

I climb into his arms as he wraps my legs around his body. I hold the back of his neck and hover close, nearly brushing my nose to his. "I wish it had been me that night on your bed. What would you have done if you'd caught me?"

He reaches behind me, and I hear the lock click. "Given you the licks you deserved." He breathes out.

My heart spins inside my chest, and I love the double meaning behind that. I wish I had been the one on his bed. I wish I'd known how to listen to my instincts, because from the start, it was him I noticed. The first time I saw him up close in the garage during the scavenger hunt. That first time—while everyone else was scared—I just kept thinking how smart he was. That he wasn't some ruthless nobody who thought small and just liked to cause trouble. That whole time he had Clay in his clutches, I kept thinking that he was stronger than anyone I'd ever known.

He lifts me higher by the backs of my thighs, looking up at me. "You pitying me?" he asks. "Tell me this isn't about that."

I hold his face, gazing into his chocolate eyes.

"Tell me you want it," he begs.

"I wanted it that night in the garage so badly," I state. "I wanted you to put me in the back seat and do it slow, again and again." I harden my voice. "And I don't want anyone else touching you."

I know the woman he was talking to at Mariette's yesterday is of little consequence, but she's around, and she's available if he needs it.

I don't like that.

"I take care of you," I tell him. "Your restaurant, your food, and I'll ride you early in the morning, and let you take off my panties in the middle of the night if you wake up hard."

I crash down on his mouth, savoring the taste of him before I slowly move over his lips, gripping his hair at the back of his head. He groans, holding me tightly and pushing his tongue in, forcing my teeth to part.

Tingles spread down to my toes. "Oh God . . ."

The heat of his mouth spreads all over me, and I move faster, not able to get enough. I kiss and nibble, and then I force his head back so I can have his neck. I kiss over his vein and up to his jaw, tasting it with the tip of my tongue. The stubble on his face brushes against my lips, and I don't know what happens, but I bite his jaw, not even thinking anymore.

"Mine," I say. "I'm the one who touches you."

He hugs me tightly, his possessive fingers digging into my ass and waist. "Fuck," he whispers. "Fucking God, Krisjen, we have to stop. You don't belong with me. You're too young."

I kiss him more and more. "I decide that," I pant, dragging my nails over the muscles in his back. "And you don't tell me no. You let me have whatever I want." I leave small kisses on his cheek, his jaw, and the corner of his mouth. "I belong to you."

And he covers my mouth with a long, deep kiss, and neither one of us can stop.

He kisses my forehead, my cheek, and I want him to go faster—harder—but I don't want to be fucked, either. Not our first time. I love the slow agony of anticipation. Of him learning my body and me learning his. When is he going to suck on me? Strip the rest of my clothes off? Spread my thighs apart?

He drops me to my feet, smelling my hair as he takes my hand and guides it inside the hem of my underwear. He presses my fingertips to my clit. "Do that," he murmurs. "You're pretty when you do it."

When did he see me . . . ?

The couch pops in my head, but then I remember. I did it for him in the garage. *The hose.*

He reaches inside a drawer in his dresser and pulls out a little device. He hands it to me.

I hold the hot pink vibrator, the word "Vibe" written on the side. I glance at him. "This is mine."

He took this from my bag? When? I search my brain, but I can't remember the last time I saw it.

He whispers in my ear, "Sorry. I just didn't want you using it with anyone else."

I remember making a joke last spring in front of Trace's family about how I used the vibrator after he would leave me unsatisfied. Macon was in the room when I said it. He didn't forget. My cheeks heat, and my heart races at the same time.

Taking my hand, he leads me to the bed. I stare up at him as I twist the knob and hear the vibrator buzz to life.

His eyes swallow me whole, and I can't see anything else but him. I barely even register crawling onto the bed, lying down on my tummy, and sliding the vibrator inside my underwear, against my clit.

His chest heaves in heavy breaths as my thighs immediately grow hot.

Raindrops beat against the windows and walls, but the only sounds filling the room are my moans as I start rubbing myself into the vibrator.

Propping myself up on one elbow, I rock my hips, pinning the toy between the bed and my body as I reach back with my hand and push the underwear below my ass. He watches me, entranced, and I thrust, grind, and slip my hand back down to keep the vibrator in place. Tingles spread low through my belly, and I feel the orgasm start to build. I moan, dropping my forehead to the bed and keeping the toy pinned on my clit.

I dream of days when he's out working and I just can't wait, and he comes home to catch me playing on his bed. And then suddenly, I'm all he's thinking about as he steps in and closes the door to punish me so loud the bed breaks.

I fuck harder, rocking my hips as the heat of his eyes falls on my ass. I glance over for a split second, seeing the long ridge of his cock outlined against his sleep pants as it grows big and hard.

I slide the other hand down between my legs, holding the little vibrator with both hands. The orgasm crests, I suck in a breath, little gasps escaping as I thrust hard once. And then again. And then . . .

He flips me over, yanks my toy away, and I whimper as he pulls off my panties.

"Macon . . ." I gasp and then groan. "No."

I didn't come.

But in a second, he's licking one of my nipples and sliding a finger inside of me. And then another one, stretching me and hitting deep.

I dig my nails into his bed. *Yeah.*

A phone rings over on the dresser. His. That's not my ringtone. But he ignores it, and it eventually stops as his hot mouth descends over my stomach and lands between my thighs. Moving his two fingers in and out, he kisses my clit, licking it, and then kisses it again. I tremble, my thighs quivering.

"Please . . ." I beg.

But the phone rings again, and Macon bites my outer flesh in frustration.

I cry out, grabbing hold of his head to keep him there, but he pulls away. Charging over to his dresser, he looks at his phone and swipes, setting it back down. "Fucking Trace," he growls, ignoring the call.

I sit up, propping my hands behind me on the blankets. "Come back to bed."

He turns, and I see sweat glisten on his neck as he gazes at me and doesn't blink. It only takes a moment, though, and he's pushing his pants down his legs and fisting his cock.

My eyes flare as I watch him stroke it and walk to me like it's a threat.

He comes down on the bed, and I fall back, grabbing his hips to guide him in between my legs.

The phone rings again.

"Goddamn that kid." He breathes out, looking in the direction of the phone still on his dresser.

But I arch up, licking and kissing his jaw. "Don't kill him."

He takes my wrists and pushes me back, pinning them above my head. "I won't, baby," he tells me, hovering over my mouth. "He brought you home to me."

God, yes. I love knowing Macon wants me. I like knowing that he liked what he saw months ago and wanted it.

The phone rings again, and Macon shoots off the bed, going for the phone, but everything throbs, and I need him inside of me *now*.

"Macon . . ." I whine.

And he turns back, seeing me, thighs spread, wet for him.

He lets the fucking thing ring and comes back, kneeling between my legs, and grabbing my hips, yanking me down. I should just tell him to mute it, but I can't wait.

"I kind of wish those rumors they say about me were true," he says. "If you'd been submitted to me at eighteen, I would never have let anyone else have you."

He presses the head of his cock to my entrance, leans over me, and thrusts. I cry out, tipping my head back as he stretches me and fills, thrusting deeper every time.

"Fuck," he whispers, pinning my wrists above my head again. "I would've kept you for me."

I roll my hips, searching for his mouth, neither one of us wanting to take it slow anymore as the heat in the room builds and builds.

"Do whatever you want to me," I whisper. *Because I keep what I want, and I want him.* God, I want him.

I find his lips, savoring the feel of his skin and the taste of his tongue.

"Wider, Krisjen . . ." he pleads.

I let my thighs fall wide, while he kisses my mouth, my neck, and sucks a breast into his mouth again. He tugs at a nipple, and I arch up, keeping it in his mouth. *God, I love it when he does that.* I pull my wrists out of his hold, taking his waist in my hands, and pull him in, burying his cock deep inside me.

I moan, and he growls, propping himself above me to stare down at my body as we fuck.

The phone rings. We ignore it.

"Macon . . ." I moan.

It rings again. He seethes. But I beg, "Don't stop."

I stare up into his eyes, my hand around the back of his neck, but it rings again.

He jerks away. "Goddammit!"

And I cry a little when his heat leaves me and the bed.

He grabs his phone, knocking over things on his dresser in the process, and answers. "Fuck!" he growls, holding the phone to his ear. "What?"

"Saints just crossed the tracks!" I hear Trace shout from here.

Macon breathes hard, turning toward me and walking back for the bed.

I bite my bottom lip and then . . . I swing around hanging my head over the side of the bed and grabbing him with my mouth as he comes in.

"Oh, fuck," he groans, just realizing what I'm doing.

He stands next to the bed as I suck him down, and he leans over me a little, burying his cock in my mouth. His hand caresses my breast.

"Yeah, so, um. . . ." Trace stutters, and I realize Macon just blurted that in his ear. "They took a left. My guess is they're going to the cemetery."

"What do I care?" Macon rubs his thumb over my right nipple, pumping his dick into my mouth slowly so he doesn't hurt me.

He groans again. "Oh God."

"Are you . . ." Trace starts to ask but stops. "Never mind." He pauses, then continues. "What do you want us to do?"

"Pull back."

"But—"

"You heard me," Macon snaps. "Just leave it."

"They're searching for the treasure."

"It's not in the cemetery," Macon says.

My eyes pop open just as he yanks the phone away from his ear and tosses it on the bed.

"Not anymore," he murmurs to himself.

The treasure? That was one of the rumors I asked him about when we ate in the kitchen that day. It's true?

I swirl my tongue around his tip, tasting myself on him. Loving that he tastes like this, because he was inside of me.

"I taste good," I say softly.

He reaches down and lifts me up, onto my knees, and brings me into his body. "Yes, you do," he whispers over my lips.

He kisses me, sucking me off my own lips and digging his fingers into my ass.

"So the treasure is real?" I ask, remembering what he just said to Trace. "They'll rip the place apart, you know."

He holds me tight. "It'll take more than that to get me to leave this bed tonight."

We kiss, our arms circling each other tightly, and I can't tell which limbs are mine and which are his. I love this with him. I love that there's nothing better than tonight. I love—

A boom hits the air, followed by another one, and we jump, pulling away from each other's mouths.

Still holding each other, we turn our eyes out the window and toward the bright glow of an explosion somewhere behind Mariette's. On a road? In the swamp, maybe?

"Oh my God," he mutters.

The fire burns big, and I stop breathing for a second. *Trace. Dallas, Army . . .*

I look at Macon. "We have to go."

I pull the hood of Liv's raincoat over my head as Macon and I dash out into the street. We climb into one of the trucks, water streaming down his face and onto his black T-shirt as he turns the key.

He spins the wheel to the left, and I grab the dash and the door as he swings around the street and charges down the road, toward the bar and the motel. The door to the firehouse is up, the small truck inside gone. Some of the volunteer fire department must've already sped out to the fire.

But instead of veering left, past Mariette's and toward the explosion, he slips into a muddy parking spot and leaves the engine running. "Come on."

He jumps out of the truck, and I push open the creaky door, hopping out.

Heading up the steps before me, he opens the door, and I walk in behind him.

People clamor and shout inside the restaurant, and we look around for familiar faces, but all I see are staff, tourists, and a few people from the Bay.

But then I see them. Army, Dallas, and Trace push through the kitchen door and charge through the dining room. I let out a breath, relieved.

Macon dives behind the lunch counter, pulls out a pistol, checks for bullets, and slips it into the back of his jeans. My heart leaps into my throat.

*The gun.* The one from his nightstand. I haven't returned it yet. I guess it's a good thing he didn't think to grab it before we left the house.

He pulls his T-shirt over the weapon and moves toward the door again, his brothers following.

The others slip out the door, but I move in front of Macon before he can leave. "It's a diversion," I tell him.

He just murmurs, "Stay here. I don't want you at the house alone."

He doesn't even look at me as he tries to leave again.

But I repeat, "It's a diversion."

Whoever they are, they're keeping the Jaegers' attention occupied while something else goes down. They're not here to start a fight. He doesn't need the weapon.

He reaches around me to push open the door, and I take his hand in mine, coming for his mouth. "Be careful."

But he pulls his hand out of mine. "Not here."

He brushes past me, leaving Mariette's, and I look after him, watching them all climb into their trucks. They speed off, and I feel the heat of peoples' eyes on my back, but when I turn around, no one is looking.

Okay, maybe like three are.

I look around to find Jessica smiling at me. Summer looks but doesn't smile.

I search the room. *Where's Aracely?*

Santa Maria. That's what Trace said. If he's right, Aracely would be there.

I bolt, running out of the restaurant, down the wooden steps, and into the rain. I splash through puddles, diving down the dark dirt road and into the night. The woods creep in on both sides, and I know there are wetlands behind the trees off to my right. But I stay on the road.

I run, not seeing anyone around. The boys' trucks are long gone.

But I don't go toward the explosion. Jetting down a small path on my left, I let my hood fall off, seeing the grooves of tires that have recently come through. The road is tiny, but BMWs and Audis fit just fine without even scraping any branches on their way.

I push my hair out of my eyes, feeling water soak my toes through my sneakers. Headstones appear up ahead, and I leap through a thin row of trees. Stumbling into the graveyard, I quickly look around for cars, flashlights, or people, but I don't see anything yet.

I know Aracely is here. She jumped at the chance earlier this year to get in a Saint's face. She's not missing this. I hunch over, staying low, and step through the overgrown weeds and ivy that climb the old burial markers.

Names engraved hundreds of years ago sit on granite half-buried in the soil after centuries of sinking into the land, while others are so faded and eroded from weather that you can't read anything. I've been here once, with Liv and Clay, because hiding things in graves was actually one story that was true. There are cases of liquor in one of the crypts. Macon buys it illegally and supplies it to the bar because sometimes St. Carmen likes to fuck with his supplier, so he needed a stash. Liv knows where it's at. One night last summer, we raided.

But a treasure? I didn't think that was true. I'm still not buying it. If it were significant, Macon could quite possibly be the most powerful person south of Washington, DC. Why would he not use it?

I spot two flashlights dancing in the dark ahead, and then headlights pop on. I stop short.

But before they can see me, someone grabs me and yanks me down to the ground. I lock eyes with Aracely, seeing her sister and a few others in her regular pack all lying on top of graves, hiding behind headstones.

I scoot in with her, tucking myself behind a marker.

"You on our side or theirs?" she asks me.

I shoot her a look. "What do you think?"

She stuffs something in my hand, and I look down, the moonlight peering through the clouds to show me a pair of steel knuckles. *With spikes on the outside.*

I gape. "Are you serious?"

She shrugs, picking up a baseball bat and flipping onto her side to look around the corner.

I slip on the knuckles in case I have to poke someone, but I'm not interested in making anyone bleed.

"You know, Macon wouldn't approve of this," I tell her.

She flashes me a dirty look. "The only thing I need a man to protect me from is a life sentence. He can clean up the evidence when I'm done."

Heh. I'm actually fine with that. As long as we can get rid of them before he and his brothers show up. Iron doesn't need company in jail.

Flashlights bob a hundred yards away, moving around graves, searching.

"How would they even know what grave to dig up?" I ask Aracely.

She sits up on one knee and zips up her fitted jacket. "When you're not stupid, and you have an endless amount of resources available to you, anything is possible." She wipes her muddy hands on her jeans and pulls a beanie over her head. "You inventory the graves, find the conquistadors, and then you discover one had a mistress, and the love letters between them are sitting in the St. Carmen Museum today. When a woman in those days bears you three sons and shares your bed for twenty-eight years, you trust her, even in death."

Oh my God. "You think the treasure is real?" I ask her.

"He didn't tell you it wasn't." She pins me with a look. "Did he?"

My face falls. *Jesus.*

Have they always had it? Or did they just recently find it? Does everyone over here know it's real? Has she actually seen it? I have so many questions.

She pulls the hat down, and I realize it's a mask that covers everything except for her eyes. Her friends follow suit, everyone getting their feet underneath them. I hop up onto mine, ready to follow.

I glance at Aracely. "You're not slashing their tires, are you?"

"No, I want them to leave."

Wise.

"So, what are we doing, then?" I ask.

She looks at me, grins, and then . . .

She leaps to her feet, the others following, all of them holding their hands in the air, howling from the top of their lungs.

What the hell? I crane my neck to see them sprint at top speed across the burial grounds. Toward the invaders.

The beams from the flashlights jerk in our direction, and I catch site of a blond ponytail whipping as some girl runs.

I shoot off, racing after Aracely and sucking in breath after breath. *This is dumb.* Someone's going to get hurt. Or arrested.

We charge through the rain, Aracely throwing her arms behind her head, getting ready to smash someone's face in.

Some teenager—I think he still goes to Marymount, actually—scurries backward, holding out his hands. "No, no, no, no!"

Aracely swings the bat down, and I watch in horror as she smashes down on the hood of the dude's Tesla. A dent sits like a crater in the middle.

"Oh my God!" Emaline Truax drops a shovel, coated in the dirt they disturbed. She swings the sledgehammer they brought with them, but I'm on her before she attacks. I shove her, the hammer dropping into a puddle, but then I hear someone growl and spin around. A guy is behind Aracely, trying to pry the bat out of her hands. I race over, leaping onto his back.

"Ah!" he growls.

I wrap my body around him, putting him in a headlock, which is pretty much all I know from wrestling with my siblings.

He throws me off, and I crash to the ground, the spikes of my knuckles sinking into the mud.

Car doors slam, headlights glow bright, and tires spin as the intruders escape. A truck, and then another one, speeds in as they peel off.

Aracely looks over at me. I smile, watching them turn tail and run. She grins, too. Liv and Clay would be proud of me.

Trace jumps out of his truck. "You got rid of them?" he asks Aracely.

I rise to my feet, about to walk over, but Aracely pulls me out of the way. "Careful."

I look down, seeing the pathetic start of a hole they tried to dig. I read the headstone. *El . . . des . . . a . . . fio? El desafio.* Challenge? Dare? Duel? I should ask Paisleigh. She knows more Spanish than me now.

"Thanks," I tell Aracely.

But someone takes my shoulders and twists me forward. "Are you okay?"

I look up, meeting Army's eyes.

But Aracely speaks up. "Yeah, I'm fine," she tells him, starting to walk away. "In case you ever wonder. Ever."

I watch her pick up her bat and start to leave the cemetery, the spark of pain on her face clear as day. He didn't see it, though. The twitch in her eyes when he brushed past her like she wasn't here.

I don't have a chance to go after her. Macon strolls up, his jaw clenched and his eyes hard on me. "I told you to stay at Mariette's. What did you think you would accomplish?"

Army drops his hands, but I don't think Macon even noticed him. He's looking at me like he looks at Trace sometimes.

I swallow. "Getting rid of them before you showed up."

"Am I in the habit of doing stupid things that I need to be protected from myself?" he chastises. "They could've hurt you. Taken you. I can suffer a few lost headstones—some holes in the ground—" He gestures to the earth underneath us. "Because it's all about the long game, and not a single person in my fucking house understands that!"

I startle, his growl piercing my ear. I don't think my parents have yelled at me like that. Ever.

I don't think it would hurt like it does with him, though.

"I wanted to help," I explain. "I just—"

"When I need your help, I will ask for it," he snaps. "I don't need someone else to babysit. You understand?"

I recoil, a feeling like I want to hide washing over me. He's looking at me like I'm stupid.

He likes me in his kitchen and in his room. Not anywhere else.

"Take her home," he orders.

Santos, who I didn't see arrive, steps up.

I can't look at Macon. "I have a car," I say, and start to walk past him.

"And make sure she doesn't leave," he calls out.

Santos takes my wrist, but before I can pull away, I hear a voice. "Don't touch her," someone else says.

I look up at Trace. Eyes hard, he stands tall—taller than I've ever seen him—and everything goes quiet. Even the rain.

Santos releases me.

Trace takes a few steps closer to his brother. Macon turns to face him.

"You can talk to us like that," Trace says. "Because sometimes we deserve it, but she's not your property."

My eyes sting. Macon stands toe to toe with his brother, getting in his face.

Trace stays rooted. "I won't hit back," he tells him, "but I'm not gonna back up anymore."

I almost smile.

"With her," he says to Macon, "you have to be gentle."

"You taking her back?" Macon dares him.

*Taking me back*. Like I'm an object who doesn't speak.

I look away, but I see Trace turn to me out of the corner of my eye. I meet his gaze.

"Can I have you back?" he asks.

I open my mouth, but I don't say anything. I don't want to start up with Trace again, but I also love that he's asking. It feels like something has changed inside of him.

He steps over, takes my hand, and says, "I'll give you a ride home."

He starts to lead me away, but I pull him back and hug him tight. My chest fills up with something, and I don't know what it is, but it feels good. I wish we'd started like this. As friends. "I love you, too," I whisper.

I take off Liv's raincoat and turn to Macon, stepping closer. "You weren't going to keep me, were you?"

He stares.

I force down the lump in my throat. "If I make love to you . . ." I lower my voice. "I don't think I'm ever going to want anyone else." I gaze at him, desperate for everyone else to disappear so he'll let me touch him. "Will you keep me?"

His chest falls hard.

I want him to keep me, but something is holding him back. Maybe it's my age. Maybe he thinks his health will be a burden on me.

Maybe it's something else.

But I can't sleep in his bed tonight.

"Aracely," I call out over my shoulder. "Would you take me home?"

I leave, catching up to her. Both of us jump into her car, and I lock my door because I don't trust myself if he tries to pry me back.

Trace was right. I need him to be gentle.

We take off, the radio playing music, and I almost tell her to stop a hundred times. He's prideful. He won't come for me. He would rather suffer for twenty years than admit he needs me with him. He won't come to St. Carmen.

He would never cross the tracks for a woman.

Soon, we're out of the Bay and climbing up into my neighborhood, the rain a steady but light fall.

Aracely hasn't said anything.

I finally speak up. "You're in love . . . with Army." I look over at her. "I'm sorry. I didn't realize."

She holds the wheel with both hands, keeping her eyes trained out the front windshield. "You weren't supposed to. He certainly doesn't."

"And you certainly don't beat around the bush with me," I muse. "So why have you with him? Why don't you tell him?"

"I did," she replies flatly. "When I was fifteen."

Oh.

"He was nineteen at the time and laughed in my face. I told him again when I was eighteen and when I was twenty."

"Didn't you go out with Iron and Dallas during that time?"

She dated them both somewhere in there.

But she just plucks a cigarette out of her pack in the console. "Yeah, well . . . that was never about love. For them, either."

I watch her, and I'm more and more curious about her as time goes on. She didn't want to stay close to the family. She wanted to stay close to Army. Any way she could. Cleaning their house, working their restaurant, dating Iron and Dallas . . .

Maybe Army would find out he misses her if there came a time when she wasn't around. She strikes me as the type who, unlike me, knows exactly what she wants to do with her life.

We pull onto my street, and she says, "I can do better anyway. Clay's dad is single, right?"

I burst into a laugh. We swing up to my gate, and I see through the bars that the house is dark. Paisleigh and Mars are at my grandparents', and if the gate is closed, my mom is still gone. "Five-five-eight-three-oh-two." I tell Aracely the code.

She looks at me, lifting her eyebrows for a second like she didn't expect me to tell her. All my friends have the code.

She punches in the numbers and waits for the gate to open before she speeds through. Winding around my driveway, she stops in front of my door.

I'm about to ask if she wants to come in and make margaritas, but she speaks before I do. "What was he like?" she asks, staring at the steering wheel. "Army?"

I drop my eyes. "Please don't ask me that."

But she argues, "You owe me. Was it good?"

I unfasten my seat belt, but I don't leave.

"Is he big?" she whispers, sounding so small all of a sudden. "Where does he touch?"

My chest aches, not because of the questions, but her tone. She wants to know because she wants to know how he'd be with her.

"You're going to get everything you want." I meet her eyes. "I wouldn't say that to everyone, but I don't think you'll fail."

I climb out of the car and dip down, peeking back inside through the window. "He won't be able to stand it," I tell her. "When he falls for you."

A smile peeks out at the corner of her lips, and I slam the door, heading inside.

# 26

## Macon

Do me a favor, man." Dallas runs his hand through his hair. "Please?"

The music pounds, and I move my eyes around the room, glaring but not seeing anything but her in my head.

"Get laid," he tells me, gesturing to the women at the table near the jukebox. "Pick one. Pick two. You need something warm. A *woman*. Not a kid."

A kid . . .

*Exactly.*

Krisjen Conroy acts like a fucking child. Just like Trace. Instead of admitting she did something wrong, she gets pouty and leaves. What was I thinking? That's how all of my days with her would be. Putting up with an endless stream of bullshit because she's fun to fuck?

I bite the inside of my mouth. Hard.

*A kid . . .*

That kid . . . is a fucking planet.

God, I never wanted something so much until her. The light spilling through the windows in my room cast this purple glow on her skin tonight. All I saw were stars. Another world.

"I thought you liked her now," Army gripes to Dallas.

"I do like her," he replies. "But she was never going to stay. None of them stay."

A blonde with a high ponytail, wearing a yellow tank top, holds my eyes. I ball my fists under my arms.

"She'll marry rich," Dallas continues, "and we'll eventually be no more than a passing nod on the street. We'll be mowing her lawn someday."

*She'd fucking love that, wouldn't she? Paying me to come to her house . . .*

"She's theirs," he goes on.

*Allowing me to step inside her shiny, white foyer so she can write me a check . . .*

"Not ours," he finishes.

I drop my arms and shoot off, seeing the blonde at the table sit up straight with a smile playing on her lips.

But I veer right, heading away from her and straight out the goddamn door.

"Macon!" Army calls behind me.

Followed by Dallas shouting, "Where are you going?"

I pull my keys out of my pocket and head for my truck, but a thought occurs to me, and I head inside the house instead. Running up the stairs, I dive into my bedroom and whip open the closet door. Pulling out the garment bag, I unzip it and pull out the black suit I wore to my parents' funerals.

I stopped attending them after that, and haven't touched these clothes since, priding myself on being a working man. I never wanted to look like I was trying to be better than the rest of Sanoa Bay.

I don't know why I want her to see me differently. I'm not ashamed of being a worker. Trace wears jeans and T-shirts. Iron, too.

Army wears shirts as little as possible, and Dallas knows he'll get laid with just a smile.

I want her to know I'm not them.

I pull the gun I retrieved from Mariette's out of the back of my jeans and walk over to my nightstand, about to drop it in the drawer when I notice the one that I had stashed there is missing.

My brothers always knew it was there. It's been there for years.

She's in my bed for a week, and it's gone.

I guess I have to go after her now. I need the gun back.

I smile a little, dropping Mariette's in the drawer in its place and undressing.

I don the suit, picking out a black shirt and black tie, and run my fingers through my hair. Grabbing my keys, I head back down the stairs and out the door, to my truck. Climbing in, I set off, speeding across the tracks to St. Carmen.

The broken dirt gives way to crumbling concrete that slowly turns into fresh blacktop, and I go from hearing the tires under the truck to hearing nothing.

The shop windows are all dark, rain shimmering like fireflies under the streetlights, and I keep my eyes forward as I pass turns that I haven't taken in years, and businesses I was never good enough to shop in.

It still baffles me that I opted to send Liv to school over here. I just knew it was the way out. I couldn't afford it yet with Dallas, and Trace had no interest in his education. Plus, I owed Liv.

We didn't grow up together, so she never really knew me, and I didn't make it easier. She had goals, and I wanted one person in the family to go to college.

But I made sure she never gave that school a reason to call me over here. I wanted to step foot in this town as little as possible.

And now, here I am . . . starving for one of their daughters.

I swing into her driveway, seeing a couple of lights on, and race around the patch of grass in the middle. The tires scream as I halt in front of her door.

Hopping out, I leave the keys inside and straighten my tie.

I press the doorbell.

Checking my phone, I read the time—11:03.

She said her siblings were with her grandparents. And if her mother came back early, then oh well. I guess we're doing this tonight.

Krisjen appears at the sidelight window, but she quickly moves out of sight. "I don't want to see you," she calls out.

I reach my arms out and grip the doorframe. "Well, I want to see you!"

"I don't care!"

Is she fucking kidding me? Does she know what it takes for me to come over to this shithole?

"Go home!" she yells.

But her voice is distanced.

Like she's moved away from the door.

*Good.*

I don't take time to think. I release the doorframe, take one step back, and shoot out my nice fucking leather shoe and kick the goddamn door.

It takes two more kicks to get the splintered wood to break away, and I charge in, seeing her in the middle of the foyer, breathing hard and wide-eyed as she scurries back, putting distance between us.

The alarm splits my ear, blaring shrill and loud.

I head straight for her.

"Are you crazy?" she growls.

God, she's cute in a ponytail.

"Turn off the alarm," I bark.

She folds her arms over her chest, not moving.

I narrow my eyes as the shrill scream of the alarm cuts through my brain.

*Goddammit . . .*

A phone rings, and I dart my gaze to the wall where a landline phone is posted next to the alarm.

She stands there.

"Answer it," I tell her.

They'll send security if she doesn't.

But she just tips her chin down, a challenge in her fucking beautiful eyes.

*Son of a bitch.*

"Krisjen . . ."

The phone rings four more times and then stops. She smiles to herself.

Twisting around, she punches a code into the alarm and the shrieking ceases. Spinning back toward me, she flexes her jaw. "It's like a three-minute response time," she says. "Better say what you gotta say quickly."

"Who said I wanted to talk?"

She shakes her head at me.

*Motherfucker.*

In two seconds, I'm in front of her, taking her hips in my hands and getting down in her face.

She scowls up at me. "You're not old enough for me."

I kiss her, taking her face in my hands and moving over her lips, hungry to get lost in her again. I press into her as she groans into my mouth.

Where is her bedroom?

But she rips her mouth away. "I can't be what keeps you alive." She breathes out. "I can't take care of you. I can't even take care of myself."

"I don't want you to take care of me!" I growl, pulling her into me. "I don't want you to make me soup and clean up after me and tell me what to eat and what not to drink! I don't want you to do the things a mother does!" I hover over her lips, starving as I lower my voice to a whisper. "I want you to do the things a girlfriend does."

Her eyebrows pinch together, pained, but her gaze on my mouth is just as desperate. Hot and sweet and crazy.

But strong.

So strong.

I was made for her.

"Touch me." I rest my forehead to hers. "And kiss me and come to bed in pretty things, or nothing, or my fucking sweatpants, for all I care, because God, you look good in them." I trail my mouth up her cheek to her temple. "And smile at me when you're happy, and yell at me when you're mad, and ride with me on the back of my bike in the rain." I come back to her eyes. "Drag me to dumb shit like plays and couples' game nights and stick your tongue in my mouth whenever possible."

She expels all the air in her lungs, tears welling, and I can see the smile hiding behind her stubborn mouth.

Her eyes drop to my lips again, she comes in, and then . . .

Red lights flash across her face.

She pulls away, and I look behind me, seeing the fucking red and blue gumballs of their neighborhood rent-a-cops.

I turn back to her, but she's moving away, a coy look in her eyes. "I don't think you have these cops on your payroll," she taunts.

I match her steps. "Call them off."

"And let them think they can leave me alone with you?"

She backs up, around the stairs, and I stalk her. The front door hangs open, the frame splintered. It's an obvious break-in. They will take me in.

"Krisjen . . ." I scold.

She smirks. "I'll tell Trace."

Like he's her protector now. She's daring me.

I arch a brow. "I raised that boy to share."

"You just want your turn, is that it?"

My turn? I break into a smile, the police lights getting closer.

She falters, seeing my amusement. "What?"

I shake my head. "Nothing."

She continues to back up, and I match her step for step. "What if I'm pregnant?" she asks.

I pause, my heart beating faster. "Are you?"

"I could be," she says. "It would be one of your brothers'."

No.

It wouldn't.

"It would be mine," I tell her.

She breathes out a laugh. "Do you think Trace would agree that his child belongs to you?"

She better stop fucking talking about having anyone else's kid.

"It would be mine," I bite out. "Trace had a vasectomy as soon as he turned eighteen. He doesn't want kids."

She slows her steps. She didn't know that.

"And Iron and Army always wrap it up," I inform her. "I had to feel you."

"But you didn't come inside of m—"

I cock my head, and her chest caves.

I didn't come inside of her . . . tonight.

She swallows. "You."

*Yeah.*

Her breathing hitches as she backs up more. "You son of a bitch. How could . . . Why did you push me away? I was yours!" She glares at me, pained. "I would've been yours in a heartbeat. A thousand more times! You acted like you didn't want me in the garage that night we fixed the car. Why didn't you say something?"

"You knew it was me." I stop in front of her. "You always knew it was me. Do you think I didn't notice you months ago? How you'd hold your breath every time I walked in a room? You knew it the next morning when I sat down at the table and the jolt hit your heart, because it hit mine, too." I search her eyes. "The hyperawareness we have around each other. You knew the moment it happened that you didn't want it to be anyone else."

She shakes her head as if in denial.

Knocks sound on the broken door. "Hello?"

"Are you pregnant?" I ask in a whisper.

She just keeps shaking her head frantically. "Why didn't you say something?"

"If you have my kid, there's no escaping me, Krisjen."

She looks up at me. "Why didn't you say it was you?"

And my eyes fall to her pink mouth and those lips that were wrapped around me just a few hours ago.

I'm so fucking hungry for her. "There's no escaping me no matter what."

"We're coming in!" a man shouts.

She wets her lips, her eyes darting between me and the door, and I wrap my arms around her. I yank open the door under the stairs, and shove us inside.

"Carsten Security?" the guard calls from inside the house. "Anyone home?"

I close us inside the dark room and back her up against the wall, her whimper falling across my lips.

"Hello?" someone calls out.

She opens her mouth, but I touch it with mine. "Shh . . ."

Shoes squeak against the marble floor outside the door, muffled talking, but her heat travels through my hand, and I suddenly can't catch my breath. I want to be inside of her.

"Swamp shouldn't cross the tracks," she bites out.

But I take her head in my hands. "You're Swamp now, too," I say. "You're ours."

Tears fill her eyes, and I capture her mouth, her moan drifting down my throat as she gives in to it and kisses me back.

A man calls out again, "Carsten Security!"

She pulls away from my mouth, breathing hard as I nibble her jaw, her neck, and then her fucking lips again. She sighs. "Macon . . ."

I lift her up into my arms, guiding her legs around me. "How could I tell you it was me?"

She wraps her arms around my neck, kissing me.

"Hello?" a guard calls out, footfalls hitting the stairs above us.

"You didn't hear me come into the house that night," I tell her. "You didn't stop."

I felt like shit, and I walked in and saw her so beautiful on the couch. Her hand under the blanket. Her shirt pulled up and her breasts and skin . . .

"The way you were with yourself," I explain, "it was the way it should be. It was like it always should be when someone touches you. The way your body moved, the way you breathed . . ." I catch her bottom lip between my teeth. "It's why we're alive. That's how it should be."

I'd seen women touch themselves before, but she was so soft. I could feel the heat from her body across the room. I forgot everything—all of my problems—for a few minutes.

"And then you spoke, and took everything I was thinking out of my head, and my insides took over," I say. "I wanted you under my skin and your scent in my head. I couldn't think. I did what we do when we're dying. We rage, and I felt it on you, too. I had to hold you."

She gazes at me, so much beauty and love in her eyes.

"I just couldn't let it happen again," I tell her. "I couldn't keep you and bring you into my shit."

"Is anyone here?" shouts one of the guards.

She kisses me so softly, brushing her mouth over mine. "I wasn't made for anyone else," she whispers, holding me tight. "I belong to you."

*Women love being owned by a good man.*

Am I a good man?

"Bite me," I beg over her mouth. "Feel me between your teeth."

Parting her lips, she catches my bottom lip between her teeth. My cock twitches.

She tilts her head and touches her lips to the corner of my mouth. Barely a touch. Soft, gentle, quick. I close my eyes. "Again," I tell her.

She does it again, and an electric current rages underneath my skin. She kisses my cheek the same way. My jaw, my temple, between my eyebrows, the other corner of my mouth . . .

Her breath, her sweat, her taste . . . everything is inside of me.

I inch her shirt up, my cock swelling at the sight of her breasts. God, I want to fucking eat her up.

My hand covers one, and I kiss her, cutting off her little moan.

Her tits press against my chest . . . I have to have her now.

Lowering her to her feet, I plant my hand on her stomach and push her into the wall. With my other hand, I unbutton her shorts and draw down her zipper. Grazing my lips over her temple, I tell her, "Take them off."

Squirming against me, she pushes her shorts down her legs, her shirt still up above her breasts.

"Now the underwear," I tell her.

Holding my eyes, she slides them down, letting them fall to her feet.

Lifting her high again, I wrap her legs around me and carry her, laying her body down on a small table. Extra dining room chairs are also stored off to the side, an old grandfather clock, and some cardboard boxes.

I whip off my jacket, rip open my shirt, and drop everything to the ground as she arches her back, pushing her tits to the sky and looking so fucking eatable. I slide my eyes down, my dick throbbing painfully at the sight of exactly where she feels so good.

Something between a whimper, a cry, and a moan escapes her. "Macon . . ." she begs for me.

And I come down, biting the soft flesh of her pussy.

"Ah," she cries, clawing her thighs.

"Hello?" the men call again. "Who was that?"

*Fuck.*

I lick and taste her, sucking so hard because I can't stop. I can't fucking stop. I bite everywhere, my teeth aching to feel her, and then stick my tongue inside of her.

"Ah!" she cries out again.

"Carsten Security!" they call out. "Identify yourself!"

*Goddammit.* Can I please have this woman in fucking peace?

Unfastening my belt and ripping open my pants, I pull her down to the end of the table, plant my hand over her mouth, and press the head of my cock to her tight little entrance.

Her moan vibrates across my hand, and I lean down, sucking on one nipple before moving to the other.

And then I thrust, sliding deep inside.

"Oh," she groans behind my hand.

I close my eyes, warmth spreading through my stomach and down my legs. My heart pounds inside my chest.

I slide out and then in again, over and over, faster and faster, until the table is banging against the wall, and her thighs are damn near touching her breasts.

Her tits bob back and forth, and I can't get deep enough. "Fuck," I breathe out. "Krisjen . . ."

I kiss her nipples, her hot breath wetting my hand over her mouth as I smooth my thumb over her clit, soft and slow.

"You want me to stop?" I ask her.

She shakes her head.

"You gonna listen from now on?"

She shakes her head.

I smile. *Of course not.*

I pound into her, coming in and gripping the back of her hair as I dive deep into her mouth, kissing her.

"Oh, Macon," she moans, jerking as I work her clit. "God, I . . . I . . ."

She's coming.

"It's okay," I growl. "Fuck it. Scream."

I shoot up, taking my hand off her mouth, and fuck her hard, yanking her down on my cock over and over again.

She cries out, her body tensing, her muscles hardening, and her pussy contracting around me as I slide in again and again.

"Oh God!" she shouts, sliding up and down the table.

My dick pumps with heat, cum starting to spill, and a hard groan lodges in my throat.

But then there's a knock at the door. "Hello?"

I don't stop.

The table rocks against the wall, and I lean a hand down on the table, riding her. Her body goes limp as her orgasm fades away.

"Just a minute!" I bark at the cops.

"Who is that?" one calls. "What's going on?"

"We're not done!" she cries, tipping her head back. "Please, just a minute!"

I stutter, spill, and release a heavy groan, coming inside of her as I thrust through it.

"Fuck." I let my head fall back, sliding in and out slower and slower as my release drifts through me and everything starts to relax.

But before we're done, she sits up and wraps her arms around me, her hair damp with sweat and in her face as she kisses me.

I circle my arms around her, touching her everywhere I can reach. *God.*

She pulls back but keeps her mouth an inch from mine. "I . . ."

But whatever she was going to say fades on her lips, and I get it.

There are no words.

Other than I want to do that with her a thousand more times. And slower, much slower.

I step back, doing up my pants, and she hops off the table, quickly slipping on my black shirt with missing buttons.

She opens the door and steps out, and I stay behind, fastening my belt.

"Ms. Conroy, are you okay?" I hear one of the cops ask.

"Yes, everything's fine," she laughs out. "I'm really sorry about this. My boyfriend . . . Well . . ."

"Your boyfriend?" the other asks.

I open the door all the way, seeing the security guards notice me as I step up to her side.

"Macon Jaeger," one says.

I know him, but I don't remember his name. They both know *me*, though.

"Is . . . everything cool?" the one I recognize asks us.

"Yeah." I nod, hooking an arm over her shoulder so they know what's mine. "I'm sorry. It was my fault."

They look behind them to the busted doorframe and back to her again. "Are you sure?"

She leans into my embrace and puts a possessive hand on my stomach. "I'm okay." I can feel her blush. "Thank you."

They hesitate, but eventually nod and start to turn around. "We'll have to call your parents to let them know we responded," one of them says as they walk for the door.

Krisjen nods. "Good luck with that."

She walks toward the stairs, glancing at me. "I'll be in the shower. Hurry."

I drop my eyes to the cut of breast peeking out through the piece of shirt she neglected to hold closed, and feel my body grow hot again.

I turn to the guard, a flash of amusement crossing their faces. I follow, seeing them out. "I'll secure the door."

"Don't be setting off any fire alarms tonight, either, huh?" one teases as they both leave.

And I can't help but smile with him. "We'll try not to."

---

Her sheer curtains glow white as the moonlight spills into the room, and I hold her to me as I stare up at her canopy bed. White fabric is draped around the frame and cascades down the four posts like some bed in a fairy tale.

Her sheets feel like water. Soft and precious and gentle, like a cloud for a doll.

"I need to get you back home," I tell her, threading my fingers through her hair. "This bedroom is unnerving."

A quiet laugh escapes her, but she keeps her head on my chest. "Why?"

"It's reminding me that you're nowhere near my age." I stare up at all the fabric. "Something I forget a lot, given the things I just did to you."

She still has a math book on her bedside table, for Christ's sake. I'm feeling a little weird about how she just rode me backward.

She lifts her head. "Have you ever been with someone with a thirteen-year gap before?"

I almost smile, because no, I haven't, but almost immediately, the smile fades. That's not true, actually.

She stares at me, her own amusement dying. "I'm sorry," she says.

"For what?"

She drops her eyes, opening her mouth to speak but then closing it again. I tense.

She swallows. "Army . . . told me, um . . ." She meets my eyes. "He told me about the husband and wife who made you and him an offer."

I shift, looking away.

But I can't move. She's on top of me.

"He didn't say as much," she goes on, "but I eventually figured out you must've—"

"I'm clean," I say. "If that's what you're worried about."

She doesn't falter. "I wasn't worried," she tells me. "I know you'd never put me in danger."

But she keeps her eyes fixed on me, and the room suddenly feels too small.

"How many?" she asks me.

I press my teeth together and grind for a split second. "I don't want to talk about it."

But she pushes me. "How many times did you do it?"

"What did I say, Krisjen?"

She shuts up, but even though I'm holding her, she feels far away now.

The past is depression. I can't change it. Why bother thinking about it?

Maybe we would've eventually been okay if I hadn't gone that far, but what if we hadn't been? I took care of my family, and I'd do it again.

Maybe.

I don't know.

I struggle to breathe, and without thinking, I grip her tighter.

It wasn't the sex that was hard. I just didn't like not being seen. I wasn't someone to them. They would never have spoken to me in public. They never would've held a door for my sister or thought about me after I left the bed.

I close my eyes, breathing hard as I tuck her head back into my chest. "A few," I finally reply in a whisper.

"A few like three, or a few like ten?"

My throat is so dry. "A few like six," I say.

I wait for another question, but she just lies there, her arm draped over my chest and her hand on my shoulder.

I draw in a deep breath. "She passed the news on to her friends," I tell Krisjen. "It didn't go on longer than a few months. I got cash and used it to buy other things I didn't mind selling."

A couple of them were nice to me. They fucking talked to me, at least, and it became clear they were just as miserable in their lives as I was. They had their own shit to deal with, and we were able to forget about our lives for a while.

But a few of the others . . . Jesus.

Everything was so dark in the Bay at that time. One of the St. Carmen women wanted me to pretend I was her son. One liked to hit me. A lot.

"I'd always had spells where I didn't feel good, but God," I go on, "I felt like an ugly piece of shit walking out of that first house, Krisjen. I never felt so worthless."

Growing up, I acted out just like my brothers, but not with sex. Not ever with sex. Sex was important. That was always my hang-up. I had to be able to connect.

"I could wash it off my body," I tell her, "but not out of my head, and I was in a hole I was never gonna crawl out of. I hated being here. I hated the sight of the world." I just go on, spilling my guts and getting it out, because if she knows, then she'll know more than even Army, and I want her to know me best.

"I couldn't pay the bills," I continue. "Dallas was drinking, Liv and Trace were constantly fighting . . . The house came crashing down on my head every time I walked through the fucking front door." I force down the lump in my throat. "It wasn't the first time I thought about it, but . . . it was the first time I really wanted to do it."

Like a fucking coward. When you feel like shit, it's hard to remember a time when you ever felt good, and I left every one of those women thinking life would always be like that.

It wasn't, and there were good days, but I'm so tired sometimes.

"He watched the whole fucking thing," I murmur. "He instructed me on how to treat her. How to be rough with her. Told me what he wanted me to do to her, where to kiss her, how hard to . . ."

I feel one of her tears fall onto my chest.

I exhale hard, my hand going into her hair, fisting it gently. “So I dived into my head and thought about someone else. Another girl.”

“Who?”

I shrug. “No one in particular. A Saint. Someone I wasn’t supposed to have. Someone sweet and innocent.” I rub her scalp. “Always with sunshine in her eyes and smiles that felt warm.” I rub my thumb along her cheek. “I just didn’t know she was real.”

She lifts her head, looking at me.

I soften my gaze. “I’ve been dreaming about you for a long time.”

Her kind eyes smile at me. “Well, since I was like ten or eleven anyway.”

“Oh, Jesus Christ.”

She laughs and climbs up my body, straddling me. She just had to remind me how old she was when I was twenty-four.

Leaning down on one hand, she holds my face and looks into my eyes. “Life is going to kill you eventually.”

I gaze up at her.

“It’s going to kill us all,” she says. “But you’re a monster, you hear me? They will have to rip you from this world. You’re strong in your head, and you’re strong in body, and you . . .” She pins me with a hard stare that takes my breath away. “You. Do. Not. Stop. You will *never* stop.”

I don’t blink.

“They will all know . . .” she tells me, “that if you’re not dead, then you’re not done.”

I suck in a breath, catching her as she comes down on my mouth. I kiss her, arching up, the power of her lips coursing through mine, into my head, and down my body.

I grow hard underneath her, and she reaches down, fisting my cock.

"And I'm not that sweet and innocent," she teases.

I gasp as she strokes me, and I grab her ass in both hands, pressing her into my body. God, I could fuck her ten more times tonight.

But I meet her eyes, coming in to nibble her mouth. "You're not sweet and innocent? Is that so?" I taunt.

I pull away, seeing her disappointed look when I crash back to the bed. I pick up a stuffed toy between her pillows and hold it up. "And what the fuck is this?"

She sits up, her beautiful naked body on display, but her expression looking oh so sweet and innocent. "A taco." She grabs it away from me, holding it to her body protectively. "I mean, obviously."

I pick up another one, which she grabs.

"A burrito," she says.

And another one.

"Broccoli."

She snatches them all away, and I'm tempted to ask what possessed her to buy a stuffed broccoli toy, but then she'll tell me, and I really don't care as long as she keeps them off our bed at home.

I pluck the toys away from her and throw them to the side. Taking her hips, I push up and suck on her breast as I fit myself back inside her for the fourth time tonight.

She pants, moving up and down my cock. "I would scold you and say we need some sleep now," she tells me.

"But I'm hard again."

"And I'm the one who takes care of you."

I press my lips to hers, slipping my tongue into her mouth and dying for more. And more and more.

"Swim to me," she says.

*More.*

I don't stop. I will never stop.

# 27

## Krisjen

He pulls away as I try to thread his necktie around his collar. "Don't bother," he says. "I'm just going home."

But I smile, feeling my cheeks warm. I stand on a chair in front of him in just my underwear, and he squeezes my ass with both hands, pulling me in.

"I like it." I start to tie his tie, which I learned how to do last spring when Clay wore one to the debutante ball. "You in these clothes does to me what me in my underwear is doing to you right now."

I shift ever so slightly, brushing my thigh against his hardening groin.

He moves in, taking my nipple in his teeth, and my stomach drops so fast I let out a small laugh-gasp. He sucks and kisses, and I close my eyes as my body starts to stir again.

I'm a mess. An exhausted, happy, delirious mess. My hair needs to be combed, and my body needs to be washed. He was inside me more than he was out last night.

And I miss him already.

Clay's mom once told us that young people—especially young women—fall in love too easily. Too quickly. I thought I loved Milo. Even when he was cruel.

Then I learned. And I kept learning. Every time Macon sat at the table. Stood at the kitchen counter. Walked into a room. Lifted a bottle to his lips. Ran his hand through his hair. Looked at me. Didn't look at me.

Worked in the garage too long. Didn't eat his food. Moved around the house at night.

What makes him different from anyone else?

"Krisjen . . ." he whispers, his hot breath caressing my skin.

And I hold his head in my hands, grazing my lips over his forehead.

That's what's different. I always hear him. Even when he says almost nothing.

I'm glad I'm not pregnant. Yet, anyway. I just wanted to see what he would say.

But I want to make sure he loves me, and I want a chance to make certain he wants it. What he said that morning in the bathtub about being worried that he would fail a woman and his children . . .

I would want to make sure he's happy about it.

I get back to work, dressing him as his hands roam down my thighs and back up to my waist.

I tighten the tie and fold his collar over. "Garrett Ames sees a boy who doesn't deserve a seat at the table," I say, meeting his eyes and steeling my voice. "But you're a man who's worked hard to get where he's at, and . . . you don't sit."

He holds my gaze, and I smooth out every crease and make sure the folds in the lapels of his jacket are cut like knives.

"These clothes show that you know you're going to take anything you want," I state. "I mean, it worked with me last night."

He snorts.

"I like that everyone outside your bedroom sees this," I say, "and I'm the only one who gets to see what's under it when you crawl into bed with me at night."

He rushes to hide the smile consuming him, pulling me close and burying his face in my breasts.

He licks, and I lean into it as he moves up my chest, to my neck.

Nerves fire between my thighs, like goddamn lightning. "Just one more time?" I beg.

He growls, digging his fingers into my ass and sucking my neck hard before he pulls away like he's in pain.

His cock strains against his pants, and I whimper, batting my eyelashes.

He laughs. But then commands me, "Pack up the kids and anything else you need. Understand? My mother's old art studio is theirs. Until the renovations are completed. Then they can have their own rooms."

*Pack up the kids . . .*

"But my parents . . ." I retort.

"They know where to find us if they ever want to be parents again."

I stare at him, some kind of throbbing going on under my skin that's making me hot and excited and in awe of him. Just like that. Moving three Conroys into his house. He's a good man.

But then I process exactly what he said. "Wait . . . Did you say *renovations*?"

He nods. "The old wing. We're going to rebuild it. Dex will need a room. So will Iron when he comes home."

I stare at him.

"You're going to make me buy more suits, aren't you?" he gripes, because he can probably see the emotion that I'm feeling at how he's making plans, holding his head up, planning for the future . . .

I nod frantically, diving down to his mouth but not kissing him right away. Just hovering and breathing for a few moments before I sink my lips into his.

He's trying. That's all I need to hear.

He mumbles in between kisses, "And no fucking taco on our bed, please."

He accidentally kisses my teeth as I break out in a smile. I bite his lips.

"Might get you a stuffed alligator, though," he teases. "Because that's what you are. A little alligator."

I keep biting, his mouth, his jaw, his neck . . . "Nom, nom, nom . . ."

He rumbles with a laugh as he nibbles my breasts and grips my ass again. "Krisjen . . ."

My skin burns for him. My arms feel empty already.

"Macon . . ." I groan, arching my back and letting my head fall so he can suck on me. I hold his head to my body. "One more time."

A screech hits my ears, and I pop my eyes open, seeing my mother standing in my open doorway.

"Oh my God," I gasp, jumping down from the chair. Macon reluctantly lets me go as I grab my pillow and hold it to my body. *Shit.*

"Oh my God," my mom says.

I glance at Macon, but he's not looking at either of us. Just staring at the ceiling as he straightens his jacket, unfazed.

"Mom . . ." But I don't know what to say to her.

Her travel case lies on the floor on its side, her eyes turning angry as she looks between Macon and me. She was supposed to be back days ago. I knew she could show up anytime. I don't know why I just stopped thinking she would.

She'll freak out because I'm with a Jaeger. She'd be happy if she found Jerome Watson in here with his hands all over me.

I start to head her off before she can speak. "Mom, I—"

But then I hear Macon's voice. "Hello, Cara," he greets my mother.

My gut knots. What?

I look up at him. He knows her?

She bursts into my room, her hair cascading in loose waves because of the one perm she got years back. She usually straightens it, but it's clear she came from a beach. An island somewhere. She has a tan.

"What have you done?" she yells at Macon. Then she turns to me. "What did he do to you? What did he tell you?"

"What . . . ?"

She shoves his chest. He arches back a little but doesn't stumble. As if he was expecting it.

"You don't get to have my daughter!" she bellows. "How dare you! You thought you could have one of us? You thought you could lay your hands on her?"

Her hand flies across his face, and I tense, my brain slowly unraveling what's happening in front of me.

He rubs his jaw, turning his head back to face her. "I remember you liking my hands on you."

My stomach drops, and the room tilts in front of me. "What . . ." I draw in a deep breath, one after another as I remember his words from last night. *Her friends*, he said.

Macon looks down at me, but I don't meet his eyes.

He'd said the woman passed him around to her friends. One of them was my mom. Why didn't he tell me?

"You don't get to fuck her!" my mother yells.

But I'm shaking my head, even as Macon turns me to face him and covers my ears with his hands. He holds me close as she shrieks.

"How dare you!"

Her words are muffled, but I can still hear her. I squeeze my eyes shut.

She hurt him. She preyed on him.

Why didn't he tell me?

I hug the pillow. What are the odds that he happens to fall for the daughter of the woman who coerced him into sex?

I stop breathing for a second. What are the odds I just happen to go to bed with the same guy?

I look up at him. "How long have you known who I was?"

His jaw flexes.

I pull away from his hands over my ears. "How long?"

"He targeted you!" my mother says.

Macon holds my eyes, shaking his head slowly.

"Because he hates us," she goes on. "Because he likes playing with our women like we're his toys."

"There was nothing I liked about you," he hisses at her.

He moves back in, grabbing my face and holding my forehead to his. "Get in my car," he whispers. "Don't get dressed. Bring nothing. Just get in the car."

"She's not going anywhere—"

He yanks away from me and walks into my mother, forcing her to back up. "I don't want to hear your voice. Speak again and you'll regret it."

She sucks in short, shallow breaths, visibly shaken.

And for the first in a long time, I'm reminded of his reputation. People are afraid of him for a reason. Maybe not back when she paid a young man who desperately needed the money, but life didn't make him a monster. People like her did.

My mother backs away and takes out her phone. "I'm calling the police."

She runs from the room.

But he stays.

I search his eyes. "How long have you known who I was?" I ask him.

He stares down at me, and when he squares his shoulders, I know. "I've always known who you were."

My mind floods with every moment I was in his house, at his table, working his restaurant, bringing him meals, throwing myself at him that night in the garage . . .

He knew I was her daughter.

"You sent Army after me to offer me a job that night," I say, remembering what Trace said. "Were you going to use me?"

"If I were going to use you, I had a lot of opportunities," he says. "I could've let you make that video with my brothers."

He takes my face again.

"I sent Army after you that night because I liked you," he whispers. "Because I wanted more of you. Because I'd never seen a woman be so soft with herself and touch herself like that. Because I didn't want you to be where I couldn't see you every day."

My lip trembles. Why didn't he tell me? Was he ever going to?

I don't realize a tear has spilled until he wipes it away with his thumb. "I wanted you close, because when you cried, I could feel it and knew this place was going to kill you, too, and for the first time in a long time, I was protective. I wanted you in the Bay where I could keep you safe."

I believe him. It sounds like him. And Macon is not someone who ever feels the need to lie.

But I believe everyone. That's my problem. I assume everyone is good and honest with pure intentions, and I can't remember a single time when that's worked out for me. I'm naïve and stupid, and I don't have a lick of street smarts like Clay or Liv. Or like Aracely.

I still think unicorns just might exist, and Macon would set a Christmas tree on fire.

He shakes his head, seeing it in my eyes. "Don't do this. Don't."

"How many times?"

He blinks hard. "Krisjen, please."

"How many?" I bark.

I need to know how many times they were alone together. Did he have her in the shower? Where did she touch him? Did he kiss her?

Tight-lipped, he replies. "A few."

"A few like three, or a few like ten?"

He drops his eyes. "A few like I blocked it out."

I laugh bitterly, backing away. "She must've liked it."

He must've been doing enough right that she kept coming back. Why didn't he tell me? He knows everyone I've slept with. He knew before we did anything. I don't need his list, but I should've known about my fucking mother!

He inches toward me, but I back up, tearing my heart apart with that one step.

I love him.

But I'm confused. I need to think.

"Krisjen, I was a kid," he pleads, "with an unbelievable weight on my shoulders. I never wanted to think about it again! And years later, there you were. In my house. All the time. With your bare feet and your pretty smile. Your music, your candles, your happy little fucking heart, and I never imagined this would happen!"

I drop the pillow, covering my face with my hands. Images assault me of them in bed together. They must've had conversation. Foreplay. A few laughs. Some part of him had to enjoy it, right?

*Oh God.* The tears stream. I can't think about anything else. They're all I see. I'm always going to see them in my head. I'm gonna be sick.

"You should've told me," I sob. "You should've . . ."

"What?" he growls. "I should've what?!"

I startle, dropping my hands and looking at him through teary eyes.

"Should've stayed away from you?" he yells, advancing on me. "Should've let you go? Is that what I was supposed to do?" And he sweeps his arm across my desk, sending all my shit to the floor. "Just fucking let you go?!"

I breathe hard as my pencils and pens roll over my chair and onto the floor.

He grabs me, snaking an arm around my waist, the other hand

holding my face. He kisses me hard, stealing my breath, but he releases me before I start fighting him.

He stares into my eyes. "Your mother is just jealous that you never had to pay me," he says in a low voice, filled with disdain. "It was quite my pleasure, actually."

And he throws me off, wiping me off his mouth and taking out a bill from his pocket.

He backs away, leaving it on the corner of my desk before he walks out the door. "I'll let Dallas know he's up."

# 28

## Macon

I charge out of the house, yanking off my tie and ripping open my shirt.

Whatever buttons were left after last night fly off in the driveway. *Fuck her.*

She has screwed her way through nearly every bedroom in my house, slept with family members I see every day. And she wanted to do it. There is nothing I wanted about Cara Conroy. So much so I could barely look at her daughter when she started hanging with Trace last spring. Every time she was around, it was a constant reminder of St. Carmen. In a way that Clay never was.

I swing open the door to my truck and climb in, starting the engine and peeling out of the driveway as fast as I can.

It's light out, way past dawn, but I don't know what time it is. The guys might be at work by now.

My hands shake, but I don't know why. I'm not fucking mad. Or upset. I feel nothing. She's nothing. Not special.

Traffic blurs in front of me, and I blink, feeling my eyes wet. I dig the heel of my palm in to clear my vision. *They'll probably be at work by now.*

The road stretches in front of me, trees breeze past—cars—and I'm on autopilot. One arm stretched out with a hand on the wheel, the other propped up on the door, my hand gliding through my hair over and over again.

*"Don't." I jerked away. "I don't like that."*

*I tongued the inside of my lip, tasting my blood.*

*She squeezed my neck. "Just get hard," she tells me. "That's your job."*

I can't breathe. It hurts. My head is throbbing. Fuck.

A horn honks, and I snap to, veering to the side of the road. I stop and drop my head in my hand, tensing every muscle to keep the pain at bay.

I didn't think about it for years. Every time it crept in, I pushed it away, not because what I had to do was so horrible, but what they wanted from me was.

People fuck for money all time, but they weren't paying for sex. They were paying to fuck a servant. A nonperson.

I'd never had sex with a woman I didn't like before that. I always knew her. Liked her. There had never been a one-night stand. It had never made me feel bad.

And after a while, I didn't see Krisjen as anything other than what she really was. Beautiful. A good person. She's bright and amazing. St. Carmen no longer existed when I saw her.

The last thing she deserves is me. She should have someone good. She deserves a clean slate.

I'll never get out of this fucking hole I'm in.

She'll never look at me the same.

I don't know how I get home because I don't remember the streets or the traffic lights, but I drift through my front door, hearing, "Hey."

I turn my head as my brothers rise from their chairs, fully dressed. They blur in my vision, but I see Trace's smile. He looks five again when he smiles like that.

"Damn . . ." he says, looking me up and down approvingly. My shirt is ripped open, and I don't know where the tie is.

"You stayed the night," I hear Dallas say. "Must've . . ."

But they all stop, their smiles fading as they look at my eyes. I turn away and start for the stairs.

I'm sweating. My clothes stick to my skin. The ceiling feels too low.

"What happened?" Army moves toward me.

"Nothing." I climb the steps, afraid to look back at him. My hand shakes. I grab the railing to steady it.

"Why don't you guys go—"

"I'm just gonna take a shower," I choke out, my pulse racing in my ears. "I'll follow."

"Macon . . ."

"Go to work. All of you," I call out, trying to lighten my voice. "I'm close behind."

I can't breathe.

The door opens, and I turn, taking a long look at Trace's face. He raises his eyebrows.

"Put some beer in the cooler." I force a smile. "It'll be a hot day. We deserve it, right?"

"Psh, yeah." He smiles wide and races out the door, Dallas following, and I twist back around, heading for the top.

Army still stands there, watching me. I know he is.

"Macon . . ."

"I'm right behind you," I say, not looking back. I reach the top and walk to my room. I step inside, close the door, and lock it.

I see my bedside table and barely feel myself walk toward it. But I don't open the drawer.

Not yet.

I sit on the bed, letting the sunlight Krisjen always leaves spilling into my room cut into my brain. I wince at the glare in the corner of my eye, and the way it's too hot on that side of my face. No clouds outside. I hate clear skies.

I rest my elbows on my thighs, draping my arms over my legs as I bow my head.

There's dirt under one of my nails. I feel it like it's a seed burrowed in there.

Sweat dampens my body. It's so hot.

And every follicle of hair feels like it's being pulled from underneath my skin.

Hair hangs in my eyes. Dirt on my shoes. I can feel it through the leather.

I'm sick of the dirt roads. The thought of seeing them again feels like a ten-ton weight on my shoulders.

All the same, all the time.

And food and people and the years and the talking. So much fucking talking. It's all the same, every time. Every day.

Tomorrow won't be any different. Neither will next week.

My eyes burn as I stare at the drawer. I vaguely feel my phone vibrate, but I cancel the call without looking and drop it on my bedstand.

Krisjen was right. She couldn't keep me alive. I was always going to end up here. I thought if I had her, it would be more than this, because I wasn't finding a reason to stay for them. For the Bay. I fail here. Every day is just more bullshit. I'm shit.

People don't love me. They're scared of me. They need me. My brothers might be attached to me, but only because I've always been here. Every moment of their lives I've been here, taking up space, on their case.

The phone buzzes again. I pick it up, ignoring the call.

I zone in on the wood grain handle of the drawer.

It could be over in one minute. Less, even. I could just stop.

I just want to stop.

The sun scorches my eyes, and I close them.

They'd get used to functioning without me. They may even feel guilty about the sigh of relief they'll feel when I'm not around. But they'll feel it.

I was never compassionate. Patient. Kind. I'm someone people put up with. Was I ever tender with her?

*I was.*

*It was real.*

*She felt it, too.*

*She liked me.*

*She was always looking, even though I acted like I didn't see.*

I shake my head. *No.*

*No.*

*She's kind. She's good at being kind.*

*It was fucking pity.*

*I'm so much less than what she could have and she knows it.*

*She's just kind.*

*She won't want . . .*

I swallow hard . . . *me in . . .*

I growl, digging my fingernails into my hair . . . *five years.*

"Krisjen . . ." I gasp.

I yank open the drawer, my heart pounding and my head splitting, but I hear a voice.

"Macon?"

I look at the phone on the table.

"Macon, are you there?"

*Iron?*

I pick up the phone, and it feels like fifty pounds as I lift it to my ear.

"Are you there?" he says again.

I can't talk, but I'm breathing hard. I pull the phone away from my ear, seeing a number I don't recognize.

"How are you . . ." I clear my throat. "How are you calling me?"

"A friend has a cell phone."

I missed the sound of his voice.

"I thought if you saw the prison on your caller ID you wouldn't answer."

He's right. I wouldn't have answered. I hate that he knows that about me. "You need . . ."

But I stop, about to ask him if he needs money but deciding to shut my fucking mouth. He can have whatever he wants.

"Are you safe?" I ask, the tears straining my voice.

"So far, so good."

I was worried about Iron in prison, but not because of his safety. When people like him go to jail, it's only the start.

"You know," he starts, "I was thinking of that time you took me to the Cocoa Beach Air Show."

I remember. Sand. Clear day. Lawn chairs, kids with earmuffs, aviation geeks with their binoculars and coolers.

"Just you and me." His voice softens, and I can tell he's smiling. "I had wanted to go the year before, but Dad was just too busy. I know he tried, but it was what it was."

Yeah. My parents had suitcases. Up in the attic, never used.

"We never got to go anywhere, and I just wanted to see it, because of the pictures I'd seen online," he tells me. "I didn't think it was real. Like planes and pilots and people who had adventures like that every day were something that only existed in movies. It was the first time I realized how big the world was. And what people can do."

We don't even use the suitcases now. We don't go anywhere. They don't even ask.

"Those planes flying in formation," he goes on. "All the people in uniforms . . ."

I listen, still hearing the sounds of the jets whooshing past, slicing through the air.

"Everything in the Bay was draining, and that day was so full of energy." He pauses and then continues. "The music, the crowds . . . You probably don't remember it, but I never forgot what a good day that was."

It was. It was noise that wasn't stress. It was distracting. I didn't think about home all day. I remember noticing that on our way back home.

"It was a good day, more so because you smiled a lot," he says. "I felt special. Like it was something we both shared, and I don't know why that felt so important, but it did and it stuck with me. I remember thinking we'd be closer because of it."

I close my eyes.

"I've had too much time to think in here already," he says. "I forgot how I wanted to be one of those pilots someday. Be a hero. Do brave things." He pauses. "They wouldn't take me now, would they?"

A knife slices my heart.

He's a felon now. The military doesn't take you with a record.

He breathes hard, and I grip the phone, forgetting the drawer.

"You don't realize how badly you wanted something," he tells me, "until you find out that it's no longer an option."

I stare at my shoes.

"I'm sick of regret.

"Sick of just surviving," he adds. "But I'm going to be a pilot. I don't know how." His tone is steady and resolute. "And I don't care if you don't support me, but every path has to be carved by someone, so I'm making a new one."

Something stretches my throat.

"I'm not coming back to that house just to exist," he states. "You understand?"

I smile, just a little.

*If I'm not dead, then I'm not done.*

I can do this.

If he can do this—keep going—so can I. It's going to be over eventually. No one lives forever. I can do more before I go.

I can show my family that we keep standing back up. I've got another fight in me.

Drawing in a lungful of air, I rise off the bed and whip off my jacket. "I'm building you a new room," I say. "If you're not home on time, I'm painting it lavender."

I hear a muffled chuckle. "Well . . . I also like peach."

I smile. "Talk soon."

"Yeah."

I hang up, tear off my clothes, and wrap a towel around my waist. Opening my bedroom door, I yell. "Aracely!"

In a few seconds, I hear her footfalls on the stairs, and she appears at my door. Her eyes drop to my towel, and she almost looks away.

I swipe up my shirt and hold it out to her. "Have the . . ."

But I stop, taking a moment to correct myself. "*Would you please* have the buttons on this fixed?" I ask her politely. Then I hand her the pants and jacket. "And take this suit to a tailor as a reference for sizing. Have them make me three more. You pick the fabric. Shirts, ties . . ."

Her face falls a little, but I don't linger for questions. Swiping my phone off the bed, I hand that to her next. "Put this on the charger. And find a time on my calendar next week to talk to me. You'll start handling my schedule, and we need to talk about you taking over managing Mariette's." My brain floods with everything I want to do, and my mouth can't keep up. "I'm giving you joint control with her. Understand?"

Her eyes go wide, but then I see it. The smile. She nods.

Taking the pants back from her, I dig out my wallet and slip out a credit card.

I hand it to her. "Go buy groceries and text my brothers to be home by six for dinner. No stopping at bars."

She takes the card. "What do you want me to make?"

"I'm cooking."

Her arms fall, and for a second she looks like she's going to drop the clothes. I shove the pants back at her and start to walk away.

"And . . ." I fire back. "Start organizing a . . . like a block party or something. Let's get everyone together. The whole Bay."

Her eyes bug out again.

I narrow mine. "Are you writing this down?"

She fumbles for a second and then gestures to her head. "I got it," she mumbles.

I walk toward the bathroom but point to the suit in her hands as I go. "And have that cleaned."

"Are you sure?"

I shoot her a look before I close the door, knowing she can smell Krisjen's perfume on it as well as I can.

I twist the shower handle, pull off the towel, and step under the spray, inhaling hard as the cold water rushes over my skin.

I force full, deep breaths, even, in and out, as I fist my hands and feel the rush of the ice charging my body.

*Just one more day.*

I can stay for one more day.

Like my mom did.

# 29

## Krisjen

I wanted to leave with him—the second he walked away.

But how could this have not been about revenge? How could he not hate everything I reminded him of?

I sit against the wall, hugging my knees and feeling the shorts and sweatshirt that I threw on, but have no idea if it's the Florida State one or the Hilton Head one. It's gray.

All the times he wouldn't look at me. Speak to me. Of course.

It wasn't because I was a Saint. It was because I was me. Part of her. He'd look at me and see her hair. Her nose.

A tear spills over, dripping down my face. He couldn't stand the sight of me.

I lock my fingers together and bow my head into my hands, shaking with cries I won't let out.

He must've thought I was a real piece of work, playing at his house like it was some kind of fucking theme park.

But when he did look at me . . .

When I found him racked with pain and saw the tears.

When he held on to me at night and then quickly let me go when he'd wake up and realize.

And then go right back to wrapping himself around me the next night. And the next. And the next.

When he finally started talking to me, and wanted only me near him. Only me.

He tried not to see me. Tried not to get close. Tried not to look at me or talk to me.

He didn't want revenge.

He didn't want me to find out and knew I would at some point.

He knew I'd hurt him when I did.

I never deserved him.

Lifting my head, I watch my curtains blow in the breeze pouring into my dark room. It can't be much past noon, but the clouds hang low outside, making the light on my walls gray with hues of blue.

I follow the light past the fabric hanging from my four-post bed and over the keepsakes—a carousel, stuffed animals, and pictures of parties, trips, and ceremonies. Past the displays of medals and ribbons I got for every swim meet or spelling bee I participated in.

Because every artifact was like another addition to the résumé of my life that proved I was alive. That I did things. That I was accomplished, and that made me valuable.

Proving I was living my best life distracted me from the realization that this room could never fit the proof of all my failures.

And knowing now that only one matters.

Rising to my feet, I wipe a tear from under my eye and cross the room. I rip the bulletin board off the wall, followed by my rack of karate belts from when I was eight. The last five are missing, because I quit, but I still display them like it was some big deal.

I throw the carousel onto my bed, scoop up every stuffed animal, and throw any picture that doesn't have someone I love in it into the pile. I grab hold of my sheer bed curtains and start yanking, tearing them away, balling them up, and adding them to the junk. Gathering up the four corners of my blanket, I pull the sack off my bed and stuff it in my closet. Some of it will get disposed of in the garbage, and some things I'm not sure if I ever want to see again. I just want them out of sight right now.

I stare in the mirror, seeing myself for the first time all morning. His mark is on my neck, and my lips are puffy. I fold them between my teeth, noticing how sore they are. I didn't notice when I woke up with him this morning. I pull my phone out of my back pocket—no calls or texts.

Clutching it in my hand, I leave the room, tucking my tangled hair behind my ear as I head downstairs. My mother hasn't come back to my room, but I know she's in the house. Macon won't be able to tell her and me apart in a few years. *Fifteen-hundred-dollar heels, married to a banker or a lawyer . . .*

I do the math in my head real quick, remembering that my father doesn't think Mars is his son, but Mars was born long before Macon's parents died. Macon was off in the military. I didn't think it was him anyway. Thank God.

A blender whirs in the kitchen, and I head in, leaning against the doorframe and folding my arms over my chest.

My mom holds down the lid as the yellow slush spins like a whirlpool inside the machine, and I can smell the tequila and the citrus.

She stops the blender, glances up briefly, and pours a glass without missing a beat. Walking it over, she hands it to me and I take it.

Strangely enough, I feel no anger toward her. None at all.

I hold the drink to my nose, smelling the Cointreau and agave syrup. My mother makes the best margaritas. "You always were a wonderful mixologist."

"It's good to have a skill."

Mine has yet to present itself.

She walks back to the island, filling a glass for herself. I don't take a drink.

"You know, I never really thought about it, because it wasn't like I had a choice," I tell her, "but if anyone had ever asked me, I would've said that I liked you more than Dad. I still do. You know why?"

She fits the pitcher back onto the blender base and lifts her eyes to me.

"Because you eventually win," I reply. "You always claw your way back to the top. It was the only quality I ever hoped I inherited."

She takes a long drink, and I step forward, setting my cup down with the island between us.

She drops her eyes. "The affair only lasted—"

"It wasn't an affair." I tighten my fists around the back of the wrought iron chair, making my knuckles ache. "You and your friends victimized a young man who'd just lost his parents and was trying to support his five siblings."

She stares at me, no change in her expression.

I go on. "And you don't care about it any more than you care that I hate you for it. All you care about is that I fall into line."

That's why she wanted him away from me. Oh, I can fuck Macon Jaeger all I want. I can pay him for some fun. Someday. *After* I give Jerome Watson a couple of kids and make his house a home. Then she'll encourage me to have all the fun I want. Discreetly.

"I'll meet with Jerome Watson," I tell her.

Her eyebrows lift.

"And I will get you a settlement from Dad."

"How—"

"What does it matter?" I blurt out. "You'll be well taken care of."

A small smile crosses her lips, happy that I'm taking care of business.

*Oh, yes, I am.*

But I'm not finished yet. "On two conditions," I tell her. "You go to the house in the Keys until further notice. And . . ." I harden my voice. "You sign over the house."

"What?" she asks.

"To me."

"You've got to be kidding—"

"Or I'll tell everyone what you did to him," I say.

"You think that will shock them?" She looks about ready to laugh. "Like your father or anyone else in this town doesn't have secrets of their own?"

I set my phone down on the island. "Everyone."

Her face falls, her eyes shifting to the phone.

She breathes in and out for several seconds, her jaw clenching over and over again. "Mars and Paisleigh—"

"Will stay with me for now," I reply. "We'll discuss guardianship once I touch base with Dad."

We stare at each other, and I know everything she's thinking. Her children are leverage. She doesn't want to give that up. Relatives will pity her—give her money—if she has children to support.

And deep down, she really does care. Not as much as Mars and Paisleigh deserve, but if something happened to us, she'd cry. Genuinely, I think.

But I also know she doesn't want this anymore. She married him, never thinking he'd take off with someone else. She would give him a home, kids, and the respectable family image, and he'd give her the life. He's the one who broke the deal.

She wants to be free. She's still young, after all.

Besides, Bateman and I have been taking care of the kids 85 percent of the time for the past nine months anyway. She's already gone.

"Okay," she says. The tone is clipped, but she agrees.

She turns and takes out a pan, setting it on the stove. "Can I make you some lunch?"

"Pack," I tell her. "Go now."

She twists around, shocked.

I start to walk away. "I'll let you know when I talk to Dad."

I take a right out of the kitchen and head toward my father's office, passing the hidden room under the stairs. I don't look, and I don't look back to see if she's coming after me for a fight. I know she'll leave. She wants what I promised.

And I wouldn't fight anyway. I feel no anger. That's for people still trying to make it work.

I walk into my father's office, leaving the door open as I traipse over the area rug to the desk. Sitting in his chair, I yank open the bottom left drawer and sift through all the files until I come across one labeled *Auto*. I slip it out.

I need to find my car title so I can sell it. An old Rover won't support us forever, and I will still need a car of some sort, but I don't need that expensive one. And I don't want my dad's old car. I don't want anything of his. I should be able to get forty thousand for the Rover. Finding it, I slip it out and set it aside, replacing the folder in the drawer.

But I spot another one labeled *Financials*. I pause my hand over it. I'm sure he took anything of any consequence, but then again, how would we know? My mother and I aren't very smart with this stuff. If he hid money—assets—it would be worth a look. Then I'll know what I can ask him for, because he won't want my mother's divorce lawyer discovering that on their own. Hiding assets is illegal.

Stealing a cigarette from the box on his desk, I light it as I start to sift through the papers, but my stomach sinks almost as soon as I start.

It's going to take forever to make sense of what I'm looking at, and there are so many accounts. Things for his businesses, papers for his family's investments, stocks, bonds, real estate, and while everything is in his name, except our house, which he gave to her, I have no way of knowing if there's anything she's not aware of. She didn't stay involved. She let him do what he wanted. Trusted him with the money.

I stuff it all in a folder to keep it in my possession in case he comes back for it and pick up my phone to call Clay's dad. He might be able to help me understand this.

But then I see the word "Assets" and pause. Peering down into the drawer, I spot another folder and pick it up.

*Household Assets.*

Flipping it open, I scan a slew of certificates of authenticity and insurance policies—for art, antique silver, jewelry, even items of clothing.

But I see my name.

Then I see it again.

And my heart starts racing as I piece together what I'm looking at.

I grab my phone and bring up the screenshots that I took from his email. I didn't study everything yet, but I swipe through the pictures, remembering seeing something.

I stop. *No, it was a text.*

I go through the texts with his girlfriend, reading one that I glimpsed but didn't think anything of when I originally saw.

**Was that everything?** she asks him.

I have no idea what she's talking about, but they must've just talked in person and are continuing a conversation.

**There's more,** he tells her. **It's not in her or my name, though. I'll get it back from Krisjen afterward.**

Something builds, climbing my throat, and I start shaking. And then . . . I laugh.

I plant my hands on the desk, cigarette smoke streaming up into the air as I bow my head and break into laughter that I can't keep quiet.

I pick up my phone and text Clay and Aracely.

**I recently acquired a six-hundred-dollar bottle of wine. Get over here. Both of you.**

Holy shit.

I smile. This doesn't change my fate, but it will ensure Mars and

Paisleigh can govern their own. I drop the phone to the desk, fold my arms over my chest, and take a long drag of the stale cigarette. *Fucking yes.*

"Oh my God!"

I jerk my eyes to the door, seeing Paisleigh.

"I'm gonna tell Mom you're smoking."

I blow out the cloud and grin at my little sister. "I got a better idea." I snuff out the cigarette. "Let's dance."

I don't have to sell my Rover. My father was hiding assets, after all. Not a lot, but enough.

Just enough.

"I must say," Jack Hewlitt says, "you could've gotten more at auction."

I sign the papers, handing each to him one by one. He leans against the edge of his desk while I sit in a chair, using it to write on. "I'm not interested in waiting."

I've spent the past two days liquidating two paintings, one sculpture, and the entire wine collection, and I did find a small account in my name. I transferred the funds to one my father doesn't have access to. I haven't asked him why he put the stuff in my name. I know why.

He knew he was leaving her. A long time ago.

And he assumed I wouldn't notice before the divorce was final. He was almost right.

I didn't find anything in Mars's or Paisleigh's names, and there's more that I own, but I'm not going to sell everything off yet.

"No waiting, huh?" Mr. Hewlitt teases. "Leaving the country?"

I smile small. "I'm not going anywhere."

He hands me my copy of the documents, and I shake his hand. "Nice doing business with you."

"And you," he says. "These will fetch a good profit. Thank you."

A *great* profit. I sold them to him for much less than my father paid, and art doesn't go down in value.

I rise, my earring swaying across my neck, and I wet my lips, because the lipstick coating my mouth feels dry like clay. I slip my forearm through the handles of my Gucci bag and take my paperwork with me.

My phone rings, and I nod a goodbye to Jack.

Fishing the phone out of my bag, I see my father's name on the screen. I changed it to *Lachlan Conroy* instead of *Dad* months ago.

"Hello?" I answer.

"You've been busy."

I shudder a little at the curtness of his voice. I almost forgot.

He always sounds like someone who's jetting from one meeting to another. A little rushed. Distracted. Bothered. He doesn't have an accent, but he adds one on purpose. Just on a word here and there. An inflection at the end of a sentence maybe. Sometimes it sounds Scottish. Most of the time it's some weird concoction of British and Bostonian.

"Krisjen, listen to me—"

"No." I walk slowly, heading to the front door of the gallery. "We have asked for you. Mars and Paisleigh have asked for you, but now that I'm selling property you hid in my name . . . Now I warrant your attention?"

It's in my name. I'm eighteen. He can scramble to get back what I haven't yet sold, but he'll have to find it first. The first thing I did was hide everything.

"We should talk," he tells me.

I agree.

"Wolfe Room," I state. "Tonight. Eight o'clock."

"How do you know about that room?"

I hang up, walk out the door, and step onto the sidewalk. How does he know about that room is the question?

I'm glad I didn't let him keep me on the phone. Part of me still remembers back when he was a good father, and it hurts. Paisleigh has never known that version of him.

The wind blows through my hair and across the sliver of stomach left bare in my sleeveless white blouse. I step in my heels, one foot after the other in my tight, white pants, barely noticing the boys until they're there.

Army. Dallas. Trace.

My heart leaps in my chest. It's been days, but it feels like years. The Bay seems so far away.

Army isn't wearing a shirt. A major no-no on Main Street in St. Carmen, and Trace wears a green T-shirt. It matches his eyes.

I see them, they see me, and I slow, thinking they're going to stop. Time halts as I wait for it.

But they don't.

And neither do I.

Army passes me, his familiar eyes following me over his shoulder as he goes.

Trace and Dallas veer around me, glancing at me but continuing without a word. My heart splits.

I don't know if I keep walking, or how I get to my car down the street, but when I look back, they're gone.

And that's how easily things can change.

# 30

## Macon

"A little higher," I tell Santos.

He grunts, exhaling, "'Kay."

We lift the beam, the sun beating down as we balance high on the scaffold and I drill a bolt through the wood. The handheld tool stutters, signaling the bolt is tightened.

"Got it?" he asks.

"Yep."

He releases the beam, taking out a bandanna and wiping down his face. People work below, the walls rising quickly while Dallas pulls up with a truckload of Sheetrock.

"Five extra bedrooms, huh?" Santos laughs. "You making plans?"

"Just making room for the unexpected."

"Yeah, that's usually how babies happen."

He laughs again, and I let him. The new addition onto the house will fill up faster than we know, and I want it to be ready. Iron will get out of prison, and I don't want the lack of space to be an excuse for Army to leave. Or Dallas or Trace. Liv will always have her room here, but at least I can count on that one not to give me any surprise nieces or nephews until she's absolutely ready.

"You know," Santos tells me, "my wife's sister does interior painting. When it's time to drywall and decorate, I could have her stop by to meet you."

I rotate the wrench, tightening the bolt.

"She's pretty. And a good girl."

I stare at the beam.

"It wouldn't be a date," he assures me. "Just one night y'all happen to work late and then you take it from there. I'm sure you remember how."

I shift my gaze up, seeing him grin. I think everyone in the Bay is under some impression that I'm fun now because I'm speaking more and getting air once in a while. I even fucking smiled at a kid yesterday. He looked like I was about to eat him.

Santos laughs when I don't play along, and we move on to the next beam.

But just then, I see Jasmine walk Dex past the house.

I climb down.

"Hey, is Army home yet?" she asks.

"Soon." I sweep the kid up into my arms. "Leave him with me."

She hands me his bag.

"You've been paid?" I ask.

"He took care of it this morning." She rubs Dex's cheeks, giving him a big smile. "Have a good weekend," she singsongs.

He giggles, and I take him inside, hearing the grandfather clock chime four o'clock. I stop in front of it to let him listen. He stares at the face, knowing that's what's making the sound, and I watch him, because it's cute. He loves it so much. I already decided to try to find him a cuckoo clock for Christmas. One with beer-guzzling dancers. He'll go apeshit for that.

Dropping his bag, I take us into the kitchen, set him down on the counter, and turn on the water, checking the temperature. Pumping soap into his hands, I give myself some and show him, like we do every time, how to lather and wash his fingers.

He tries to stick his hand in his mouth, and I take it back, helping him rinse.

"Da-da, da-da."

"Soon, man," I tell him.

It's funny how he has his dad's hair and mom's eyes. I have my mom's, too. Dallas, Trace, and Iron better reproduce with brown-eyed women. I'm tired of being a minority in this house.

We dry off, and I sit him in his high chair, taking out the steamed broccoli, chopped avocado, and bites of grilled chicken mixed with mayo and ranch dressing that Army left this morning. I spread it out on his tray, and he starts eating, while I make him a cup of water.

Walking over, I raise every window in the kitchen and move to the living room, doing the same in there. I close my eyes and inhale, my shoulders relaxing a little.

But my eyes stay closed. It's good she stayed away. She ghosted Mariette and hasn't come back for her toothbrush, her paycheck, or her dress.

Gone. Nice and clean. That's the best way.

I shake my head, opening my eyes. Starting some music on my phone, I head back into the kitchen, seeing Dex kick his feet and eat as I start to slice the loaf of bread.

The front door opens and closes, and Trace enters the kitchen.

"You're done early," I say.

"What's this?" He lifts the lid on the pot on the stove, sniffing the chili. "Mmm."

"Tech Advantage called." I place the bread on the table as Army and Dallas stroll in, everyone making themselves a bowl. "They wanted a cleanup tomorrow for an event next week."

"I have a . . ." Trace starts to make an excuse but then stops. "Nothing."

I study him for a second, and then pull Dex's high chair up to the corner of the table between me and Army. We all sit, Dallas digging his spoon into the chili.

"There's shit going on at the beach," he explains to me. "Trace wants to be there."

But Trace interjects. "It's fine. I'll do the job."

He stares down at his food, and I'm not sure what the hell is going on. I mean, I know I've been yelling at him to grow up for years, but now that he is . . . I dig in my eyebrows.

Dallas chimes in again. "I'll fill in for him."

Trace gapes at his brother. I dig in my eyebrows deeper. *What. The. Fuck.*

"Are you sure?" Trace asks him.

Dallas shrugs, shoveling food in. "I'm not doing anything else."

"Thanks." Trace finally puts on a happy face. "I'll get you back."

"What the hell happened while I was gone?" someone says.

We all look up as Liv leans in the doorway with her hands in her pockets.

"Hey!" Trace shoots up, grabbing her in a hug like she wasn't just home three weeks ago.

He sits, and she whips off her black jacket, heading to the stove for a bowl. "I leave for college and y'all turn sweet?"

"What are you doing home?" Army asks her.

"Christmas."

"That's this month?" Dallas looks around the table. "Shit."

She scoops chili into a bowl, sniffing it as she puts the lid back on the pot. "Ugh, what did you do to my recipe?"

"I taught you how to make that, you little shit," I mumble.

"You tried to," she fires back.

She swings her leg over the chair at the end of the table like she's climbing on a horse and sits. I glance up briefly.

"Table is feeling empty without you and Iron." Trace hands her some bread. "And Krisjen."

"Thanks." She takes a slice and then looks around. "Where is Krisjen? At Mariette's?"

I chew, the table falling quiet. No one has mentioned her since I came home that morning. They knew to leave it alone.

"We saw her in town today," Dallas finally says. "She looked different."

"Gorgeous, actually," Army adds.

"Like glass," Trace mumbles over his food. "Beautiful, shiny, fucking glass."

He sounds angry.

"All the Saints look like that," Dallas tells him.

I push my spoon through the chili, feeling eyes on me. When I look up, Liv is watching me.

"But when they love you," she muses, "you've never had anything softer in your arms."

My heart stops.

"Like they're so grateful when someone is gentle with them," she almost whispers.

I feel my pulse in my stomach, seeing Krisjen in my head. In my house, in the tub next to me that day, in my restaurant . . .

"Yeah, well." Army rises. "Fuck it."

He carries his bowl to the sink, and like Trace and Dallas, he hasn't asked me what happened with Krisjen, but unlike Trace and Dallas, I'm not sure he cares. And I deserve it. He liked her. Even if he did offer to fucking share her.

"I was thinking we could all go for a ride tonight," Liv says. "We all have bikes. They have the food trucks at Delgando Beach, and the weather's pretty perfect."

Trace perks up, but I feel his eyes on me as if waiting for me to allow it.

I finish chewing and stand up. "That's a good idea."

Trace slaps the table. "Hell yeah."

"No girlfriends," I hear Dallas order.

Army turns. "I'll get Dex in bed later and see if Aracely can come over to sit with him."

"I'm going to go get some more work done outside first," I tell them.

Dallas stands up. "I'll help."

I point to Trace. "You got dishes."

I start to leave, hearing Liv and Dallas argue behind me. "No girlfriends? I can't tell Clay she can't come, Dallas."

"She can't come!"

"We want you to ourselves for a while," Trace points out.

"Ugh, fine."

I shake with a laugh, stepping out the front door. Heading back to the addition, I pull on some gloves and look up at Santos. "Your wife's sister . . ." I say. "When the walls are ready for paint, send her by."

He smiles, and I start climbing up the scaffolding.

We descend the stairs.

My brothers' and sister's boots scuff the cement steps behind me on our way down to the unmarked black door. I tilt my head, cracking my neck.

It's been a week.

Garrett Ames wants an answer to his proposal to buy land in Sanoa Bay.

And he'll meet only on his turf.

*The Wolfe Room.*

It's a secret underground meeting place where the real parties at Fox Hill Country Club happen. It's on the lower level of the clubhouse, but anyone passing by on the golf course would just assume it was an employee entrance. Or a utility room. Very few members—or their families—know what happens inside.

But Liv does. Army didn't want me to bring her, given that Milo Price and Callum Ames tried to hurt her in here last spring, but this time she has us.

And Milo Price has a scar. For now.

They'll both pay. They just don't know it yet.

I knock twice, and in just as many seconds, the door swings open.

Garrett Ames greets us with a smile. Sickly sweet. Like spit filled with sugar. "Please, come in."

He steps back, making way, and I glance at Jerome Watson and another man sitting at a round table with five seats. The other one looks vaguely familiar, but before I can place him, Garrett speaks up.

"I'm surprised you agreed to meet here."

"Well," Trace says. "We wanted to see inside."

And then he proceeds to look up and around, wide-eyed, like if we pinch our pennies, maybe we can golf here someday, too.

"Wow," he coos.

I contain my smile but feel the pride all the same.

"Excuse us for being late." I set my helmet down on the round table and sit in an empty seat. "We were out on a joyride."

Jerome Watson eyes me, amused. "All of Tryst Six, huh? Oh. No, I forgot. There's only five left now."

*For now, fucker.*

My siblings pull up chairs from around the room, and while I'm tempted to take a long look around the infamous place in person, I refrain. They don't need a reminder that I've never been here before. They know.

"Let's hurry this up." Ames pulls out a chair, unbuttons his suit jacket, and sits. "The markets are about to open again in Tokyo. I need to get on the phone."

I never noticed the smell of the leather of all the Jaeger jackets—mine, Army's, Dallas in Iron's, and Liv in my old one (Trace prefers a T-shirt)—but I smell it now. The muscles in my arms feel ten feet thick.

An attendant stands at the wall behind Ames, his hands locked in front of his body as if he's ready to pour a drink or pull out a chair.

I glance at the only other person at the table, and my pulse kicks up a notch.

Lachlan Conroy.

I knew who Krisjen's father was, but I would've known him anyway.

She has his eyes. Why is he here?

"The same deal is on the table," Ames starts off, and it takes a minute to bring my gaze back to the meeting at hand. "Two hundred acres, you know what I'm willing to pay," he states. "I'm playing ball, because this is faster than going through the government, but I *can* go through the government."

I don't have the authority to sell the land. It's owned by several Sanoa Bay residents. But I am head of the community council, and I'm just about the only reason they haven't sold their stakes yet. I can persuade them.

Or dissuade them.

I study the scar on his jaw. A groove with three lines. Like a shooting star. It's faint. Not the first thing you see when you first meet him, but I've known that it was there for a while.

His eyes gleam. "I will get what I want, Macon."

"For three times the price you're offering to pay me."

"What I'm offering to pay you is twice what they will when they take your land."

He's not wrong. He knows it, and he knows I know it.

I avert my eyes to the side, but I sweep over the corner of the room, at the top, near the ceiling. The fiber-optic lens hidden in the stag antlers. It records everything.

And judging from the things that just happened in this room last night, I'm guessing they don't know it's there.

"That star on your jaw." I tap my fingers on the table. "I have the same scar. It comes from my father's ring when he hits you."

Army shifts to my right, and I see him look at me. None of them know where I got mine. I have a lot of scrapes. We all do.

"It was an accident with me," I tell Ames. "We were both upset, I hit him first, but not many people have that mark. What did you do to him?" I cock my head. "He wasn't typically violent."

My father hit me twice in my life, and both times he was defending himself. He forgot he was wearing the ring that day.

Ames stares at me flatly. "Do we have a deal?"

"Was it over my mom?" I press. "When I was a couple of years old, she worked in your parents' house for a time, right?"

Dallas's breathing grows heavier behind me.

I go on, "My dad said one night she came home and never went back. What did you try with her?"

Liv shoots out of her chair, but I hold out my arm, pushing her back down.

"You wanted a piece of her, didn't you?" I say. "Did you get it?"

I feel the heat rolling off Army and Trace, hear Liv's knuckles crack. Ames went after our mom, like his son, Callum, went after my sister last April.

"If you got it," I tell him, "I suspect you wouldn't still be so angry."

He's been targeting us for as long as I can remember.

"Callum has a taste for our side of the tracks, too." I clear my throat. "He's your heir, correct?"

His eyes pierce like a raptor's.

"Your *only* child," I say. "Correct?"

Not correct. He has another son. At least one other one. It would create a fucking mess for Garrett Ames if Callum ever found that out.

But before Ames can react, there's a knock on the door.

I tense. Santos is outside. One call away if we need him.

The attendant crosses the room and answers the door. Jerome Watson rises from his chair before I even look.

"Krisjen," he says.

I turn my eyes over my shoulder, seeing her for the first time in days.

*Glass.* Did she look like that last year when she and Liv were in school together? She wears a black tennis skirt and a matching tight sleeveless shirt. I take in every inch of golden skin on her neck, her arms, and her thighs. I was everywhere on her. Just days ago.

Why is she here?

"You're dressed for golf," Watson says.

Her gaze drifts to me but faces forward again, like she doesn't recognize me.

"I like night games," she tells him.

He gestures for her to sit. "Me, too."

She doesn't take the seat offered, and I try not to glare at him. Did he invite me here because she would be here?

Liv looks around, and I can tell—same as me—she's trying to figure out what's going on.

"Krisjen—" her father starts.

But she cuts him off. "I'll deal with you in a minute."

She stands in front of the table, addressing Watson only. "I want my own room."

I freeze. *What the fuck?*

"Until I'm ready to share yours," she tells him.

A truck sits on my chest, but I don't shift my eyes off the table. Jerome knew he was meeting with one of us tonight and decided to kill two birds with one stone. He wanted me to see this.

Liv sits up. "Krisjen, what are you doing?"

Krisjen doesn't reply.

Jerome Watson doesn't sound fazed. "What else?" he demands.

"My brother and sister come with me."

"What?" her father speaks up. "Where's your mother?"

But no one pays him any mind. My head swims.

"Your sister," Jerome tells her. "Your brother should be away at school by now."

"What the hell is this?" her father barks.

Good question. It seems Krisjen has realized she can do better. I shouldn't care. She never lied. She knew she'd give in.

"Why would I still want you?" Watson asks her, suddenly playing hard to get.

He may not know she fucked Army and Iron, but he does know about Trace. My stomach twists with knots.

Fuck her.

I clench my jaw before speaking. "Whether you marry her or not," I tell him, "you're going to want a piece of her. Trust me."

And now he knows I had her, too.

Her father pounds the table with his fist once, and Dallas laughs under his breath. Krisjen doesn't move.

I stand up, collecting my helmet as my brothers and sister get up with me. Screw this. I wasn't going to give Ames anything anyway, but now, I hope there's a fucking war. They're all going to bleed.

"I will get the land," Ames says, warning me before I bolt.

"The hard way, then," I say in a low voice. "I'm in the mood for a fight. A long, loud, expensive fight."

"There may be losses."

"As long as you're okay with that," I tell him.

Trace chuckles, and Dallas stretches his arms in the air. "Ah, this is going to be fun."

I kick my chair back, hearing it tumble behind me. "And the stock market in Tokyo is closed all day," I tell Ames as I walk out. "It's Saturday there."

# 31

## Krisjen

I'm glad he leaves quickly.

It takes everything not to watch him as he passes me. As I absorb the last I'll probably see of him for who knows how long.

I will see him, though. Maybe at a stoplight a year from now. On Liv's social media when she's home with them next summer. Maybe he'll have a kid someday, and I'll have a kid, and I'll see him across the field as they play on opposing sides.

I will see him, though. He's not done yet, and I'm satisfied with that. I can be satisfied with that.

But I still feel like my insides are bleeding.

I draw in a breath, hear the door close, and look at my father. "Are you going to raise the kids?" I ask him. "You and your girlfriend?"

He lifts his chin, his discomfort at discussing this in front of his colleagues evident. But we don't have to discuss anything.

"They stay with me," I tell him, taking out the check from a pack I found in his desk. "Say yes."

"We need to talk."

"We will." I set the check, already made out, on the table. "Say yes."

He inhales and exhales three times, and then nods once, barely.

He might be willing to go the distance with me and Paisleigh after he's remarried and has set up house properly, but he doesn't believe Mars is his, and it doesn't matter, because I'm not discussing it. We're a package deal.

I slide the check over to him. "And pay her off."

He drops his eyes to the check, taking in the sizable but fair amount I wrote out. She won't acquiesce for anything less.

"I left her the house to sell," he says.

"You mean the home where your children live?" I fire back. "Fuck you."

Garrett Ames chuckles and then takes a sip of his scotch.

"Krisjen, what has gotten into you?" my father growls in a near whisper.

He's embarrassed.

I don't retreat. "Take out your Montblanc," I order him.

*Take out your fucking pen and sign it and this is done.* He'll be free.

He doesn't break eye contact until he has his pen out and starts signing it.

He pushes it back over to me, and I take out my phone, log into my bank account, and scan the check, immediately depositing it.

I put both the check and my phone away. "If it doesn't clear, the next check will be bigger."

His jaw flexes, but he keeps his mouth shut, slipping his pen back into his breast pocket.

"Have your lawyer draw up the papers," I tell him. "Bring them when you come to see your kids next Saturday. I'll make sure she signs them quickly."

"Krisjen."

"Please leave," I say.

And I lift my eyes to the wall behind him, done dealing with him tonight. Two down, one more to go.

Buttoning his suit jacket, he walks out, slamming the door behind him.

Jerome tsks. "Not as sweet as I thought."

I cock my head. "Y'all are handfuls."

He laughs, but I don't.

"So why the change of heart?" he asks.

"Well, I'm not going to college."

I pull out one more thing from the pocket of my skirt and step forward.

"And I promise you, you'll get everything you pay for," I tell him, placing the key on the table. "On one more condition."

Jerome reaches out to pick it up. "And what's that?"

I slide it away from him. "Not you." And I push it toward Garrett Ames instead. "You."

He picks it up and turns it over, examining it. "And what's this a key to, little girl?"

I leave quickly, worried they'll try to make me stay. I know the stories, heard about the sharing that goes on among the adults. I never asked my mother and will not ask Clay if she thinks her parents took part in any of it. I don't want to know.

I don't want anything to do with it.

*The adults . . .*

Like I'm not one of them now.

My plan worked perfectly tonight. Everything went in my favor. The tears well in my eyes in spite of the wins.

He left. So quickly. Left me in there. With those men. In that room. In *that* room. God . . .

I walk down the drive, toward my Rover, barely noticing the people on the green. "Krisjen!" I hear someone call.

I look right as a crowd of night golfers congregates a hundred yards away, one person waving their golf club in the air. I think it's Clay. Did Liv join her?

I came dressed to play for their biannual fundraising event—if nothing else, as an excuse to get out of the meeting if Jerome tried to keep me—but I just want to go home. I need to think.

I know I did the right thing. Right? This is what's right. It sucks, but it's right. He'll be safe now.

But then he's there.

In front of me. Walking to me as I stop at my car.

"Does he have enough money for you?" Macon asks, climbing the incline of the driveway, up to me.

He didn't leave. I don't blink, but I feel the tears in my chest. *He stayed.*

"You look good," I whisper.

He does. The bags are still there but getting lighter. He's sleeping.

As soon as I drove up and saw the bikes parked along the edge of the driveway, I got nervous, but I was also happy to see him riding. With his family.

He stops when he reaches me, his body pressing into mine as he gazes down at me. "How many square feet did he promise?"

God, I love his eyes. Everyone notices the green eyes on his brothers, but Macon's make me feel like I'm tucked away in a cabin, deep in the forest, under a quilt, and it's raining. It feels like a memory, but it's not. I've never been to a cabin.

"You're all riding," I say, unable not to smile a little. I'm glad he's getting out. He looks strong.

"Does he have brothers, too?" he says.

My chin trembles. He looks so good. "I don't know," I admit. "But he won't want anyone else touching me. At least for a while. At least until . . ."

He touches his forehead to mine.

"Until?" he gasps.

But he already knows.

Grabbing me in both hands, he lifts me up and pins me to the tree. I wrap my legs around him. "What was one of the rumors about me that you said you heard?" he whispers over my jaw. "That I'm gonna breed you all out?"

I hold his face in my hands. "I love you."

His scent fills my head, and I close my eyes, my hair like a curtain falling between us.

"You could be carrying one of ours right now," he says, hovering his mouth over mine. "My brothers and I had a lot of fun with you, after all."

I brush my nose to his. "I love you," I whisper.

"He's going to get you nice and used."

I kiss him softly on the lips, and I feel his body tremble under my hands. "I love you."

"I would father all of your children," he murmurs.

I press my lips to his forehead, trailing kisses down his temple, down his face, and to the corner of his mouth.

"Summon me every time you want one." He breathes hard, digging his fingers into the backs of my thighs. "I'll happily work for you."

Leaning in, he kisses my forehead, sets me back on my feet, and leaves me there.

"I love you," I mouth long after he's gone.

# 32

## Macon

I sweep through Mariette's kitchen, Aracely keeping pace behind me. "When does the menu change?"

"January."

I flip through her inventory, scanning the numbers and cost. "You getting orders in?"

"Already done," she says.

I shoot out my arm, passing her the papers. She should've asked me before she bought a bunch of shit she wasn't sure I'd approve.

But that's what I hired her for, right? To take initiative?

She's wasting no time, either. In the last two days, she's redesigned the restaurant menu, moved the accounts over to a new system I can access on any device, and hired a new server. To replace Krisjen.

I push through the back door of the empty restaurant, the night air cool and loud with life.

"I also want to talk to Mariette about extending hours starting in the spring," she says behind me.

"Whatever you want."

It'll cost more to stay open longer, and we'll need a bigger staff, but let her see if she can make it worth it. I'll know in the first month.

She disappears off somewhere, and I look over, seeing Torres heading into the bar with his arm around his wife.

"Macon, come on!" he calls out.

I flash him a dirty look, to which he laughs and heads inside. I've never been fun at bars. That's what he knows.

But if I go in there, I'll get drunk. And missing her will be unbearable.

Gabriela Minor kicks a soccer ball across the street with her six-year-old little sister. I stop, checking the time on my phone.

It's after ten. I look at her. She looks up at me.

Then she claps her hands. "Okay, bedtime!" she tells her baby sister.

She takes the girl's hand and helps her kick the ball back to their house. I move along, toward mine.

I should be proud of her. I know it sucks to have to babysit all night while your mom works, and most fourteen-year-olds just want to get the kids in bed so they can watch TV and be left alone. She plays with her sibling like I never did with mine. She's a good kid.

I hear the music before I even step inside my foyer, but as soon as I do, I shut off the playlist on the TV and toss the remote back onto the table. Trace sits up on the couch, and I think there are girls on each side of him. I don't look. "Move it to the pool," I tell them all.

I head into the kitchen, and Dallas leaves with someone as soon as I enter. I don't see Army. He's probably upstairs with Dex.

Filling a glass with water, I drink it down, refill, and drink more.

The lights in the pool out the window glow under the water, and in no time, someone is cannonballing into it, the lawn chairs quickly filling up as the house empties.

This is the time of day I used to love. Family in bed. House quiet.

World in bed. World quiet.

It feels like forever ago that she'd get in her pajamas and grab her pillow, but then she wouldn't use it. I was her pillow those nights she slept in my room.

Someone glides into the kitchen, their reflection creeping up behind me in the window.

I turn my head, looking down at Summer, a server at Mariette's. Krisjen trained her. Blond hair, early twenties, long tan legs in shorts, and her feet in skates. I stare down, my heart pumping harder in my chest.

"I was going to track down Krisjen to return them, but they fit me." She rolls her feet back and forth as she holds the counter behind her. "We should all wear them."

Her arm brushes mine, and her eyes are filled with heat as she looks up at me, waiting.

She licks her lips and cocks her head, and if I don't look at her face, I could almost envision it's Krisjen. Same beautiful skin. Same toned thighs.

I swallow the rest of the water in one gulp and leave, walking up the stairs and opening my door. Before I close it, I hear Van Morrison playing in Army's room. He plays it when he rocks Dex back to sleep.

Leaving the light off, I turn on my shower and push my jeans to the floor. Stepping in, I wash my hair and body, bowing my head under the spray and letting the heat pour down my back.

*I love you.*

I plant my forearm on the shower wall, leaning my head in. I still feel her whispers against my mouth. She kept saying it, brushing her lips over mine.

That's what I'll miss. More than anything. Her kisses. Without thinking, my mouth opens, feeling her tongue prying for entry just like she's here.

I drop the handle of the faucet, ready to turn it to cold like I'm now in the habit of doing at the end of every shower, because the cold drives every thought out of my head, but I can't turn it. I fist it, pushing myself to just do it, but the heat feels perfect. She's here, right where she's supposed to be. I can feel her smile against my mouth.

Instead, I turn off the water, wrap a towel around my waist, and walk to my bed. I leave a trail of water as I go, hearing music playing out by the pool. I sit on the edge and drop my head into my hands, hating how hard I am for her. Hating the ache in my chest, and the pain in my heart.

*I love you.*

She just kept fucking saying it.

My eyes sting, and I close them, not noticing my door opening until light streams in from the hallway. I stare as a pair of white skates with orange wheels glides into my view, and when she's in front of me, I slide my hands up her smooth calves. Her touch lands on the back of my neck and slips farther up as I press the top of my head into her thighs.

*I love you.*

She just kept saying it like she hadn't agreed to be his minutes before. Does she want me? Does she really think she wants me after everything I've done?

I brush my fingertips up her legs, hearing her breathe hard and her little whimper escape.

I lift Summer's leg, and then the other one, pulling off the skates and holding them both in my hands. "Leave," I tell her.

She stands there, waiting, but I don't look at her face. I should let her stay. My brothers wouldn't kick her out of their rooms, but I can't look at anyone other than Krisjen in my bed. Not yet.

I don't know when Summer leaves, but in a minute the room is dark again, and I'm gazing down at the skates.

Krisjen doesn't want me. She wants to fuck me. Inside and out.

I hold a skate in each hand. "You found new ways to break me."

I tie the skates together by their laces and set them next to my door. Ripping off my towel, I pull back the covers on my bed, about to climb in, but a beeping sound chimes outside the window and I stop. It's the sound large trucks make when they're backing up.

Prying the curtain aside, I crane my neck, but all I see are the people around the pool, partying with their music. Trace walks across the deck, looking toward the street like he sees something.

In less than a minute, I'm jogging down the stairs in jeans and slipping on some shoes. Opening the door, I immediately see workers placing signs and cones. The writing on the truck reads *Department of Transportation*.

"Fuck, what now?" I mutter, stepping outside.

I bolt into the street, slipping my T-shirt over my head as I approach one of the guys in a neon yellow shirt. I see Trace and Liv make their way, as well, out of the corner of my eye.

"What the hell is this?" I demand.

The road worker looks at me, grit all over his face from wherever they were earlier in the day. He points to another man, and I head over.

The guy wears a yellow vest over a long-sleeve blue UV shirt. "What is this?" I ask him. "What's going on?"

He turns to me. "Sorry for the noise," he tells me, directing another worker. "We won't be long. I promise. Just dropping off some things for the morning."

Morning? What?

"We'll get started early, I'm afraid," he calls out over the truck engine. "About five a.m."

I glance at Trace, then Dallas. Both of them look at me, blank.

"Here's the schedule," the man says, thrusting a packet of papers at me.

I sift through, seeing it's a stack of the same sheet. For passing out and posting, I assume.

I scan the notice. *Lane construction.* Atlantic View Avenue, Bay Hawk Road, Seminole Point, and Seascape Court. For the next two weeks. Lane closures.

They're paving the roads.

"The streets will need to be clear," the man goes on, "including that parking lot tomorrow." He points to Mariette's. "I know it'll suck, but we'll move quickly. You shouldn't be inconvenienced for too long."

"So after six years of me petitioning the city council, you're just now, all of a sudden, getting to work?"

"I never know where I'm going until they tell me, sir." He starts to follow his crew, still placing cones to detour traffic. "Someone pulled some strings for you."

I look past him, locking eyes with Clay, who stands next to Liv.

"Was it your father?" I ask her.

She shakes her head. But she looks nervous.

"We'll see you bright and early," the guy shouts, waving as he continues his work.

The truck turns, taking a right down Bay Hawk, and I need to know if we're getting sidewalks, signs, and streetlamps . . .

This isn't a coincidence.

I walk up to my brothers and sister, the noise from the truck fading away. "What did she do?"

They stare at me, Dallas and Trace glancing at each other, and I don't know who knows what, but someone knows something.

"She traded her house," Clay finally answers. "Garrett Ames will back off for five years."

He'll back off? He's not standing in my way of getting roads or trying to take the land?

For five years?

I narrow my eyes. "And what am I supposed to do with five years?"

She shrugs a little. "Find a way to make the land more valuable to the government than whatever Garrett Ames would do with it," she says. "She bought you time."

It doesn't make any sense. "He gave up a nine-figure deal for a house?"

"No." But it's Liv who answers this time. "Krisjen threatened to give *us* the house as an alternative. We could find a million things to do with it that would drive down property values in their neighborhood."

The wheels in my head turn. *Yes, we could.* He would not want us owning property in St. Carmen.

"And Jerome Watson gets her," Liv adds.

I gaze at the papers in my hand, crumpling the edges in my fist.

"She doesn't need to sell herself to him," Clay says. "Her parents hid some of their assets in her name. She's been liquidating. She'd never sell herself to him for money."

I swallow the lump in my throat.

"But she'd do anything for you," Trace murmurs to me.

It's not meant as an accusation, but I feel the slice all the same.

I've wanted roads for these people my whole life. I've begged for it, but we're not taking it like this. She doesn't get to swoop in and save us. I save us.

I need to see her.

In minutes my family is back to their party, and I'm crossing the tracks again. The gate to her house is open, but I don't question why. Speeding down her driveway, I spot a large truck in front of the house, *Bayside Moving* written on the side.

Clay wasn't lying. She gave away the house.

The windows of the home are dark, and the truck is sealed shut for the night, but the ramp is down. They're still loading furniture. There's time to stop this.

I bang on the door over and over again. *Come on.*

There's no answer. Where is she?

Where are the kids?

I knock again, but there's no answer. No one's here.

I take out my phone and dial one of the many numbers I vowed never to contact again.

"Hello?" Cara Conroy answers.

I walk back to my truck. "Are you in town?"

She hesitates, and she may have forgotten my number, but she knows my voice. "I'm not far. Why?"

"Two Locks," I tell her. "One hour."

# 33

## Krisjen

Why can't I get it right? It's wrong every time.

And I've tried following the recipe several times.

Dipping my finger in again, I bring it to my mouth, sucking off the filling. It's not even close to Mariette's key lime pie. What the hell is she putting in it?

I pick up the note card she wrote out for me and study it. She gave me a bogus recipe. I know it. I'd keep a secret like that to myself, too.

I add more lime juice and stir.

"Are you listening to me?" Clay asks. "You can't go through with this."

She sits at the kitchen island of her mom's new beach house, watching me cook. I've been staying here with Mars and Paisleigh for two days while I search for a more modest place. Not that we had to leave our house, but it was never a home. Not like that little cottage Trace showed us that night. I want them to live somewhere like that.

I swipe the filling with my finger, tasting it again. The nerves in my jaw joints perk up, and I shrug. It's got more punch at least. I pour in more juice.

"Krisjen!"

I glance up and start stirring again. "He doesn't love me," I tell her.

I said it to him several times. He didn't tell me once.

"Is that what you think?" she snaps. "How could he not love you?"

"You don't know everything, Clay." I pour the filling into a pie shell. "I'm not what he needs. I owe him."

"Krisjen—"

But my phone rings, and I hurriedly drop the bowl back to the counter, thankful for the interruption.

"Hello?" I answer quickly.

"Hey, it's me," Bateman says. "The kids never showed up at your grandparents'."

"What?"

I step away from the pie, checking the clock on the wall. It's almost seven. They got out of school four hours ago. Mars texted me that they were there.

"Your grandma didn't think anything of it," he goes on. "With your parents and such, she figured wires got crossed, but I found Paisleigh's homework in my car and called to see if I could drop it off. It's due Monday. That's when we realized we didn't know where the kids were."

I slip my feet into my flip-flops and grab my keys. "Have you called my parents?"

"Both of them," he replies. "Your dad's not answering, and your mom said . . . that they're in the Bay."

"What?" I blurt out, feeling Clay's eyes on me. "Why would—"

"I don't know," he says, sounding breathless. "Do you want me to call someone?"

I hook my purse over my head and mouth to Clay, "Gotta go."

I push through the screen door, jogging down the porch steps. "Not yet," I tell him. "Keep your phone on you just in case."

"Got it. Let me know when you have them."

"Bye." And I hang up.

Why are the kids in the Bay? And how does my mother know that?

What's going on?

I hop in my car, the sky black, not a star visible. The thick air breezes through the open windows, but I let my hair fly in my face, too busy dialing the entire way over to the Bay.

Mars doesn't answer. My mother doesn't answer. I hesitate, tempted to call Army. I don't want to face Macon.

But I call him anyway.

The phone just rings. No voicemail picks up.

I race toward the Bay, thunder rolling across the sky as I keep calling Mars and my mother over and over again.

Headlights flash, and I glance in my rearview mirror, seeing a car behind me. I slow, watching them drive up alongside and as soon as I recognize Army's truck. I exhale, a little relieved.

He tips his chin at me, and I swerve to the side, slowing to a stop. He does the same, pulling over in front of me.

He hops out and heads back to me, leaning on my open window. "I was just on my way to retrieve you."

"Where are Mars and Paisleigh?"

"I'll take you."

I narrow my eyes.

His gaze falls down my body, but in a way that feels condescending, not leering. "Follow me," he says.

I open my mouth to speak, but I close it again. I just need to get to my brother and sister, and then I can figure out what the hell is going on.

I watch as he climbs back into the cab of his truck, no other figures visible inside, and I hesitate only a moment when he hits the gas.

I ride his tail, turn left, and then follow right, but instead of continuing to the Bay, he takes another left. He pulls into the marina, slowing over the speed bumps. I follow, my heart beating faster. Something isn't right. They're not here. Why would they be here?

He coasts into a spot, and I park next to him, shutting off the engine and exiting quickly.

He waits for me near the bed of his truck.

I look right and then left, hearing the boats rock on the water, the weight in the air heavy. "Army . . ."

"It's okay," he says. "The kids are fine."

I follow him down the walkway and onto the dock, passing sport boats and yachts, and stopping at a deep-sea fishing boat. He steps onto the deck, holding out a hand to help me. I glance past him, not seeing anything inside the dark cabin.

I ignore his hand and hop on, walking past him and sliding open the door.

I stop.

Men crowd the living room, and I gaze around, recognizing most of them as they all turn their heads to look at me.

Jerome Watson. Garrett Ames. A lawyer named Stewart Cole.

Trace. Dallas.

Macon stands in the center, wearing a dark suit with a navy blue shirt and a black tie. His arms are crossed over his chest.

"You keep the house," he says.

But he's not talking to me.

He's talking to Garrett Ames.

"I keep the five years," he continues. "Once that time is up, if the land is not appraised for at least three hundred percent above your initial offer, you get it. No argument."

I rush in. "No."

But they keep going as if I'm not there. "Say it again," Garrett demands, gesturing to everyone in the room. "Say it again, in front of them all."

"*No* argument," Macon repeats.

What the fuck? Does he have any idea what I went through to protect him?

Macon shifts his gaze to Jerome Watson. "Stop looking at her."

I glance, seeing Jerome turn away from me.

Garrett Ames holds out his hand, and Macon shakes it, the gesture by no means friendly. They both know Macon won't break his word. Garrett is making sure everyone sees it.

In a moment, they're gone, leaving only the Jaegers still on the boat.

I charge up to Macon. "What did you do?"

"Bought you back." He tips my chin up. "You weren't yours to sell."

I shake my head. He took me off the table and put every person living in the Bay on it instead. How could he do that? Five years to make the land valuable is something, but it may not be enough. What if he can't pull it off? I'm not worth that.

"Where are my brother and sister?" I ask.

He picks up a cigarette and lighter. "Making up their new beds and decorating their new room."

His mother's art room . . .

I back away, toward the doors. "I'm taking them home."

"They are home." He lights the cigarette. "I have power of attorney. Do you?"

"What?" I breathe out.

Power of attorney. He could've only gotten that from one of my parents.

He slides a document across the side table. I walk over, pick it up, and read it as he waits.

My mother is the grantor. She's given him authorization to act on Mars's and Paisleigh's behalf in her absence. It doesn't mean he has custody, but he has more than me. I haven't gotten around to making this legal with my parents yet.

"I just paid a lot for you," he whispers. "Come here."

How much money did he pay her for this? On top of what I got her from my father, my mom has to be sitting pretty fucking well right now.

I hear Dallas in the background. "The whole Bay paid for her."

I drift to Macon. "How much?" I ask him. "How much did you pay her?"

The smoke curls toward the ceiling, his eyes locked on mine.

I pull the ties on my cover-up, letting it fall to the floor. I stand in my two-piece swimsuit that I wore on the beach earlier today. "Enough for all of you to get your uses out of me?"

His chest rises and falls in heavy breaths, and I reach behind my back, tugging the strings of my top. Pulling it away from my body, I stand in the middle of the room, topless. The guys are silent behind me.

"Enough for you to do whatever you want?"

"Enough for me to get you knocked up," he whispers. "I want a kid, and I want it from you."

I almost choke on a lungful of air. My stomach drops, and I barely notice him snuffing out his cigarette and lifting me into his arms. The room spins.

Is he serious?

"Wait outside," he tells his brothers.

He carries me away, and closes us off into a back room and sets me on my feet. I can't look up at him. I'm afraid.

He smooths locks of my hair through his fingers and brushes my chin with his thumb. "You would've been his wife?"

I try to speak, but it takes a moment. "Or your revenge," I say quietly. "Is that what I am?"

Does he love me? Does he want me?

His hands glide down the sides of my torso, over my belly button, around my hips, and up my back. Then he brings them back around, his thumbs brushing the undersides of my breasts.

But all I really feel are his eyes. Nothing feels as good as him looking at me. He pulls me into him and kisses my forehead.

"How long do I have to pay?" I ask.

He pushes my bottoms down my legs, backs me up to the bed, and pushes me down before he strips off his clothes. "Until you're dead."

I crawl back on the bed, away, but he comes down on me, pressing me on top of the covers. I plant my hands against his chest as he stares down at me, already hard and pressing between my legs.

I dig my nails in, and he cocks his head.

"What if I was looking forward to being Mrs. Watson?" I taunt, lifting my chin. "What if I wanted him?"

He forces my leg out, grunting as his groin presses against my warm center. "If you ever fucking say that to me again . . ." he growls.

And then he thrusts his hips, pushing inside of me. I gasp, feeling his hard cock inside me, stretching me.

I push at his chest but don't push him away. He pumps his hips, thrusting between my legs, sliding in and out, and then he dips down, sucking on my right nipple.

My eyelids flutter.

I watch him lick and bite as he drives into me faster and harder, fucking me like he owns me.

"I'm scared of you," I whisper. "A little."

*Still.*

If I ever fucking say *that* to him again—taunt him with Jerome Watson—what will he do? Kill someone?

"But I think you like me, too." He breathes over my skin. "Just a little. Don't you?"

It's not really a question. He knows the answer.

My legs fall wide, I circle his waist with my arms and arch up, catching his bottom lip in my teeth.

He trembles, slowing. "I'm scared of you, too."

*I know.*

Flipping us over, I straddle his cock and dive down, kissing and licking his stomach, his chest, and his neck. Then I roll my hips, taking him back inside me as I gaze at him and rock nice and slow.

"She didn't try to touch you, did she?" I say.

I don't want him to ever have to speak to her again.

He digs his fingers into my hips, tipping his head back as he tries to guide my hips faster and faster. "No one touches me but you."

Only me.

"Krisjen," he groans. "Faster."

"No."

I want him slow.

He grits out, "Fuck."

Slow and soft, I slide up and down his cock, my orgasm teasing as I start to rub myself. He watches me, and then I feel his muscles tighten.

"Faster," he begs through his teeth.

I let my head fall back, loving the feeling of him wanting me.

I bounce, and he shoots up, both of us wrapping our arms around each other. I fuck him, holding him to me as the heat builds in my stomach. I drive my thighs into him again and again, crashing my mouth down on his as I start to come.

I whimper and moan, both muffled in the kiss, but when the orgasm rocks through me, I open my eyes, seeing him staring. Watching me.

I roll my hips nice and slow, my lips layered with his as he grips my ass, presses me hard against his groin, and . . . spills inside of me.

He growls against my mouth, not kissing me back as I leave pecks on his lips and feel him throb between my legs.

He falls back on the bed, taking me with him, and I just want to curl into him for the rest of my life. He wants me. I know he wants me.

Does he love me?

I lean over him, kiss his eyes, between them, and down his cheeks. Taking his mouth, I kiss him, moving over his lips, savoring every second.

I pull back and look down, and for a moment, I swear I see a smile, but then not. He blinks, his expression hardening, and he moves out from under me.

Sitting up, he swings his legs over the bed and picks up his clothes, starting to dress.

I sit cross-legged, holding the sheet up over my body. "Look at me."

He keeps his back to me. What's wrong?

"Macon, look at me."

He shakes his head. "How can you look at me?" he says barely above a whisper.

He rises, pulling on his pants and still not meeting my gaze.

"I'll always see you," I say, but my voice is gravelly with tears. "Even when I close my eyes."

I told him that less than two weeks ago.

He sits back down and pulls on his socks and shoes. I cover his back, wrapping my arms around him. "I know you hate me. What she did to you . . ."

He pulls my arms off him, grabbing his shirt off the nightstand and standing up again. "I knew exactly who you were when you slept next to me all those nights, Krisjen."

I sit back as he slips his arms into the shirt. "When you rode on the back of my bike and sat at my table and fed me and filled my house with your fucking perfume. I knew who you were from the start."

He still wanted me. Knowing I was her daughter.

Then why doesn't he say it? *Tell me you love me.*

How could I not look at him? "I was made for you," I murmur.

I stare at his back, waiting for a response. *Just say it. Please.* If he loves me, then everything is okay.

"Just get dressed." He stands up, leaving his tie but pulling on his jacket. "They'll take you back to the house." He faces me as he pulls on his jacket but still doesn't meet my eyes. "If you don't sleep with me, you sleep alone," he says. "You live with us now."

He starts to leave, and I wrap my arms around my knees. "I'll get my pillow."

He stops, his hand on the knob.

I smile, a little sadly.

I'll be in his bed. I'll always be in his bed.

I know my mind. He thinks there's too much baggage, and he thinks I'm too young. But he's stuck in his bullshit. He feels too guilty to claim me, but he can't let me go. I don't want to lose time. Does he want me the way I want him?

I swallow through the tightness in my throat. "I always thought I was some special little shit growing up," I say.

He still doesn't face me.

"I was told I was smart," I tell him. "That I would take on the world and everyone would know who I was. I would be someone great, and no one would be outside my sphere of influence."

Adults tell every kid they're significant. We want to believe it.

"But the thing is . . ." I go on, "I'm not unique. I was never that smart. I'll never be an astronaut, or the captain of a ship, or a professor of biology or philosophy. I'm not a good athlete, and I'm fine seeing mountains and operas and Alaska just on TV."

None of that is what I wanted out of life. I want none of what I was taught to want.

"No one will remember me after I'm gone," I say, "and I'll never be someone kids learn about in school."

I drop my eyes, heat covering my cheeks and my pulse racing painfully.

"I just want to love you." All I can do is whisper. "That, I will do beautifully."

# 34

## Macon

I leave the room, pulling the door closed hard. I dig the heels of my palms into my eyes, trying to push back the tears. *God, I fucking love you.*

She's perfect.

And I know, without a doubt, I shouldn't keep her. She knows nothing of all the possibilities that are out there for her. She won't still love me in five years. Was I serious? Do I want a kid with her?

I don't want her having anyone else's.

Fuck it. This could be it.

This *is* it.

I can't stop. I'm not even going to try, and if I end myself someday, it won't be because of my shit headspace. It'll be in the wake of ruining her life, because no matter everything that will go wrong, the time I have with her will be worth it.

I button up my shirt, tuck it in, and fasten my tie, leaving the boat.

Clay sits on the hood of my truck, my sister leaning back between her thighs.

I toss my keys to Army.

Trace, Dallas, and I head for the doors.

“Take Krisjen home,” I tell Liv. “Our house.”

“What are you guys doing?”

I jerk my chin at Army. “Let’s go.”

He climbs in the driver’s side.

“Macon.” Liv follows me. “What are you doing?”

I yank open the passenger-side door. “Get home.”

She watches us, Clay jumping off the car and standing next to her as we all climb in and Army hits the gas, backing up.

Liv knows enough, and that includes knowing better than to press harder for answers. She’s got a lot to lose. I don’t want her involved.

I take one last look at the boat, picturing Krisjen at home when I get there, but she won’t be in bed because she doesn’t fucking listen. I smile a little. I’ll fight with her all night if she wants. As long as she doesn’t leave.

We take off, and I turn down the music, catching Trace in the rearview mirror. He wears a knit cap, a plaid collared shirt peeking out the top of his zipped-up leather jacket. I’ve never seen him in a collared shirt.

His face is turned out the window.

“You don’t have to come,” I tell him.

He nods, still looking outside. “I know.”

Like Krisjen and Liv, I never wanted to break the illusion that we were good people.

Army glances at me and then back to the road. “Are you sure about this?” he asks. “The more we do this, the easier it becomes. That’s a slippery slope.”

I comb my fingers through my hair and straighten my tie. “It should’ve been done last spring,” I state. “He’s a threat to their safety.”

“And he can’t be stopped,” Dallas chimes in behind me. “Not in one piece anyway.”

Dallas and Iron are one side of the same coin. There's a detachment inside of them. If they make up their mind it needs to be done, then there is no choice.

Army and Trace are the other side of that coin. Loyal, but their conscience takes up a lot of room inside them.

Liv is a mixture of both. Things need to be done, and she accepts that she'll feel like shit about it sometimes.

I'm not sure which one I am yet. I always felt like shit hurting someone, but I felt the same watching TV.

"I'll do it," Dallas announces.

"I'll do it," I say.

I don't want his hands dirty any more than necessary.

I look over at Army. "You have Dex. You don't need to be here."

Last time, he didn't have a child to worry about. I would understand if he wanted to back out.

He focuses on the road. "We all have things to lose."

I watch him out of the corner of my eye as we cross the tracks, rain speckling the windshield, and his silence fills the car in a way that Dallas and Trace probably don't even notice.

We haven't talked much the past week. I don't think I even knew where to start any better than he did.

He knew where my head was at last week.

That morning I came back from Krisjen's.

He watched me walk up the stairs, and he knew.

I was glad when he left, but now it's all I think about.

He left.

"I'm sorry," I whisper.

Army darts his eyes to me, and I open the glove compartment, pulling out a pair of black leather gloves.

"For everything," I tell him, pulling them on. "It's all yours as much as mine. You can take anything you want."

He steals glances at me, trying to watch the road.

I swallow through the needles in my throat. "Just not her, okay?"

He's quiet. He doesn't say anything.

*He's mad.*

But then he says, "I want my own room."

I smile to myself.

Yeah, I guess it's ridiculous he shares a room with Dex.

"You get first dibs," I assure him.

The new addition will be ready before the summer. Mars is sharing a room with his little sister right now, but he'll also need his own space. As will Iron when he comes home. That leaves two rooms left.

"It's a bad time of year," Trace tells us. "Water levels will be low, and the gators—"

"He won't be found," I say.

I know what he's worried about, but we've done this once before. Not dozens of times like the rumors say. Once.

Nothing makes it out of the swamp.

We coast back into the Bay, around the village center, and deep into the dark green brush. Willows and oaks spill onto water shimmering in the faint moonlight, and rain spatters the dark surface. A wake is kicked up as an animal moves underneath the water.

We pull alongside the road, park, and exit the vehicle, walking to the wooden bridge in the black forest.

Milo Price sits on his knees in the middle, Santos gripping the back of his collar.

I stop in front of them, my brothers behind me. "Where was he?" I ask Santos.

"The motel."

I look down at the piece of shit who tried to assault my sister, and who made Krisjen bleed. The motel isn't a brothel, but he acts like it is.

It's a good place to disappear for a few hours, though. Guys like him can afford fancy hotel rooms, but the sleaze of a seedy, well-used mattress is half the turn-on for them.

I gaze at the scar running down the side of his face. My sister's girlfriend did that, but that was never the end of it. He should've known we'd come for him eventually. We don't trust St. Carmen police to protect anyone but St. Carmen assholes.

Milo smiles at me. "You had to wait for me to come over here."

I nod. "Traffic cams and such."

There are cameras everywhere. If they track his last location, they can track him to us, but when he comes to the Bay, traffic cams lose sight of him long before he crosses the tracks. From there he could've gone anywhere. There's no proof that he came here.

"Well, let's get it over with," he spits out. "It'll take more than five of you to give me a beating I can't take."

"I'm not going to hit you."

His smile falters, but still . . . he doesn't seem afraid.

Santos hands me a hunting knife, heat coursing down my arms as I take it. I squeeze my fist around the hilt.

"Can I ask you something?" I peer down at him. "Why do you pay for it? Sex, I mean."

It isn't always Bay women he's fucking, but whoever it is, he's coming to the motel and he's paying them.

"It doesn't look like you've had any trouble getting tail for free," I continue. "Is it because it makes it a job for them? To please you?"

I never asked the women who paid me.

But he shakes his head. "No," he tells me. "When I pay them, they're animals." He pauses. "*Farm* animals."

My fingers ache around the hilt.

He shrugs. "When I'm done eating, I just shove the sloppy, sticky dish under the shower for their next fuck."

My mouth goes dry.

I grab his collar, yanking him from Santos. "Thank you for your honesty."

I rear the blade back, my eyes on his throat, but then she's there, slipping between him and me. Footfalls race over the bridge behind me, and I can only assume it's my sister and Clay.

Krisjen grips my shirt at my stomach, her eyes looking up at me and pleading.

"Get out of my way," I growl. "I won't make the same mistake as my father."

If he had put my mom first, she wouldn't have spent twenty years dying from the inside out. I'm not giving Milo Price a chance to succeed the next time he comes for my sister or Krisjen. Family comes first.

I glare at Price, but I hear the tears in Krisjen's voice. "The only mistake would be doing something that risks you being taken from me."

No one will take me from her.

"Look at me," she begs, and I see Liv out of the corner of my eye. "Look at me."

I meet Krisjen's blue eyes.

"I love you," she whispers. "You're the only thing I've ever been sure about. I love you so much. He doesn't have anything you have," she whispers. "Look at what you have."

Her gaze flits around me, and I don't have to look to know my family is everywhere. My brothers, my sister, my friends—safe and alive.

"We come first," she commands, and then leans in, whispering. "And his day will come."

"Krisjen and I can fight our own battles," Liv adds.

My hand shakes with the knife. This has to happen. He has to go.

"Don't leave me," she begs. "You're not going to want to look at me"—she presses her body into mine—"through a piece of glass."

An image of me talking to her in jail and not being able to touch her flashes in my mind. An image of her sleeping without me.

That's not what a man does.

I grind my teeth together. She's right. Making sure that I'm always at her side comes first.

I lower the blade and release Milo. Wrapping my arms around her, I pull her into me and press my mouth to hers, gripping the back of her scalp and holding her so tight, she groans.

God, I love her. I bury my face in her hair. I love her so much.

"You're smart," she murmurs in my ear. "You'll figure out how to get rid of him. Bide your time."

Damn right. I hold her to me, pressing my lips to her forehead.

"Enjoy your whore," Milo bites out. "You dirty piece of Swamp shit."

Balling my fists, I pull back from Krisjen, holding her eyes.

And she sees it. "Macon . . ."

"I won't kill him." I kiss her again and then push her behind me, dropping the knife and grabbing Price by the collar, hammering my fist down onto his face.

"Oh, Jesus," my sister gripes.

Milo falls to the floor of the bridge, and I raise him up again, hitting him so hard, a slice of pain hits my knuckles like I've been stabbed.

I shove him to Santos. "Get him in the truck."

He throws him over his shoulder and carries him off the bridge. We all follow.

"What are you doing?" Krisjen asks.

"Just taking him home."

We climb into the cab of the vehicle, Santos and Milo in the bed with Dallas and Trace and the women in the back seat.

Army drives as rain starts to fall, but we're in St. Carmen's town center before it starts to pour. We cruise past restaurants, the dress shop where Liv worked, and the Harbor Point Fishing Boat. We coast through the roundabout.

People eat under awnings on the sidewalk and watch us pass, and I'm guessing that it's my truck, and not that we're speeding, that catches their attention. Coasting into a parking space, Army ignores the meter, and we both hop out, heading to the tailgate. Dropping it, I take Milo from Santos and don't even bother standing him up. Dragging him as he kicks and tries to get his feet under him, I haul him over to the police station, seeing Chavez slowly descend one step at a time down the station stairs.

I drop Milo at the foot of the steps. "Tell your superiors to keep their trash out of the Bay," I tell the officer.

Milo spits blood, coughing as he tries to stand up. "Arrest him," he sputters.

"Shut up," Chavez warns him.

Milo pushes himself to his feet. "Arrest them!"

I turn, finding Krisjen, but then her eyes go wide.

"Macon!"

I look behind me, seeing Milo come with his fist cocked. He hits me to the ground, my cheekbone slamming against the pavement. I wince, the cut in my skin spreading like a fire over my face. I try to push myself up, shaking my head clear, but I see something out of the corner of my eyes and look just in time to catch his leg before he kicks me.

I grab him, yank him, and push myself up, slamming him in the jaw.

He falls to the ground, and I climb to my feet, a crowd growing around us. Chavez remains on the stairs.

I circle Milo, waiting for him to try again.

He rises, zones in on me, and then . . . He shoots off, rushing me.

Slamming into me, he pushes us to the pavement, and I feel the pebbles in the street dig into my leg. My elbows scrape against the road.

We roll, I straddle him, my blood spilling onto my clothes from the cut in my face. I punch once.

And then again. His eyes roll into the back of his head, and I stand up, take him by the collar, and drag him back to the steps.

Chavez looks down at the kid, not moving to help him.

I take a step back, and another. And another.

Milo is stupid, but he's a fighter. It's always fun with someone who doesn't know when to quit. The next time will be especially enjoyable, because he'll be older. As will his friend Callum Ames. Taking them down will be an actual challenge. Thank God.

I lean against the tailgate, looking at the diners as the cops spill out of the station, and Bay people who work in their restaurants stand paused with their trays.

Liv holds Clay's hand, and I pull Krisjen back into my body, hanging an arm over her shoulder.

"I love you so goddamn much," I whisper.

She leans her head back against my chest. "I suspected."

And I smile, kissing her hair.

The next morning, we still haven't slept.

We stayed up all night, talking about our favorite holidays, our worst memories, if we believed in God, my favorite body part of hers, and why the electric bill has more than doubled since she started staying here the past couple of months. We agreed. It's her long hot showers.

And we spent a lot of time not talking. Hours not talking. We need to leave this bed, though. If only because I want to look forward to her tonight.

I hold her to me, grazing my fingers up and down her back. "We should wait to have kids," I say. "Okay?"

I don't want to talk about this now, but she may take my previous statements as an invitation to stop birth control.

"Do you want them?" I ask her.

She lifts her eyes to me, nodding. "You?"

"I think so." I'm almost thirty-two. I don't want to be an old father, but I don't want to be a bad one, either. "I should . . . I need some time."

I feel good today. I feel better a lot lately, but it might not last. I can't make her any guarantees. I'm not ready for kids. Not yet.

She touches my face. "I want you to talk to someone."

I shift underneath her. I really don't want to do that.

"I'd be destroyed if anything happened to you," she whispers. "You need someone who knows what they're doing. Will you try?"

I swallow hard. I'll do anything she wants me to. Not that I'd be okay losing anyone in my life, but I can't lose her. I want us happy.

Every day doesn't have to be easy, but I want her to know every day that I love her.

"Okay," I reply.

She smiles, and I feel her body relax in my arms.

"I'll be a handful, you know," I warn her.

And I don't even mean the moods.

She laughs. "I've got two hands."

She slides on top of me, kissing my lips. "I know who you are," she says. "And I want every minute of it."

I grip her ass, rubbing her over my groin. "You sure?"

"Oh, baby, I won't be a picnic, either." She kisses me deep, slipping her tongue in again and again. "But you like pains in the ass."

I break out in a smile. They seem to be my lot in life.

Just then, we hear a bellow outside the door. "Ah!" someone shouts.

Was that Mars?

There's pounding on the stairs, and then I hear Dallas. "Get these clothes out of the dryer!"

We hold each other, listening.

"Macon!" Trace calls out. "We can't live like this. We're going to need another bathroom. Like, yesterday!"

Yeah, we need the addition to the house finished, like, yesterday. We're at full capacity.

I bury my face in Krisjen's neck, rethinking my desire to leave the bedroom at all. Ever again.

But she pops up, straddling me. "Oh, can we get a Christmas tree today?"

I shake my head. "I'm not stepping foot in that shithole of a town right now."

She flashes me a bold smile along with her breasts. "Good things do come from that shithole." She wiggles her eyebrows. "You know you like to slum."

I arch up, kissing her chest, her neck. "My little princess from the wrong side of the tracks . . ."

She circles my neck with her arms, both of us stirring again.

But just when I think I've successfully distracted her, she pulls back and looks down at me. "Tonight," she tells me. "We'll take everyone out for food, pick out a tree, put the kids to bed, and then we'll break into Mariette's for dessert and have sex on one of the tables."

I chuckle. *Fine.* "With the skates?" I ask, hopeful.

She smiles wide, but then stops me as I start to kiss her neck again and glances over her shoulder to where they lie on my bedroom floor. "Hey, how did they get in your bedroom, by the way?"

I crash back on the bed, squeezing my eyes shut. "Ah, shit."

Fuck. I totally forgot about that.

"Macon?"

"I can explain," I rub my eyes. "Just give me a sec . . ."

But she grabs my throat, her eyes zoning in like bullets. "Explain . . . what?"

"Nothing happened."

Her scowl deepens. "*What* didn't happen?"

I hold up my hands in surrender, loving everything about having her in my bed with me, and trying to keep the laughter at bay.

She'll be a handful, indeed.

And I'm here for all of it.

# EPILOGUE

## Krisjen

***Four Years Later***

I think I'll marry Army next. Or Trace. He's agreeable and teachable. Why not? It'll be great.

Or . . . I could just run the Bay on my own. The newly widowed queen who steps in, because *she's a fucking widow now, because she's going to kill Macon Jaeger!*

"I need a shower," he says, laughing as he comes through the door with his brothers.

I pull my thumbnail out of my mouth and spin toward him as I stand at the window.

He drifts into the dark house, the grandfather clock chiming 5:00 a.m. "Let me wake up Krisjen first."

But I grab the framed picture of us, me in his arms, my legs wrapped around him, my happy smile peering over his shoulder as the camera captures only his back. *Good times. Better days.*

I throw it across the room, but it just clips his shoulder.

He rears back, stumbling, but then rights himself and looks in my direction. "Ow." He rubs the spot it hit. "What the hell?"

"You're two days late!" I bellow.

His face falls, and he holds out his hands like he's trying to wrangle a horse. "I'm sorry, okay? I . . ."

But I grab the coffee-table book of Mammoth Cave that I got

in Kentucky, because we just closed our eyes and picked a place on a map for our honeymoon.

I throw it as Army, Trace, and Dallas back up, out of the way. I grab the remote, a magazine, and a potted plant, and hurl every single one at my husband. He ducks out of the way as Trace chuckles at the scene.

"I told you it would be unpredictable," Macon argues.

"And I told you to get a satellite phone!"

I hurl a candle, throw Dex's soccer ball, and pick up the crystal bowl Clay got us for our wedding, but stop and put it back down. It's pretty.

"Worrying my ass off, wondering if you were shot or strangled or kidnapped or sinking to the bottom of the ocean," I yell. "And I can't call the cops!"

He moves in. "Come here."

"I'm not a fan of you right now!"

"Steel stomach, remember?"

Ugh! I stomp on his foot, and he grunts, clenching his teeth. Grabbing me, he swings me over his shoulder.

I flail, kicking. "Let me go!"

"Go to the bar for a while," he tells his brothers. "I need to deal with this one."

And I feel a slap on my ass. I flinch and then growl.

"Might get loud . . ." Dallas taunts.

"Don't you spank me in front of them!" I shout.

"Don't worry, Krisjen." Trace chuckles, and I hear the door open. "We know you're the boss of him."

Laughter fills the air as they drift out of the house, and Macon spins around, carrying me up the stairs.

Tears spring to my eyes. I was so worried. Every second. At any moment, he could've been gone forever, and I might never know what happened to him.

"Let me go." I slap his ass as I dangle there. "You deserve the silent treatment for the next two days after that stunt. Because that's how long it's been since I've slept!"

We reach the top, and he carries me into our bedroom, closing the door.

"Let me down!" I yell.

His hand grips the back of my thigh, his fingers crawling inward as he kisses against my jeans.

"I thought you were giving me the silent treatment," he teases.

I clamp my mouth shut, pouting and trying to keep from crying out of relief as I hang there.

"We got the containers," he whispers.

Fine.

"Then they pushed us overboard and tried to sink our boat," he says.

I suck in a breath. *Oh God.*

That's what I'd been afraid of.

I understand that these black-market deals to get lumber, steel, cement, and pipes—which all the local suppliers were either withholding or were overcharging for, thanks to Garrett Ames—could be dangerous, but I always hope Macon's reputation will precede him.

But every once in while we run into a dealer who would just rather take the money, try to kill them, and sell the items they already sold again. It's bad business, but when they're coming from overseas, they don't care. They'll never see you again anyway.

"We took their boat instead," he tells me. "I marooned them on Coral Cay. For now."

Coral Cay is a small island with about one tree for shade, but otherwise it's pretty barren. There's nothing and no one, and if a ship or a Cessna does pass by—which is likely, given that it's only a few miles off the coast—they'd hide. Anyone Macon sticks there doesn't want to be caught anyway. There's food and water, and he'll go back in a few days once he's found a cargo ship that he can stash them on to get rid of them.

It could've easily turned bad, though. It's only a matter of time. What would happen to us if Trace had been lost? Or Army? It's not just Macon I worry about. Losing anyone would devastate him.

He presses his lips into my thigh. "This is all I thought about out there in that black water," he whispers. "Guns pointing at us . . . The depths below . . . I had to get back to you."

A tear drops to the floor, and I wipe my eye.

"Still not talking to me?" he goads.

He puts me back on my feet, drops to his knee, and unbuttons my jeans, pulling them down below my ass. Yanking my underwear to the side, he sweeps his tongue up my flesh, and I gasp, gripping the dresser at my back. My clit starts to throb.

"Do you think I'm going anywhere?" he asks.

Tears fill my eyes.

He bites and plays with me. "You think that I'm going to widow my young bride and let another man have this?"

He tugs off my clothes, stands up, and then yanks my shirt over my head as well as his.

"Talk," he growls in a low voice, pressing himself into me.

I press my lips together.

He takes my jaw in one hand, lightly squeezing both sides. "Your husband told you to open your mouth."

He squeezes and squeezes until I have fish lips, and I'm almost laughing.

But I don't. I've lived with four years of close calls like this. I'm entitled to a little pouting.

"Or maybe you weren't worried at all." He releases me. "Maybe you think I was with another woman the whole time."

My eyes flare. That wasn't even a thought, but now the image is in my head. Son of a bitch.

He grinds himself into me, holding my waist. "Feel what you do to me, Krisjen."

I feel it.

The hard ridge in his jeans that just appears every time I'm naked. Or when I walk around in his clothes, or reach into a high cabinet and my stomach shows. Or bend over and my thong shows. Or sit in his lap or help him in the garage. He loves seeing grease on my face.

"You don't think everyone knows Macon Jaeger's little Saint has him wrapped around her little finger?"

I flex my jaw, my heart swimming.

He leans in. "Tell me what I need to hear," he whispers.

*No.*

"Say it," he demands.

*Nuh-uh.*

He caresses me everywhere, finally coming up to cup my face. "All I could think about was this."

He comes in to kiss me, and I whimper, putting my hands on him.

"Baby . . ." he begs.

The sound of his voice is desperate, and I can't help it anymore. The relief floods me, and I wrap my arms around him.

"Mine." I press my forehead to his.

"That's what I want to hear."

He whips me around to face the dresser mirror, and I break into a smile as he hugs me to his body and buries his face in my hair. It's his comfort move. How he feels safe.

"I love you," I tell him.

Turning me back around, he holds my eyes as he lifts me into his arms and carries me to our bathroom.

I hug with my arms and legs as he leans over and starts the shower, shrugs his jeans off, and steps in. He closes the door, the shower inside dark with the black tile I picked when we added it to our many renovations of the house.

Liv's old room no longer exists, Macon and his brothers having to tear down the walls to make a hallway toward the new wing.

Liv and Clay are looking into buying an old, abandoned lighthouse a few miles away, but we have a few spare bedrooms in case they ever sleep over. Dex has his own room, Paisleigh has a balcony, where she likes to imagine she's Juliet, and Mars opted to have his room in the attic. There's a window that leads right to the tree where the old treehouse still sits. They built the wing around it, keeping a small courtyard in the middle on the lower level. Mars likes to sleep in the treehouse. Still. At sixteen years old.

Macon puts me down, and I soap up a loofah, starting to wash the sweat and ocean off him.

"I'll get the satellite phone today," he finally says.

"Thank you."

"You really fucking love me, don't you?"

I dart my eyes up to his, watching his proud smile spread like he has me right where he wants me.

I tear my eyes away from the way the suds drip down his golden skin and push him down on the stone seat of the shower. His eyes gleam as he watches me drop to my knees and take him in my mouth.

He exhales, holding my head to his body.

*Yes, I love you. And I'm never losing you.*

It was a long road for him to learn how to manage everything that goes on in his head, and some days he forgets how altogether.

But he knows that I love him, and that another good day is coming.

Once he found a doctor who didn't aggravate him—and got to know them—it got a lot easier for him to keep talking to someone.

He knows he's not alone. They check in with each other regularly.

And the time between one bad day and another has gotten longer and longer, and there are so many days when he's the one taking care of me.

We're lucky.

Every time I feel him, smell his skin, see him crook his finger with a smile on his face, I'm so goddamn lucky I found him.

"Mama Kris!" a kid yells.

I pull my mouth off my husband.

"Can I have pancakes?" the kid, Mato, from across the street, yells. I see a dark form peek around the bathroom door. "Willow says I can't!"

Macon looks at me. "What the fuck?"

But the kid can't see us clearly through the frosted glass. It's fine. I stand up. "Of course you can have pancakes," I tell the six-year-old. "It's too early, though. Go home and get ready for school. I'll be downstairs soon."

"'Kay!"

And he slams the door on his way out. I look down at Macon as he runs a hand through his hair. "You need to talk to that kid about not coming into our bedroom."

"I did."

I lean down to kiss him.

But he just gives me a scolding look. "How did we get into a situation where we're feeding eight kids who aren't ours every morning?"

I slide my body on top of his, straddling him. "Kids can't concentrate in school if they're hungry," I tell him. "If they don't do well in school, they don't become doctors, lawyers, and presidents. We're in this for the long game, baby."

He laughs, and I know I won.

It wasn't really a big deal to start out. Willow and Mato's dad is offshore working most of the time, and their mom has odd shifts at the hospital a lot, so I started having them come over here for breakfast. A few other kids started joining them. Kids need a well-rounded breakfast. Maybe if I'd tried not to starve myself so much in high school, I would've done better in math, too.

I reach underneath me, stroking my husband and fitting him inside of me.

"I'm getting to be an old man." He sits up, holding me close. "I can't have scares like that when my dick is hard."

I place his hand on my breast. "An older man is the only one who knows what to do with this."

And I slide his hand down my body that he's kissed and tasted every inch of thousands of times, because he knows how to appreciate a woman properly.

We kiss, and I sink down on him, but then I stop.

Holding his face, I caress his cheek with my thumb, feeling his eyes on me.

But I can't look, because if I look at him, I'll chicken out. "I want a baby," I say.

He's silent. I keep caressing, finally forcing my gaze up.

He stares at me, his expression unreadable.

"Can I have a baby?" I ask him.

We avoided the subject for a long time. I wasn't in any hurry. I had plenty of time, and I loved having him to myself.

But I also know he avoided the subject because he was scared.

I wait for him to argue. Or to make some excuse about why we should wait longer.

Or worse, to tell me he doesn't want children at all.

He doesn't say any of those things, though. Taking my hand, he puts it against his chest, over his heart. "Say that again."

I feel the beat in his chest quicken.

I smile just a little. "Can I have a baby?"

He hardens even more inside me, and gasps, "Yes." Then he kisses me hard and deep, moving slowly over my mouth.

I start to rock on him, but then a knock hits the bathroom door. "Macon! Krisjen!"

I startle at Trace's voice, pulling away from the kiss.

"We're leaving at nine!" he bellows.

I wince. *Shit.*

Iron. I completely forgot.

I start to move away, but Macon pulls me back down. "Where do you think you're going?"

"There's so much to do," I whine.

Breakfast and backpacks, and I'll need to log in to check that Mars handed in his assignment because he always forgets. Then there's groceries to stock up on.

But Macon locks me in, pressing his cock up inside me. "Fuck no," he gripes. "We pick up Iron today, *and* then there's Callum-fucking-Ames . . . This shitshow of a summer starts tonight, and I need another fucking minute alone with you before that."

He kisses me through my laughter, and our quickie—which never turns out to be very quick at all—commences as I roll my hips and pant on top of him. Iron is finally coming home—after getting an extra four months for bad behavior, and Callum Ames is finally returning, or that's the word.

It's going to be a hot summer. If Macon gets through this without going to prison himself, it'll be a miracle.

He touches my lips with his. "I love you," he says.

I hug him. "Mine."

# ACKNOWLEDGMENTS


To all the women I grew up with . . .

To my mom, who always finds a solution.

To Grandma, whose thirteen hundred square feet are still the most magical place I've ever been.

To my aunt Carol, who always shows up for people.

And to my stepmom, who showed me the way.

I'm grateful for everything that went right, but more for everything that went wrong.

I learned, so thank you.

To all of the women who help make my stories possible—Jane Dystel, Lauren Abramo, Kerry Donovan, Adrienne Ambrose, Lee Tenaglia, Claudia Alfaro, Elaine York, Christine Porter, Ashlee O'Brien, Michelle Chu, Ivette Portillo, and Vibeke Courtney—thank you for finding me and for helping me be here.

Turn the page to enjoy a bonus scene from Dallas . . .

*The scene takes place during* Five Brothers, *after the Bug Jam.*

## Dallas

I don't think I dislike Krisjen. She's not boring.

I would've thought she'd fight back. At least defend herself against those girls at the Bug Jam. Aracely says she didn't, though. She just took it, and I find that perplexing.

But more so because she kept getting up.

I smile, the cool sheet sinking between my legs and resting against my groin. I tuck my arm underneath my head, staring up at the shadows of the branches outside fluttering across the bedroom ceiling. I've been in bed for hours, but I'm not tired.

I exhale, my chest slowly caving. I don't understand her, but I like being perplexed. I like it a lot.

My phone buzzes on the floor below me, and I roll, reaching over the edge of the bed and recognizing the number immediately as I grab the phone. A grin pulls at my mouth, and I lie flat on my back to answer.

"Hi," I say.

"You texted."

"And you called."

I knew he was watching. The live cam above the visitor's center captures a one-eighty of the grounds, and although it wouldn't have been easy to find me in the crowd, he only had to look for motorcycles. Luckily for him, Krisjen dragged us all out today, so I was there.

Callum Ames could watch me bringing her into the parking lot from his frat house at UPenn. He knows my bike.

"And you answered," he replies.

"You jealous?"

"You alone?" he teases.

I can't hold back the smile now. "You mean is her sore, sweaty little cunt in bed next to me?" I taunt. "Not yet."

I know what he's thinking. What he's been thinking since he saw Krisjen on my bike through the webcam.

"You don't want her."

His deep voice darkens, something sinister touching his tone. It's only been a few months, but he sounds different.

I hope he doesn't come back at Christmas. Or next summer. I want to run into him again when he's a man. When life has fucked with him a little more.

"You don't know what I want," I retort.

"I know what you like."

"I like women, too," I point out, "and that always pissed you off, because you knew you could never be everything I wanted."

His voice drops to a whisper. "Don't say that."

My chest tightens, but only for a moment.

Callum Ames was one of a million mistakes I wanted to make before my life was over, but he wanted to be the only one. It was almost a year and half ago. I was twenty. He was in high school. It shouldn't have happened.

"You remember the first time you laid your hands on me?" he asks, his voice softening.

"A right hook into your jaw."

I remember. A brawl between a couple of his little rich prick friends and a couple of us.

"It was raining . . ." he goes on.

The water drenched his shirt. I could see right through it. His hair turned dark blond when it was wet.

My cock swells. I glide my hand down and stroke it under the sheet. "Raining like it is tonight."

"Saints versus Swamp," he tells me. "Out in the woods, it was dark, we were soaked."

"My people were ripping yours apart . . ." I tease.

"We were fighting, and then . . ." He grunts, and I can almost feel him. "My dick was in your mouth."

I bite my bottom lip. "You couldn't get enough. You came so quickly."

He was hard immediately. We'd fought, found ourselves alone, and then . . .

"And then you pushed me into the back seat of your car," he says, "came down on my back, and sucked on my neck."

"And covered your mouth while I fucked you."

My cock fills my hand, so thick and hard, tenting the sheet.

I was fast. But I was gentle. His shirt was gone. I don't know where. His jeans halfway down his thighs. His wet hair hanging in his eyes. He was breathing so hard he couldn't talk, and I was breathing so hard I couldn't think. I didn't expect it.

"So tall," I say to him in a low voice. "So dashing. Future CEO, hedge fund king, oozing power someday with your cocky smile in your five-thousand-dollar suits that women will get wet just looking at. Wish all your frat boy friends could see how hard you get for me."

"So hard the next week too when I pinned your fucking face into that same seat and fucked you right back," he taunts.

I smile. *Yeah, you did.* Iron saw the bite marks on my back and just shook his head.

"Are you hard now?" Callum asks. "I am."

A hand slides up my leg and fists my cock. "Oh, I can't take it," Jessica coos, pulling the sheet aside and grinding her naked body along mine. "This is getting me horny again."

My heart jackhammers, and I grab her thigh, pulling her over me. "Sit on it."

The other end of the phone is silent as the girl who was asleep next to me fits my cock inside her again and sinks down on it.

Warmth coats my body like a blanket slowly descending over my skin, and I groan, closing my eyes and arching my back a little.

"Fuck yes," I say into the phone.

"Oh, yeah," she moans, starting to ride me. "That feels good."

Rising up, I wrap one hand around her waist and suck her plump tits. She whimpers, and I flick my tongue over her nipples.

Callum breathes in my ear. "What I did to Liv last year was a dream compared to the pain I will bring when I come home," he says, all the need and heat in his voice gone and replaced with rage. "I will be the end of you, Jaeger."

I chuckle, falling back and watching the girl's tits bounce as she thrusts her hips up and down my cock. "If you're still thinking about me in three and a half years," I tell him, "I'll be laughing my ass off . . ."

I hang up, tossing the phone aside and gripping her hips in both hands as I close my eyes.

*. . . and I'll be ready.*

If you enjoyed *Five Brothers*, keep reading for an excerpt from

# TRYST SIX VENOM

*Tryst Six Venom* is a sapphic love story between Macon's sister Liv, and Clay Collins. It takes place about six months prior to the start of *Five Brothers*.

# Clay

The cut at the corner of my mouth stings. I tongue it, slouching in the wooden chair as I gaze past Father McNealty's empty seat in his office.

God, it's better than a drug. The feeling swirling in my gut and my heart pounding like I'm dangling a hundred feet in the air, only holding on by a single hand.

*She's better than a drug.* I always knew she had it in her.

"If you ever come near me again," Olivia grits through her teeth in the chair next to mine, "I will cut you."

I look over at her. The orange juice she threw at me stains her white Polo, too.

But I almost smile, seeing the tear in her sleeve. I fought back, didn't I?

"Cut me?" I taunt, watching her as she watches me graze my hand up the inside of my thigh, dragging up my school skirt. "Where?"

I pretend to rub myself, moaning.

Her mouth twists into a snarl. "Cunt."

I turn away, smiling to myself. *Dyke.*

Sitting up straight, I hold up my nails, inspecting the damage. It took three teachers to pull us off each other. My only regret is that she didn't start this shit after school when we wouldn't have been interrupted. I'm in every bit as good a shape as she is. This could've gone on for hours.

The second bell rings, and now we're officially late for fifth period. Where the hell is he?

"They're going to research it, you know?" Liv says, and I can see her looking at me out of the corner of my eye. "Find out where that video came from, and when I take this online with my receipts, the entire fucking world will be calling for your head. Especially since I'm only seventeen."

*Fuck.* I forgot about that. She's a minor.

I pick at the chipped red nail polish, ignoring the skip in my heartbeat. "And who will believe you?" I turn my head, meeting her dark eyes under her long, black lashes. "I'm Clay Collins."

Blond and just like a bomb. Everything the administration loves to parade around in their recruitment brochures.

Her eyes narrow.

I look her up and down. "And you're a dumpster rat probably looking forward to a long and illustrious career turning tricks on the dirty floor of her shitty house."

Olivia launches out and grabs me by the back of my neck. I gasp.

I clutch the arms of the chair for support as she pulls us face-to-face, and I harden my jaw, looking into her eyes. The dark brown lights up with flecks of gold as she glares at me, and I can smell the peaches in her long black hair.

My heart pounds so hard. *Yes.*

*Like a fucking drug.*

She stares at me with fury, and I brace myself for impact when I know I should pull away.

But I don't want her to let me go. It took so long to get us here.

I hate Olivia Jaeger. I fucking hate her, and I'd happily never love anything if I could hate her my whole life. My eyes pool with tears, and I don't know why.

But I don't blink.

*Come on.* My chin trembles. *Come on.* I want this.

The juice she threw at me still drips from my skirt, and I close my eyes at the burn in my scalp where her fingers are curled into my hair under my ponytail. *Come on.* I open my mouth, feeling her everywhere. Almost tasting it.

Bitter but beautiful, like Valium on my tongue. That's what she's like.

I open my eyes, a tear spilling over, and I see her watching me, a mixture of anger and wariness in her eyes. Like she's unsure about something.

A voice carries in from the office, and Liv pushes me away, releasing me as the door to the headmaster's office opens.

I shake my head as I sit back in my chair. *Wimp.*

"Father McNealty is held up with the mayor," Mrs. Garrison tells us, remaining in the doorway. "He will speak to both of you in the morning, so don't think you're off the hook. Go to the locker room, change—"

I rise before she's finished, grab my cell phone off his desk, and walk past the old bag.

"And get directly to class," she yells after us as Liv and I walk through the office toward the door. "If I get another whiff of one more fight between you two, I'm calling your parents to pick you up!"

But we're already in the hallway, the door swinging closed behind us. I don't turn around, and I don't slow down, charging down the empty hallway as teachers drone on in their classrooms, and I descend the stairs, finding my way to the locker room.

Jaeger's on my tail the entire time, though, and I feel her eyes on my back. I hope she jumps me again.

I hope she does.

I push through the door, the offices and locker room empty as everyone is already outside. I stop at my locker and dial in the combination, throwing it open.

"Just had to be orange juice, didn't it?" I gripe, pulling my Polo off over my head. "Everything is sticky."

It's down in my goddamn socks. These saddle shoes are vintage. If she fucked them up, I'll make sure not even her lowlife brothers can protect her.

She digs in her locker—which is unfortunately in the same row, because Coach keeps lacrosse together—and I stalk over to the cabinet, pulling out a spare Polo.

"You know," I tell her, fumbling with a clean shirt, "if you didn't want everyone to see, then maybe you shouldn't have been practically fucking her in public."

"We weren't fucking," she growls, glaring at me. "As you and everyone else clearly saw. I guess if I didn't want people filming, I shouldn't have expected as much as some simple manners from a stupid, useless cow."

I slip my arms into the shirt. *Stupid, useless . . .*

But I pull it back off and throw it at her. "This should fit your fat tits. Take it."

She catches it, and I yank another shirt out of the cabinet, making sure it's a small.

She sets the shirt in her locker, checking her face in the mirror that hangs on the inside of the door. A trickle of dried blood coats the ridge of her ear, and I try not to look at her as she wipes it clean.

A tiny pang of guilt hits me, but I push it away. She made me bleed, too, didn't she? It's not my fault she has to line metal up her ear with all her dumb piercings. She came at me first.

I lick the cut at the corner of my mouth again, glancing over and watching her throw the bloody wipe on the ground, her lips twisted in anger.

But the fury is in her eyes, too, and I know she's still upset.

I pause, confusion seeping through. I know I deserved her anger.

I'd have been furious, too. And I honestly wasn't going to post the video. That wasn't my plan originally, but . . .

I grind my teeth together and close my eyes, blinking long and hard. Olivia kissed that girl everywhere. *Everywhere.*

I stare off into my locker, the bra like sandpaper on my skin. I peel it off, dropping it to the floor.

I mean, if I did that with my boyfriend in a public place, I'd be a slut, right? I might even get into trouble, because sluts don't represent Marymount at lacrosse games.

Marymount girls are good girls. We're discreet.

And now she knows.

I stand there, the air grazing my bare breasts as she digs in her locker.

She brushes down her blue, green, and black plaid skirt as chills spread across my body. She tightens her high ponytail, fluffing up the messy hair and smoothing out the loose tendrils that hang around her ears, the posts and small rings there glinting in the lights as the flesh of my nipples hardens.

I can't look at her, but I see everything.

She stops moving and lets her head fall, both of us breathing in sync. Quiet and alone, but so crowded.

"Why do you want me to hurt you?" she asks, her voice suddenly soft.

I don't blink.

*Why?*

*Why?*

My chin trembles. *Because . . . at least it's something.*

At least I have that.

My brother's picture hangs inside my locker door, and I absently rub my thumb over the faint hidden tattoo on the inside of my middle finger. He would've been fourteen this month.

My insides shake, and I grab the prescription bottle, tapping out a ten-milligram blue pill. I pop it into my mouth, the bitter dust starting to dissolve on my tongue before I swallow.

I pull out a clean sports bra and pull it over my head, followed by the shirt as she takes off her dirty one. And I can't help but look.

The contours of her stomach are tight and smooth, and I slide my eyes down her legs, the curves on the backs of her thighs mesmerizing.

But then she holds her hand out to me, and I look up, seeing a package of wet wipes. I stare.

"You want them or not?" she barks.

"Piss off."

And she throws it. The package hits the side of my head, and I growl, letting it fall to the ground.

"There's a drop of blood on the back of your neck, dumbass," she tells me.

I almost laugh. What? Does she feel guilty about hurting me or something? It's not like she should. I got her good this morning, didn't I? That video had eighty-five thousand views before I took it down at three a.m.

But, of course, by then it had already done its damage. What's on the internet stays on the internet somewhere.

Jesus, what did I do?

I grab the package off the ground and pull out a wipe. "Where?"

She pauses a moment, staring at her locker, and then stalks over, taking it out of my hand. Pushing me back around, she wipes off whatever is on my neck, and my thighs are burning with her touch. *God . . .*

"It's going to take every ounce of pull I have to protect you," she says. "You know that?"

Protect me?

"Once my brothers find out what you did," she warns, "their women will rebuild your fucking face."

"I'm not scared of Tryst Six," I say over my shoulder.

My father eats that side of town for breakfast.

But then I hear the click of her blade behind me, and I stop breathing.

"Take out your phone," she tells me.

"What for?"

I turn around, meeting her eyes, both of us eye to eye.

Her arm hangs at her side, the blade in her hand. "Do it." She cocks her head, calm. "I'm sure you have notifications by now."

Notif—

*What did she do?*

I quickly turn around and grab my phone out of the locker, turning it back on.

It lights up, loads, and in a moment, I hear dings and see tabs pop up.

Clicking on one, I watch as YouTube loads, my heart pounding hard as the same video I posted—and deleted—starts playing again. The jewelry in Olivia's ear glimmers in the moonlight, and her flowing white tank top makes her slender neck look warm and tan as she bends it back for the girl to kiss.

The account is registered to Vaudevillian Vix—not me—and it already has seven thousand views.

I drop the wipes. "What did you do?" My eyes lock on her.

"You wanted it up, so it's back up."

"But I took it down," I growl.

Goddammit, I took it down. I look back at my phone, scrolling the comments. Why would she do this? When did she do this? Before the fight? After?

"They won't trace it back to you," she assures, walking back to her locker and tossing the knife in. "It came from my phone."

So why repost it then, if not to screw me over?

"Take it down." I charge over to her. "Take it down now."

I don't want people to see this. It was a mistake.

"You're not scared of Tryst Six?" She fixes her lip gloss in the mirror, extra red against her black shirt and black hair. "Well, I'm not scared of you, baby. Do what you will. Leave it up—forever if it gets you off." She turns and looks at me. "Every degrading comment and joke is for your pleasure, so enjoy it."

*Son of a bitch!*

I push her aside and pull her phone out of her locker. "Take it down now." I hold her phone out to her, but before she can take it, I pull it back and swipe the screen, trying to do it myself. "Unlock this!" I yell at her. "Goddammit, Jaeger!"

She pushes me back into the locker and grabs her phone. "Scared now?" she taunts. "Huh? Feel violated when you've lost control of your property? How does that feel?"

I raise my hand, pointing in her face and shouting, "Take it down!"

But she grabs my wrists and twists them behind me, and I whimper at the ache as she backs me up into the lockers again.

"Because why?" she whispers in my face. "Say it. You're afraid, aren't you?"

I shake my head. She presses her forehead into mine hard, but I push back, giving as good as I get while I try to wrangle my hands free.

"You're afraid because your life is sad, and you want to gut anything that's different." Her breath falls on my lips, and I feel a light layer of sweat cover my back. "Anything that makes you feel strong, because at least it's not dull, and it's too painful not to feel, isn't it? You're afraid of me because someday you're going to wake up and remember that that video is still there, but I'm not, am I? I'm gone, living, and you're not, because your brain is still in the fucking gutter."

A sob lodges in my throat, and my body shakes.

She shakes her head at me. "You're just afraid."

"I'm not afraid," I tell her. "I'm . . ."

But I swallow, pushing the word back down my throat.

*I'm* . . . Tears fill my eyes, and I tighten every muscle in my body, forcing myself to get my shit together.

But I'm lost. She's holding me, and I'm lost. She's not leaving. Not in six months. Not ever!

She stares at me, and I clench my fists behind me as our noses brush, and I hover a moment from her lips. "Livvy, I . . ."

She can't disappear. Time will stop. It has to. I can't see her go. I . . .

My mouth rests open, the need to feel her overtaking me. I can't . . .

I can't . . .

I can't stand it. I touch her mouth.

I layer my lips with hers—grazing, brushing, inhaling as she stops breathing and I just feel her and feel every inch of my body suddenly burn like a firework about to pop.

And then, all at once, we're in the shit.

She releases my hands, and we both grab on to each other as she pushes me into the lockers again, our arms and hands wrapping around one another as her mouth sinks into mine.

I moan. *Yes. Fuck, yes.*

Our legs thread together, the heat between her thighs hitting my center, and she slips her hands under my skirt, grabbing my ass through my panties as we go at each other, kissing and nibbling and grinding.

"Liv . . ." I whimper.

I lick her tongue and groan, kissing her hard and fierce and closing my eyes, because everything is spinning, and my body is on a roller coaster. I'm fucking flying right now.

She lifts my leg, and I can't stop. Grinding and panting as I slip my hand up her shirt, pulling down her strap, so I can get my hand inside her bra. She dives down to my neck, and I tip my head back, letting her have it all. I want her. I want to feel her and kiss her and touch her everywhere.

Our lips come back together, again and again, eating each other up, kissing frantically. I brush her nipple, and my clit throbs.

"You gotta be fucking kidding me," she whispers, shaken. "Are you kidding me right now?"

*I know, all right? I know.* I wasn't afraid. I was . . .

Jealous. I've wanted this since we were freshmen, that first day we met, before the fighting started.

And when I knew she liked me, I was so happy, but . . .

Ashamed. Tears spike my eyelashes, even with as happy as I am right now. I was so ashamed.

She brings one hand up, grabs the back of my neck, and takes my bottom lip between her teeth. I pause, savoring the fire blazing inside my body.

Our foreheads meet again. "We have to stop," I murmur.

I fumble and squirm, trying to push her away, damn near wrecked because I'm aching for this. I don't want to let her go.

But she doesn't let me. "No," she bites out in a whisper. Her mouth crashes down on mine again, and I can't fight. I hold her head, soaking up how soft she is. How beautiful she smells and how hot her mouth is.

I barely notice as she lifts up my skirt and yanks down my panties just enough to bare my sex, but then she fiddles with her own clothes between us, and in a moment, she's on me. Her pussy rubs against mine, and I pull away from her mouth to moan as she grinds on me, the friction of our skin agonizing.

Agonizing but perfect. It's hot and wet and . . .

She grips my ass, her head dipped into my shoulder as I wrap my arms around her neck and meet her rhythm, both of us fucking against the lockers.

"Ugh!" I cry out as she goes at me.

I'm consumed. This is what it feels like. This is what right feels like. It was always wrong before. Kissing someone. Letting them touch me. I never had that burn low in my belly.

I was never hungry.

Until her.

I sink into her mouth again, kissing, sucking, tasting . . .

At least there's this. I thought hating her was enough. If I couldn't have this, at least I had her attention. Even if it was bad.

At least I could destroy what I was going to lose anyway in three months when we graduated, and I couldn't look at her every day anymore.

But God, I do hate her. Her smile and her red lips. The way she smudges her dumb eyeliner, making her eyes look smoky and captivating, and her wild hair that always looks like it flew through the wind before she put it up in a ponytail.

Her olive skin, how her bracelets make music every time she moves, her chipped black nail polish, and those stupid biker boots with all the buckles she wears that make her legs so hard not to look at.

The way she rolls her skirt up, and I can't pay attention in Calculus.

I hate it all. How every part of her looks like it has a taste.

I whimper as our pace gets faster, and I feel and hear her breathe hard, in and out as the friction turns heavenly.

And this isn't even all we can do to each other. "God," I pant.

She hovers over my mouth. "Come to my shitty house tonight," she demands. "Sweat with me between the sheets?"

I nod. "Yeah."

I want to sneak out. Into a dark place with Olivia Jaeger and do things.

All night.

But then a voice pierces the air. "Oh, I know!" someone says.

I pop my eyes open, stopping. *What?*

Giggles and laughter follow, and I hear the creak of the locker room door.

*Oh, shit.* Ice courses down my veins as everything goes cold. This can't . . .

I can't . . .

Oh my God.

Another voice follows. "And then he was like . . ."

*Fuck!*

I push at Olivia. "Get off me."

She stumbles back, and I reach under my skirt, pulling up my underwear.

*Jesus Christ.* I'm just a world of stupid today, aren't I? Anyone could've seen us.

I step back over to my locker, avoiding Liv's gaze as I check myself in the mirror, righting my clothes again and tightening my ponytail.

I see the wet wipes on the floor and kick the package back over to her.

Sweat seeps out of my pores as girls round the corner just in time, and I look up, seeing Amy and Krisjen.

They stop, bags slung over their shoulders as their eyes dart from me to Olivia, noticing us there.

"Hey," Amy says.

Both of them stare at Liv, struggling to contain their smiles until Amy finally breaks down in laughter like the cat that ate the canary. Another punch of guilt hits me about the video. I cast a glance at Olivia and see her ignoring all of us as she pulls on a short, black leather jacket.

She won't meet my eyes.

"Are you okay?" Krisjen asks me, giving my back a sympathetic brush of her hand as she passes to her locker.

The knots in my stomach start to ease. I don't think anyone saw us.

The last time they saw me was when I was walked with Jaeger to the front office after the fight, so I'm sure they want to make sure I'm not in trouble.

"Are you kidding?" I steel my spine and swipe my finger under my eye, fixing my eyeliner. "Nothing is tastier than a piece of cake."

They both laugh at my jibe, and I dart my eyes up again, finally catching Olivia's.

Her head is turned toward me, staring at me with a mixture of pride and wrath.

Someone clears their throat, and I blink, seeing Amy turned toward Olivia.

"Would you mind?" Amy asks her.

Liv looks over her shoulder at her.

"I don't feel comfortable changing in front of you," Amy explains.

I clench my jaw.

But Liv remains silent.

It's on the tip of my tongue to dull the embarrassment for Liv and tell Amy no one wants to look at her pancake nipples, but . . .

I don't. Liv stands there for a moment, as if waiting for something, but I just ignore her and finish touching up my face.

Her locker door slams closed, and I jerk, seeing her move out of the corner of my eye and walk toward me.

She strolls past, knocking my shoulder with hers as she goes. "Don't cross the tracks."

And then she's gone, her threat hanging in the air as the locker room fills with the P.E. class coming in.

I almost laugh. She's rescinding her invitation for Night Tide, I guess.

Lucky for her, I love getting on her bad side.

Copyright © Penelope Douglas

**Penelope Douglas** is a *New York Times*, *USA Today*, and *Wall Street Journal* bestselling author. Their books have been translated into twenty languages and include the Fall Away series, the Devil's Night series, and the stand-alones *Punk 57*, *Birthday Girl*, and *Credence*, among others.

VISIT PENELOPE DOUGLAS ONLINE

PenDouglas.com

PenelopeDouglasAuthor

𝕏 PenDouglas

Penelope.Douglas